The
Hanging
Committee

PUBLISHING

First Edition published 2024 by

2QT Limited (Publishing)

United Kingdom

Cover Design by Charlotte Mouncey with photography from istockphoto.com

Printed in Great Britain by Ingrams UK

A CIP catalogue record for this book is available from the British Library

ISBN 978-1-7385640-6-4

THE WISSTINGHAM MYSTERIES

A CRIME SERIES

BOOK 3

The

Hanging

Committee

NIGEL HANSON

To Sheena
with very best wishes
N Hanson

LIST OF MAIN CHARACTERS

Commander Selwyn Fitzgerald: Owner of Wisstingham Hall & Estate

Sebastian Fitzgerald: Selwyn's nephew

Amanda Sheppard: Librarian & Sebastian's fiancée

Miriam Cheyney: Wisstingham councillor & Selwyn's fiancée

Eleanor Delaney: Elderly library assistant

Christine Lagrange: French friend of Eleanor

Theo Patterson: Vet

Mrs Soames: Wisstingham Hall housekeeper

Detective Chief Inspector Stone: Hopestanding CID

Gabriel Montand: French vigneron and farmer

COMMITTEE MEMBERS

Roland Hawtry: Retired headmaster

Charlie Pembroke: Retired police officer

Francis Mboko: Businessman

Celia Rossiter: Fashion editor

Marcia Phelps: Artist

MINOR CHARACTERS

Julia Smyth: Wife of Theo Patterson

Detective Sergeant McBride: Hopestanding CID

Superintendent Nelson: Hopestanding CID

PREFACE

For Jonathan Crawley the day had just gone from bad to worse. Late for school, he had had a roasting from the teacher, his returned homework was littered with red pen crosses and terse comments and now, this encounter with his nemesis. He had hoped the detention he had just come from would have ensured an uneventful journey home today, but no, Hawtry had been waiting for him.

As he squatted against the stone wall of the railway bridge, Jonathan gazed wretchedly down at the blood spatters on his school shirt. He glanced in both directions but there was nobody around to help. Finally, reluctantly, fearing his next action would further signpost his defeat, he fished out his handkerchief and pressed it to his nose.

The bullying had been going on for weeks now, without a word of complaint from Jonathan.

Seated on the top of the wall opposite, Hawtry laughed and threw a stone at his unhappy victim. 'You're a coward, Crawley, a fucking cowardly wazzock!' the boy jeered. 'Your sort shouldn't be allowed to breathe.'

Jonathan said nothing. Hatred simmered behind his stare, his mind fixed on the daily question of if, and when, this fearful persecution would ever end.

'In fact you know what I'm going to do? One night I'm going to burn your house down, then you and that horrible fat mother of yours will fry.'

At the threat to his mother the dam finally burst. His face now convulsed in hatred, Crawley sprang up and rushed across.

Hawtry's smile instantly gave way to surprise and alarm. He launched himself down to the ground and landed a punch on the oncoming face. Crawley reeled backwards. Blood began to trickle down his chin. Hawtry pounced on his cowering prey, grabbed him by his shirt and tie, swung him round and pushed him hard against the wall. Tears now coursed down Crawley's face.

'Get on the wall and stand on it,' Hawtry yelled.

'Please, please no,' pleaded Crawley.

'Do it or I'll kill you,' Hawtry hissed as he made to close in on the wretch.

With uncontrolled sobs the terrified child hauled himself up onto the wall and stood there petrified. He stared in tearful fear at his tormentor.

'Now walk along to the end.'

Crawley started to reach out his hands in final supplication but stopped as Hawtry bared his teeth and, with a raised fist, advanced. Crawley turned. Shaking and hesitant, he began to shuffle along the parapet. When he was halfway along, Hawtry gave a shout. Crawley, still quaking in fear, glanced round in panic. Hawtry had started to run towards him, a sneer on his face. Crawley turned and unbalanced. His arms flailed in the air. He screamed then plummeted to the railway line below. There was a sickening thump.

Stunned, Hawtry froze for a moment then forced himself to look over the wall. Below, across the railway track, Crawley's twitching body lay on its back. Blood had spurted from the mouth. The lifeless eyes stared upwards, unfixed, the look of terror still frozen on the face. Below the head a pool of blood began to spread across the sleeper and gravel.

Hawtry felt cold. His lips quivered. He looked furtively around for any witnesses but none could be seen. His natural reaction was to run for help, but what was the point? Crawley was dead, wasn't he? He looked around again then back down to the inert body. The unblinking, accusing eyes stared back up at him.

He tried to reason against the waves of conflicting emotions and wild thoughts that rampaged through his mind. *I didn't intend to kill him. I didn't touch him. It wasn't my fault if he couldn't balance properly. He could have jumped down and run away. It was just an accident.* But if he went for help and said it was an accident, the police were bound to find out the truth. Then he would be sent to jail. He had heard stories about what happened to people in jail. Horrible stories.

If he just walked away, the police would surely think Crawley had just climbed up there of his own will then fallen. As for the blood on his face and shirt, he was covered in it now, anyway. There was nothing to link *him* to it.

With further thoughts of self-exoneration and excuses, convincing himself that he would get away with it, Hawtry hurried home as quickly as he could. He only hoped the trembling would stop before he got there.

Chapter 1

Seated on his favourite bench in Wisstingham estate's lake garden, Commander Selwyn Fitzgerald forced a faint smile at Mustard's futile attempt to chase a duck. It quacked angrily away into the sky, while the beagle barked after it. The weather was fine, the surroundings idyllic, but for Selwyn it was not the 'God's in his heaven and all's right with the world' moment it should have been. He glanced at the rather crumpled letter he still held in his hand, eagerly snatched up from the salver in the hallway and hastily opened as he set out with the dog for his walk.

'How much longer are they going to take?' he grumbled as, with an angry frown, he began to re-read the letter.

'We very much regret that we are still unable to grant your application to excavate on the recreational land presently leased from your Estate. This is due to further delays in the completion of the two land transactions, as further requests for information have now been received from the Land Registry. This also means ownership of the crypt site cannot pass to your estate at the present time, both parties having agreed that the two land transfers should be concurrent.

Please rest assured we are doing everything in our power to expedite matters.'

not approve and would bien sur kill him with his shotgun or his bare hands. Well, Yvette is pregnant and the man must to marry her very suddenly and by force. It was in strict intimacy for the honour of the family.

There has not been so much excitement in the village since the mayor fell off some scaffolding at the Mairie.

Otherwise, there is not much news. I work hard in the pottery, to make the usual things for the Christmas markets. There are also some new things I make in pottery, small houses, for the fair this year. I so wish you could be here to sit and talk as I work, like before.

Maman is now very infirm and neglects the vineyard. She depends very much to her manager Marcel to take care of the Domaine. My Christian try to help but so soon he get very tired. Rarely does maman even spend time in the pottery. She often curse my grandfather for leave to her the Domaine. It was really not his fault. I fear things cannot continue like this for very long.

I hope your father is in good health and that you are content with your new home and life.

I miss you very much and was desolated when you departed. We spent so many happy times together, you teached me English and I teached to you pottery.

Please write soon and stay safe and well

Christine.

Eleanor gazed at the letter for a moment then sniffed back a budding tear. From the daybed came a rustle and grunt as her father woke and stirred. He sat up slowly, cleared his throat and ran a hand through his crop of white hair as he looked over in Eleanor's direction and smiled.

She smiled back and folded the letter into its envelope. 'Had a good nap?'

He shook his head, struggled to rise, tottered, then fell back onto the daybed.

Eleanor hastened over to him. 'You must be careful father, at your age.'

'You're no spring chicken yourself,' he replied as she helped him up and across into his chair. 'You shouldn't be burdened with looking after me. You should be doing something better with your life, or at least what's left of it.'

'Nonsense. I'm still fit enough to look after you and I like being here.'

'What? In this backwater?'

'There's enough to keep me busy with the translation agency taking off as it is. Besides, there was nothing to keep me in France.'

He leaned his head slightly to one side and eyed her keenly. 'Are you sure?'

She stared back at him then glanced away. 'Well,' she paused for a moment. 'Well yes.' She was conscious of the envelope in her hand.

The father held her gaze, widened his eyes then, in the absence of any response, looked away. 'Alright, as long as you're sure. What's for tea?'

Pleased at this rare indication of an appetite Eleanor smiled. 'How about a cheese omelette and some oven chips?'

He nodded and she made her way to the kitchen.

***

Her hand poised on the polished brass handle, Eleanor paused for several moments to peer through the door's glass window. Finally, she pushed it open and entered Wisstingham library. Once inside, she stood rooted to the spot in the spacious open hall and stared in amazement at the interior.

The highly-polished, dark wood shelving and furniture harmonized with the Victorian floral-patterned floor tiles. In contrast, though still in harmony, the white ceiling was picked out with elaborate swirls of relief moulding, framed by an equally exotic cornice. On the tiled floor in front of her, a yellow patterned image of the tall leaded window was picked out by the rays of sunshine that streamed in.

Eleanor looked over to the reception desk. She paused uncertainly before setting off to join the small queue, the sound of her footsteps on the tiles only adding to her hesitancy.

Her handbag clutched tightly, she was about to turn and retreat to the relative anonymity of the street when someone nearby spoke.

'Good morning, madam, can I help you?'

She turned to face the owner of the soft, deep voice whose smile seemed to be mirrored in her twinkling, hazel eyes, framed by Cleopatra-styled hair.

'I'm Amanda Sheppard the librarian. I hope you don't mind my saying you looked to be a little lost.'

Eleanor returned the smile, lined eyelids crinkling as she peered over her glasses. 'Oh, you're just the person I was hoping to speak to, if you can spare a moment or two.'

'Of course I can, do please come this way.' Amanda led her past the desk and down a corridor. She unlocked her office door and once inside offered to hang up her visitor's hat and coat, then motioned her to a chair. As Eleanor adjusted her hair and straightened her cardigan, Amanda sat down at her desk.

Opposite her, the elderly lady rested her hands neatly over the handbag on her lap. 'My name's Eleanor Delaney and I've come to enquire if I might be of use here. In a voluntary capacity,' she quickly added, on noticing the librarian's brow wrinkle.

Amanda looked taken aback, but pleasantly so. 'It's kind of you to offer. What sort of tasks do you think you might be suited to doing?'

Eleanor smiled. 'Well, I like to think I have a wide range of attributes, dear. I have a languages degree and run my own French translation agency, so I'm fairly adept with computer work and IT. I'm numerate, fairly active and can make a good cup of tea or coffee. And I also bake delicious cakes, or so people tell me.'

Amanda stroked her mouth as she stared at her visitor. 'How well do you get on with people?'

'I used to work in my father and mother's…' she paused for an instance, 'in their shop.'

'Oh, where was that?'

'Beziers, in France.'

Amanda suddenly rose. 'I'm so sorry, I never offered you any refreshment. Would you like a tea or coffee?'

'No, that's okay. I'll be going for a bite to eat, shortly.'

Amanda resumed her seat. 'I tell you what, if you haven't any other particular commitments, how about you join me for lunch and we could chat over it?'

The eyelids crinkled in a smile again. 'That sounds like an excellent idea, my dear.'

At the Mazawat café, the two women resumed their conversation over a sandwich and pot of tea served by Gwen, Amanda's erstwhile rival for her fiancé's affections, though that flame of the waitress's had long since flickered out.

'You were telling me about your family,' Amanda prompted.

Eleanor put down her teacup and stared at in silence for a few moments. Then she glanced up at Amanda and smiled. 'A bit of a sad story my dear, and I wouldn't burden you with it. Suffice to say we had our problems, enough to drive my parents apart. Eventually, they divorced and my mother returned with me to live in France where I was brought up. Mother then met a younger man and they married.'

'And yourself?' Amanda enquired, hesitantly, 'Are you married?'

Eleanor shook her head, slightly vehemently, Amanda thought. 'No, I never met the right person.'

'What made you return?'

'My mother recently passed away. Then her husband committed suicide. It was very upsetting.' Eleanor rummaged in her handbag for a handkerchief which remained in readiness, in her hand.

'I'm so sorry,' murmured Amanda.

'Other than a very good friend, there was nothing left to really keep me in France. I didn't want to continue with the shop and, in any event, my translation business had really started to grow. It's all online so it doesn't really matter where I'm based. Also, my father now really needs someone to take care of him. So that's why I'm here, my dear.'

Amanda frowned, 'it sounds like you've got a full-time job as it is, what with the translation and your father, without having time to come and help us out at the library.'

Eleanor leaned across and placed a reassuring hand on Amanda's. 'The agency work doesn't take up all my time, by any means, and my father has a daily carer who comes in. Anyway, I need to get out of the cottage and I want to become involved with the local community, so working at the library would seem ideal.'

'How much time do you reckon you could spare us?'

'Perhaps three days a week, though it might need to be a bit of a moveable feast.'

Amanda readily nodded agreement. 'Well, as long as it's on a voluntary basis I'd be delighted to have you on board. I'm afraid I haven't the budget or a staff vacancy to take anyone on permanently, though goodness knows we could do with an extra pair of hands. Of course, being in possible contact with the public, particularly children, we'd have to go through the usual vetting procedures. I assume you'd have no objection to that and that you've no skeletons lurking in the cupboard?' She gave Eleanor a look of mock suspicion then smiled.

Eleanor smiled back. 'I can assure you the skeletons are well hidden. I don't know how the procedures can work with someone who's just come from France, but I imagine there must be some way, since we're all in the EU.' Anyhow, do vet away and you'll be in a very safe pair of hands.'

'There's just one thing I should warn you about. I'm due to go to Canada soon on a six-month exchange, so during that time you'd be working under Mary, my assistant. She'll have control of any decisions whilst I'm away. If you could call in tomorrow, I'll be delighted to introduce you to her and get things moving. You'll need to bring in some identification and we'll arrange to get some photos done for the clearance.'

Eleanor nodded and smiled, 'That's quite alright dear.'

A time arranged for their next meeting and delighted to have found such a pleasant, cheerful and unsalaried addition to her staff, the librarian could only insist on paying for lunch.

***

The following day, bounding up the steps to Hopestanding Central Library, Amanda was about to push through the swing doors when she was nearly bowled over by a gargantuan young woman with the slogan 'Food Quarter' emblazoned across her sweatshirt. With no apology but rather an angry glare at the librarian, she hurried on down the steps.

Must be the Quarter's official taster, mused Amanda as she entered the building. Once inside, she grimaced at the sound of Mayor Henderson's introductory speech in progress and the embarrassment of her lateness. She quickly palmed her hair into place and crept as surreptitiously as she could to join the listening audience of invited guests.

'…and accordingly, I'm truly delighted to open this first Hopestanding Arts Festival which I hope, nay I am certain, will be a total success,' he continued. 'If you would like to view the exhibits in the upstairs galleries then join me in my parlour for refreshments afterwards. That's through the first floor connecting bridge to the town hall and follow the signs. Thank you, ladies and gentlemen.'

Amidst the applause, general hubbub and shuffling of the crowd, Amanda threaded her way to the staircase. There she was intercepted by her boss Miriam Cheyney. 'Not like you to be late, Amanda,' she commented, though her smile belied any criticism.

Nevertheless, Amanda apologised. 'Sorry, we had a crisis at the library. An old man collapsed. He's alright though.'

Miriam nodded and they both started up the stairs. 'This event's made me wonder whether Wisstingham could host its own festival,' Miriam observed.

'Just what I was thinking on the way here. We've got the exhibition room, and the village green for some open-air venues. Perhaps something could also be set up at the hall.' She stopped in her tracks, causing Miriam to halt and look at her. 'What if it was to coincide with the opening of the hall?' Amanda further suggested, which prompted Miriam's eyes to widen.

'What a brilliant idea,' she exclaimed, then quickly glanced round to see if their conversation could have been overheard. Satisfied that it hadn't, she leaned into Amanda. 'Let's see if we can make it a reality, shall we?' Amanda nodded her agreement and they continued upstairs.

As a consequence of the conversation, Amanda subsequently found herself scanning the assembled great and good in a somewhat different light, searching out

Gwen arrived with two place settings and a backward glance at the café frontage, beyond which the man was receding from view. She turned to face Amanda who had been watching her and the dreamy expression on her face. 'That was the new vet, Theo Patterson,' she pointed and confided as she wiped the table and set the places.

Eleanor cast a glance in the direction she had indicated.

Once alone, Amanda gave Eleanor a smile and leaned closer to murmur, 'I think our waitress is going to be disappointed. I'd heard about the new vet and that he and a local horsewoman Julia Smyth are an item. She's from one of the local landed gentry families, so she'd prove pretty stiff competition, I reckon.'

'I imagine so. I suppose he's what you young people would refer to as dishy.'

'Yes, but not my type.' She smiled involuntarily as her thoughts homed in on her fiancé Sebastian Fitzgerald, with whom she'd only recently been reconciled.

Minutes later, Gwen arrived with their food and they ate in silence for a while. Amanda was intrigued to watch Eleanor as, with deft flicks of the tip of her knife, she discarded morsels of food to the edge of her plate, though Amanda could not discern what crime they had committed. She resumed the conversation. 'Whilst I'm away, I've agreed that a group of people can use the Exhibition room for meetings, probably once or twice a month. They're going to try to kick start an Arts and Crafts Festival and Exhibition for Wisstingham. I met them earlier this week at the Hopestanding Festival and we're meeting later this week, so I hope you'll be able to be there so I can introduce you.'

'I'd be only too happy.'

'Then, whilst I'm away, I'd appreciate if you could look after them and be their contact. Mary will deputise for me and be the one to make any decisions in my absence, but I reckon she'll need all the support she can get.'

Eleanor beamed. 'Of course you can count on me, dear,' she murmured and smiled across at Amanda before continuing with her meal.

Chapter 3

'Any post, Mrs S?' Selwyn Fitzgerald's hopes were once more dashed by the housekeeper's shaken head as she shuffled into the study with her boss's elevenses.

''fraid not, Commander.' She placed the tray on the plan chest and gave him a sympathetic smile. The daily enquiry had been going on for over a fortnight now. 'Would that be the council's letter yer still waitin' for?'

'Thanks Mrs S. Yes, it certainly is,' came the dour reply.

'Them folks 'as never been known to do anythin' in an 'urry,' the housekeeper warned as she turned to leave the room. 'I reckon as 'ow St Peter 'imself would be twiddlin' 'is thumbs waitin' for any one of that lot to turn up.'

Selwyn stared gloomily at the silver teapot and the tray's contents for a moment. His spirits lifted slightly as he spied the plate of shortbreads.

Nearly two months had elapsed since the agreement in principle was reached with the council. For him, Wisstingham Council's formal letter of agreement to the land transfer, and approval for his excavation work on the neighbouring recreation land, was long overdue. No doubt still tied up in red tape with the Land Registry. Not that there was any certainty he would find the family's long-lost treasure buried either on the recreation land or in the crypt, but after all the negotiations and final agreement, the delay and suspense were now well and truly beyond a joke.

There was a tap at the door which opened simultaneously to reveal Sebastian Fitzgerald. 'No letter then, Gov?' he enquired as he spied the expression on his uncle's face.'

Selwyn shook his head then glanced at his watch. 'Got time for a cuppa before you set off?'

'Just about.'

Selwyn moved over to the plan chest and started to pour out two cups. 'It's not just the infernal delay, those planning blighters are beginning to cause friction between Miriam and me. She wants me to press on with the plans to open the hall and I'm bally well refusing to do anything until they do their bit and sign on the dotted line. If their estates people can't move things along, what confidence can I have that their finance wallahs will come up with the funding towards the works to the hall, to open it? Anyway, let's change the subject. 'Is she all packed and ready?'

'Yes, she is,' Amanda answered from the door as she walked in, a small rucksack slung over one shoulder. 'The cases are in the hall.'

She was immediately followed by Mrs S with an extra cup and saucer which Selwyn took from her. It only took one look at Amanda for the housekeeper to fumble in her apron pocket for a handkerchief to staunch her oncoming tears.

With a smile, Amanda approached her. 'Dear Mrs S, I'm only going for six months, I'll be back before you know it.'

'Yes, but it's Canada. That's round the world and there's all them bears and wolves and things. And all that snow. Miles and miles of the stuff.'

Amanda wrapped her arms, as far as she could, around the ample frame of the sobbing woman. 'There, there now. I'll be perfectly safe. There's nothing to worry about.'

Mrs S broke gently away from the librarian, forced a courageous smile then broke into more sobs as she waddled out of the room. Amanda slowly shook her head as she watched her go.

Some ten minutes later the trio left the room and headed to the entrance hall where the pantomime of departure from Mrs Soames unfolded. Finally, with the Jaguar fully laden, Selwyn, Sebastian and Amanda set off for the airport to the farewell and tears from Mrs S, whose handkerchief alternated between waves in the air and dabs to her eyes.

***

Detective Chief Inspector Stone gave a cursory nod to the constable who had raised the cordon tape for him to duck under. He strode towards the small group of officers who surrounded the covered corpse. 'What have we got then, McBride?' he enquired of his sergeant.

'Another jumper, sir. Pretty grisly. Female, probably in her mid-forties. Only one witness so far, a driver, who was parking on the top floor and saw her jump, called it in. Doyle's taking his statement. The pathologist's on his way.'

Stone sighed and averted his gaze from the growing pool of blood seeping from under the edge of the covering. He gazed upwards at the concrete monstrosity that was Hopestanding's one and only multi-story car park. 'Bloody place should have been knocked down years ago,' he grumbled.

'Or at least made suicide proof,' added McBride. He reached into his pocket, pulled out a plastic bag and offered it to his boss. 'Suicide note found in her coat pocket.'

Stone eyed it warily. 'What's it say?'

'Blames her husband who's been having an affair. It also accuses him of physical violence and mental cruelty. Says she just couldn't take it anymore.'

Stone pocketed the bag, looked back down at the body and shook his head. 'Why can't they just take a pill or do something less messy? Have we got a name?'

'Elizabeth Carey.'

'Any children or other dependents?'

'There's no mention of any in the note.'

'Then you'd better find the husband and break the news. Get a full statement, if he's in any fit state to talk. Check to see if he's got any previous or if there've been any previous complaints. Also check with social services.'

Both men looked round at the approaching pathologist who padded towards them in his protective gear.

'Good morning gentlemen,' he greeted them, 'what have we got here?'

McBride filled the pathologist in as he knelt to uncover and examine the body. With narrowed eyes and compressed lips Stone looked reluctantly on.

***

Since the first day she had set eyes on him, in the veterinary practice, Julia Smyth's determination to take possession of Theo Patterson had never wavered or diminished. Hers was a greedy and hungry appetite, so she took every opportunity during her visits and consultations with the practice to meet and ensnare their newest recruit. Fortunately for her, since she ran her parents' stables during their prolonged absences in Spain, these encounters were fairly frequent. That her father was one of the landed gentry, and had both a partnership and an office in the practice, further facilitated such meetings. Therefore, it was only a matter of weeks before the couple were indeed, as Amanda had mentioned, an item, having in fact consummated their relationship in that very office.

It was during a meal they had booked at Qwik Qwak that Julia decided to move in for the kill, during the course of crispy duck and pancakes, to be precise. With a toss of her straight blonde hair, she leaned forward and fixed eager eyes on Theo, who had just spooned a dollop of hoi sin sauce onto his plate. Her tongue ran slowly along her full lips as she pushed her hand across the table towards his. With a quizzical look he put his hand on hers and stared back into her widened eyes.

'You do love me don't you, Theo?' she asked.

He frowned slightly. 'Of course I do.'

'Enough to marry me?'

His hand was removed, whereupon her smile vanished and she stared down at her plate. 'Obviously not,' she murmured.

He stared at her for a moment then hastily reached back for her hand and leaned in towards her. 'Hey, I do love you. It was just a bit of a surprise. We're doing fine. We've plenty of time for that.'

She regarded him through filmy eyes. 'Not that much time, darling. Time's racing by and mummy and daddy want to see me settled. They're planning to move out permanently to Spain but need to know I can manage the estate here. They don't reckon I could do it on my own, without at least someone to turn to.'

Theo stared at her for a moment. 'But we could live together, couldn't we?'

She gave an adamant shake of her head. 'They're too old fashioned for that, I'm afraid. It would have to be all or nothing. That's also how I feel.'

'But what about my job? I couldn't give it up just to help run the estate.'

Julia fixed his gaze and grasped both his hands in hers. 'You'd have the best of both worlds. After we're married, daddy will transfer his partnership in the practice to you, then the saving in money will enable you to take on a junior, so that you'll only need to work part time there.'

Theo's eyes narrowed. 'You've got this all worked out, haven't you? Have you discussed this with him?'

Julia nodded. Her eager eyes were back.

He stared back at her. He'd have to think hard and fast. If he was to delay and ask for time to think about it she'd explode and cut him off completely. He'd seen how she could behave if she didn't get her way. He would probably also have to say goodbye to his job. Life wouldn't be worth living here. If he said yes, he'd be made up for life. A partnership in the practice and a life of luxury. More than he could ever otherwise achieve. She was fun to be with and if he was not in love with her he was very close to it. The sex was great and imaginative and she certainly had a good appetite for it. There were risks, he knew that only too well, and what if it didn't work out? Well, by the sound of it the family wouldn't want any scandal so, if it didn't, there'd be plenty of money to buy him off. What the hell! It was all too good to say no to.

With narrowed, anxious eyes she watched him rise, and come round to her side of the table. Her expression totally changed as he then got down on one knee.

'I've no ring to offer you, right now, but will you marry me, my love?'

Julia beamed, rapidly nodded her head and with welling tears bent to give him a lingering kiss, to the accompaniment of applause from the nearby tables.

***

ELEANOR'S DIARY ENTRY 23RD. MARCH 2011

Terrible news received today. Christine's husband is terminally ill with cancer. Apparently one minute he's fine, goes to see the doctor with something he considers minor and within a few days he's told he only has weeks to live. It's so hard to believe. He's always been such a lively person. What on earth will she do without him. She has her pottery but I can't see her devoting the rest of her life to that.

If only I could be there to comfort her. But much as I long to fly over to be with her, there's things here that need to be done, particularly with Amanda away.

Life is so very unfair.

Father's decline is slow but distinct. Marian tells me he sleeps more and his bouts of confusion and forgetfulness are longer, which I have also noticed. He's a dear thing and in the light of bitter experience, how I wish mother had not taken me away from him. If only they could have come through the nightmare together. After all, neither of them were to blame.

It sounds like everything went well at the first meeting of the festival committee. My tea and scones certainly seemed to go down a treat before it. And I think Amanda really appreciated my involvement. It appears Hawtry got elected as committee chairman with Francis MBoko, a woman whose name I can't remember – must find out about her — and Charlie, (God bless him. How he makes me laugh!) the first members. It all seems to be going in the right direction and in Amanda's absence I fully intend to make sure it continues to do so, as far as I can from the sidelines.

From what I heard they're going to be the founder members of the main committee and also one called *The Hanging Committee*. Sounds a bit grisly but apparently it's to oversee the choice and display of the exhibition entries. Hanging of the pictures, I suppose. Then there are going to be other groups to organise finance, health and safety, (naturally – must have that!) logistics like toilets, refreshments, car parking and one for marketing and publicity. Sounds quite a to do.

I'm not sure I'll be making scones, biscuits and tea for all of them!

***

APRIL

'Do those two know each other?' Francis MBoko asked Roland Hawtry as they watched Charlie Pembroke and Eleanor deep in conversation in the corner of the room.

Roland smiled. 'I don't believe so. I rather think he's keeping her and therefore the plate of biscuits to himself. That's at least his third.'

As if on cue, Eleanor gave Charlie a smile and farewell pat on the arm then broke away to bring the biscuits over to the two men who each readily liberated one.

'These are delicious,' commented Roland. 'Did you make them?'

Eleanor gave an appreciative nod.

'Well, it's very kind of you to look after us like this.'

'Not at all,' Eleanor replied in her thin voice. 'There's plenty of tea and coffee in the flasks over there. Do you live in Hopestanding?' she asked Francis.

'Yes, I've a penthouse apartment in the new development on the Wisstingham road.'

'You must have been lucky to get that,' said Roland. 'I'll bet that was in high demand from the minute it went on sale.'

Francis' brilliant white teeth flashed a smile. 'Right on! It was my project so the apartment was spoken for from the very start.'

Roland's eyebrows rose. 'Really? So, you're a builder?'

'Architect and developer,' corrected Francis.

Further conversation was halted as the door swung open to reveal a middle-aged woman whose piercing blue eyes anxiously scanned the room. She shrugged off her camel coat, hung it and her scarf on the coatrack, then hurried over to the group. Tall and slender with high cheekbones, she had short wavy chestnut hair and a cupid's bow lips. 'Am I late?' The question, directed at Roland, came out in a husky breathless voice.

'Not at all, Celia,' he reassured her. 'We're making the most of our host's kind hospitality.'

'Let me help you to some tea or coffee,' offered Eleanor and handed the biscuits plate to Francis.

The newcomer's anxious eyes visibly relaxed. 'Thank you, a coffee would be lovely, milk no sugar, please. I thought I was going to be late. I swear that traffic gets worse each week.'

Charlie, who had given up on the contents of the notice board, now joined them and the biscuits. 'Hello, it's Celia isn't it?'

She nodded, 'Hello everyone.' Her glances to the men still bore a hint of apology.

Eleanor arrived with the coffee and a plate of croissants which Charlie eyed hungrily. 'I'd better leave you good people to it,' and, to a chorus of appreciation, she departed.

'Did anyone read about that poor woman who committed suicide?' asked Charlie, after a few moments.

Francis nodded. 'The inquest you mean?'

'I'm surprised the husband wasn't arrested,' added Roland.

Charlie shook his head. 'Nothing they could charge him with and prove.'

'It was common knowledge he used to beat her. And he was having affairs. She might have committed suicide but he as good as killed her. Surely to goodness there's something the police could do,?' said Celia, bitterly.

'Obviously not or they'd have charged him already,' Charlie replied.

Celia pursed her lips. 'Then there's no justice.'

'But there should be,' declared Roland.

'Yes, there should,' echoed Francis.

The awkward silence that ensued, as each person was drawn into their own thoughts, was finally broken when Roland said, 'Well, I suppose we'd better get started.'

The meeting that followed began, however, on a sombre note.

***

had outweighed any unnecessary exposure to the risk.

A lot of research had gone into establishing Carey's routine. It had not helped that, for a while after his wife's death, there had been no fixed pattern to his movements. However, once he had returned to work on a regular basis, in his small workshop, a suitable opportunity presented itself, particularly as he often worked late into the night.

Carey was not scared of being alone in the darkened building once the other occupants had left. Combined with a large frame, his customary brute force gave him all the confidence he needed. His fists had always proved useful and been readily applied numerous times, in a variety of circumstances, over the years.

But the brute force was to prove to be of no avail. It would have been if he had thought to peer through the darkened windows of the car parked next to his, but it was late and he was tired. So, the gun levelled at his head in the dead of night, as he was about to get into his car, was a strong persuasion for him to cooperate and accompany the four people back to the building he had just left.

Once inside, he was bound and gagged, three of the figures, now hooded, awaiting the fourth who had mounted the metal staircase and headed along the open landing to a position immediately above them.

Several minutes later four hooded figures stood in silence watching the corpse, divested of its redundant bonds and gag, as it hung from the balustrade, the body twitching and swinging in its death throes. On the cheeks of only one, however, did the tears freely flow. As the body slowly rotated, the bulging eyes seemed to stare down in accusation at each of its executioners. But not for long. Shortly after, the figures were gone and the corpse was all alone.

***

The wiry Scot leaned sideways, his bloodshot eyes glued to the television. His left arm blindly groped by the side of the armchair for one of the cans of lager. On the stained coffee table in front of him lay an empty whisky bottle, alongside the uncleared debris from yesterday's dinner.

The hand finally connected and, moments later, a hiss momentarily blocked out the football commentary as he pulled the ring back.

Russell McNabb, disgraced and sacked Chief Engineer of Wisstingham Council, deserted by his wife, still redundant and likely to remain so, took a swig then passed a bony hand across his mouth and heavily stubbled chin.

Two months back, he'd have killed for this much time off work. His life had been a string of property development schemes, all of which Tyson, their erstwhile council leader, assured him were a done deal. Until the interfering bitch of a mayor had exposed a deal which hadn't quite reached completion. And now Tyson, also sacked, was gone with the wind and Miriam Cheyney, her mayoral year over with but still a Councillor, was free to make a fucking mint out of her grandiose fiancé's estate. All the money Hirst had given McNabb was long since gone, as were Hirst's chances of buying the land off Wisstingham Hall and making a killing with his development plans. Another enemy for that fucking commander.

'Awa ya bastards,' he growled at the screen as another goal slammed home from the opposing team. He unsteadily placed the can on the coffee table. Energetically he rubbed his face with his hands then passed one through his thinning hair. He smiled as he recalled the deal he'd made the previous day for the rent of a garage on the edge of the town. His crusade to bring about Cheyney's ruination had entered its next phase.

However, after the breakdown of his marriage and the despair and chaos into which he had rapidly fallen, through his many alcoholic hazes, the distinction between ruin and death had become distinctly blurred.

***

'So, you've no idea where he is?' queried Selwyn, fairly certain the answer would be 'no'.

Mrs Soames closed her eyes and exhaled deeply. When re-opened, those same eyes glared at him. 'If I knowed where 'e was you wouldn't 'ave needed to ask me. 'e's not at the cottage cos I checked and I'd 'ave already chased 'im round 'ere sharpish, if 'e was. 'e went off to work this morning, cheery as yer please, and I reminded 'im to be back in good time.'

Selwyn gave a submissive nod. 'Amanda won't be pleased,' he murmured as he headed to the front door.

'Tell me about it!' replied the housekeeper, which shocked Selwyn into a surprised glance as to where on earth and how his housekeeper had picked up the expression.

'She's not going to be pleased at all,' he murmured to himself as he eased the Jaguar down the drive.

Sure enough, when Amanda saw Selwyn standing alone outside the airport arrivals door, with no sign of Sebastian, her smile instantly vanished. Nevertheless, it briefly returned as she hugged the commander.

'Hello dear girl, so lovely to see you. 'fraid Sebastian couldn't make it. Got the briefest of messages on the way here. Don't know where he is. Must have been held up with something really important because he was so looking forward to this moment.'

'It doesn't matter,' Amanda lied, still hopeful, despite her expectations of his being there with kisses, hugs and the engagement ring now lying in tatters.

At his insistence, Selwyn trundled Amanda's suitcase across the car park. As they neared the car he stopped and turned to her. 'I have to warn you Sebastian's not been himself for some time now.'

Her eyes widened. 'What's the matter? Is he ill?' a touch of panic in her voice.

'I don't really know. He's become very insular and broody. Spends a lot of time on his own. I don't know whether it's because he's missing you. Reckon it's bound to be. He seems very unsure of things and people. I don't think there are any problems at work. I've wondered if all that's happened to him, over the last few months, has finally come home to roost.'

For several minutes, as they drove from the airport, neither of them spoke. Amanda feared her fiancé's absence – was he even still a fiancé? — and no communication to explain why he was not there, could only betoken diminished affection for her.

It was Selwyn who eventually broke the silence. 'There've been a good number of bookings for the fishing chalets whilst you've been away. Got Sebastian to thank for much of that. And the farm's doing quite well.'

'That's good.'

'So, what did you think of Canada? What did you get up to?'

Amanda's reply, though lengthy, interrupted by occasional queries from Selwyn, lacked any real enthusiasm, such that when she'd finished, Selwyn briefly glanced at her and smiled. 'You've not to worry, Amanda. I'm sure once you're back with Sebastian he'll bounce back to his old self in no time at all.'

Bounce is certainly what Mrs Soames seemed to do — as far as her frame would allow — as she hurried from the kitchen on hearing the hall's heavy front door creak open. Wiping her hands on her apron and with the widest smile she had worn for a long time, she waddled up to Amanda, briefly held her by her arms to give her a good look, then clasped the girl to her ample bosom. 'Oh my dear, 'ow lovely it is to see you again,' she exclaimed, tears beginning to trickle down her rosy cheeks. 'God love you ducks, you must be famished, I'll 'ave a cuppa and yer favourite sandwich ready in a jiffy. Just to put you on.'

Amanda smiled back at her. 'Oh it's so lovely to see you again, Mrs S. Thank you, that'll be just perfect.' All the while her eyes and ears were anxiously attuned for sight or sign of Sebastian, irrationally ignoring the fact that his car was not outside.

'Right you are,' Mrs S cheerfully replied, wiping her eyes only after the commander told her they would be in the drawing room, and had led Amanda away.

'Any news on the excavation front?' she asked, once they were settled.

Selwyn's jowls drooped in harmony with his downturned mouth. 'Not a peep from the council. Blithering idiots! It's taking longer than Napoleon's retreat from Moscow. Caused no end of friction between Miriam and me. She's wanting to plough on with opening the hall to the public and I'm stalling until the blighters come good.' He was nevertheless pleased to see the genuine smile his tirade had brought to Amanda's face.

'Any changes here, since I left?'

'Oh yes, employed a new quarry manager, Jeremy Kemp. First rate chap. Ex-sapper, like Bilton was. Also got a new Estate Manager, Sean Morrisey, big as a barn and smokes like a chimney but excellent background. Comes from the Killingden estate. I think you'll like him. He's got an artistic bent. Something of a painter. I'll introduce you to them as soon as you've settled back in.' He leaned forward. 'Just one thing, which Sebastian will no doubt tell you about in more detail, Fellowes Industries is up for sale.'

'Oh no. Will his job be safe?'

'He certainly doesn't seem worried about it. I'm sure he'll be okay. He's done an excellent job running it.'

'Poor lamb. It's just been one thing after another for him.'

Selwyn nodded. 'Very true.'

News on further developments would have to wait. Mrs Soames was the first to interrupt the conversation as the door swung open and she trundled in a trolley heavily laden with a tea service, sandwiches, biscuits, fruit and cakes.

'Good Lord!' Selwyn exclaimed as he rose to assist, though appearing to have no idea just what he should do. 'What a spread.'

Hardly had the trolley's contents been transferred to the

coffee table, when the sound of the front door opening and closing drew their attention and eyes to the drawing room door. There was the rising sound of running foot-steps down the parquet corridor. The door was flung open and a breathless Sebastian burst into the room. His gaze immediately homed in on Amanda who rose, her eyes glued on him and her mouth parted in surprise and anticipation. He hastened over to her, gazed briefly into her eyes, gave her an urgent kiss then wrapped her into his arms where he held her for some time.

'I'm so, so sorry,' he eventually murmured, though the relieved smile she gave him signified no necessity for the apology. 'There's been a murder at the offices and one way or another I've been tied up all day. I get the impression Stone thinks I'm responsible just because the building's got something to do with me. It's been like Rourke's Drift with all the press there and it's all been pretty bloody.'

'Oh my gawd,' exclaimed the housekeeper who appeared to look to Selwyn for some sort of reassurance, though there was clearly none forthcoming, rather a barrage of questions.

At your offices? 'When was this and who? Have they got someone for it?' Selwyn asked.

Amanda, who had drawn Sebastian down next to her on the chaise long, put a hand up to interrupt to ask, 'How about that tea, Mrs S?'

'Quite so,' agreed Selwyn. So, back on familiar territory, Mrs Soames busied herself pouring, serving, handing out plates and offering the sandwiches around.

'It's a tenant of one of the small units,' Sebastian explained. 'Our cleaner found him hanged from the first-floor passageway, poor woman. They thought it was suicide at first, but now the police think it's murder. They've been questioning everyone all day. That's why I couldn't get away, but they told me not to say anything about it.'

'Who was it?' asked Amanda.

'A chap called Carey. He was the husband of a woman who committed suicide while you were away. Jumped from the multi-storey car park.'

Amanda shuddered. She remembered the earlier near fatal events at the Fellowes building, the previous year, when she had been shot by Monaghan and Sebastian was nearly killed. The building and its past seemed to be still intent on casting a shadow over them. She had an uneasy premonition that this was only the precursor of another dark chapter in their lives.

***

Despite Selwyn's and Mrs Soames' best efforts to persuade Amanda and Sebastian to dine at the hall that evening, they were determined to celebrate Amanda's return with a meal at Qwik Qwak.

It was there, over aperitifs, that Sebastian drew the engagement ring from his pocket and proposed once more. The delighted librarian only too readily accepted and, after an absence of over six months, happily returned the ring to her finger.

However, as the meal progressed Amanda was conscious that there was something different about him. At first, she put this down to the day's events, but by the end of the meal she was convinced that this was not the case. Although the conversation and his attention to her did not flag, Sebastian somehow seemed more distant and sadder than she had ever known him. It was almost as if a part of him was absent and closed off from her. Her thoughts kept drifting to Selwyn's earlier comments. Her question to Sebastian, if everything was alright with him and their relationship, yielded a very positive reply. He asked many questions and seemed keen to hear her anecdotes, but somehow the intensity of his affection for her did not seem the same as it had been. She knew better than to challenge him on this. Their relationship had to settle in again.

Nonetheless, she was to brood on her misgivings and his unchanging detachment, which she later noticed was not just confined to her company, for many days to come.

Chapter 4

After a final wave goodbye to Selwyn, as he stood at the top of the stone staircase in front of the hall's impressive oak door, Miriam Cheyney eased herself into the driving seat of her BMW Z4 sports car. It had been an enjoyable evening, even if she had had to restrict her intake of wine. For once, the spectre of the council's long-awaited completion of land transfer documents, together with the excavation approval, had not made a visitation to the dining table and their conversation. She dearly wished Selwyn would understand that different departments were dealing with the land transfer and the hall opening projects, and that he would get a move on with the hall opening work. There was no doubt the transfer documentation would come through, and there was much to be planned and done before the first visitors could set foot over the hall's threshold. Miriam was certain that Selwyn's stubborn refusal to commit to anything would find him wrong-footed when postman Pat finally delivered. Then it would become all hell and no notion to get things moving.

But the evening had been friction free. Selwyn's insistent invitation for Miriam to stay the night, very tempting though it had been — and at most times successful — was insufficient this evening to outweigh the convenience of being at her own house for the early morning start she had to make. It was already later than she had planned to be home, so she put her foot down as she left the estate.

The weather had turned bad. A light drizzle was accompanied by gusting wind. Driving along the Hopestanding road, through the rain-spattered rear window Miriam became aware of headlights that had steadily approached from behind. Not that it mattered, she would soon turn off onto the quiet country road, a useful short cut to where she lived.

Minutes later, Miriam felt a pang of irritation when the car also turned off behind her. Its headlights were now even closer. Whilst not dangerously close, it was beginning to feel uncomfortably so. She accelerated but the following car maintained the same distance from her. Although now distinctly uneasy, she resisted the temptation to speed up even more. Without any roadside lighting, the limited visibility was hampered by the frequent bends in the road. Miriam would have normally thought it fortunate that there was no oncoming traffic, in such bad weather on such a narrow lane, but her growing fear now made her think otherwise.

On a long bend, the car, which to Miriam now definitely appeared in pursuit of her, approached close enough to almost touch bumpers. It pulled out and accelerated alongside. Miriam was forced to veer to the very edge. All too late, she caught sight of a fallen tree branch on her side of the road. The other car held its position alongside. To avoid the branch, Miriam was forced to brake sharply, the tyres skidding on the tarmac before she swung off the road then jolted over the rough ground.

Terrified, she gripped the steering wheel for all she was worth. Her foot was down flat down on the brake pedal, which did not seem to work. The car still seemed to just plough on. As she was bumped about, all she could do was stare helplessly through the windscreen. Suddenly, out of the darkness loomed a tree. Miriam furiously turned the wheel. She felt icy cold. The car narrowly missed the trunk. It finally came to a halt. Her heart pounded as she sat breathless and shaking, unable to move. She glanced towards the road.

From the other car, now parked, the driver had emerged and was hurrying towards her. As he drew nearer, Miriam made out the shadowy figure's dark balaclava. She also saw a moonlit reflection from something long and shiny in the figure's hand. Still powerless to move, perspiration trickled from her brow. Her clammy hands were still glued in terror to the steering wheel. Miriam could only watch as a hand reached out to open the car door. That was the last thing she saw.

***

'Are you busy? Silly question I suppose. Course you are. Wouldn't be here otherwise, would you?'

Eleanor turned from her computer screen to see Amanda framed in the doorway with a slightly mischievous smile, her eyes twinkling.

'Of course I'm not too busy for you, my dear. After all, you're the boss.'

Amanda glanced conspiratorially around then approached her. 'It's a bit of a cheek really. Nothing to do with work but it would help me out no end.' She handed her a computer printout and leaflet. 'This is what I need translated, the promotional material for the fishing chalets for the website. I just wondered, well hoped, really, if you might be prepared to do a French version of it.' She gave Eleanor a 'pretty please' look.

'I'd be delighted to, dear. Are you expecting some European customers then?'

'I don't see why not. It's a pretty part of the country and we've got coverage on some of the major platforms. I'll pay you.'

'You certainly won't. It will be a pleasure. It won't take me any time at all.'

'Well, perhaps a complimentary fishing permit then?'

Eleanor giggled. 'Can you see me wading into the lake to gaff a 20 pounder?'

'Not likely, you'd be trampled underfoot by the other anglers if you hooked one of those. Alright, if nothing else, the next lunch is on me. Better get back to work, I suppose.'

As Eleanor leafed through the material she could hear Amanda happily whistle 'Hi ho, hi ho, it's off to work we go' as she returned to her office.

***

To those who knew her, Celia Rossiter was a great success. One of Hopestanding's daughters, born and educated there, she had risen through the ranks of journalism to become the editor of a leading London-based fashion magazine. She dressed in the most elegant clothes, dined at the best restaurants and could be seen at most of the major national events such as Wimbledon, the Henley Regatta and the Cheltenham Gold cup. She had a penchant for champagne and fine wines, went to most of the London theatre opening nights and drove a Mustang GT convertible.

In her earlier years, Celia had had had a roving eye for men and an almost insatiable appetite for sex, which had brought her to the beds of many lovers, though never to the altar, being so enamoured with the male species as to never manage to remain faithful to one, for very long.

However, all was now not as it seemed. Mentally scarred after being mugged late one night on a London street, and disillusioned with the ineffectiveness of the police in hunting down her attacker, she was left to harbour a deep-seated abhorrence of violence against women. She had watched more than one dear friend suffer violence in her lifetime, and it had enraged her to witness the long and usually unsuccessful route to court and ultimate justice. Accordingly, in her later life she had shut herself off from the company of men.

Celia was well spoken with a slightly nasal voice and a habit of keeping her mouth open in a smile as she listened to people.

On retirement, she had gravitated back to her hometown and immersed herself in a number of local causes and committees, as well as the local amateur dramatic group. With her knowledge of marketing and journalism, she would have been best placed to join the festival sub-committee dealing with marketing and promotion. However, after her encounter with Roland Hawtry and the others at the Hopestanding festival, she was convinced their steering committee would provide her with a greater sense of fulfillment and had expressed a preference to join their group.

With her parents deceased, she lived alone, her only company a large Persian cat called Catastroff.

This was the woman who now pushed open the door to

Wisstingham library and strode to the reception desk for her appointment with Amanda.

Once inside the librarian's office, Celia seated herself in the chair from which Amanda had hastily cleared a pile of books. 'It was good of you to find the time to see me. Roland asked if I'd fill you in on what's been happening – he's had to go away for a few days — but you must be very busy after an absence of, er six months, wasn't it?'

Amanda nodded. 'Yes and not at all, I'm only too pleased to meet you at last. I've been looking forward to an update. I hope Eleanor Delaney looked after you all.'

There was a momentary pause as Celia appeared to size Amanda up. 'She has indeed. Eleanor's a most remarkable woman.'

'She certainly is. We're lucky to have her. How's Roland getting on with the committee?'

'He's an excellent chairman. I think everyone reckons he's the ideal man for the job.'

Over coffee and biscuits the two women discussed the progress and plans for the festival. As the meeting progressed, forthcoming though Celia was, Amanda had the distinct impression she was holding back on something. Something she wanted to broach but was afraid to do so.

Finally, when it appeared they had exhausted the flow of information, with a slight frown and fixing Celia's gaze Amanda asked, 'Is there anything else you want me to know, or want to ask?'

The unblinking blue eyes stared back at her, the silence between them fractionally too long before Celia confirmed there was nothing else, though to Amanda, it appeared the woman looked a tad uncertain.

***

Selwyn slowly replaced the receiver and slumped down onto the sofa opposite the telephone table. His eyes had a hunted look. He stared at the phone for several moments, transfixed in shock and wild thoughts. He would probably have stayed there longer had it not been for the soft shuffle of Mrs Soames footsteps as she approached, with wrinkled brow. 'What is it, commander?'

He looked up at her in complete bewilderment. 'It's Miriam. Someone found her in her car. It must have been just after she left here. She's in hospital.'

'Oh my gawd!' Mrs Soames swayed for a moment before Selwyn sprang up, took her arm and supported her down onto the sofa. For a few seconds they sat in silence. The housekeeper took the Commander's hand in hers and patted it soothingly, 'What 'appened? How badly is she?'

'They don't really know, it was the police who just rang. It seems she swerved off the road. They're looking into it.' He rose, 'she's sedated at the moment and they said to wait to hear, but I must see her.'

'Shall I come with you?'

'No, Mrs S, but thank you. Best not to go mob-handed.' She forced a smile for him and he hurried off.

'There's no physical harm, as far as we can see,' the doctor reassured Selwyn as they stood by the bedside. 'The sedation should last for probably another hour. You're welcome to wait if you want to.'

Selwyn thanked him and sat down in the chair beside the bed. Hardly had the doctor gone before DCI Stone appeared. Selwyn made to stand but the other gestured for him to remain seated.

'Hello Inspector,' Selwyn greeted him.

'It's Detective *Chief* Inspector now.'

'Congratulations. I didn't know.'

Stone shook the proffered hand. 'Yes, it was most unexpected. Between you and me, I think it was a bit of a political move. It's suiting the Superintendent's plans to keep me on whilst knowing that I'm not likely to be there for very long. But I'm not objecting. It'll help the pension.'

'Perhaps Superintendent Nelson was thinking of that also?'

'I'm not sure they're that philanthropic but you never know.' He gazed down at the sleeping patient and rubbed his mouth, 'this is a strange business.'

'It's good of you to take a personal interest. I assume this would normally dealt with by one of your officers.'

Stone shrugged away the appreciation. 'Don't mention it. The councillor's one of our important citizens and anyway, we go back a bit now, don't we?'

'Do you know what exactly happened?'

'We won't be certain until we've been able to question her. It appears she swerved off the road and blacked out. Another driver found her sometime around 11pm. Had she been with you?'

'Yes. She left about 10.45. She had an early start in the morning, and before you ask, she'd had one small glass of wine with her dinner.'

Stone nodded. 'As confirmed by toxicology, well within the legal limit.'

'Do you have any other details?'

'Not really, just that the driver who found her said that before he rounded the bend, his headlights picked out a figure who appeared to be running from the direction of the car. By the time he'd got closer, he saw whom he presumed was the same person, drive off at speed.'

Selwyn exhaled deeply. 'So, it could be foul play.'

Stone shook his head. 'Not necessarily. Maybe the other person thought about helping, but just didn't want to get involved, as soon as they realised they might have to speak to the police. Maybe they'd been drinking or been doing something they didn't want to be found out. An assignation perhaps.'

'So, you don't know whether it's a man or woman.'

'No.'

Selwyn stared down anxiously at his fiancée's serene face. 'And you've no idea what made her drive off the road?'

Stone cleared his throat. 'It may be nothing to do with it but our officer found an area of the road that had a lot of leaves on it and nearby, a large tree branch that looked like it had been freshly broken off. Of course it could be nothing to do with it. Something that had happened earlier.'

Selwyn saw the DCI glance at his watch. 'The doctor said she's likely to remain sedated for another hour.'

'In that case I'd better get back to the station and return later for a statement.' The two men exchanged glances.

'I really appreciate your involvement, chief inspector.'

Stone offered one of his infrequent smiles. 'Don't mention it, sir.' At the doorway he turned back. 'Rest assured we'll do all we can to get to the bottom of this.'

Early evening found Selwyn seated, nursing a glass of malt whisky as he stared at the setting sun through the windows of the garden room. Mrs S entered to ask if the commander was at home to a visit from Detective Chief Inspector Stone.

Selwyn jumped to his feet. 'By all means Mrs S, show him in.'

A minute later, the DCI appeared. It had been some time since his last altercation with the housekeeper. She now appeared to be well disposed towards him, so he accepted Mrs S's offer of a cup of tea, in preference to the stronger drink Selwyn had proposed.

'Any new developments?' Selwyn asked anxiously, after Mrs S had gone.

'I understand you stayed with the patient for a little while.' Stone sounded somewhat guarded.

Selwyn however, was easy with the question. 'Yes, Miriam kept waking then dozing off again. She was in such a sorry state I didn't attempt to press her on what had happened so I left her to sleep.'

Stone appeared to relax. 'Well, commander, I've just managed to get some information from Ms Cheyney. She remembers a car following her and nearly colliding with a branch in the road. It appears the other car positioned itself alongside her such that to avoid the branch she would have to veer off the road.'

'The bastard!'

'She reckons it was a man and remembers he was wearing a balaclava, though she couldn't give much more of a description. It appears he approached the car and she caught sight of something in his hand. He was about to open her door and that's all she can remember. We're assuming he saw the other car approaching so he scarpered sharpish, but not before moving the branch off the road. It wasn't there when our witness arrived.'

Selwyn's eyes narrowed. 'Tyson,' he hissed.

'I don't think we should be jumping to any conclusions,'

warned Stone, 'though that is one line of enquiry we're pursuing.'

'Either Tyson, that engineer, or Hirst. It's got to be one of them.' Selwyn insisted.

'As I said, let's not be hasty. We're looking into all possibilities.'

It was perhaps fortunate for the commander's equanimity that further discussion was abandoned as Mrs Soames waddled in with the tea tray.

On his departure, the DCI promised to keep the commander as fully informed as he could, whilst urging no direct action on his part.

To Mrs Soames consternation, when she came to clear away the tea tray, the commander, with glass and bottle, had emigrated to the study. From behind the closed door strains of Bill Evans' 'What is there to say?' could be heard, a sure sign that her boss was in low spirits.

''e'll be givin' that whisky bottle a bit of a smackin', this evening,' Mrs S murmured to herself as she shuffled off to the kitchen.

***

'Oh my goodness, what on earth's happened?'

Amanda's face turned in the direction from where the anxious query had come, as she pressed to staunch the flow of blood.

Eleanor hurried into the office, plonked down the two coffee mugs on the desk and reached out for Amanda's arm.

'It was my silly fault. I dropped a file on the vase and cut myself on it trying to rescue the flowers.'

Eleanor sat the injured librarian down, examined the

cut and snatched a couple of tissues from the box on the desk. 'Hold these tight against it and I'll get the first aid kit. Where's it kept?'

'At the front desk.'

'Wow, thank you, that was expertly done. I'm sure the NHS would snap you up,' said Amanda, after the wound had been cleaned, dressed and bandaged.'

Eleanor, who was now mopping up the spilt water from the desk, gave an abashed smile. 'You don't get to my age without learning a few things. I'm only too glad I was here to help, dear.'

'I'm only too glad you were on hand. I can't stand the sight of blood, especially my own. I also want to thank you for looking after the festival committee whilst I was away. They can't speak highly enough about you and your home-made cakes. They've gone down a bomb.'

Eleanor tried to deflect the compliment with a shake of her head. Amanda regarded the bandage. 'Not bad enough to get me out of doing next year's budget, I suppose. It's a horrible job. Each year you trim things to the bone, then the next year you have to get even lower. A bit like limbo dancing.'

Eleanor let out a little snigger. 'I'm sure you'll work wonders.'

Amanda reached for her coffee. Eleanor did likewise, studied it for a while then announced, 'I'm afraid I won't be coming in after this week. Not for a while, anyway.'

'Is there something wrong? Is it your father?'

She tried to smile away Amanda's alarm. 'No, not really. He's got to a stage when he needs more specialised care, so I've managed to find a place for him in a local care home. No, I need to go back to France for two funerals. My friend

Christine has lost both her husband and her mother.'

'Oh my God. I'm so sorry. What happened?'

'They weren't connected. The mother had dementia and her husband cancer. It's so unfortunate it all happened at once. If she wants me to, I shall stay for a while until things are more settled for her.'

'Oh dear, Eleanor, my deepest sympathy. I hope it all works out. We'll miss you and I do hope you'll come back to us when you return.'

'Thank you, dear. I most certainly will.'

***

Francis threaded his way with the drinks through the crowded bar. Over the crowd, the top of his head was clearly visible to Charlie as he watched his approach. Francis flashed a smile as he placed the pints on the table. 'It's heaving,' he commented as he sat down.

'You forgot the nuts,' Charlie observed, with a wry smile.

'Leave it out, mate.' Francis delved into his jacket pocket and dropped two bags onto the table.

'Cheers.' Charlie raised his glass, Francis responded then tore open one of the packets and Charlie followed suit.

They sat in silence, chewing before Francis glanced across at Pembroke. 'Don't seem like another year, does it?'

Charlie nodded then started a coughing fit, pulling out his handkerchief. Francis looked on with a concerned expression. 'You alright?'

Charlie nodded, returned his handkerchief and took a mouthful of beer. 'Yeah, must have been those nuts.' He stared reflectively at his glass. 'It sure doesn't seem like a year's gone flashing by.' He looked back at Francis, picked up and raised his glass. 'To the boys,' he toasted.

Francis raised his glass. 'To the boys, God bless 'em.' He quickly replaced his glass on the table, his lips pursed. Charlie placed a reassuring hand on Francis's arm.

***

OCTOBER

The arrival of Mrs Soames in the library, carrying a bulky, manilla envelope, was to be the highlight of the commander's day. That however, was only after he'd expressed concern at the pained expression on the housekeeper's face.

'Oh don't you go concernin' yourself, commander. It's just me various veins. They're playin' up somethin' chronic today.'

This triggered his own mental concern as to just how Mrs Soames was going to be able to cope when the hall was opened to the public. But he was wise enough not to open the lid on that particular box, at least for the present. 'Well, you just take it easy Mrs S, we don't want you doing any damage to yourself.

The housekeeper indulged him with a smile and the envelope, then beat a shuffling retreat muttering, 'Chance'll be a fine thing what with all there is to do,' once she was safely out of earshot.

Selwyn quickly tore open the envelope and hastily glanced through the beefy documents. His eye's widened in parallel with his grin. Here they were, the land transfer deed, and the excavation permit for the recreation land.

The door opened and in walked Miriam. Her pale face gave way to a tired smile as Selwyn discarded the documents onto the table and hastened towards her. 'Should you be up, old thing?'

She gave him a mock glower. 'Less of the "old thing" if you don't mind. I may look a crock but it doesn't follow I am one, yet.'

They kissed and with his arm round her, Selwyn escorted her to the chaise longue. 'How about some tea?'

She nodded and he was about to move over to the bell-pull, when he remembered the varicose veins. 'Have a read at those,' he motioned to Miriam, then set off for the kitchen. He had just reached the hallway when the sonorous bell to the front door rang. 'I'll get it, Mrs S,' he called out in the direction of the kitchen, at the doorway of which Mrs S had appeared.

Moments later Selwyn stood in the entrance hall with DCI Stone, Mrs Soames still detained in the doorway by her curiosity.

'Could we have tea for three please, Mrs S,' asked the commander. 'Just give me a shout and I'll come and get it.'

Mrs S gave him a withering look. 'You certainly will not,' she muttered as she turned back into the kitchen.

'And what brings you here?' Selwyn asked as he led the DCI down the corridor, their footsteps resounding on the highly polished parquet floor.

'I just thought I'd drop by to fill you and Ms Cheyney in on progress regarding the accident, as far as I can.'

With an inward smile Selwyn reflected on how often, and under what variety of hostile circumstances, the DCI had previously trodden the same corridor over the past couple of years.

'Councillor Cheyney, how nice to see you up and about,' Stone addressed Miriam, when he had entered the room. 'How are you, now?'

'Good days and bad days, I'm afraid,' Selwyn cut in, 'but steadily improving,' he hastily added, on catching Miriam's frown. 'Soon be back up to snuff, eh?'

Miriam nodded just as Mrs S entered carrying a laden tea tray.

'I told you I'd…' Selwyn's comment tailed off as he noted the housekeeper's expression. 'That's very kind of you.'

Another glower as the housekeeper departed.

'Now what can you tell us?' asked Selwyn, once the trio were seated and served.

Stone cleared his throat. 'From our enquiries, it would appear the tree branch was broken off and placed in the road deliberately, sometime not long before you arrived on the scene, councillor.'

'Please, call me Miriam.'

'Have you found who was responsible?'

'I'm afraid not, sir. We found some evidence at the scene and have interviewed someone…'

'McNabb?' Selwyn interrupted.

'I'm not at liberty to say.'

'Oh, come on man. After all Miriam's been through, both now and before, surely to God you can be more open with us?'

'I'm sorry. I can't divulge that at this time.'

Selwyn rose, paced over to the window and stared out on the wildflower meadow. Then he turned and exhaled his frustration. 'Alright then. Does this evidence prove who was responsible?'

'The evidence, as it stands, can't put anyone away.'

Selwyn stared at Stone, glanced at Miriam then turned back to the meadow. 'Jesus Christ!' he muttered, his frustration back with a vengeance.

'I'm sure chief inspector Stone's doing all he can,'

observed Miriam.

'Thank you, councillor.'

Although Selwyn maintained his hard stare at the meadow he knew Stone had risen, from the sound of the change that now jingled in his pocket. It was a leitmotif which, with memories of how often he had heard it before, seemed to strangely reassure the commander. He turned. 'There's only two people who I reckon would be in the frame, that's Tyson and that chap McNabb.'

'Three if you count Hirst. He was also in on the skulduggery with them,' Miriam pointed out.

'He has been ruled out of our enquiries,' confirmed Stone.

Selwyn moved forward towards him. 'And what of the other two?'

'All I can tell you is that McNabb appears to have left the area, months ago. So far, we've not been able to trace him.'

'There you are. It's got to be Tyson. He's the bastard that got away with it, last time.'

'Selwyn.'

'Sorry dear.'

'What I can assure you of is that we're doing all we can to find and charge the guilty party. It's certainly not a case of any error on your part councillor, so if you have to make a claim on your car insurance, the incident log will record that. I have the incident number for you.' He handed her a slip of paper.

'Well, at least thank you for that,' said Miriam.

'Tell me,' Selwyn enquired, 'have there been any further developments over that death at Fellowes House?

'We're treating it as murder, commander.'

'Wasn't he the chap whose wife committed suicide, recently?'

'He was.'

'So, possibly a revenge killing?'

'That's one possibility we're looking at. I must admit that when we found that the company your nephew works for is based in the building, we did wonder whether the death was in any way connected with past events.'

Selwyn frowned. 'But you've discounted that now, haven't you? After all, the only connection is that Sebastian's company leased out the unit to the dead man.'

'Yes, we're satisfied the link was only coincidental.' He glanced at his watch. 'I'd better be making a move.' He turned to Marion, 'Councillor, I would recommend you take every precaution. I'm afraid we can't offer you police protection, so do take care. Try, as far as possible, to be accompanied by someone whenever you venture out.'

'Easier said than done, though I appreciate your advice. Please keep us informed of any further developments.'

The DCI promised he would and was shown to the door by Selwyn. There, before he left, Stone confided in the commander. 'Off the record, I'm sure, if you were in my position, you'd be doing everything to keep tabs on Mr Tyson and his movements.'

'I'm sure I would,' at which the two men exchanged knowing nods and parted.

By the time he had returned, Miriam was already leafing through the documents.

'So, at long last things are on the move,' he enthused, once they had both read everything.

'You mean opening the hall?' prompted Miriam.

'Well, er yes.'

'Your first thought was your treasure hunt, wasn't it?'

Selwyn gave a sheepish nod.

'You're not going to neglect progress on the hall are you?'

He looked at her and smiled. 'I take it that's an instruction rather than a request.'

She smiled back and tapped the tip of his nose. 'I would say so, my love.'

'So be it. I'll get the files out and set up our first steering committee meeting. You, me, Sebastian and Amanda. Then, at the appropriate time, I suppose we'll jolly well have to include Mrs S and Sean. But for now, with the land transfer in the bag, I think we should celebrate with a drop of bubbly, what do you think?'

It was difficult to know whether it was the effect of the champagne, or excitement at the start of the project to open the hall, that seemed to have brought some colour back to Miriam's cheeks. However, it was certainly more the prospect of a start to the exploratory excavation on the recreational land that was responsible for the subsequent spring in the commander's step.

***

The date of the next Wisstingham arts festival committee meeting coincided with Eleanor's return to the library, following her return from France. Amanda was happy to see her again and the faces of the committee members, particularly Charlie Pembroke, appeared to register equal pleasure as they crowded round the coffee urn and the freshly made cakes she had brought in.

'It's so good to see you again,' Amanda greeted her. 'And you've saved my bacon remembering the meeting was today. I'd completely forgotten to get some refreshments in.'

Eleanor's eyes wrinkled in a smile. 'It's my pleasure, dear.'

'Did everything go alright?'

Temporarily distracted by Charlie Pembroke who, from across the room, gave her a smile and thumbs up sign, Eleanor returned the smile then turned to her boss. 'Oh yes, dear, it all went as well as it might. And do you know,' she rubbed her hands in evident glee, 'Christine's agreed to come and stay for Christmas. I'm so looking forward to it.'

Roland, in his role of chairman, was now chivvying the committee members to go into the meeting room. Amanda turned to Eleanor. 'It looks like the meeting's about to start, why don't you come and sit in on it? I'm sure no one would mind.'

Eleanor gave her an abashed look. 'Oh no. I couldn't possibly. It's not my place. I'll just clear up out here.' With that she scurried off to collect the empty cups, saucers and plates, whilst Amanda joined the others.

'Still here?' asked Eleanor as she poked her head round Amanda's office door, late that afternoon. 'Nothing wrong is there?'

'No. What makes you ask that?'

'Well, I was on my way home and I could see you were still here, but there's no sign of your car. The car park's virtually deserted.'

Amanda looked at the clock. 'Heavens, is that the time? No, it's all fine. My car's in for service. Sebastian said he and Selwyn would sort it all out. I'm due to ring him when I'm ready to be picked up.'

'Oh, you don't need to bother him. I'll drop you off.'

Amanda looked doubtful. 'It's at the hall. It'd be out of your way.'

'That's not a problem, dear.'

'Goodness, this is impressive,' commented Eleanor as she drove into the hall's drive.

'Yes, they knew how to lay these places out.'

On their arrival, Sebastian was already descending the stone staircase. 'I was getting worried. Thought you'd forgotten to ring,' he said to Amanda, through the open passenger window.

She closed the window, got out and gave him a kiss. 'I nearly did. Come and meet Eleanor.' She made the introduction through Eleanor's now open window.

'Thanks again, Eleanor,' said Amanda.

'It was a pleasure dear, and nice to meet you, Sebastian.'

He stared after the red Fiesta as it disappeared down the drive. 'HEN, what an appropriate number plate,' he commented as he led up the steps.

'What do you mean?'

'Mother Hen?' his tease rewarded with a light punch on his trouser seat.

'Just watch it, buster,' she chuckled. 'Eleanor is a lovely, caring lady.'

Chapter 5

The jingling change announced Stone's striding approach down the corridor towards his office. As was his custom, he eyed his reflection in the glass window screens he passed, checking on hair, moustache and tie. Whilst he could not be called dapper, he took a pride in his appearance, his shortness of stature and rotundity made up for by his smart appearance. Or so he thought.

His passage was interrupted by DS McBride who came bowling out after him through one of the doorways. 'There's been another one, guv.'

'What?' came the disgruntled reply. Stone continued without slowing.

McBride kept pace, by his side. 'Another hanging.'

They came to an abrupt stop. 'Where? Don't tell me, Wisstingham Hall.' Stone's widened eyes seemed to stare in defiance of an affirmative reply.

'No, Milbrook common.'

Stone's shoulders visibly slumped. 'Thank God for that. You'd better fill me in on the way there.' He began to hastily retrace his steps to the lift, McBride still keeping pace as he briefed his boss.

By the time they arrived at the scene, the pathologist was already knelt by the body.

Stone turned to a constable. 'Who was first on the scene?'

He nodded in the direction of a DC who appeared to be taking a statement from a man. 'It was Johnson, sir.'

'Get him over as soon as he's finished.' He looked back down at the body. 'Any ideas who he might be?'

Noone could shed any light.

'Do we know if there were any witnesses?' asked Stone.

The constable turned and pointed. 'Just the chap with Johnson.'

Stone turned his attention to the pathologist. 'Cause and time of death?'

'I'd say between ten pm and midnight. As to the cause, well all my money's on strangulation but autopsies do sometimes throw up surprises.'

As Stone contemplated the corpse, his thumb and finger teased at his moustache. He knew that face from somewhere but just could not make the connection. He was now joined by Johnson. 'What about the ground? Any sign of imprints from steps, or anything used to get him up there? Any tyre tracks?'

'Nothing like that, sir,' replied Johnson.

'Perhaps he was just hoisted up there,' suggested McBride.

'If so, there'd probably have been more than one of them involved. What about footprints?'

Johnson shook his head. 'Loads of imprints where the grass has been trodden down but no prints as such. I reckon half of Hopestanding could have walked through here over the past few days.'

'Oh, that's just dandy,' exclaimed Stone.

Thanks to a fingerprint match with the police records, within a couple of hours the dead man had been identified as Justin Welton, a recent guest of one of Her Majesty's prisons, news of which caused DCI Stone to slap his forehead. 'Of course it was him, how the hell could I have missed that?' As his memory took over, he became completely awestruck. He stared distractedly through his office window.

'There've been a lot of villains through here since he was caught and banged up,' McBride tried to console his boss who now started to pace and jingle up and down his office. 'It's got to be a revenge killing, surely,' offered McBride, as he watched his boss, somewhat like a tennis match spectator.

'I don't reckon it's a simple as that,'

'Why not, sir?'

Stone paused to look at his subordinate. 'Because the two men who would have the perfect motive for the killing each have the perfect alibi.'

McBride, frowned and stared at him.

Stone resumed his seat and eyeballed the sergeant. 'Ten years ago, Welton was convicted of killing two young men in a road accident whilst under the influence of alcohol. The victims happened to be the sons of Charlie Pembroke and Francis MBoko respectively, both of whom I should point out were with me last night at a masonic function, from 8pm until the early hours.'

Nevertheless, the formality of interviews with the two men took place. DCI Stone had had to stand down from the proceedings, replaced at the interviews by Superintendent Nelson.

Pembroke had almost laughed off the very idea that he, as a successful police officer with an unblemished record, could have stooped so low as to have any involvement in the killing. That his ex-colleagues could even think he might have been involved was ludicrous. Yes, he had been mortified by the loss of his son and harboured a loathing of the offender, but no he'd had no involvement. It would surely only have been a matter of time before the toerag would have encountered some form of retribution from other quarters.

Charlie had reminded his interrogators that Welton, a known drug dealer and police informant, had crossed his criminal associates only a couple of days before his drunken car accident. Furthermore, when arrested, he had pleaded for protection. It was indeed fortunate for him that his remand and subsequent sentence had provided this.

Mboko, when interviewed, had been far more taciturn but had been adamant that he too had not been involved. He was an architect and a respected member of the local business community, certainly not a member of the criminal fraternity. He would not know where to start to arrange a killing and the proof of his whereabouts at the time of the murder spoke for itself. Had he been in league with Charlie Pembroke in arranging the murder? Absolutely not. Charlie was a police officer and would never involve himself with something like that.

Looking on through the one-way mirror to the interview room Stone had nodded at this comment.

No, MBoko was not sorry the man was dead. And yes, he had hated Welton for the death of his son, but time had moved on, as he also had and now intended to do, if his interviewers were quite finished.

At the subsequent briefing in the DCI's office, whilst the

two men had not been discounted from their enquiries, the emphasis was to be placed on the investigation of Welton's old contacts.

***

DECEMBER

Eleanor could barely contain her excitement as she stood in front of the barrier at the airport arrivals. Every time the large, opaque glass door slid open to disgorge more passengers, she felt a thrill of anticipation. This would instantly subside when a stranger was revealed, generally encumbered with baggage.

Since she had arrived quarter of an hour before the plane was due to land, Eleanor remained in the same position for almost an hour before the door opened and Christine Lagrange finally appeared. As she walked through, Lagrange's sharp, brown eyes scanned the line of waiting people and picked out Eleanor who had burst into a wide smile and was waving furiously.

Christine had come well prepared for a British winter, her long, fawn camel coat set off by a matching woollen scarf wrapped twice round her neck. Henna coloured hair peeped out from the sides and peak of a red Breton cap.

Her lips, red with lipstick, cracked a smile when she spotted Eleanor and she hurried round the end of the barrier to reach her. 'Bonjour ma chère,' she almost sighed. She temporarily abandoned her cases for the two women to exchange kisses on both cheeks and embrace.

Eleanor then grabbed the handle of the larger case and they headed for the exit. 'How was your journey?'

Christine gave a little shrug as she walked. 'Ca va, it was no delays.'

The journey to Wisstingham passed in almost constant exchanges. When they actually arrived and drove through the village, Christine's delight at the pretty, thatched cottages and gardens manifested itself in a series of oohs and aaahs. 'Is like Midsomer,' she observed, which brought a contented smile to Eleanor's lips.

Once inside Brackshaw Cottage, Eleanor helped to carry the cases upstairs. They were abandoned in the guest bedroom while Christine was given the grand tour, her final verdict being that the cottage was just exquisite, which afforded Eleanor much relief and pleasure.

As the December days drifted by, Eleanor delighted in showing her friend around Wisstingham, Hopestanding and the surrounding countryside. She introduced her to the library, though not to Amanda who at that time was very busy. She showed her the town hall and, from its ornate metal gates, gave her a glimpse of Wisstingham Hall. They sampled the delights and menus of the village's three pubs, The Happy Rat, The Phantom Hound and the Ferret and Wardrobe. They dined both at Qwik Qwak and the Mazawat café, which became a firm favourite of Christine's.

It was to the Mazawat that on one grey December day, with leaden clouds in the sky and Eleanor at work in the library, Christine ventured on her own.

Only three of the tables were occupied with customers, so Christine seated herself at the window table from where she could watch the comings and goings in a typical English village.

Gwen Chase, who remembered Christine from previous visits, approached with a menu.

'You're the French lady, aren't you?' the question more of a statement. 'Bonjour madame.'

'Bonjour,' Christine smiled back.

Gwen then went to elaborate lengths to slowly and rather loudly explain the menu's contents, already fully understood by her customer who sat patiently smiling through the performance. She homed in on an espresso and slice of strawberry cheesecake, without reference to the menu. Gwen then offered a few more words of her GCSE (nearly failed) French and departed.

As Christine gazed through the window, a heavily built man approached her from one of the adjacent tables. He had a round, rather pale face, even for an Englishman, receding hairline and straight, mousy-coloured, short-cropped hair, greying at the sides. His wrinkled forehead was shiny, his nose straight and bulbous and he had a prominent chin, above which he wore a glum expression. As he approached her, the expression instantly switched into a practised broad smile, his eyes slightly widened as if in anticipation. 'I hope I'm not intruding but you must be the French lady I've been hearing about. It's Christine Lagrange, isn't it?'

Christine stared uncertainly at him for a moment.

Still smiling, the man touched the back of the chair next to her, glanced at it then back at Christine.

'Please, to sit down,' she responded.

He did so and offered his hand, 'I'm Charlie Pembroke, a retired police officer.'

Christine shook it hesitantly which prompted Pembroke to assure her the mention of his career was of no relevance. 'I think we know someone in common. Eleanor Delaney. She…' he hesitated for a moment. 'She looks after me and my other committee colleagues. We're organising an Arts and Crafts festival and exhibition for Wisstingham.'

Now very much more at ease, Christine finally smiled. 'You 'ave a beautiful village, monsieur. I adore it.'

'Actually, I live in Hopestanding, nearby. It's a bit bigger than Wisstingham.'

'I have seen this town too. It is also splendid. I like very much the church.'

By the time Gwen brought the order, the two of them had eased into pleasant conversation and Charlie briefly adjourned to bring his unfinished drink.

***

Later that evening, over the dinner table, Christine described her meeting with Pembroke. Contrary to what she had expected, from Eleanour's expression this did not appear to meet with her approval, though she said nothing. It was only when Christine mentioned that she was hoping to meet with him again that Eleanor's tight smile vanished, her lips now compressed and thin. 'I think it might be best if you did not form a friendship with him,' she suggested.

Christine frowned and stared at her then smiled. 'I think you are jalous, no?'

'I am not jealous. I just don't want to see you upset or unhappy.'

'How can I be unhappy? He is a nice man. I have to have some friends if I am being here.'

Eleanor's spirits soared. She had offered for Christine to

stay with her as long as she liked. Indeed, during her stay in France Christine had said, on more than one occasion, that there was nothing to keep her there. The Domaine was now in good hands. But she had never before given any indication that she would be prepared to stay in England. Eleanor now desperately wanted to defuse the situation. She smiled, reached across the table and patted her friend's arm. 'Maybe I am just a little jealous. You are a very dear friend. I just want you to be happy. Men can be …' she searched for the right word, '…unpleasant, at times.'

This appeared to bring matters to a close and the two of them continued their meal in harmony, the conversation changed to preparations for Christmas.

***

JANUARY 2012

'Yes!' Kathy Turnbull disconnected from the call and punched the air.

This was that tedious time of the year, after the Christmas advertising had yielded a large chunk of the Chronicle's annual income, when the editor customarily instructed the reporters to seek out advertorials. These were features on businesses and organisations which would include advertising space that the contributors paid for. More space than they might normally sign up to. In exchange, the overall coverage gave far better value for money than a mere advert. And Kathy had just clinched a beauty, coverage of the local veterinary practice which would also feature the recent wedding of one of the partners to Julia Smyth, a member of one of the prominent, local families.

At first, the call to Theo Patterson had yielded not only no interest whatsoever but even a hint of hostility. Fortunately, his wife had taken over the call and insisted they should go ahead. She was prepared to pay the lion's share of the bill in exchange for the wedding coverage and Theo's recent ascendency to the partnership. The advertorial would appear in the following month's special, pull-out edition.

***

DCI Stone stared at the evidence board, a whiteboard pen poised in his hand. Around him stood various officers and at the back, sat perched on the edge of a desk, Superintendent Nelson.

Stone turned to face his audience and began to pace. Simultaneously, several pairs of eyes glanced at the clock. It was customary, on such occasions, for bets to be made as to how long it would take before the sound of jingling change would be heard.

The closest to twelve seconds was today's winner.

'So, we have two murders with a similar MO, namely hanging, with a possible similar motive of revenge. Let's deal with the most recent one first. Justin Welton.' Stone tapped the relevant half of the board and scanned his audience.

'Except in his case only, according to the pathology report, Welton had been sedated beforehand,' cut in McBride.

Stone nodded. 'Welton, who'd just been released from prison, was found dead, hanged on the morning of 19th. November. Death had occurred in the early hours. Ten years ago, he was found guilty of causing death by dangerous driving, well over the limit. He'd run into another car and killed the two young men in it.

'If it's revenge,' chimed in PC Johnson, 'wouldn't that put the men's families in the frame?'

'We all know whom we're talking about,' chipped in Nelson, 'retired CI Pembroke and Francis MBoko, but they've both got sound alibis for the time of the crime.'

'But what if they'd got someone else to commit the crime?' the PC persisted.

Stone took back control of the briefing. 'It's possible, but it's far more likely it was the victim's old associate Vincent McNulty, a known drug dealer. They'd fallen out just before the accident and McNulty had apparently threatened to kill him.'

'Any progress with that?' enquired Nelson.

'We're still checking out his alibi, though he'd probably have hired some muscle to do the job,' McBride interjected.

Stone jingled. 'Anything from the crime scene?'

'Nothing much,' confirmed McBride, 'it's a popular place for dog walkers.'

Stone tapped the other half of the board, stared at it for a moment then began to pace again. 'The first victim was one Jack Carey. He was found hanged at Fellowes House on the thirteenth of September. It was immediately outside his own business premises, within the building. Murdered in the early hours of the morning. No signs of forced entry or a struggle and no fingerprints to go off.'

For Christ's sake stop jingling, man, Nelson wanted to say and made a mental note to bring it up, later.

Stone continued. 'The victim's wife committed suicide in March, claiming she'd been driven to it by her husband's infidelity and physical and mental abuse. We've followed up on any relations or friends who might have wanted to take revenge, but none seem to fit the bill.'

'Did Carey have any previous form?' chirped up Johnson.

'No official record of any major fallings-out with anyone, grievances or anything like that, but neighbours have said the man was a nasty piece of work and could easily get aggressive. The wife was always quiet and kept herself to herself. There were reports of his shouting and occasional screams from the wife, but everyone was too frightened to intervene or report anything.'

'Possibly some lover or vigilante taking revenge for the wife?'

Stone looked across to McBride. 'That's something that's being looked into, isn't it McBride?'

'Yes, but there's no indication she was playing away.'

'What do we know about the ropes?' asked Stone.

'The same in both cases,' another officer replied. 'A common brand, found in a number of DIY stores, boat-yards and online. We've made enquiries about any recent purchases in the area and are following them up.'

'Okay, any questions or observations?' Stone looked around the group but nothing was forthcoming. 'Alright, Then, let's wind this up. Keep on it, everyone.'

***

FEBRUARY

Despite Eleanor's opposition, which had resulted in two further bouts of disagreement between the two women, the budding relationship between Christine and Charlie

Pembroke showed signs of almost coming into flower. Christine had reaffirmed her wish to remain in Wisstingham and declared again that there was nothing left for her in France.

In confirmation of this, late January had seen her return briefly to France to put the Domaine up for sale. A good time to do so, the Notaire had confirmed, since it would allow a prospective purchaser to benefit from the year's wine harvest.

The older woman's affection for Christine had grown ever stronger since her arrival in Wisstingham, and her fear of losing her ever more acute. Eleanor had therefore concluded it was better to surround Christine, the object of her affection, with as much comfort, happiness and interesting diversion as possible, and to make her so reliant upon her that Christine would not wish to leave.

Consequently, on one dreary afternoon Eleanor's cheerfulness was in marked contrast to the gusting rain she battled through to arrive home. She divested herself of the wet overcoat, umbrella and shoes in the cottage hallway. The 'Hello Christine' she shouted, as she headed to the kitchen to make a pot of tea — her friend had by now had been fully converted to this very English refreshment — was replied to from the living room. Eleanor hummed as she brewed the tea, set the tea tray and placed that week's copy of the Chronicle on the tray.

''ow was your day?' Christine greeted her as Eleanor entered the room.

'Very good indeed, dear,' came the enthusiastic reply. 'There's something here I'm just dying to show you.' She poured the tea, seated herself next to Christine, put the supplement on one side and began to eagerly search through the Chronicle. She found what she was looking for, folded the paper to more clearly display the advert and with a triumphant smile handed it over. 'There's a pottery in Hopestanding that's for sale or lease.'

Christine read the advert then looked up at her friend. Her frown of uncertainty did nothing to dampen Eleanor's spirits.

'But I have not the money to do this,' Christine objected. 'Not until I sell the Domaine.'

'That's not a problem. I can pay for the lease and the legal costs. It would be my present to you. It would be like old times, two of us together whilst you work.'

Christine appeared to dreamily consider the prospect. Then she frowned, 'but I cannot let you to do that.'

'Of course you can. I will be so, so happy to do it.'

Christine's smile, coupled with her now watery eyes, signalled total agreement. Eleanor promptly reclaimed the advert and made a call to signify their interest in viewing the property.

Over dinner, the women excitedly discussed future plans and possibilities. Even the opportunity to create something for the forthcoming arts festival was mooted. It wasn't until later in the evening, when conversation was finally exhausted, that Eleanor sat down to work on a translation. Christine curled up on the daybed, her legs under her, and started to leaf through the newspaper's supplement.

'Merte! Mon Dieu!' she suddenly exclaimed.

Eleanor's head spun round in her direction. 'What is it?'

Christine was already up and bringing the opened article to her. 'This veterinaire, I am certain this is the 'usband of Yvette Montand.'

94

Eleanor took the paper from her and scrutinised it. 'Oh my God, I think you're right. But it can't be.'

'Bien sur it is.'

While Christine stood over her, Eleanor read the article. Finally she looked up. 'But this would make him a bigamist.'

'Exactement!'

'Unless he's already divorced?'

Christine sniffed her disbelief. 'Pas possible, not in the time.'

'So, what do you think we should do?'

'Tell it to your police.'

Her fingers pressed against her lips, Eleanor stared into space and pondered.

'What you think?' Christine prompted.

'I think it may be complicated for the British police to bring a case of bigamy. They will need to investigate and get evidence of what has happened in France. I also wonder what good it will do for Yvette Montand. Perhaps he already provides financial support for her. If he is charged with bigamy, he will surely lose his job and freedom. Then it will be Yvette who will suffer.'

It was now Christine who paused to think. 'Oui, yes, I think you are right. I will go to see him.'

Though somewhat nervous of the matter being dealt with by Christine, who had a tendency to be impulsive, Eleanor was reluctant to get herself deeply involved, so she simply agreed with her friend, imploring her to be very careful in what she said and did.

Chapter 6

The procession seemed to have gone on all that Saturday morning, much to the amusement of Mrs Soames and Amanda. First one man would appear, then the other, each carrying something out through the rear lobby to the car and trailer parked in the garage courtyard. At one stage, Sebastian's appearance, with a metal detector in one hand and a pick slung over his shoulder, prompted Amanda to burst into 'Hi Ho, Hi Ho, it's off to work we go.' This provoked a sideways scowl from her fiancé and a comment of, 'not funny.'

Nor, it would appear, was the commander particularly taken with the smile on his housekeeper's face as she watched him lug a generator along the corridor. 'Nothing to do then?' he challenged, his sunken jowls accentuating the normal hang-dog expression.

This drew an equally challenging response. 'Plenty to do, commander, but I reckons as 'ow my first job is to get Amanda 'ere to look on 'er Amazin thingumajig…'

'Amazon,' corrected Amanda.

Mrs S gave her a frown. ''er Amazon thing, to find a brighter coloured doormat, seein' as 'ow folks don't seem to see the one that's there and use it.'

Selwyn, who had now put the generator down and welcomed the brief respite, glanced along the parquet floor. Much of its pristine polished surface now bore testimony to the dirt that had been tramped in that morning, thanks in no small part to an earlier downpour.

'Got a good point, that woman,' came his murmured admission.

By now, Sebastian had arrived. 'That's the lot, guv,' he panted, then picked up the generator, with no protest from his uncle, and set off to the trailer with it.

'I've got you some provisions,' Mrs S offered, 'but 'ow about a nice cup of Rosie before you go?'

'Capital idea.' This. Selwyn thought. would also be an opportunity to find and fill his hip flask.

'I'll serve it in the drawing room, but mind as 'ow you take your shoes off at the end of the corridor,' Mrs S instructed, as she waddled off to the kitchen.

'What's the plan of campaign?' queried Amanda, once tea had been served.

Selwyn pushed home the cork on the bottle of Jura, screwed the top on the hip flask and deposited it into the inside pocket of his Norfolk jacket. 'Firstly, we'll peg out the excavation area from the recreation ground survey plan, check it out with the metal detector, then start digging.'

Amanda glanced over to Sebastian who gave her a 'guess who'll be on the end of the spade,' look, which caused her to smile.

'We'll both share the work,' Selwyn added, with a slightly injured expression, having caught the exchange.

'And what if you don't find the treasure?'

Selwyn shrugged. 'We'll just have to restore the ground and put it down to experience, dear girl.' He drained his cup and consulted his watch, 'well, my boy, we'd better get to it.'

As Sebastian carried the picnic hamper to the car, he almost salivated at the thought of all the neatly packaged sandwiches and items of food it doubtless contained. Mrs S packed a hamper like no other. With both that and the equipment safely loaded into the car, their departure was waved off by Amanda and Mrs S.

'Now for that mop,' murmured Mrs S as she headed back into the hall.

After what had been a long and arduous day, it was not until after seven pm when Selwyn and Sebastian, weary from their exertions, finally drove into the courtyard. After Sebastian had locked the gate, they unloaded the bare minimum of items, leaving most of the tools and equipment ready for the morrow, then headed into the hall.

They were barely halfway down the corridor when Selwyn was halted in his tracks by the appearance of Mrs Soames as she sallied forth from the kitchen, not so much by the sight of her, as her instant perusal of their footwear and doubtless the cleanliness or otherwise of it.

So, he dutifully bent to take off his muddy boots, prompted Sebastian to do likewise. They then retreated back to the door to deposit them there. In their stocking feet they approached the housekeeper who now stood with her arms akimbo. 'So 'as it been a good day, commander?'

'Tiring, Mrs S, tiring.'

'Did you find anything?'

By now, Sebastian had returned from the kitchen where he had deposited the basket and bottles on the table. 'There's certainly something there but we've not got down to it yet,' he explained.

'Well I'm sure as 'ow you will. There's a casserole and

dumplings keeping warm for you, when yer ready.'

Selwyn rubbed his hands. 'Splendid Mrs S, just the ticket. We'll freshen up first and have a quick snifter.' He shot her an anxious glance. 'That's if it'll not be keeping you too late.'

She glanced at the clock. 'Oh that's alright, my Reggie'll be about to watch his Migraine programme. That foreign detective,' she added in response to Selwyn's quizzical frown.

'Maigret you mean?

'That's it. So, you get yerselves sorted out and while yer doin' that, I'll clean your boots up. But just this once, mind. This isn't going to be a regular thing.'

'Of course not, dear Mrs S,' Sebastian quickly cut in. 'That's very kind of you.'

'You be off with you.' She headed in the direction of the boots, determined to have the last word.

Generous though the measure of whisky was that Selwyn poured for his nephew, when they reassembled in the drawing room, it clearly did nothing to improve his demeanour.

'Are you okay, dear boy?' Selwyn asked with narrowed eyes.

'It's work,' Sebastian muttered and downed the drink in one.

'Yes, well it does that to us at times, I suppose.' Selwyn took the nearly empty glass, went to top it up then handed it to his dispirited-looking nephew.

For a while they drank in silence. Sebastian's reticence obliged Selwyn to ask, 'Come on, what is it my dear boy? Spill the beans.'

Sebastian looked him straight in the eye. 'I've just been made redundant.'

'What? That just can't be. Surely.'

'It's true, I've had an email from Fellowes Industries' new owner. Says they're not going to renew my contract and they're going to pay me off for the present one.'

'And who the hell's that?'

'Jeffrey Hirst.'

Selwyn was dumbstruck, but only for an instant. 'The bastard! The utter conniving bastard! What the hell does an undertaker know about electronic technology? It's purely vindictive to get back at me.'

'It was *you* that backed out of the land sale and scuppered his development plans.' Sebastian's misery was momentarily relieved by the sight of his uncle's bulldog expression.

'That was Miriam really. She's the one who exposed him and his council cronies.'

'Well, whatever the reason, I'm well and truly stuffed.'

'Nonsense, there's more than enough work here to keep you fully employed.'

'Thanks, guv but that's not the point. It's the career I chose and was good at, all gone. I'm just bad news,' he added, on reflection.

'Rubbish. Absolute tommyrot. It's not your fault that he's done what he's done, and what about Amanda?'

'Sebastian slowly shook his head 'she'd be better off without me. I'd probably only screw her life up, like everything else.'

Selwyn went to place a hand on his shoulder. 'Come on dear boy, you mean the world to her, and to me,' he said, softly.

Sebastian looked up at him, on the verge of tears. 'It's true. I didn't do anything to protect my mother. It was because of me that you nearly lost all the estate's money. I almost got Amanda killed by Monaghan and if it hadn't been for me, Lucian would still be alive. I even screwed things up bringing Archie Fox back here. And now I've lost my job. I'm sorry, I'm just not hungry. I'll see you tomorrow.'

Selwyn called out to no avail as, with bowed head, Sebastian forlornly headed for the door. He left the commander to wonder whether he should warn Amanda of what had happened, or if that would be an interference he should not make. What Sebastian had said and implied greatly troubled him as to what he intended to do.

***

Most of the waiting customers speculated about the one woman who sat in the veterinary surgery without any animal. One of these people was Selwyn, there to present a rather boisterous Mustard for his annual injection. At one stage, the beagle managed to get close enough to sniff the woman's shoes before the commander pulled him back, with an apologetic smile which the woman acknowledged.

Perhaps a saleswoman, thought one nearby woman, though she did not appear smart enough for that.

Come to collect a pet she'd left here, thought another.

Eventually, she, the last person left in the waiting room, since she had engineered to have the last appointment of the day, was called into Theo Patterson's consulting room.

'Mrs Lagrange, how can I help you,' he enquired, slightly puzzled that she was not accompanied by a pet. He frowned, disturbed at being unable to recall where he had seen this woman before.

'It is more your wife you should to 'elp.' Christine's voice was distinctly frosty.

'Julia? What do you mean?'

Christine eyed him, coldly. 'Your first wife Yvette and her child.'

Patterson's eyes widened as he now recalled the woman and his jaw momentarily dropped, though he tried to lightly dismiss the accusation with a condescending smile. 'I'm sorry, I don't know what you're talking about. You must be mistaking me for someone else.' He stood up. 'Now if there is nothing more you came about.'

'Menteur. Liar. Seat yourself, Monsieur, there is no mistake. You are married to Yvette Montand and 'ave a child with 'er. Now you marry another woman. That is against the law, no?'

Patterson resumed his seat and exhaled deeply, no trace of humour left on his face. 'Now look, the marriage was forced upon me and not a proper one. It would not be recognised as such. So, if you don't mind, I must ask you to leave.'

Christine held his gaze for several moments before she gave a full gallic shrug of shoulders, face and hands. 'Very well, it will not be a problem for you if the police and your English wife are to 'ear of this, no?' She rose and half-turned towards the door.

Patterson jumped up, his fists clenched. 'Now look here, you can't just come in here, threatening me. What's this got to do with you anyway? Who the hell do you think you are?'

She gazed steadily at him. 'You know well who I am. You come to our village and try to use my friend and me. You ask for a job and borrow money you do not give back. You are bête to desert Yvette and your child then to marry again.'

Patterson stared at her then lowered his gaze. His shoulders drooped as he collapsed back down into his seat. He breathed in deeply then exhaled and ran a hand through his hair. 'Alright, what do you want? What will it take for you to keep quiet?' Although he nearly spat the words out his demeanour was one of resignation.

'I want that you will to pay money for your family.'

'Blackmail,' Patterson murmured. His head drooped. 'Okay, I will send them money.'

Christine wagged her finger at him and shook her head. 'No, no. You will pay the money to me and I will send it to Yvette. Then I know it will to arrive.'

Patterson glared at her. 'How much?'

'Three hundred and fifty euros every month. You will to give it to me, each month in big notes.'

Patterson's eyes widened. 'That's ridiculous. It's too much.'

'I do not barter with you. C'est ca.'

He rose again and glared at her, his teeth bared. 'You bitch!'

Undeterred, Christine smiled. 'And you are the bigamist, monsieur. I will come tomorrow and you will give to me the money in the car park, after the surgery closed. Then I come each month on the same date.'

Patterson seethed, his teeth gritted, but he could only nod his acquiescence before she made for the door, still smiling.

Christine was in a state of near euphoria as she described her day's work to Eleanor, when she had returned from visiting her father. Eleanor however, who would have much preferred her friend to have kept quiet about the whole affair, showed little enthusiasm for the venture. It was only their shared experience and view of the man, supported by the village gossip that Patterson had allegedly forced his attentions on Yvette at the outset, which elicited in Eleanor a sense of justice that the man was now being made to pay for his sins.

'Why you are not 'appy for me?' Christine demanded, annoyed at her friend's indifference.

'I don't want to have any trouble over this. I know it is perhaps a good thing for Yvette but it could ruin everything.' She glanced at her friend. 'For both of us,' she added.

This statement was robustly refuted by Christine who confirmed that the first payment to Yvette would be sent by tracked mail to her home address, within the next couple of days. There would be no address or explanation given other than a brief note saying the money was for her and the child.

That same week this glitch in the smooth-running of the women's relationship was almost entirely eclipsed when Eleanor signed the lease on the pottery. For Christine, the chance to move in, equip the place and start work was a godsend. Over the past few weeks she had begun to feel hemmed in by Eleanor. She had continued to show resentment and apparent jealousy, incomprehensible to Christine, at her continuing friendship with Charlie Pembroke. The pottery now gave Christine the space she needed. It would also provide the opportunity for Charlie to visit without the visibility their Mazawat meetings attracted, which always somehow seemed to get back to Eleanor. The last time this had led to another unhappy exchange between them.

'Why can't you just be content with what we have together. Just the two of us?' Eleanor had demanded.

'I like the man and you make me feel smothered at times, I need more freedom,' had been Christine's response.

'But you will have freedom with the pottery.'

Christine had given her a tired look. 'Sometimes you make me feel you want more from me than I can give to you.'

This comment had brought tears to Eleanor's eyes which the guilty friend had sought to expunge with an embrace, kisses and a reassurance that she and Charlie Pembroke were just casual friends. As such, their friendship would never be allowed to get in the way of her relationship with Eleanor.

***

It had been Selwyn's idea to arrange the dinner party. Just the four of them, Miriam, Sebastian, Amanda and him. Mrs Soames had been delighted at the news of the dinner party. This provided the opportunity for her chubby fingers to leaf through the well-thumbed copy of Leith's cookery, for gastronomic recipes suited to the occasion.

The official agenda, apart from enjoying some time and a good meal together, was to share information and thoughts on the opening of the hall and what progress they had made.

Selwyn's other undisclosed purpose was an attempt to rally the spirits of his nephew. His redundancy appeared to have been the final straw in the downward spiral he had started upon months earlier. It appeared his estimation of personal failure and worthlessness was at an all-time low. This had now pitched him into a dark place from which nobody, not even his fiancée, had been able to extricate him. On the contrary, the greater the efforts made, the more he distanced himself from his rescuers, such that even Amanda was left to walk on eggshells in his presence. Selwyn therefore feared that Sebastian might well not even show up for the meal.

For the opening of the hall, Miriam's brief covered the marketing, publicity, grant applications, sponsorship and finances. She was now in fine form and fully recovered from her earlier trauma. Her eagerness to open the hall, putting it well and truly on the national map of stately homes and raising the profile of Wisstingham, remained unabated. The grants had already been agreed in principle and the anticipated revenue would significantly enhance the estate's income.

Selwyn was involved with the finance side of the project and the planning of the changes to the day-to-day procedures and routines, together with the physical changes to the hall and estate that the opening would bring. He was, however, becoming increasingly frustrated at the bad weather and lack of progress with his excavation works on the recreation area. He was acutely aware that the clock was merrily ticking away his limited tenure of the site.

Although not directly connected with the opening, it was nevertheless hoped that any major discovery would feature in the publicity material and perhaps an exhibition on the day.

Sebastian's sector of the opening project covered security, communications, electronics and the IT systems, as well as monitoring progress against the action plans the team had committed to. Despite the abundance of time now available to him, it remained to be seen how much progress he was actually making, a matter to be approached by the other members of the team with great caution

For Amanda, aspects of signage, the descriptive information panels, publicity brochures and displays fell within her remit, together with the coordination of VIP and other invitations to the opening day.

'To Mrs Soames and her superb dinner,' Selwyn announced as the housekeeper finally placed the cheeseboard on the table. He stood to toast her with his wineglass. The others followed suit whilst the smiling but bashful Mrs S blushed to the roots of her hair as her hand batted away the compliment. 'Oh go on with you, commander, it weren't nothing special,' she fibbed, then armed with the crockery and cutlery from the previous course, scurried back to the kitchen in a cloud of dimly discernible, murmured appreciation.

'Which neatly brings us to the one aspect we haven't so far discussed,' said Selwyn, his face grown serious as he sank back down into his chair, 'That of the cafeteria and catering arrangements.' He glanced at his fellow diners on whose faces similar expressions of apprehension now appeared. There was a momentary silence as each contemplated the elephant in the room.

Amanda cleared her throat. 'Is Mrs S still adamant that she wants to run the whole show?'

'I'm afraid so,' replied Selwyn.

'That's just not going to be practical,' observed Miriam. 'Much as she's brilliant at her job, she won't be able to handle her daily domestic and catering duties *and* the cafeteria. That's going to have to be contracted out.'

'But if she had enough staff?' suggested Amanda.

The commander slowly shook his head. 'It wouldn't work, I'm afraid. Much as I love the dear woman, she wouldn't be up to it. She's not one for delegation nor is she exactly a people person.'

He glanced at Sebastian who merely grunted. Seeing more was required of him, he added, 'You're bang on the money there. She'd probably go through the staff like a dose of salts and if anyone didn't like her food, or was critical, she'd end up becoming our customer prevention department.'

'Nevertheless, we're going to have to deal with this pronto, we're running out of time. eight months sounds a long time but there's an awful lot to get done. We've got to find a satisfactory compromise with her, somehow. The architect's champing at the bit to finalise the café layout and the relationship with the kitchen, so she'll have to be involved in those discussions.'

'Good luck with that one,' Sebastian murmured, which drew a frown from Amanda.

Selwyn glanced hopefully round the table. 'So, any ideas as to how we handle it?'

'You'd better leave it to me, to open discussions,' Miriam suggested. 'I think it needs a woman's touch.'

Selwyn gave a smile of relief. 'Capital, that woman.' He rubbed his hands. 'Now let's do justice to the cheese-board. Anyone for port or a liqueur? Then we can discuss progress.'

On this point it was not only the Commander who studiously avoided glancing at Sebastian.

***

The drive from Hopestanding's drab and ever-so-concrete, multi-storey car park to Wisstingham Hall, where she was due to lunch, gave Miriam ample time to reflect on the meeting she and Amanda had just attended. It had certainly been successful, topped off by a final assurance from the Arts Council representative that the support funding application for the opening of the hall was looked on favourably.

The relationship between the councillor and her subordinate Amanda had changed dramatically from its rocky start. It was now a firm friendship built on liking, mutual trust and respect, developed through the various hardships and challenges they had faced together.

'And now for lunch,' Miriam murmured to herself as she drove into the garage courtyard, parked up and switched off the engine. She reached for her handbag and briefcase from the passenger seat, nimbly stepped out of the car and set off for the side entrance to the building.

As if through a sixth sense, or maybe her acute hearing, the housekeeper sensed the luncheon guest had arrived. She put down the kitchen towel, shuffled out of the kitchen and had started to make her way down the darkened corridor when there came a flash of light from the other end of it. This was instantaneously followed by the sound of an explosion and a piercing scream. Simultaneously, there was an explosion of glass from the rear door into the corridor, then only the persistent screaming.

Mrs Soames, though shocked and terrified, rushed down the corridor. She pulled open the door, as best she could, over the shards of glass. Outside, she was greeted by the sight of the burning wreckage of Miriam's car and next to the door, her body covered in blood, the poor woman continuing to scream.

'Oh my God!' came the commander's voice from behind Mrs S. He knelt by his fiancée's side and tried to both comfort her and determine how badly she was injured. She in turn flung her arms around his neck and turned her bloodied face and bewildered, terrified eyes to him. Her screaming had now abated into heavy, uncontrolled sobs as she pulled his head close to hers.

'Ring for an ambulance and the police, Mrs S,' he instructed, over his shoulder. He gently turned his fiancée's face to examine the cause of the bleeding. 'Miriam, can you move, old thing? Do you feel anything broken? Can you move your limbs?'

She released him, gingerly moved her legs and arms then nodded.

Selwyn glanced nervously at the smouldering car which fortunately was some distance away. He knew he shouldn't really move her before the medics arrived, but remaining near the car might prove the worse of two evils. 'Come along, if you feel you can stand, and let's get you inside.' He carefully helped her to her feet. Though she was now trembling, he managed to support and guide her through the damaged door and into the hall.

'They're on their way,' Mrs S assured him as they reached her by the telephone table. Her worried gaze focused on Miriam. 'I'll get you some tissues and how about a cup of Rosie?'

'Excellent idea, maybe also something a bit stronger, eh, my love?'

Though still trembling, Miriam managed a slight smile and nod.

'Also fetch the brandy, would you please, Mrs S. The Hine, mind. I'll take her into the study. Oh, also some warm water, a towel and the first-aid box.' He turned back to Miriam. 'Let's see if we can't get you cleaned up a bit.'

For the rest of the day the hall, particularly the garage courtyard, was a scene of intense police activity. No lesser person than Superintendent Nelson made an appearance by which time Miriam had been driven off to hospital, accompanied by Mrs S. He assured Selwyn that no stone would be left unturned (an ironic turn of phrase, it struck the commander) in determining the cause of the explosion and, should there be one, the perpetrator of the crime.

DCI Stone however, was later far less forthcoming with any such positivity. Nevertheless, by close of play, he was more practically forthcoming than his superior. He confirmed that preliminary findings showed the car had been destroyed by an incendiary device, with more details awaited from the forensics team.

Once Selwyn had made his statement, he was able to dash off to the hospital where Miriam's injury, mainly attributable to having been thrown against the door by the force of the blast, had been dealt with and dressed. It was the shock and temporary hearing impairment that had yet to be overcome.

'You're going to stay safe with me until you're fully back up to snuff, old thing,' Selwyn insisted as he guided Miriam, her head bowed, to the Jaguar. As she followed them, Mrs S could not suppress a smile. For her, the Commander's words immediately conjured up a vision of a reprise of her role of matron-in-charge, this time of Miriam's recovery.

'Some good food, care and plenty of rest and you'll be up and about and back to your old self in no time,' she predicted, once settled in the back of the car. Fortunately, she was unable to see the look of concern on Miriam's pale face, in the front, and the sparkle of merriment at the prospect, in the commander's eyes.

***

Mouthing the ritual, Charlie Pembroke watched as the new candidate was initiated. A movement caught through the corner of his eye caused him to glance towards his guest and old police colleague, Roger Stone. He was scratching at a mark on his apron. He stopped, glanced at Charlie, offered him a fleeting, guilty smile then straightened in his chair to concentrate on the ceremony.

Afterwards, in the bar, after the meal and their congratulations and chat to the new initiate, they took their drinks to a table in the corner.

'Everything alright?' Charlie enquired after a slurp of his IPA.

Roger grimaced and scratched the back of his head. 'It would be if we could get anywhere with these two murders. Ordinarily we'd have had them cracked by now. And the admiral's constantly breathing down my neck on budgets.

Charlie smiled. 'Nelson still there then? I'd have thought they'd have pushed him upstairs by now, somewhere he couldn't do any harm.'

'No such luck. He's like the poor, always with us. Never been off my case since all that long-running pantomime started up at the hall. Charlie, you've never seen anything like it, bodies were piling up. Our guys and the armed response unit were there so often they might as well have taken up residence. And all the time Nelson was constantly chewing my ear about overtime. Bloody idiot.' Roger paused to take a drink.

'I read about the happenings at the hall.'

'Who on earth didn't? And then the final debacle, when two people got trapped in the tombs in the crypt on the priory site and damned near became bodies.'

Charlie stopped mid-slurp. 'You what? I never heard about that. Where the hell was it?'

'Near the industrial estate. Just off the Copworth village lane. All the same business tied up with commander Fitzgerald and his wretched estate.'

'No love lost there, then.'

Roger pursed his lips. 'Oh, the chap's okay, I suppose.'

'What's so sticky about the recent murders?'

Stone studied him for several moments, pondering whether he should confide in him. *Charlie would have been a strong suspect for one of the murders, but he had the perfect alibi. Anyway, he was one of us, the good guys. He'd been a copper for more years than Stone cared to remember and he'd worked closely with him. He had to be sound and safe enough.* Roger took a quick look around them then threw Charlie a weary glance. 'There doesn't seem to be any connection. We'd thought they might both be revenge killings but…' He paused to consider his words. 'Well, let's be honest. You know the score. The two people with the best motives for the second one were you and Francis but you couldn't have had a better alibi.'

'It didn't stop them questioning me though.'

'They had to, as well you know. Got to stick to procedure no matter how futile it might seem.'

Charlie shrugged. 'It was alright for me but it upset Francis, raking up the past.'

'I can imagine, but it had to be done.' Now resolved to let him into his confidence, Roger continued. 'On the first murder, we can't find anyone who might have a motive for revenge. Unless he rubbed someone up the wrong way. It sounds like he was a really nasty piece of work, but none of the relatives fitted the bill and all have been ruled out.

'And the second?'

'Aside of you and Francis,' the only leads we seem to have are the villains the victim associated with. He was an informant and had had a run-in with Vincent McNulty, remember him?'

'I should say so.'

'Well, they'd fallen out just before the accident and McNulty had apparently threatened to kill him,' replied Stone, 'but he and his mob have got their alibis sewn up tight as a drum.' He glanced at Charlie. 'If you and Francis hadn't been with me that evening, you two really would have been in the frame.'

Charlie let out a sigh. 'Don't I know it.'

'What would you have been doing if you hadn't been with me?'

Charlie scratched his head. 'Oof! Let me think.' He took off his glasses, laid them aside and massaged his eyes and face. The glasses back on, he stared at his colleague. 'I'd probably have been watching the tv or working upstairs in the study.'

'And no one to vouch for you.'

'I suppose not. Course, I might have been out for pint with Francis. Then we'd have had an alibi.'

'Funny how things work out,' reflected the DCI.

Further conversation was halted by the arrival of two other Masonic colleagues of Charlie.

***

Selwyn leaned against the side of the Land Rover and watched as the labourer dug deeper into the earth. His mind was transported back to the day when he similarly watched the efforts of Fred Ferris. That fateful day when the trunk was excavated. His thoughts wandered off along the subsequent trail of events that led from the find.

'Summat down 'ere,' came a voice as the digging stopped and the labourer knelt to examine his find.

Selwyn felt a jolt of excitement and caught his breath. 'What is it? Go careful with that spade. Let me see.' He moved to the edge of the pit as a hand appeared and deposited a rusted piece of metal. Instantly deflated, the commander stared at it with sagging jowls and bent to examine it. It was a simple, long, pointed cone of metal.

'Anything?' came the voice from the curly-haired head, the face noticeably tanned despite the time of year.

'Yes, it's certainly something,' Selwyn replied, too intent on scrutinising the pikestaff head to register the banality of his reply.

'Then I'll carry on digging,' whereupon the labourer reached for a pick and swung it high in the air. This instantly galvanised Selwyn into the present and action.

'Whoa! Not the pick. Go gently for goodness sake. Let

me see.' He approached the excavation and stared down. 'Ease the soil with the fork.'

The man shrugged and tossed the pick to one side. He glanced at his watch, reached for the fork and began to dig.

Two hours later, the frustrated labourer had loaded the tools into his Land Rover and departed. He had become exasperated throughout his excavation as the commander repeatedly halted operations to take numerous in situ photos of the items, as they were revealed. Selwyn only hoped the chap would return the following day, though was confident he would, as he was yet to be paid.

On the ground before him, on top of the plastic sheet Selwyn had optimistically brought, were not what he had been in search of, throughout the years. Instead of the family treasure he had dearly hoped to find, lay a pile of military relics, he assumed from the English civil war. Pikestaff heads, the shafts long decayed away, muskets, swords, helmets, and even a small cannon, complete with cannonballs. A significant find in themselves and certainly valuable in their own right, but not the real treasure he had been searching for. None of the silver chalices and plate, jewellery, silver and gold coins, fine armaments and finery that legend and some of the old archives had mentioned.

Selwyn's further disappointment had been Sebastian's absence. He had promised to be there but failed to turn up. Nor had there been any message to confirm and explain his absence. What made it worse was that Selwyn was not even surprised.

In the fading light, the labourer long since departed, Selwyn began to carefully load the finds into the trailer.

When finished, he stared despondently at them. No doubt Miriam and Amanda will be pleased, he thought. I suppose they'll make a fine display once they're cleaned up.

As the pale rays of the winter sun finally disappeared and twilight descended, the Jaguar and its cargo made its way back to Wisstingham Hall.

Chapter 7

MARCH

A loud metallic clatter, followed immediately by a piercing shriek which Selwyn all too clearly recognised, brought him swiftly to his feet. He dashed from the study into the hallway. As he hurried towards the staircase, an alarmed Mrs Soames emerged from the kitchen, holding a large saucepan, probably the instigator of the whole proceedings.

Mrs S was the first to arrive at the crouching figure seated on the lower steps of the staircase. Her bowed head was cradled in her hands. 'Just a pan I dropped, dearie. Nothin' to fret yer 'ead about,' she crooned as she placed a comforting hand on one of the huddled shoulders. With a final, 'There, there now,' the housekeeper retreated in deference to the commander whose sad but kindly smile Miriam's tearful eyes took in.

'I'm sorry, I'm sorry,' she murmured, with a pleading look to her fiancé as he seated himself next to her and stroked her hand. 'I was just coming to see what you brought back from the dig.'

'Perhaps it was too soon,' Selwyn consoled her. This was the first time she had left the security of her room since the return from the hospital two weeks earlier. 'I'll help you back upstairs.'

'No!' The hint of defiance in her tone pleasantly surprised him. Miriam could be a feisty woman, at times.

This appeared to be a welcome departure from the weary docility she had displayed since the explosion. Her softened eyes met his and she smiled. I'll be alright in a minute. I just want to be with you.'

He kissed her lightly on the lips, forgetful of the housekeeper's presence, until she cleared her throat. ''ow about a nice cup of Rosie?' The suggestion was warmly welcomed and Mrs S promptly disappeared, with her smile, into the kitchen. An arm round his fiancée, Selwyn guided her to the lounge.

'I'm sure it's getting better,' Miriam said, once they were settled on the Chesterfield, her words more a question than statement.

Selwyn nodded. 'I know it is. Just needs a little more time, old thing.'

Visibly brightened, Miriam smiled and playfully tapped him. 'Less of the old, if you don't mind. Anyway, things have got to move on or the opening will be a fiasco.' She wrinkled her nose at him. 'And that's just not going to happen.'

'That's the spirit.'

However, her expression darkened. 'Any word?' she ventured, in lowered tones.

Selwyn sighed. 'I'm afraid nothing much. I rang Stone who said they'd so far drawn a blank with Tyson. Although he didn't have an alibi for the time the device must have been placed, they couldn't uncover any evidence and he's threatening to go after them for harassment.' He gazed at her for a moment, his feelings of love and compassion now in combat with those of anger and revenge. 'Of course, I could introduce him to the business end of my grandad's elephant gun.'

This drew a weak smile. 'Better not, Selwyn.'

'Why not? I'd be able to mount him on the wall. A real trophy. Wisstingham's biggest bastard.'

Her giggle warmed Selwyn's heart. 'Okay, we'll leave it up to Stone.'

Miriam squeezed his arm. 'So, changing the subject, what about a recce of the find?'

Selwyn sprang to his feet. 'Absolutely. Just got time before Mrs S brings in the tea. I managed to get the stuff cleaned up as best I could, without damaging anything, though it'll need more expert attention, particularly the leather.'

They made their way along the corridor. 'Shan't be a moment, Mrs S,' he called in at the kitchen doorway, as they passed. Through the long gallery they continued, rays from the sinking sun casting long, coloured beams of light through the stained-glass windows. Selwyn's shoes tapped out on the tiled floor as they passed through into the old tack room where his find was arranged. Carbines, helmets, swords and breastplates were stood in line against one of the walls. On the long table were arranged a variety of pistols, leather belts, pikestaff heads, powder flasks and even a collar of bandoliers.

Selwyn smiled to see the delighted expression on Miriam's face as she slowly took in what she saw. She studied each of the items on the table, turning them over and bending to peer at many of them. Finally, she returned to his side, slipped her arm through his and stared at them all, in silence. 'It's absolutely fantastic,' she eventually announced. 'They'll make a wonderful display.'

'Not what I was looking for, though,' complained Selwyn.

She gently nudged his side with her elbow. 'Grumbleg-uts. Some people are just never satisfied.'

Any further happiness was short-lived as the loud ring of a bell from the kitchen, to announce refreshments were ready, caused Miriam to start with a brief cry. She instantly cowered against Selwyn then looked up at him. Her expression brought home to him that they had yet some way to go on her road to recovery.

***

JUNE

Never before in his life had Theo felt so trapped. Even the sight of his naked wife kneeling in front of him, as she undid his belt, her smile and hungry eyes leaving nothing in doubt as to what was about to happen, could disperse the thoughts and fears that assailed him. Julia was insatiable in everything she did. The ever-inventive sex that left him shattered and exhausted, the boundless energy with which she undertook horse-riding and other physical activities. She expected no less from him. Then there were the parties and hectic social life. Their whole life together was being run at a break-neck pace and he was increasingly struggling to keep up.

Julia had everything planned out, a whole route-map for the rest of their lives. When the children would be born and how many, their schools. He had begun to harbour thoughts that the marriage had been a big mistake, but to extricate himself from it would be to lose his position and job at the surgery. And without the job and money, that French woman would spill the beans. Then he would be charged with bigamy. Julia would see to that if the truth came to light. He would be totally ruined and could go to prison.

Whilst he could prevent that by staying put, the black-mail was sure to come to light, anyway. Between that and Julia's demands and expensive tastes, he was being gradually bled dry. Even now Julia was beginning to ask questions about what he spent his money on. It was only a matter of time... God how he loathed the Lagrange woman. He wanted and needed her dead.

From down below came a soft moan as Julia worked on him, her roguish eyes lifted up to his. He smiled down at her, gently stroked her hair then closed his eyes and feigned growing pleasure. *After all, there's a whole surgery of drugs and implements I can use. It's just a case of getting her in the right place at the right time and that shouldn't be difficult at all.* She arrived for the money every month, after the surgery had closed, to meet him in the woods at the end of the car park. The place was always deserted.

He opened his eyes and smiled at the prospect, a smile that Julia mistook for an indication that they had reached the next phase of their love-making.

As Julia took charge of the proceedings and pushed him backwards onto the bed — she was always the dominant one – Theo's mind drifted to the previous evening. He had left the surgery early and driven to the pottery which, according to the recent edition of the Hopestand-ing Chronicle, had re-opened under Christine Lagrange's ownership. There, he had waited in his car until the pottery lights went out and Lagrange had exited. She had locked the building, got into her car and driven off. He had followed her and now knew where she lived. One way or another, she was a marked woman, for sure.

Julia's moans and panted demand of 'Come on big boy, tally ho, give it to me, good,' as widened eyes stared down on him from her hungry face, brought him quickly back to his present reality. There was nothing for it but to act. The blackmailer would have to be silenced once and for all, and quickly.

***

The Wisstingham Hall project team's initial meeting had been hard work. Miriam had been in fine form and had confirmed that the Arts Council funding application had been successful. The council were consequently fully committed to their funding offer. Miriam's indisposition had however inevitably impacted on progress in obtaining sponsorship funding, which she hoped would now accelerate.

Amanda had made excellent progress on the design of advertising material, programmes and publicity posters.

Sebastian's contribution, however, had been so lack-lustre and inadequate an exasperated Amanda had voiced her condemnation of his apparent lack of interest and progress. The costings for the Wifi system and EPOS systems for reception and the cafeteria were way behind schedule, as was just about everything else he had committed to. Even Selwyn had also been moved to make comment. Sebastian had appeared to be on the verge of leaving the meeting but refrained from doing so, though for all his subsequent interest and involvement in the further proceedings he might just as well have done so.

Rather like the mountain going to Mohammed, thought Selwyn as he and the architect later gathered up their papers and drawings for the next meeting. As usual, it was a meeting both men dreaded. Their numerous previous attempts to encourage Mrs S to see the impracticality of her management of the cafeteria, in conjunction with her other duties, had met with complete stonewalling, failure and hostility. The woman was the project's veritable King Canute.

It had been agreed from the outset that any meetings involving Mrs Soames, and external agencies such as the architect, should be held in the kitchen.

'Gets me all flummoxed sittin' at a table in posh surroundings. It's not natural. My place is in the kitchen or waitin' on. If its somewhere else, I feel proper peculiar and can't consecrate,' she had argued at the outset.

Whilst it was true that the family's more informal progress discussions, including Mrs S, had taken place in the garden room – and even then she was ill at ease – all more formal meetings saw her jittery and, at best, monosyllabic in her contribution. What frustrated the architect was that the housekeeper's involvement was more a question of keeping her onside and informed, rather than drawing any meaningful contribution from her.

'She can be as obstinate as a mule if she sets her mind against something,' Selwyn had warned him, at the outset.

Selwyn gave the architect a knowing glance as they made their way down the corridor to the kitchen. 'Are you ready for it?'

The other grimaced. 'As ever one can be under the circumstances.'

'Never mind, there'll be a first rate cup of tea with biscuits.'

'We might need something stronger.'

'We'll save that for afterwards.'

The architect grunted his accord. 'Your good lady's looking so much better.'

'Nearly fully up to snuff, I reckon.'

They entered the kitchen where, ready and waiting, Mrs S was seated at the table. Her busy hands sought to straighten an already perfectly smooth tablecloth, her lips tightly compressed. In the centre of the table, on an ornate metal stand and beneath a knitted cosy, stood the teapot, alongside it the sugar bowl and a plate of freshly baked shortbreads. Teaplates, teacups, saucers and spoons were neatly arranged on three sides of the table.

Contrary to her normal practice, Mrs S remained seated as the commander entered. He glanced at the table. 'Expecting us then, Mrs S?' The somewhat lame attempt to break the ice appeared to not even scratch the surface.

'Of course, commander.' She watched icily as the two men found space to deposit their papers and drawings.

The architect gave her a broad smile. 'Good morning, Mrs Soames. I hope you're well.'

Mrs S sniffed. 'Good morning. As well as a body might be, thank you for askin''. She turned a kinder eye on the commander. 'Would you care for some tea, sir?'

'Capital idea, that woman.'

The tea now poured, the architect rose to unfold a couple of drawings which he put hesitantly in front of the housekeeper. She dutifully fished into her apron pocket and with much ceremony put on her reading glasses. She peered at the drawings and sniffed.

'This drawing shows the new layout for the cafeteria area and the kitchen. Not your kitchen,' the architect quickly added, 'the one to serve the café.'

She eyed him coldly. 'An' what's wrong with this one for the café?'

His indulgent smile appeared to cut no ice. 'Oh this would be far too small and not in the right place, anyway. We couldn't have such long journey times between the kitchen and café area. Also, it would adversely impinge on the hall's use of the kitchen. Couldn't have two cooks in the same area, now, could we?' His brief dismissive laugh made Selwyn cringe inwardly.

The housekeeper's glaring eyes shifted from the architect to Selwyn. 'What's this about two cooks? I won't be wantin' another cook. A girl to 'elp, maybe?'

Selwyn now groaned, inwardly. Slowly, in a patient, controlled voice, he replied. 'Now Mrs S, we have mentioned before that there would need to be a chef for the cafeteria but that you would remain as the halls' cook, er chef,' he quickly corrected himself.

Mrs S slowly rose. She appeared to try to take her anger out on the straightening of her apron. 'So, I'm good enough for the 'all but not good enough for the café, eh?'

Selwyn's raised hand silenced the architect. 'Mrs S, please sit down,' his tone such that she complied. 'The demands on your time, if you were to be in charge of the cafeteria, would be such that you would not be able to look after the hall's requirements. We expect hundreds of people to visit, each day. If you were to run the café, I should be obliged to find someone to look after the hall.'

The poor woman's lips started to quiver as she stared at her boss.

'But I couldn't bear for you not to be looking after me and the hall. That's why I would prefer that the cafeteria had someone else looking after it. You would then remain in charge of all the hall's requirements. A far more responsible position.

Mrs S put a hand to her mouth. She continued to stare at Selwyn as she slowly took in what he had said.

'And, if you were agreeable,' cut in the architect, 'some of the finer things for the café, such as cakes, biscuits and other specialties, could be made by yourself. They could be branded as Mrs Soames' delicacies.'

'With a girl to help you out,' added Selwyn.

The housekeeper looked from one to the other then dreamily stared across the room. She surveyed the kitchen, sniffed once more and pulled the other drawing towards her. Although upside down, she scrutinised it. 'That seems to be a far more sensible arrangement,' she conceded, now smiling, 'though I reckons my kitchen would need updatin'. Any more tea?'

***

JULY

'I'm off now,' Eleanor called upstairs as she put on her coat. 'You're not going to the pottery today then?'

'No, this cold is too bad for that,' came the muffled voice from upstairs.

About to leave, Eleanor spotted the envelope on the hall table. Each month the envelope that appeared briefly there before Christine posted it to France, on her way to the pottery. Eleanor slipped it into her handbag and departed.

Later, on Eleanor's return, Christine was seated in the lounge, wrapped in a blanket with a box of tissues in close attendance.

'What 'appened to the envelope?' were Christine's opening words as Eleanor entered.

'I posted it for you.'

'But that is something I do.'

Eleanor stared at her, surprised at the vehemence of the protest. 'It doesn't matter who posts it, does it? You're ill so I did it for you.'

'But that is for me.' Christine insisted.

'Well, it's done now. There's no need for us to fall out about it.'

Christine regarded her with dreary, watery and wary eyes. 'Desolee. I am sorry, It is the cold,' she eventually apologised.

Eleanor smiled. 'Let's have a drink and forget all about it.'

***

Sebastian warily scanned the gloomy crypt as his torch-light flitted across the walls and stone coffins. Selwyn's torch similarly swept the interior, but more methodically, picking out the corners of the room. Despite the time of year, it felt clammy and impervious to any of the sunshine and warmth the summer might surround it with.

The excavation on the recreation site had long since been abandoned, its hidden treasures which the old map had suggested might be there, now discovered and safe. The ground had been reinstated and the hoardings taken down. After a somewhat tetchy handover meeting with the council's park and recreation manager, the area had been restored to the general public's use.

Accordingly, after some deliberation, and with the priory site now in the estate's ownership, Selwyn quickly turned his attention to the crypt as a possible hiding place for the family treasure. 'We'd better get some method into this,' he told Sebastian. 'You start at that wall and work your way round in a clockwise direction and I'll start from the diagonal corner, in the same direction.'

'And what exactly am I doing?'

'Run your torch slowly up and down the walls looking for any irregularities. If you find any, use the marker to mark the spot at eye level.'

It was some time before they were seated on one of the coffin lids, sampling Mrs Soames' tea from a flask.

'About a dozen points I found,' said Sebastian as he delved into the rucksack for the sandwiches the house-keeper had prepared.

'About the same,' confirmed Selwyn. He took a sandwich from the proffered box. 'What we really need is brighter lighting and a generator. But if I start to get all that lot together, at the moment…'

'Miriam's going to have a humour failure,' Sebastian anticipated him.

'Absolutely.'

'We don't seem to have achieved a lot, today.'

'Yes, I'm sorry. I hadn't appreciated how much more light we'd need. I should have brought the metal detector. Anyway, we've made *some* progress. There are a couple of other things I wanted to discuss with you, but here's not really appropriate, so why don't we head back, when we've finished lunch, and take a stroll by the lake? Maybe take some refreshments with us.'

'Sounds like a plan,' although Sebastian had some res-ervations as to what exactly was on the commander's agenda.

The sun was low in the sky by the time the two men were seated in the lake garden. Banks of cloud hung on the far horizon, but there was no wind and the surface of the lake was still, other than its disturbance by the take-offs and landings of ducks and the occasional Canada geese. In contrast, the swans and cygnets made calm and leisurely progress, heads occasionally bobbing below the water level. In the distance, the tall sycamores were in full leaf.

Selwyn had equipped himself with his trusty hip flask from which he poured out generous measures for them both. Sebastian reached for the flask, which Selwyn had placed on the bench between them, raised it to his mouth and spoke into it. 'And welcome to another edition of 'Chats by the lake', listeners, with your host Commander Selwyn Fitgerald.'

'Idiot!' muttered Selwyn, retrieving the flask, though secretly pleased to see this rare touch of humour in his nephew.

'So, what's it all about, Guv?'

'I've got something I want you to do for me.'

Sebastian brightened, 'What's that?'

'I'm concerned for Miriam's security, particularly when out in the car. Is it possible to have some sort of tracking device fitted?'

'To her?'

'No, you buffoon, the car. I don't want her to know about it, at this stage. Can you sort it out?'

'Not a problem. That'd be a GPS tracker. Might cost a bit though, depending on how sophisticated you want it to be.'

'Money's no object. I want the best. But I don't want her to know. I think she'd see it all as "Big brother"...'

'…which of course it is.'

'Well, I suppose so, but I just want her safe.'

'Do you really think they'll try and strike again?'

Selwyn nodded gravely. 'I fear the bastard will. God help him if I get my hands on him. I've been wondering about getting her a gun. How soon could you get the GPS thing?'

'A couple of days, three at the most.'

'That's fine, The garage is doing the full check out next week, once we've got it registered, so they can fit it at the same time.'

'Consider it done, my liege. As for the gun, I think that'd be inviting trouble, especially after our recent history with your firearm. I think the mace, alarm and tracker are as far as you could reasonably go.'

Selwyn's jowls drooped in reluctant agreement. 'Maybe you're right.' He eyed him. 'You're in a remarkably bouncy humour.'

Sebastian's smile faded. 'It must be you. I always enjoy your company. Makes me feel…'

'Secure?'

'Yes, I suppose so.'

'And what about Amanda?'

His eyes downcast, Sebastian said nothing. He stared at the ground in front of him. 'It's just not going to work.'

'You don't love her?'

'Of course I do. I'm just no good for her.'

'You're totally wrong, my boy. You're the best thing that's ever happened to her, believe me.'

Sebastian turned and gazed despondently at him. 'It's what I said before. I'm no bloody good to anyone. I've not even got a job now. I'm just bad news to anyone who comes near me. The very last person whose life I want to bugger up is Amanda and if we stay together, believe me it'll happen, as sure as hell it will. I'm just not prepared to risk that. She deserves better than me.'

Selwyn maintained their gaze for a moment then turned away and heaved a huge sigh. 'We've been through all this before, my dear boy. It's just not true. It's just bad circumstances that are to blame, not you. Remember what you nearly lost and the joy you both felt when you got back together. Amanda would be lost without you. She needs you, I need you. You can't give up on us all. More importantly, you can't give up on yourself. You have responsibilities to me, the hall and, most of all, yourself.'

Sebastian stood and placed the small empty cup on the bench. 'I'll honour those responsibilities but I'm sorry, that die's been cast. It's just how I break it to Amanda.'

Head down, he set off alone, back to the hall. Selwyn gazed sadly after him, wondering what on earth he could do to change his nephew's mind.

**

In his hovel, for that was what the squalid rental flat had now become, Russell McNabb switched off his laptop and reached for the whisky bottle. So, the bitch had recovered and was back fulfilling her civic duties. The incendiary device had failed and so had he. It now needed more personal intervention. But that would have to wait for the dark nights. She would be bound to attend evening functions in the autumn and winter. And, by then, her confidence would have grown, together with her nonchalance. Then he would find his opportunity, take it and stick the knife in.

**

'You look in a bit of a tizz if you don't mind my saying so, dear,' observed Eleanor as a flustered Amanda looked up from her computer screen. 'Is everything alright?'

The librarian rolled her eyes and gave a tired smile. 'Everything's happening all at once. I've got wall to wall meetings for the next two days and enquiries coming out of my ears for the fishing lodges.'

'Well that's a nice problem to have, isn't it? The lodges I mean.'

'I suppose so, but I've got a booking from France and I can hardly make out what the chap's saying.'

Eleanor patted her shoulder and gave an indulgent smile. 'Just let me sort it out for you, won't you? By the way, the printers rang, the leaflets and maps are ready to be picked up.'

Amanda's shoulders drooped. 'Grrr. It's all getting a bit too much.'

'What can I do to help, dear?'

Amanda turned beseeching eyes to the old lady. 'If you could please look at the email from France and sort out the booking. It's open on the screen. The diary's here.' She hastily took it out from her drawer. 'And if the dates are free, if you could please confirm it back, with the price. They're in the back of the diary. Then if you can book it in.'

'That won't be a problem. What about the leaflets and maps? Would you like me to pick them up?'

'Could you please?'

'Certainly. Is that it? Is there anything else?'

The beseeching eyes re-appeared. 'I need to drop off

some things for Mrs Craddock, together with about fifty of each of the leaflets and maps. She's the new lady who's going to look after the actual arrivals and do the cleaning. She's near the printers. Her address is also in the back of the diary. The instructions and other stuff for her are all in that drawer.' She grabbed her purse and took out a banknote. 'That should cover the petrol.'

Eleanor smiled. 'Don't be silly, the petrol comes free. It'll be my pleasure, dear. A bit of excitement in the day.'

Amanda glanced at the clock, jumped to her feet and clasped Eleanor's hands. 'Eleanor, you're a godsend. Thank you so much. I don't know what I'd do without you.' She grabbed hold of her papers and bag and dashed to the door.

With a smile, the old lady sat down at the desk and started on the email.

***

OCTOBER

Gabriel Montand stepped down from the train at Hopestanding station. He lowered his case to the platform and with narrowed, dark eyes scanned his surroundings, his huge, muscular hand massaging his mouth. He smoothed out the crinkled piece of paper taken from his pocket, studied it, picked up his case and lumbered towards the exit. The porter, by no means a small man, cast a curoious gaze up at the Frenchman as he passed by.

Minutes later, Montand squeezed his huge frame into the back of a taxi and tried, without success, to read out his destination to the driver. With a 'Merte alors!' he handed him the piece of paper.

'Not from these parts then?' queried the driver, as they set off.

'Comment?' growled the Frenchman and the conversation eclipsed into silence.

'Foreign boxer, I reckon,' the cabbie later explained to one of his mates, back at the rank, an opinion unknowingly shared by Mrs Craddock who had, with some instant alarm, opened her front door to the Frenchman.

Only after Montand had produced a copy of the email confirmation of his hire of the fishing chalet, filled in the paperwork and handed over the cash, did she relax. He received the key and set of chalet instructions and how to find it, together with a map of Hopestanding and the neighbouring village of Wisstingham.

'Wouldn't like to meet him on a dark night,' the lady had muttered as she watched him trudge down the road.

The golden rays of the setting sun were already reflecting off the lake's tranquil surface by the time Montand unlocked the chalet and entered. With a weary sigh he dumped his case and shoulder bag on the floor. His craggy eyes took in the kitchen diner and small lounge as he wandered through to the bedroom and bathroom for a cursory inspection. He then returned to his case, opened it and pulled out the bottle of Pernod, purchased at the airport. He lumbered into the kitchen area in search of a glass and some water.

On the porch, seated on a chair he had taken from the dining area, he gazed out at the lake and the comings and goings of the waterfowl and swans as he formulated his plans for the following day.

On the basis of one postmark and his brother's research

on the internet, in Nantes, he had managed to track down the whereabouts of Theo Patterson, veterinary surgeon, leaving Gabriel to marvel at the wonders of the internet. Tomorrow, just before the surgery was due to close, he would travel there, lie in wait and confront the villain. Certainly he was very conspicuous as a Frenchman, but he had given a false name and address, and paid in cash for the hire of the chalet. As for transport, true to what the website had advertised there was a bicycle on the porch. Nothing outstanding by any means, a velo that might have seen service with La Poste, but it would suffice. It would get him wherever he wanted to go, without the expense and exposure of having to hire a car or take taxis. He would cycle to the surgery later that night to familiarise himself with the route and area, in readiness for a return the following night.

Gazing out over the calm surface of the lake, for the first time that day Montand briefly smiled, reflecting that Patterson was now within his grasp and how close he was to getting his revenge. On this latter thought the smile disappeared, to be replaced by a far grimmer expression. The revenge would be for his poor Yvette and grandson who had both died during the birth.

Montand had meant to leave it much later to set off to the surgery, but his impatience, and concern that he might stand out as a cyclist on quiet streets, persuaded him to set off earlier. It was therefore around nine thirty when, after a couple of wrong turnings, he arrived at a lane which led off a side street. At the start of the unlit lane a sign advertised the location of Hopestanding Veterinary Surgery.

In the twilight he cautiously pedalled. Another sign and arrow, further along, directed him off the lane into another lane which opened out into a car park. His expectation that all would be deserted was not however met. On the other side stood a long, single storey building from the windows of which light spilled out onto the adjacent footpath. Montand had unknowingly chosen the one night in the month when the surgery was the venue for the practice's board meeting. He came to an abrupt halt. In the entrance and to the front of the building a small group of people were talking. There was not enough light for him to clearly make out their faces.

Suddenly, he and the bike were illuminated by the headlights of a departing car. Only one of the group caught sight of Montand's face, enough for that person to recognise and instantly catch his breath, feeling as if he had been plunged into icy water.

By the time the car had driven away, the Frenchman had already taken cover behind a nearby tree. From there, once more enveloped in the darkness, he watched the group of people. One of them broke away to go inside and after a few moments, the lights inside the building went out one by one.

Before the figure returned, the others had already drifted off to their cars and started to drive away. The solitary man, whom, in the passing light from one of the departing cars, Montand now recognised as Patterson, was locking the front door.

Immediately after the last car had gone Montand hurried forward to intercept his quarry. Patterson was already running to his car. He jumped into it, slammed and locked the door and had already started the engine when his pursuer arrived and tried to grab the locked door handle. Patterson flinched away from the side window as Montand's fearsome face briefly appeared at it, before he dashed around to the front, By now the panicked vet had throttled the engine and started to accelerate away. There was a thud and a cry but he could see nothing in the mirrors.

Thoughts flashed through his mind. Should he stop and see if the man was injured? But if he wasn't really injured, Montand would attack him, for sure. Should he turn round and run him over? There were no witnesses. He could claim Montand had just stepped out in front of him, in the darkness. If he was alive, he'd come after him anyway, and all would come out, assuming Montand did not kill him first.

For a moment he dithered in indecision then decided to drive on. If Montand had been killed or badly injured, let someone else discover him.

Still in shock, Patterson was breathing heavily, his adrenalin pumping, his fear gave way to fury. The Frenchwoman had taken the blackmail money and then betrayed him. He would kill her. For sure he would kill her.

He drove to Brackshaw Cottage to where he had previously followed Christine Lagrange. The car squealed to a halt. He dashed to the front door and hammered on it.

To his astonishment it was opened by a very elderly lady whom he vaguely recognised.

Her eyes widened on seeing him. 'You,' she exclaimed.

Patterson's jaw dropped. For a second he was speechless. 'What are you doing here?' he then blurted out. Recovering himself he demanded, where's the Lagrange woman?'

Eleanor glared at him. ' What do you want with her?'

'I want to see her, NOW.'

'Well you can't, she's not here.' Eleanor made to turn away and go back inside but he grabbed her arm. With an expression of cool contempt she regarded his hand then turned back to face him. 'Let go of me this instant, or I'll call the police, Mr Patterson, or whoever else you are.'

'You smug bitch,' he sneered, releasing her. 'You're in on the blackmail too, aren't you? Well let me tell you, your friend is finished and so are you. Montand has come looking for me and I'll do for you both. You tell her that,' he fumed.

Eleanor remained completely unshaken. 'I have absolutely no idea what you're talking about. Please leave or I really will call the police.'

Patterson glared at her, clenched his teeth and his fists, but nevertheless turned and left.

***

To Amanda, the Celia Rossiter that now sat opposite her at the Mazawat café was certainly not the same person she had met the previous September. Gone was the high degree of self-assurance, the woman now shadowed by something of a haunted look.

Over the months, they had met regularly for lunch, It had always been genial though, with the benefit of hindsight, Amanda now recognised the gradual change that had come over her friend.

This lunch had been at Amanda's instigation after the Arts and Craft's festival committee meeting. Celia had appeared uncertain as to whether or not she should accept the invitation, but had agreed.

Amanda scrutinised her dining partner whose head was bowed as she studied the menu. 'Everything alright?' she enquired, as casually as she could.

Celia glanced up. 'Yes, why shouldn't it be?'

Very defensive, thought Amanda. Her facial reaction perhaps prompted Celia to add, 'Oh, I thought you meant the menu. Me, I'm absolutely fine.'

Liar, but Amanda, was not going to press the point. 'So what's the latest? Apart from the committee, that is.'

Celia gave a vague wave of her hand. 'Oh, this and that. One or two journalistic pieces for fashion magazines and the odd show.'

'Are you finding being on the committee gets in your way? You don't regret having got involved with it do you?'

'No, not at all.' Her frown appeared to indicate otherwise.

'And what can I get you ladies?' Gwen interrupted having breezed up with notepad and pen poised for their order.

'You would tell me if there was anything wrong, wouldn't you?' Amanda later asked as they waited for the coffee to arrive.

Celia's thoughts immediately drifted to that dark September night and the corpse, slowly swinging and turning, its dreadful staring eyes accusing each of those that looked on.

'Yes, I would,' her reply just a fraction too late to give credence to the words.

Once the bill had been paid they parted, Amanda sadly none the wiser as to the cause of the changes in her friend's demeanour.

***

'Got a minute, dear boy?' Selwyn enquired of Sebastian once they were out of earshot from the dining room, where Miriam was regaling Amanda with the details of her new car.

'Course.'

'Then let's head out for a stroll.' The very mention of the word magically brought a tail-wagging Mustard to his side. Selwyn smiled and stooped to pet the beagle. 'I swear he's got the hearing of a bat and could graduate in English.'

They headed out of the side door and across the yard, though the dog soon scooted off in front, on his customary heading of the lake garden. There were, after all, ducks to be disturbed.

'How are things?' Selwyn eventually enquired after several moments of silence.

Sebastian cast him a wary glance. 'So, so.'

'Which means?'

'I told Amanda that I don't see any future for us.'

Selwyn groaned. 'And?'

'She won't have it. Says I'm not going to get rid of her as easy as that. She says she loves me and that she doesn't believe I don't love her. So, until she believes otherwise, that's that. Says she's going to stick with me through thick and thin until I come to my senses.'

'Well done that girl. At least one of you has got sense.'

'I don't even have the guts to break off the relationship,' Sebastian lamented.

'Only because you love the lass. One in a million, that one.'

Sebastian stopped walking and Selwyn turned back to face him.

Sebastian sighed. 'God! I'm such a bloody mess.'

They had reached the gate to the lake garden, at which Mustard patiently waited. They walked through and the dog scampered off to the lake. Seated on the usual bench, Selwyn placed his hand on the other's shoulder. 'You'll get through this my lad. Just got to pull yourself together and think what Lucian would be saying to you. Very proud of you he was. Don't let him and his memory down. Point taken?'

The nephew's eyes closed as he slowly nodded.

'So, this is where you two miscreants have sloped off to,' a voice interrupted, a little way off from the other side of the gate.

Selwyn swung round and smiled at the sight of Miriam and Amanda as they approached. 'Guilty as charged, milud.'

Miriam stooped to plant a gentle kiss on his cheek then rose and smiled to the sky as she breathed in the balmy, September evening air. 'If I'd known it was going to be as nice as this I'd have suggested a barbecue.'

'With Munchkin here serving up some of his mean burgers,' said Amanda, who'd seated herself next to Sebastian and squeezed his arm. Sebastian sadly smiled his appreciation of the compliment.

'Sounds just the ticket,' added Selwyn, 'Perhaps we should organise a hog roast for the opening.'

'Now there's an idea,' Miriam enthused, whereupon the conversation once more reverted to plans for the big day.

Chapter 8

Throughout the day, Theo Patterson had found his attention and eyes repeatedly wander to the baseball bat he had smuggled into his office and secreted at the side of his desk, early that morning. A scalpel was also hidden under papers on the desk. He intended to be ready should Montand pay him a visit.

It had certainly not been his intention to be last out of the building that evening, but Murphy's law struck. Complications during an operation on a dog had resulted in him and his assistant having to work after the surgery had closed. After cleaning up, the assistant had rushed off. So, here he was, tail end Charlie, left alone to lock up.

All seemed quiet enough when he peered warily out of the reception room window, before he left the building. At the front door he glanced nervously around but there was no one in sight. He tried to lock the door, the action complicated by his shaking hand and grasp of the baseball bat. Behind him, Montand, surprisingly quiet for his size, crept up from round the corner and felled him with a crashing blow to the head.

***

Another person whose day had been fraught was Eleanor. After Patterson's visit the previous evening she had waited with mounting concern for Christine's return. It was not unusual for her to stay late at the pottery to finish a batch of pots for first firing, or glaze those due for their final firing, in order to have a full complement for the kiln. Once, she had not returned at all but slept there overnight on the large old sofa, to avoid disturbing Eleanor's sleep on her late arrival.

The hours dragged by. Eleanor alternated between making cups of tea that went only half drunk, pacing the room, or watching, unseeing, the television. Repeated calls and messages to Christine's mobile went unanswered, which induced Eleanor to fear that Patterson might already have carried out his threat.

By morning there had finally been a message to say all was well, that Christine had slept at the pottery and would see her that evening.

Throughout the day, unresolved questions of how Montand had discovered Patterson's whereabouts and why he had turned up, repeatedly crossed Eleanor's mind. Even Amanda had noticed and commented upon how distracted she seemed.

'One of those days, dear. You get them when you get older,' was her excuse. She wondered if Montand had tracked Patterson down from the postmark on one of the envelopes, but why had it taken so long? Maybe he had searched a national register of practising vets but surely that would have been a very cumbersome challenge, particularly for an IT illiterate farmer in France. In any event, if it had been possible, surely it could have been achieved long before now.

At lunchtime, since she had failed to make her customary sandwich, she had gone to the Mazawat. There she learned that Christine had visited the previous evening and dined with a gentleman whose description appeared to match that of Charlie Pembroke. This final snippet of news added to her anxiety over the danger, exposure and violence threatened by Patterson. It had weighed heavily on her throughout the rest of the day, such that when she arrived home her nerves were jangled and she was impatient to speak with Christine.

When Christine did eventually breeze into the cottage, it was already nearly dark. Her reaction to the news of Montand and Patterson, though worried and guarded, lacked the concern Eleanor had anticipated. She simply gave a gallic shrug and walked off into the lounge.

In pursuit, Eleanor followed and squared up to her. 'I told you it was a bad idea to make him pay money. Now look what's happened.'

'It is the letter you post that brings him 'ere,' Christine blurted out.

Eleanor frowned. The suspicion that had emerged earlier in the day now surfaced as she observed Christine's defensive reaction. Words which, from Christines' expression, it appeared she had immediately regretted saying. 'You never sent the other envelopes, did you?' the accusation murmured slowly.

'Mais oui.' Christine's assertion faltered as she coloured.

'Oh, how could you?' Eleanor stared at her. She detected no sign of remorse, rather a belligerent scowl. She sank down onto the sofa and covered her face with her hands. 'You kept the money, I suppose?'

'The man is a brute and deserve to suffer. Anyway, I am not be sure the money will to reach Yvette.'

'You have jeopardised everything. What's more, you've lied to me.'

Christine splayed her hands, 'About this yes, but…'

'Not just this,' Eleanor rounded on her, 'but other things.'

Christine pursed her lips, her hands now firmly placed on her hips. 'What is it you mean?' she challenged.

'Last night, you were not working at the pottery. You were with Charlie Pembroke.' Eleanor's mouth was set firm.

Christine threw her arms up in the air 'Oh, this is impossible. You are impossible.' She stamped a foot and stormed out of the room.

Eleanor was about to follow but paused. She would give her a little time to subside. However, before that could happen she heard the front door slam. It was now more than likely that Christine would spend another night at the pottery, or maybe even somewhere else, Eleanor feared.

***

Panting from his exertions, Gabriel Montand glared at the inert form on the floor then lumbered out of the room, his teeth bared. He paused in the reception area to study the map pinned on the noticeboard. It took him a few minutes to find the street he was looking for. The street, together with a name, which the vet had been only too ready to reveal to him. Christine Lagrange, the woman who had kept the money intended for his daughter and her baby. Now he would track her down. Lagrange who, the connard had told him, now knew of his arrival in England. He knew the woman, the potter from his village. Incroyable she should come to the same place where Patterson lived. She had to be dealt with. He had come too far. His mother had always told him his temper would do for him. Now he had to cover his tracks. He did not care if Patterson was dead, the swine deserved it. He was only too pleased that he had been able to give the bastard the truth about Yvette and the baby, to take into his grave.

Montand tore the map from the noticeboard, scanned the car park from the reception area window, then slunk out of the building to retrieve the bicycle from where he had hidden it.

He perceived luck was once more on his side as he cycled through deserted streets, halting from time to time to check his bearings.

He found Brackshaw Cottage, bounded on one side by an identical cottage and a copse of trees on the other. Across the road stood three dwellings, hemmed in by further stands of mature trees.

It was in the shadows of one of the trees near the cottage where Montand secreted the bicycle and crept towards the building. He carefully unlatched the wrought iron gate and passed through the small front garden. Through one of the lighted windows he spied two women stood by a dining table, apparently arguing. One he recognised as Lagrange, the other, although she looked vaguely familiar, he could not place. His lips tightened against clenched teeth as he shrank back and returned stealthily to the bicycle.

On his way back to the lake he pondered how he might find a way to get Lagrange on her own.

Once seated at the chalet's table he began to prod laboriously at the keys of an old laptop his brother had sent him, to bring on his travels. He cursed as he repeatedly lost the pages he had found then had to start again.

Eventually, with his discovery of a Lagrange pottery and its address on the outskirts of Hopestanding, a smile creased his rugged face. That would be his destination the next day.

***

The following morning saw DCI Stone look up from his desk as his door swung open to reveal Superintendent Nelson.

'Roger, another murder's been called in.'

Stone blinked his eyes closed, his expression reminiscent of someone with trapped wind. The Super closed the door and seated himself on the edge of the meeting table. 'A Theo Patterson, vet and partner at the Hopestanding practice. He was married to the Smyth family's daughter, so their clout will ensure this becomes a high-profile case. You'd better get down there immediately and for God's sake watch what you say to the press.'

Stone let out a long, deep sigh. He massaged his temples, put away the papers he was working on and went in search of DS McBride.

'Severely beaten up but the pathologist doesn't think that was the cause of death,' Stone advised Nelson over his mobile. 'Just a moment, sir.' He turned to McBride. 'What's happening with the staff?'

'They're in another part of the building, giving statements and the partners are up in arms about the surgery being closed.'

Stone spoke again to the mobile. He wandered over to the reception windows, as he listened, and gazed out. 'Yes, the hyenas are out there. I don't know how the hell they get to know so quick… No, I've not said anything… Three pm. Alright, I'll let them know. Do you want me there?... No, I won't say anything else to them.' Stone sneered at the mobile after he finished the call. His hands automatically sought the pockets they could not reach through the protective clothing. He rejoined McBride in the consulting room and fixed his gaze on him for a few moments while he thought. 'So, since this wasn't Patterson's room, I reckon the assailant must have chased or dragged him in here from the reception area. There's more blood here than in his own room.'

'Aye, and from the amount of blood elsewhere, it must have been him that moved about whilst being attacked, or afterwards, and not the assailant.'

'But that wasn't enough to kill him so what was?'

'Maybe his heart gave out?'

Stone shrugged. He glanced around the room then nodded to the open door of the wall cabinet. 'The lock's broken. Anything missing?'

'We've listed what was in it and the staff are checking.'

'A drug theft gone wrong, possibly?'

'Aye, maybe. Mind you, our feller was nae small. The other would have to be a big chap to take him on.'

'Or possibly more than one of them? We'd better wait and see what the postmortem has to say.'

'Aye, and what our lads come up with,' McBride motioned to the SOCO team, busy at their work.

Stone checked his watch. 'We'd better get a move on, I suppose.' He took one more look around the room, sighed then made for the door.

***

Since taking over the pottery Christine had found that by staying open into the early evening, until the homeward traffic of cars and pedestrians had tailed off, she was often able to achieve one or two more sales. Evidently, news of the late opening had spread. The extending opening times did not matter to her. There was always work to do, twice a week the loading of the kiln, most of the time glazing of biscuit-ware, pricing, labelling, ordering materials and so on. At times, it was also her refuge from her possessive friend.

Gabriel Montand had however ensured he would arrive in Cawthorn Lane some time before the advertised closing time.

At first glance of this little backwater, a newcomer might suppose that Wisstingham and maybe even Hopestanding had gathered together all their artisans and corallled them into Cawthorn lane. A stonemason's sat alongside carpenters which abutted the premises of a lady who wove wicker baskets. On the other side of the road were a picture framer, tinsmiths, a fully stocked haberdashers and wool shop, also Lagrange pottery. The latter was unique in that it was the only building that also had access from another lane to the rear of the property, through a large courtyard. The layout of the building was also unusual in that the large garage could be only be accessed from the courtyard. This connected into Cawthorne Lane by a narrow passageway which ran alongside the gable end.

As if to create a true village atmosphere, a small public garden with mature sycamore trees was located between some of the buildings on the opposite side to the pottery.

It was to this garden, in sight of the pottery, that

Montand led his bicycle, leant it against a tree and settled down on a wooden bench to watch the premises. He watched as the proprietress of the glass shop locked up and departed. As time drifted by, one by one the other businesses closed for the day until, by nearly six thirty pm, all was still, the road empty other than for an occasional pedestrian who would stroll past, more often than not on the end of a dog's lead. Only the basket weaver's shop remained open.

Montand was about to rise and walk over to the pottery when a red Ford Fiesta approached. He recognised the driver as the woman he had seen through the cottage window the previous evening. He watched as she pushed open the pottery door and entered. With a grunt he reluctantly settled back on the bench to wait.

Christine's reception of Eleanor, when she entered the pottery, was cold. 'Why have you come?' she demanded.

Eleanor gave her a reproachful glance. 'You didn't come home. I was worried about you.'

Christine shrugged, turned and hurried into the next room which doubled as a dining and sitting area. 'I have been working late. I did not want to disturb you,' she replied, over her shoulder.

'Don't you walk away from me,' Eleanor's voice raised as she scurried after her.

Christine spun round to face her. 'You try to interfere with my life. You treat me like I am child. I have a right to choose my friends.'

'I try not to interfere,' Eleanor pleaded. 'If I do, it's only to prevent you from making mistakes, because I care for you.'

Christine scowled. 'You are not my maman. I am old enough to make my own choices. That is the problem. You do not want to just be my friend. You want something more and I can not to give it to you. You smother me.'

Eleanor fixed her with a cold stare. 'How can you say that? You have every freedom. You have the pottery.'

Christine snorted. 'Pah, you always throw this pottery at me, and the car. You never let me forget your gifts.' She raised her arms in the air. 'I do not want your pottery and I do not want you. You are lesbian. I will leave you and go with Charlie. I am sure he love me. I will marry to him and you keep your pottery and your car.' She leaned forward and stuck a solitary finger in the air, her lips tightened into a malevolent 'o'.

Eleanor paled and stared at her betrayer. Tears welled in her eyes. Her dreams lay torn in pieces, right in front of her. 'But we are happy together. Please don't leave me.'

Totally unrepentant, Christine glared at her. 'I stay 'ere tonight and I take my things tomorrow, when you have left the cottage. I will leave the car, then I will go to Charlie.' She pushed past Eleanor and disappeared back into the workshop.

Eleanor let out an angry cry. 'After all I've done for you.' She looked desperately about her. Memories of all the happy times she had spent with the woman whom she loved came flooding back. She picked up one of the biscuit-fired pots that had come out of the kiln that day, and stared at it. All the happy conversations they had shared about the pottery returned to haunt her. She threw the pot, turned and hurried out of the room.

Moments later, Montand saw the pottery's front door fly open and the older woman emerge in a flood of tears.

She almost tripped over the threshold as she rushed out. At the doorway, Christine stood, arms akimbo, a defiant glare on her face as she watched the woman go.

In great agitation the distraught woman unlocked the car and with a backward, tearful glance at Christine, got in and drove away.

Montand smiled, rose and hurried across to the pottery. He tried the door which was unlocked. With a glance around he entered.

Eleanor had almost reached home when she brought the car to a stop. Her eyes still wet with tears, she gripped the steering wheel and gazed through the windscreen, battling with her thoughts. If only she had tried to be more reasonable and understand Christine's point of view. How much better to compromise than lose her altogether. She shook her head resignedly, turned the car around and started off back.

By the time she reached Cawthorn lane, the pottery was in darkness, the door closed and no sign of life inside. She was about to get out, one of the conflicting voices in her mind still urging a reconciliation at whatever cost. Her hand was poised on door handle when opposing thoughts invaded. Had she not done so much for this woman? No doubt Christine could not see the danger she was getting herself into and it was up to her, Eleanor, to keep her dear friend safe. To capitulate now would be a disaster. She must bring Christine round to her way of thinking with patience and commonsense.

Her head slowly sank in reluctant acceptance and her hand shifted from the handle to the ignition key. She would have to wait things out. The engine roared into life and the car set off back to Brackshaw Cottage.

Montand wrung his huge hands as he stared at the body. The unblinking eyes confirmed his fear that the woman was dead. There could be no doubt. And the vet. He had only set out to beat him up, to exact his burning desire for revenge. But he was most likely dead. Why had he not just given in to his temptation to just flee the fishing chalet and head for France, when he had seen the morning's television news coverage? Realisation now dawned that if he was caught, he would find himself accused of two murders. He had to get away as quickly as possible. If only he could make it back to France, he felt he would be safe.

As he did not wish to leave by the front door, he hurried into the next room to search for another exit, only to find himself treading on some broken pottery. At one side of the room he came across a pine table set with four chairs, one at the head of the table. On the other end of the table stood piles of biscuit-fired mugs and plates. Behind that end was a door which Montand found led into a huge garage and storage area. Slabs of clay, sealed in plastic, were stacked against one of the walls. He tried the garage door, which was unlocked, and opened it sufficiently to peer through the gap. The garage led out into an open yard which itself opened onto the lane. A Corsa was parked near the back gates.

He would need to make a run for it, lie low in the chalet and plan to get away as quickly as possible and not wait for his return flight home.

***

By the time DS McBride arrived at the pottery, having waited for his boss who had not appeared at the office, nor responded to his calls, the place was a hive of activity. A PC was posted at the door, another was taping off the area around the building and an officer in protective clothing was carrying items into the building from the nearby van. Inside the pottery itself, a doctor, who had apparently just finished examining a female body that lay on the floor, rose and waited for McBride to join him. 'I'm doctor Smethwick. The neighbour called me in but I think this is something for yourselves. She looks to have received a blow to the skull.'

McBride regarded the body. The apron and clothing showed no signs of disturbance and there did not appear to be any superficial injuries. He looked over towards the potter's wheel on which sat a partly finished pot. Its clay looked dried out. He glanced at the body's hands which were clean. *So, if she had been disturbed, she had had time to wash her hands.* He turned to the other man. 'Thank you doctor if you would please leave your details with the WPC there, we'll take it from here.'

'You having a special offer week, McBride?' the pathologist asked as he later entered, suited up for his work.

'Aye, two for the price of one,' McBride replied, grimly.

'Where's Jingle balls?'

'I've no idea.'

The pathologist bent to his task and the DS went in search of the WPC who was taking a statement from a tearful, mousy-looking woman in the adjoining room.

As he entered, the WPC broke off and stood to update him. 'Miss Bellamy owns the shop next door. She found the deceased this morning when she came in to have a coffee, which she does each morning before opening. The door was unlocked, the light still on and she found Miss Lagrange lying on the floor, so she called a doctor.'

'McBride eyed the woman whose handkerchief was doing sterling service. 'Did ye notice anything unusual when ye came in this morning?'

'No, I don't think so.'

'When did ye last see her alive?'

'Yesterday evening. I caught a glimpse of her in the storage area but she seemed very preoccupied. That was after her friend Eleanor Delaney had left. She works at Wisstingham library and they live together, but I don't know where. Anyway, I think Eleanor wasn't in a good mood. After the party finished and I went home, the light was still on. I nearly stopped to…' At the memory the poor woman succumbed to another tearful bout.

McBride waited for her to compose herself. 'Did ye notice anyone else arrive here, after ye invited her?'

'No.'

'Did anything happen out of the ordinary?'

The woman shook her head. 'Can I go now?' she queried, timidly.

McBride nodded. 'We'll get your statement completed and my colleague will call in for ye to sign it.'

The woman rose to leave. At the door she turned. 'There is just one thing, I've just remembered. When I closed up last night, I saw a large man parking his bike against a tree opposite. He sat on a bench for a fair while but didn't seem to have anything to do or read. Just seemed to stare into space. I don't know if that's useful at all.'

McBride's eyes widened and he slowly exhaled. 'Aye, I think that could be very relevant.'

***

'Must you do that?' Superintendent Nelson glared at DCI Stone, as if he had just brought the bubonic plague into his office.

Stone frowned in confusion. 'Do what?'

'Jingle. You look and sound like some kind of vaudeville act.'

'It helps me think,' he protested.

'Well, it doesn't do it for anyone else. Where have you been anyway?'

'Dentist,' Stone slurred. His tongue wandered off on an exploration of the still numb gum.

Nelson wondered if it would be going a step too far to insist that his officer kept less change in his pockets. 'And have your thought processes come with anything further on our unsolved murders, Roger?'

Stone shifted his stance, his discomfort heightened by a resolve not to thrust his hands into his pockets. 'On the first two deaths, the hangings I mean, we've exhausted every lead so far. The team are checking back through the witness statements to find anything that might have been missed. On the second murder, the victim's old associates have put up a stone wall and a stack of alibis.'

'And what about yesterday's suspected murder?'

'We're checking out CCTV footage, disgruntled customers at the vets, local addicts and drug dealers. We're…'

The Superintendent leaned forward across the desk and fixed him with a piercing gaze. 'Let me stop you there, Roger. All this boils down to is a lot of effort but no results. The Chief Super is breathing down my bloody neck because the Smyth family have sure enough turned this into a high-profile case. What's more, as of this morning we've a suspicious death on our hands at Hopestanding pottery. That could be four murders we've clocked up with none of them solved, so you'd better come up with something pretty damned quick or I'll be obliged to draft in some other resources, and you know what that might mean.'

Stone shifted in his chair. He knew only too well what that might mean. Restructuring and early retirement had been hinted at before his surprising promotion. He was in no financial position to weather that option, if it was resurrected. He had to continue working for at least another four years.

Nelson did not wait for a reply. 'McBride's there at the scene. I've got a meeting with the Assistant Chief, so you better get your skates on and get down there. Let me have a rundown by one pm. If it is murder, I'll need to arrange a press briefing. By the way, what's happening on the car bomb case?'

'We're keeping an eye on the main suspect, Karl Tyson but we've not turned anything up to charge him.'

'What about the other chap, the council guy? What was he called?'

'McNabb. He's nowhere to be found. We believe he left the area some time ago.'

'Well keep onto it. The Chief keeps reminding me about it.'

A pained expression on his face, the DCI rose. 'All we bloody need!' he muttered to himself as he jingled his way out of the office. Nelson gritted his teeth at the sound and the thought of the golf clubs in the boot of his car, that would not see the light of day that afternoon.

***

Eleanor frowned at the look of consternation on Amanda's face as she entered the room.

'It's the police. They want to speak with you.

Alarmed, Eleanor rose. 'Oh my goodness, what about?'

'I don't know. You'd better use my office.'

With a murmured 'thank you,' the ashen woman followed her. In the corridor, Amanda signalled to the officers waiting at reception who started towards her. Once in the office they introduced themselves and presented their warrant cards.

Eleanor turned to Amanda. 'Won't you stay with me please, dear?' she implored.

Uncertain, Amanda turned to the officers. The policewoman nodded consent. 'Certainly, if you want me to.'

Once the four were seated at the conference table, the PC was the first to speak, his colleague ready to take notes. 'Miss Delaney, we understand a Christine Lagrange has been staying at your address?'

'Yes,' Eleanor's lips trembled. 'What's happened?'

'I'm afraid we have some bad news for you. I'm sorry to have to tell you that Christine was found dead this morning at her pottery.'

Eleanor took a sharp intake of breath and Amanda reached out to hold her hand.

'How? When? What? Oh my God...' Eleanor broke off, her shaking hand covering her mouth. Tears welled up in her eyes.

The officers glanced at one another. 'It was her neighbour, the lady who has the basket weaving shop, who found her,' explained the WPC.

'How did she die?'

More glances were exchanged. 'That's currently under

investigation. Can you tell me when you last saw her?'

Eleanor tightened her lips in an attempt to hold back the grief. 'Yesterday teatime.'

'What time would that be?'

'Oh, about half past six.'

'And what happened?'

'We spoke for about half an hour, then I left.'

'Was Christine married?'

'No.'

'Do you know if she has any next of kin in the UK?'

Eleanor shook her head. 'Both her parents are dead and her husband died recently. They had no children or living relatives that she told me about. How did she die? Please tell me.'

'I'm afraid we can't at this stage,' replied the WPC.

'Did she suffer?'

The policeman shook his head. 'We don't think so. That time of six thirty was that when you arrived or left?'

'When I arrived.'

'Did she seem alright when you left?'

Eleanor paused for an instant. 'Yes, she seemed fine.'

'Did you see anyone else in the vicinity when you arrived or left?'

'No.'

'Were there any cars parked outside the pottery or nearby?'

'No, it was unusually quiet, except for some sort of function which was going on next door. Otherwise, the place was deserted. Christine kept the pottery open late as she used to work late anyway.'

The questioning continued, briefly interrupted when Amanda arranged some refreshments.

'Would you be prepared to identify her, please, Miss Delaney?' asked the PC.

'Eleanor pursed her lips and nodded. 'When will that be?'

'Probably sometime tomorrow morning. We'll let you know.'

Amanda moved towards her and put her arm round her shoulders. 'I'll take you there,'

'Thank you dear. I appreciate that. Are you sure you will be able to get away from work?'

'Not a problem. I'll prop my old cardboard cutout up at the desk. No-one will notice,' Amanda quipped, which drew a faint smile.

After the interview, Eleanor rose to leave and cast a forlorn look at Amanda.

'What are you going to do now?' asked the librarian.

'I'd better get on with some work. It'll keep me busy.'

'You'll do no such thing. Get your coat and we'll go and grab a decent coffee.'

Seated across from her in the Mazawat, it pained Amanda to watch Eleanor, her disbelieving stare focused into the distance and cup of tea hardly drunk. The digestive biscuits, her favourites, remained untouched.

'I can't believe it, I just can't believe it,' she repeatedly murmured with occasional shakes of her head. Despite Amanda's various attempts to engage her in conversation, answers were either monosyllabic or through the curtest of sentences.

Eventually, Amanda glanced at her watch. 'I'm afraid I'm going to have to get a wiggle on Eleanor. It's the festival committee meeting. Why don't you head off home?' But what's there to head off home for anyway? she immediately thought. There'll be no company. Who's going to look after her?

Fortunately, Eleanor made a sudden revival at the mention of the meeting. 'I should think not, my dear, I'm coming with you. I've not missed a meeting yet, serving refreshments and I don't intend to start now. Anyway, it will keep my mind busy.'

'And you wouldn't want me lowering the catering standards,' Amanda added, which coaxed a smile.'

'That's right and I won't let you claim authorship of the cakes and biscuits I made.'

Eleanor insisted that it was her turn to pay the bill, despite Amanda's protestations. Amanda had come to learn that at times, Eleanor could not be dissuaded from her intended path. However, having just heard the news of Christine's death, (for nothing ever escaped the Mazawat café's jungle telegraph) with genuine-sounding expressions of sympathy Gwen was even more insistent that the refreshments were on the house.

***

The same news had also evidently travelled to the festival committee members already gathering in the library's exhibition room, by the time the duo arrived. Eleanor's service of tea coffee and cakes was repeatedly hampered by expressions of consolation and sympathy from the members, particularly those of the grim-faced Charlie Pembroke.

He it was who broached the press coverage that the police were now searching for a large man seen riding a bicycle in the vicinity of the vet's and the pottery. This snippet of news appeared to Amanda to strike home with Eleanor as she cleared away some of the crockery to enable the meeting to start.

'I assume the boss is coming, is he?' Francis Mboko queried as the minute hand of the large wall clock inched to the meeting time.

'He said he was,' affirmed Charlie. 'Ah, there he is now.'

Sure enough, the tall, thin frame of Roland Hawtry could be seen through the glass doors as he hurried along the corridor.

'Sorry I'm late everybody,' he apologized when he entered the room and made his way towards the meeting table, 'my last meeting went on a lot longer than expected.'

'Not to worry Mr Hawtry,' came a voice at his side as Eleanor brought him a cup of tea, 'two sugars, isn't it?'

He glanced at her. 'Yes indeed, thank you. It's very kind of you.'

Eleanor regarded him for a moment before speaking. 'There are biscuits and some of my date and walnut cake over there. Do help yourself.'

'You're so good to us all, Eleanor,' Roland smiled then made his way to the confectionary, bearing teacup, saucer and teaspoon, and a briefcase that had clearly seen the inside of many a meeting room. Then, with a laden plate balanced on top of the teacup, he headed precariously to the head of the meeting table. He carefully deposited everything and sat down next to Amanda. 'I'm dreadfully sorry to have kept you waiting.'

'No need to apologise, everyone's been far too busy talking about the latest events. If it carries on like this, Wisstingham will find itself twinned with Midsomer.'

'Yes, what a dreadful business.'

Amanda leaned closer into him. 'The dead woman was a close friend of Eleanor's,' she whispered.

'That's terrible. I didn't know. Perhaps I should…' He looked round for her.

'I think she's probably already gone. I'll pass your condolences on, if you wish.'

'Certainly. Well, I suppose we'd better get on,' whereupon he called the meeting to order, those not already seated making a speedy move to do so.

'I thought you'd gone home,' Amanda later exclaimed when she entered her office, after the meeting, to find Eleanor staring at her computer screen.

'Oh my dear you gave me a fright. No, I couldn't bear to be on my own so I thought I'd just cross reference those books we're getting rid of. I've just finished.'

'You deserve a coffee for that splendid effort. I was dreading doing it.'

'Well, I wouldn't say no, I'm quite parched.'

'I'm not surprised. Most of those book titles are dry as a bone. Talk about past their sell-by date, I reckon Noah brought half of them ashore.' She patted Eleanor's shoulder and made for the kitchen.

'Will you be alright on your own?' Amanda later asked.

'Oh yes, I've got a lot of things to do. What will you be doing this evening?'

'We're dining at the hall, so no doubt we'll end up talking shop about the opening and how far behind we are. We seem to have adopted a methodology that the sooner we get behind, the more time we'll have to catch up.'

Eleanor smiled.

'The commander will probably drift off to his latest plans for discovering the family treasure. Miriam will chastise him for taking his eyes off the ball. He'll round on her for the council's latest shortcomings then they'll both have a go at Sebastian, poor Munchkin, for being behind programme with the IT and electronics. Mrs Soames will do her level best to persuade us into second helpings of one of her delightful sweets and that will be most of the evening gone. Then, I'll be only too happy to go home and creep upstairs to bed.' Amanda frowned. 'I don't believe I've missed anything out.'

'It all sounds very interesting,' observed Eleanor who looked more assured than she had done all day.

***

The evening, however, was not destined to turn out quite like Amanda had predicted. It was during the main course, after Selwyn, true to form, had indeed drifted off onto the search for the family treasure, that Sebastian suddenly grabbed Amanda's arm, a slightly worried look on his face. 'Hey, you know the police are looking for a chap on an old-fashioned bike. You've not got anyone staying at the chalets, have you?'

She glanced at her watch. 'The twenty second. Yes, there's a Frenchman staying in one of them.'

'You don't think…'

'Well I do sometimes,' Amanda quipped. 'I'm certainly doing so now. It's a bit of a stretch isn't it? There must be loads of people with old-fashioned bikes. I can't see how it could possibly be him.' However, the French connection troubled her, even though it was probably nothing more than coincidence.

'What do you reckon we should do?

She thought for a moment. 'Well, there are three possibilities. One is to go over there now and check on the guy, in the pitch dark, though I can't recall his name and I don't know which chalet he's in. The second is to phone the police, and the third is leave it until the morning and check it out in daylight.'

Selwyn leaned forward. 'It's none of my business I know, but it's pretty late. To go and knock up what could be a completely innocent stranger, suggesting he's a cycling homicidal rascal, or even worse, sounds a bit over the top. Equally, to send our good friend Stone down there, on what could well prove to be a fool's errand doesn't strike me as the most sensible of options.'

'Worthy and appropriate though it might be for him,' added Miriam.

Selwyn shot her a sideways glance. 'That would leave the alternative of going to the chalet first thing tomorrow, to see if the chap's the right size. He might be a midget for all we know. But if he is on the big side, we could see what he's got to say for himself. Then, if we're still suspicious, you can then call in Stone and his merry men.'

'Sounds like a plan to me, but what's this 'we'?' queried Sebastian. 'I'll be the one going along with Amanda. It's not as if I've got anything else to do,' he added, more gloomily.

'Steady the buffs, that man, there's more than enough to occupy you here, including getting up-to-date on your progress perhaps?'

''e could 'elp me polish some of them brasses and the armour,' suggested Mrs S who had arrived to clear away the second course and overheard the conversation.' The suggestion however had no takers. 'Who's for apple

166

crumble with cream, ice cream or custard?' She enquired.

A Cheshire cat smile spread across Selwyn's face. 'Well done that woman. Count me in for ice cream and the cream option.'

'Would that the two portions of crumble then?' she teased.

He smiled again and wagged his forefinger at her. 'That's just one at present. I'm sure you'll be pressing us for seconds, later.'

Mrs S tried an indignant look but failed miserably. 'As if I would do such a thing, commander. Anyway, I'm not certain as folks with 'eart conditions should have second helpings.'

'Yes, well it depends on the size of portions I suppose,' countered Selwyn. 'If your food wasn't so delicious a chap might not be quite so keen to ask for more.'

The compliment defeated Mrs S. 'Never heard so much flapdoodle in all me life,' she muttered with a faint smile as she took the remaining orders.

'How did the committee meeting go today, Amanda?' asked Miriam, during the cheese course.

'Pretty good. I think they're almost on track. Everyone appears to be working well together. There's just something I can't put my finger on that makes me wonder if I'm not missing something. No matter. There was something I was saving for later, but whilst we're on the subject here goes. There was a proposal that the dates for the festival and the opening of the hall be moved to coincide. It was suggested we could maybe host one or two festival-based activities in the grounds to maximise on cross-promotion of the two events.'

Selwyn paused mid-slice of the stilton. 'That's a rattling good idea, but we couldn't bring our date forward that far, surely.'

'It's suggested the festival date be moved back by three weeks to the weekend of 8th. December.'

Selwyn glanced at Miriam. 'Do you think that'd be possible?'

She took out her mobile and consulted the calendar. 'That'd mean we'd have to move the opening forward by two weeks.' All eyes turned to Sebastian.

'What do you reckon, my boy?' asked Selwyn.

Sebastian considered for a few moments. 'The building and services work are ahead of schedule, the catering side's got plenty of leeway and the electronics would be no problem.' He glanced at Amanda. 'What about the promotional and advertising side of things?'

'There'd be enough time.'

Glances were exchanged and Selwyn spoke. 'In that case, I say we go for it.' He raised a glass to which everyone responded likewise, followed by much animated and enthusiastic conversation.

***

There was a definite spring in DCI Stone's step as he strode along the corridor towards his office, the postmortem report on Theo Patterson under his arm. Independent sightings had been reported of a burly man on a bicycle in the vicinity of the two recent murders. Moreover, sets of matching prints had been identified at the two scenes of crime, though sadly there was no record of them on the national database. But still it appeared they were getting somewhere.

'McBride, my office now,' he called into the open office as the DCI clinked his way past the doorway.

With another murder, a suspicious death on his hands, and Nelson talking of drafting in support, Stone knew he needed to get some quick results.

'This fella that's been sighted, McBride, any further leads?'

'Not presently. We're still checking out all the B&Bs and hotels in case he's from out of town, but the bike suggests the laddie's probably local.'

'Unless he's hired or stolen the bloody thing. Check if there's any progress on the hire situation and any lost or stolen bikes. Our search for miladdo will be in the local papers tonight, so make sure uniform are on their toes.' Stone tapped the autopsy report. 'This Patterson business is a bit strange. He was given a lethal injection. Now why would someone give him a real pasting then finish him off like that? Why not just carry on beating him to a pulp?'

'There was Fentanyl missing from the secure cupboard. Is that what was used on him?'

Stone consulted the autopsy report then nodded.

'Whoever took the stuff maybe intends to use it again. What's it used for anyway?'

'It's a sedative and pain killer. Much stronger than morphine.'

'So, whoever it was must have known what they were dealing with.'

Stone rose, went over to the window and stared down at the car park. 'Any conflict between him and the other vets and staff?' he enquired over his shoulder.

'Nae anything that's being admitted to.'

'Have another word with the cleaner. They're often the ones to open up about that sort of thing. Now what about the Lagrange woman? Do you reckon it's murder?'

McBride scratched his head. 'I couldn't say. There's the broken pottery but there was no blood on it, nor on the head. She could just have dropped it if she came over ill, but the repeat sighting of the feller on the bike makes me think there's more to it than just natural causes.'

'I think you're probably right. We'll just have to see what the autopsy comes up with. I'd better go and brief the Super.' He picked up the report and followed McBride out of the office.

Chapter 9

OCTOBER

'Hey, that's Charlie Pembroke coming out of the doctor's,' Amanda commented as they drove past the local surgery, on the way to the lake.

'I didn't know it was open on a Saturday.'

'It isn't. Must be something special.'

'He's not looking too chipper,' observed Sebastian.

'You're right, certainly not his usual self. He looks to have lost weight.' Through the wing mirror, Amanda watched his dwindling reflection as he bent to unlock the security chain on his bicycle.

The sunshine's sparkle on the surface of the lake seemed somehow reassuring to Amanda as she and Sebastian headed from her car towards the fishing chalets. Ahead of them scampered Mustard, the venue of his usual Saturday morning walk a different one today. This however, still held the promise of feathered things to annoy. As the happy beagle bounded to the water's edge, several ducks broke from the lake's surface. For several moments they circled until one descended back to the water, the others soon following.

Mrs Craddock had reminded Amanda that the Frenchman they were seeking was called Gilbert Colbert. 'A big brutish-looking man,' she'd described him as. Just as well therefore, that the sunshine seemed to take the potential sinister edge off their purpose for being there.

Outside the cabin, the complimentary bicycle was propped against the timber balustrade, secured to it with the combination lock. On quick inspection mud spatter evidenced it had been in use. After each let, any bikes that had been used were always hosed down and cleaned.

'Better keep Mustard on the lead,' Amanda advised as she knocked on the door.

Sebastian tried to grab the errant beagle's collar. 'Easier said than done.'

A second knock still yielded no answer.

'Perhaps he's scarpered,' offered Sebastian.

'Monsieur Colbert?' Amanda called out and rapped once more. Still no reply. She tried the door handle and found it locked. She took out her master key and unlocked the door. With a glance back at Sebastian who nodded, she pushed the door slightly open and repeated her call. After another glance at him, she slowly pushed the door fully open and looked inside. The place looked still inhabited. A coat was slung over the back of an armchair and a leather jacket draped over the back of a chair. Of Colbert there appeared to be no sign.

Sebastian grabbed hold of Amanda's arm. 'Better let me go in first.' He tied Mustard's lead to the balustrade then brushed past her.

'Who said there are no gentlemen left?' Amanda murmured and stopped him to kiss his cheek as he passed.

He entered, Amanda immediately behind him. He rounded the corner of the entrance and looked into the kitchen diner area. 'Oh, bloody hell!'

Amanda squared up alongside him and took a sharp intake of breath at what she saw. Seated on a chair, slumped forward onto the dining table, was the form of a large man. His right arm was spread on the table, the other dangled limply by his side. The head lay on one side. From a bruised face eyes stared vacantly at the table surface. To the left of the head lay the door key and an overturned glass, the contents spilled onto the coaster, table and floor. On the table, to the right of the body, lay an insulin pen, its needle still visible.

'What a state to be in,' exclaimed Sebastian. 'He looks like he's gone ten rounds with Mohammed Ali.'

Amanda sniffed at the clear, spilled liquid. 'No smell, might be just water.'

She stepped forward and placed her fingers on the neck. 'Stone cold,' she announced to Sebastian who seemed rooted to the spot.

'We'd better report this and get out until the police arrive,' he suggested.

'Mmm, just a mo.' Amanda continued to stare at the body and surroundings. She knelt down and examined the bottom of the trousers then rose, took out her mobile and began to take photos of the scene from various angles. Next, she turned to survey the living area then moved towards the leather jacket. From her bag she fished out a pen and with it nudged the jacket front open on each side and took screenshots. She then entered the bedroom. A watch lay on the table next to the bed. She took more photos and did the same in the sitting room.

Sebastian was now fidgeting his unease. 'Have you quite finished?'

'I reckon so, Munchkin. Let's go and sit outside and call Hopestanding's finest.'

***

McBride tapped out a number he really didn't want to ring. He knew the reception he would most likely get, but that would be no better than the one he would receive for not having called. Damned if I do, damned if I don't, he thought as he waited to connect.

'Yes, what is it?' came the terse voice at the other end.

'I know it's your day off sir, but I just thought you'd want to know that there's another body.'

'Jesus Christ!'

'It's been found in a fishing chalet owned by Amanda Sheppard.'

'I knew it. I just bloody knew it,' came the outburst.

'I believe it might be our man on the bike. The chalet rental includes the use of one. Also sir, there's some information from Patterson's parents. The vet inherited some money from his grandmother and took a year out from work to go backpacking through Europe. So maybe that's the connection with the Frenchman.'

'Good work, but you'll have to deal with it,' Stone snuffled, 'I'm miles away at a wedding. God knows why, I'm feeling bloody awful. I reckon I've caught something. Keep me updated… and thanks for letting me know,' he added, grudgingly.

McBride smiled, he'd got off lighter than anticipated. Now he was clear to handle the case without Jingle balls. With a bit of luck the man would be off sick for a few days, which might just give him enough time to wrap things up. He reached for the autopsy report on the French woman. He opened and speedily re-read it. A single blow to the head at the pterion, the thinnest part of the skull, so he'd understood from the pathologist. 'And extremely thin in this case, eh', he murmured. Maybe it had just been an accident. But there was the broken pot which had been nowhere near the body. Nor had there been anything to fall against, where the pot was, or had she fallen and dropped the pot afterwards? Then there was the sighting of the man on the bike. That was just too coincidental.

He glanced at the wall clock, closed the file and set off.

Within minutes, he and a couple of PCs were on their way to the fishing lake, a destination he knew from one of the earlier encounters with the Wisstingham estate fraternity.

On his arrival, he found Amanda seated on the chalet veranda adjacent to Montand's. 'I trust you've nae contaminated the crime scene.' McBride's opening remark cut little ice with Amanda.

'No more than was absolutely necessary. I touched the door handle and the neck, to check he was dead, but nothing else, though my prints are probably all over the place since I own it and often go in. The door was locked and the key was lying on the kitchen table.'

McBride gave her a tired smile. 'I'll take your statement after I've done my inspection, so don't go anywhere.'

'Officious twerp,' Amanda muttered as he disappeared into the chalet.

It was some time before the DS finally emerged and returned to her. 'The emergency exit looks all secured from the inside. Did anyone else have access to the front door key?'

'Only myself and Mrs Craddock who does the key transfers and cleans the chalets.'

McBride started to make notes. 'I'll need her address.'

Please, Amanda bristled at his attitude.

McBride continued his questioning. No, Amanda did not know the deceased. As far as she knew he had arrived from France on the 18th. October and had booked the chalet some four weeks earlier. She did not know the man or the purpose of his visit and had not even met him, alive anyway.'

'And why were ye here in the first place?' queried McBride.

Amanda had to think quickly. She gave a nonchalant shrug. 'We regularly check on the cabins. I wanted to make sure everything was alright for our guest.'

McBride gave her a hard stare.

'So, what do you reckon?' she continued. 'There were one or two things I thought were a bit odd.'

McBride glanced heavenwards and sighed. For him this had all the hallmarks of a suicide. In all likelihood, the Frenchman had committed two murders then killed himself. Everything would appear to be neatly wrapped up and he had no intention of letting any amateur sleuths try to unravel this ball of wool. He knew Stone was not presently in good odour with the top brass. This just might be his opportunity to grab some limelight and get onto the next rung of the ladder, should the hierarchy now be thinking of pensioning his boss off earlier than intended.

Amanda noted his expression and refrained from any further comment.

'I'll need ye to come in to the station and make a statement. I'll let ye know when, in a while.

'Very well.' By now Sebastian had returned from his walk with Mustard.

'And what about you?' McBride challenged him. 'What did you get up to?'

Sebastian knitted his brow. 'I'm not sure I care for your tone.'

'I don't care what you do or don't care for. You two are magnets for trouble. You might have run rings round DCI Stone, but you won't be doing that with me. So, I'll ask you again, what did you do after you arrived here?'

Sullenly, Sebastian described their arrival and actions without mention of Amanda's photographic exploits. When he had finished McBride pocketed his notebook and pen then eyeballed each of them in turn. 'We won't be needing any fingerprints as we already have those so you can be on your way for now. I strongly recommend you don't interfere in this matter, including speaking to the press.'

'So, what have you concluded?' Amanda persisted.

'That's for me to discuss with my colleagues once we've seen the autopsy results. Now off you go, the pair of ye.'

'I feel like a scolded child,' Amanda fumed as they trudged back the car, her annoyance further aggravated by the supercilious smile on McBride's face, when she turned to look back at him.

'Do you think he killed the vet and the Frenchwoman?' Sebastian asked as they drove away.

'I don't know what the link is to the vet. Eleanor and Christine have no pets but it seems a bit too circumstantial that both this chap and Christine were French.'

'Do you think he committed suicide?'

Amanda glanced at him. 'I'm not sure. One or two things don't seem to add up, but I'll have to think about it.'

***

'A bit of luck sir,' DC Johnson addressed McBride, when

he returned to the station. 'We've located a garage that's been rented out to McNabb. Some bits of electronic stuff. No sign of him though and the owner's not heard from him for several weeks. Looks like he's abandoned the place.'

McBride nodded appreciatively. 'How did you come across it?'

'The garages were of interest to the drugs squad. They went in and when they found out who'd been there they tipped us off.'

'Better get the techies involved.'

'They're already on it sir,' the DC beamed.

'Who's the owner?'

The other consulted his notebook. 'Gordon Sullivan.'

'Is he known to us?'

'Yes, he's got previous for receiving.'

'Then let's have him in.' McBride smiled, his confidence in the future soared. If he could find McNabb and crack the bomb case as well…

***

A warm scarf wrapped round her neck and a broad smile on her face, Miriam's hair flowed free. Alongside her sat a not so deliriously happy Selwyn, as they bowled along the country lanes in her new car. Not a brand new car but new to Miriam, a Mercedes E that Selwyn had bought for her on the proceeds of the insurance claim, with a little help from the estate funds.

This had not been her first outing, but Selwyn had been insistent that he accompany her, though perhaps he now inwardly regretted the decision. He never travelled well when Miriam was at the wheel. At this time of year, despite the blueness of the sky, travelling with the top down for him was not the most sensible of options, no matter how warmly they were clad. Nor did his confidence in their journey increase when she placed her hand on his thigh and gave him a knowing glance.

His thoughts catapulted him back to the first time she had done that, when they had visited stately homes. Despite their now much greater familiarity with each other, the gentle squeeze she gave brought on the same frisson. Nevertheless, he could not help but shout, 'Going at a bit of lick aren't we, old thing?'

She grinned, replaced her hand on the steering wheel and momentarily put her foot down. 'That's what I call a lick,' she shouted.

Selwyn closed his eyes and slowly shook his head. 'Incorrigible woman,' he shouted.

She glanced across and blew him a kiss as she slowed down. 'You wouldn't have me any other way.'

He smiled. 'I don't suppose I would,' he murmured to himself. 'Just wait till I get you home,' he cautioned, more audibly.

She wrinkled her nose at him. 'I just can't wait.'

The journey continued, Miriam delighted with her car and new lease of life. The explosion now seemed very much a thing of the past. Despite his lack of optimism on this score, he drew comfort from the tracking device being in place, being tested at that moment by Sebastian, back at the hall.

***

Mrs Soames paused in her polishing of the mahogany stair bannister to look down at the commander as he crossed the hallway on his way to the kitchen. She smiled inwardly at the thought that any prospective raid on the biscuit tin would be thwarted by its emptiness, the new batch still in the oven. Perhaps the smell of them had lured him. The journey however, stopped short of her domain as Selwyn stopped to contemplate the suits of armour by the front door. He then turned to survey the ancestral portraits on the staircase walls. He gave a start when he found the housekeeper smiling down at him.

'Didn't see you there, Mrs S. Quiet as the proverbial church mouse.'

'An' there's me thinking as 'ow you were going to do a bit of mousin' of yer own, in the biscuit tin,' she responded.

Selwyn adopted a feigned look of hurt. 'As if I'd do any such thing.'

She moved to descend. 'Oh no? Anyway, the new batch should be done in about five minutes. How do you fancy a nice cuppa and a warm shortbread or two?'

Selwyn broke into a grin. 'Excellent idea that woman. I'll be in the drawing room. Bring a cup and plate for yourself.'

The housekeeper's eyes widened at this rare invitation. Must have something to say, or else he's bored, she thought, as she waddled into the kitchen. She supposed the latter since he had not apparently sought to seek her out for a discussion.

Seated on the Chesterfield Mrs Soames felt uncomfortably out of place. Selwyn seemed in no hurry to embark upon conversation as he alternated between sips of his tea and nibbles of a biscuit.

'So, how's Reggie?' he eventually enquired.

'He's fine,' she replied, guardedly.

'Busy, is he?'

'No more than usual,' the answer even more guarded.

'Does he find he has any spare time on his hands?'

'I'm sure 'e 'as. Doesn't take 'im long to get through his chores.' Mrs S peered at her boss through narrowed eyes. 'What 'ave you got in mind, commander?'

Selwyn slowly massaged his mouth as he regarded her. 'Got a marine engineering background hasn't he?'

'Ye-e-e-s.'

He leaned forward. 'You know that launch in the boat-house? Do you think he might be interested in looking at it and seeing if he could get it going again and spruce it up a bit?'

'Bless you commander, I'm sure 'e would and 'e'd give it a good go. It'd keep him from under my feet.'

'Ask him to come and have a word with me would you, please? Don't tell him what it's about.'

'Would you be working on it with 'im?'

'I'm afraid not, much as I'd like to. There's all the malarkey for the hall opening and I'm hoping to re-start the treasure hunt. If I could find that before the opening it really would be the icing on the cake. However, if Reggie needed another pair of hands at times, I'd always find somebody reliable.'

'But I thought you'd done with the search 'ere.'

'I have. I'm now going to move on to the crypt.'

Mrs S shuddered. 'Oh my gawd! Don't you go disturbing no ghosts and bringing 'em back 'ere.'

Selwyn chuckled. 'I don't think there's any danger of that and if they did come here, I'd make sure they wiped their feet before they came in.'

'It's no laughing matter commander, you shouldn't joke

about these things.' She looked appalled.

Selwyn tried desperately to smother his mirth. 'Not to worry Mrs S, we'll make absolutely sure that you come to no harm.'

She placed her cup and saucer on the tray and gave him a chastening look. 'I should think so too. I'll be back for the tray when you've finished.'

'And mind you mention it to Reggie,' he called out to her, as she reached the door.

***

The following day, Selwyn and Sebastian set out for the crypt, the Jaguar's boot once more laden with tools and equipment.

The dank walls exuded a cold that within minutes penetrated to the very bones. The eeriness and shadows that danced off the walls convinced both men that there must be a far better way to spend a wet autumn day.

With the light they had available to them, try as they might they could not find anywhere on the walls or floor that suggested a concealed space or opening. The stone coffins were far too heavy to contemplate moving, which now seemed to be the only remaining possibility to discover a hiding place below.

'I'm going to have to hire the imaging gear again,' Selwyn concluded. 'I should have done it sooner. I just felt so sure we'd find something to work on.'

'That's if we could get it down here. Not to worry, guv, there's always another day.'

'Maybe, but I hoped we might just find something before the big day,' He gave a shudder and turned up his jacket collar. Okay, let's pack up and get out of here. We'll bring some heating next time.'

An hour later they were on the right side of a warming brandy. Their conversation about the next visit to the crypt concluded, they sat in silence gazing at the flames of the coal fire that Mrs S had ensured was lit in good time for their return.

'So how are things between you and Amanda?' Selwyn eventually queried.

Sebastian shrugged. 'Amanda's not for letting me go and I've not got the willpower to leave her. I love her too much for that. But things are very patchy and a wedding date's no longer mentioned. We do have some good times but then it all falls away again. I feel such a bloody mess guv, just going through the motions in life. My self-esteem's still at rock bottom.'

Selwyn made to speak but was cut off.

'And I know you're going to give me all that grief about pulling myself together and what I mean to other people, but it makes no difference.'

'What if you were to see a psychologist?'

'A shrink? Do me a favour! If you and Amanda can't cut through the haze, I don't see how lying on a couch and spouting to a stranger's going to do it.'

'They *are* experts and it's not really like that at all. I went to see one when I was really low after Georgina died. I found talking to someone who was a complete stranger to the family was very freeing. He certainly got me round that nasty bend in my life. It's totally confidential.'

'Maybe, but I can't imagine anything they can say that's not already been said. Anyway, it'd probably cost a fortune.'

Selwyn snorted. 'For crying out loud, don't let the cost

put you off. You know I'll cover that. For my sake, will you please give it a try?'

Sebastian stared at the fire for a moment. 'Alright guv I'll give it a go. I do appreciate your support.'

Selwyn returned his smile. 'Don't mention it, my dear boy. It's the least I can do.'

***

It was late in the afternoon. Darkness had fallen and the rain continued to do likewise. At the library, Amanda received a call from reception to say there was a woman who wanted to see her urgently. There was a mountain of paperwork piled on her desk and the daunting task of compiling next year's budgets. At first inclined to put her off, when the name Marcia Phelps was mentioned an instinct persuaded Amanda otherwise. A minute or so later the visitor was shown into the office.

Marcia was a rather mousy young woman. Small in stature with a round face, she had a button nose and cupid lips. She also had a slightly anxious smile which she frequently used, as if to excuse an action or comment she had made which she feared might give offence.

She perched on the edge of the chair and began to finger the cuff of her coat. 'Sure I'm sorry to disturb you, Amanda. You must be very busy, are you not?'

'Not at all, it's always nice to see you, even if we don't seem to get much time to speak. How can I help you?'

Marcia gave the briefest of smiles and glanced nervously in the direction of the closed door. 'It's just a thing that occurred after the last committee meeting, which has me worrying like the very devil. I just don't know what to do about it.'

Amanda planted her elbows on the desk and cupped her chin in her hands. 'Why don't you tell me and let's see what's the best thing to do?'

Marcia appeared somewhat reassured. 'It was after the last meeting, with me there in the alcove fetching my coat. You had already left. Didn't I overhear Mr Pembroke talking to someone. On his mobile I supposed. He was giving out to them that they needed to keep their cool and that they — he said 'we'- couldn't be linked to the death. He was almost eating the head of whoever it was. Then Mr Hawtry walks into the room and the two of them start talking, quite cosy like. Then doesn't Eleanor arrive to clear the tea and coffee cups away. Charlie said something nice to her and I heard the three of them getting the stuff together, so I just grabbed my coat and I'm off. I don't know if anyone saw me.'

Amanda, now bolt upright, frowned and stared at her.

'So, what the devil am I to do?' The cuff was now really receiving rough treatment.

'Are you sure that's exactly what he said? You couldn't have made a mistake with the words, could you?'

'Absolutely not. It was as clear as a bell.'

'And Roland?'

'They seemed very friendly. Yer man could well be in on it, for all I know.'

'Well, as uncomfortable as it is, I think the only option you have is to see what the police have to say about it.'

'Oh, I couldn't be doing that!'

'It's either that, just keeping quiet about it, or else confronting Charlie and Roland.'

The latter option appeared to shock Marcia even more. She ceased the attack on the cuff, on noticing Amanda was staring at it, and gave her a begging look.

Amanda shrugged. 'I'm sorry Marcia, I really can't think what else you might do. Unless you want me to raise it with the police, but I would have to tell them where it came from and they'd want to talk to you.'

Marcia's chin dropped. She stared at her hands clasped in her lap. Then she looked up. 'Sure and I'll be having to think about that. Perhaps I should stand down from the steering committee, though I really don't want to.'

'What about tonight's meeting?'

'Ah, you've put yer finger on the very thing. I've kept putting off doing anything.'

'Why don't you just see how the land lies with them, whether they say anything to you or seem different, then we can discuss it tomorrow or the day after. Charlie is an ex-policeman and Roland's very respected, so I really don't think there can be anything untoward.'

Marcia chewed her lip then let out a deep sigh. 'Ah well, I suppose that's the best thing to do. Can I see you tomorrow?'

Amanda consulted her diary. 'Yes, as long as it's after two o clock.'

There came a knock at the door and one of the staff entered. 'There's a Roland Hawtry wants to speak with you Amanda, if you can spare a few minutes.'

Marcia shot Amanda an alarmed glance. Amanda nodded. 'Yes, show him in, please.'

Roland's eyes widened when he spied Marcia. He smiled at Amanda. 'Thanks for seeing me, I do hope I'm not intruding.' He glanced at Marcia. 'Two birds with one stone. I hoped to catch you, Marcia.'

Marcia visibly flinched and Amanda invited him to sit

down. He glanced at Marcia then addressed Amanda. 'I couldn't remember whether you were due to attend this evening. I've a vague recollection that you said you couldn't.'

'That's right, I'm afraid I've got a presentation do at the town hall.'

'In which case I hope you can tell me if the change of dates for the hall opening and festival is on the cards.'

'Yes, it is, I intended to text you anyway.'

Roland gave her a thumbs up. 'That's great, then we can re-examine the programme this evening.' He turned to Marcia, 'Are you intending to be there?'

Marcia flashed a glance at Amanda. 'Well, I suppose so,' the commitment given with evident reluctance.

Roland glanced at his watch. 'Why don't we grab a coffee and have a chat. We've just got time.'

She glanced at Amanda. 'Well,' she hesitated. 'I reckon so. Where would you be thinking of?'

'The Mazawat's probably the closest,' suggested Amanda.

'Then let's go in my car,' Roland proposed. 'We can't walk in this.' As if on cue, aided by a gust of wind, rain loudly spattered the window. Unease written on her face, Marcia looked across at Amanda who, with a little hesitation, gave the briefest of nods.

Marcia gave a fleeting smile to Roland. 'Ah well, alright then.' As she did so there was another knock on the door and this time Eleanor entered. 'Oh, I'm sorry dear,' she addressed Amanda, I didn't know you had company.'

'It doesn't matter Eleanor, do come in.'

Eleanor caught sight of Marcia. 'Oh, hello dear, I didn't expect to see you.' She took in the two visitors. 'You're a bit early. I was just going up to set everything out.'

'There's no hurry Eleanor, we're just off out for short while,' Roland reassured her.

This was Marcia's cue to reluctantly rise. After saying goodbyes she followed Roland out and cast one last, unhappy glance back at Amanda.

'Doesn't look too cheery that young lady,' Eleanor observed, with narrowed eyes, as she gazed at the closed door.

'No,' agreed Amanda. She regretted she would not be at the meeting and began to wonder just how safe Marcia would be in Roland's and Charlie's company.

Throughout the presentation and evening that followed, Amanda could not take her mind off Marcia's forlorn look as she left. A silent appeal for help. It was of some comfort to her that when she returned to the library to check on the car park, Marcia's car had gone.

***

When DCI Stone returned to work, fully recovered from a severe bout of flu, he immediately sensed, on walking through the station, that something was afoot. A little too much sympathy here and there, a lingering look or two, perhaps an embarrassed silence. Yes, something wasn't quite right. Nor did it take him too long to discover just what it was.

His meeting with Superintendent Nelson, after a seemingly reluctant enquiry as to Stone's health, was monopolised by praise for the way McBride had solved the murders of Patterson and Lagrange. Not only those, but the subsequent suicide of the perpetrator, which would be a mere formality at the inquest.

'The AC's well pleased, as is the Commissioner,' Nelson

beamed. All *you've* got to do is to solve the other two murders. Better get to it, eh, Roger?' With a glance at Stone's pocket, to which the DCI's hand had automatically gravitated then frozen, Nelson bent to the document in front of him and Stone took this very blatant cue to leave.

Together with those of McBride, there would appear to be at least another pair of hands poised ready to tug on the edge of the rug under the DCI. A further sting, when Stone entered the open office, was to see the self-satisfied grin on McBride's face. 'I hope you're fully recovered, sir,' he greeted his boss.

Stone merely grunted. 'I'll have a catch up with you in half an hour.' He glanced around the office. Some of the staff appeared uncertain as to whether to say anything, look happy or sympathetic, whilst others busied themselves such as not to have to look at him. With a nod to the young female DC who smiled at him, the DCI defiantly jingled his way out of the office and headed down the corridor.

***

McNabb was convinced this would be his ideal opportunity. One he had been waiting for since his last failed attempt. He had checked on the time and venue for the meeting and from the agenda he knew Councillor Cheyney was to present an item. The foul weather was also perfect. Everyone would have their heads down in the driving rain, oblivious to what cars and people were around.

He slid the knife into the inside pocket of his jacket. With the rucksack slung over his shoulder he took one last look round the dingy room. He picked up the suitcase, turned off the light and locked the door behind him.

Minutes later, his van was on the move.

***

Still concerned about Marcia and unable to contact her, Amanda was in an anxious frame of mind when she let herself into Sebastian's cottage. Nevertheless, as she hung up her coat she called out to him as cheerfully as she could. However, his response immediately signalled he was probably in one of his moods of despair, the very last thing she needed. She spied a letter that lay open on the hall table and began to read it. Another rejection to a job application.

She paused at the lounge door and took a deep breath. With a smile she entered. 'What ho, Munchkin?'

Sebastian was slouched in front of a television wildlife documentary. He looked up and offered her the merest shadow of a smile. 'Hi,' was all he could manage.

Amanda glanced at the empty plate on the dining table. 'You've eaten then?'

'Yeah. I didn't do you anything 'cause I didn't know how long you'd be.'

'I see.' In the absence of any further communication she wandered into the kitchen. She leaned with both hands against the working surface and exhaled deeply. Then she opened the serving hatch and leaned through it. 'So what sort of a day have you had?'

'Oh a real belter.'

'I'm sorry. I shouldn't have asked. I saw the letter.'

'Oh that's just par for the course, isn't it?' He leaned forward and rubbed his forehead, briskly.

Amanda returned to the lounge and knelt next to him.

She gently pulled his head towards her and gave him a lingering kiss, to which he responded as if just going through the motions. He pulled away and gave her a look she had seen too many times before.

She rose, knowing where this was headed. More laments that he is just not good enough for her. 'I'm sorry, I just can't go through this again. Not now. I'll go and stay at Nan's place, just for tonight. It'll be best for both of us.'

She hoped against hope he would respond, take her in his arms, embrace and kiss her, tell her how much he loved and needed her. But no, he merely hung his head in resignation and despair.

Within minutes she was on her way to the cottage her late grandmother had left her.

Some time later, after a meal of tinned sausages and beans she had found in the cupboard, Amanda lay curled up with a glass of merlot and a book in front of a blazing coal fire.

There was a knock on the front door. Her hopes rose. Perhaps it was Sebastian. He had come to apologise and take her back to the cottage.

Her spirits dived when, on the doorstep, she found a rather hesitant DCI Stone. 'Good evening chief inspector.'

'Good evening, I hope it's not too late. I er… I hope I didn't disturb you. I called at the hall and was told you were here.'

'Oh no, not at all. The doorbell was ringing anyway. Do come in.' The response threw him until he caught her impish smile. 'Come on in,' she insisted.

Once inside she motioned him to a chair on the other

side of the fireplace. He gazed and smiled appreciatively at the fire.

'Would you care for something to drink? A glass of wine?'

'Oh no. maybe a cup of tea?'

'With pleasure.' She disappeared into the kitchen and returned a few minutes later with the same.

'I was just on my way home from work. I thought I'd call to tell you that we've finished with the chalet, so it's no longer cordoned off.' He noticed the look on her face. 'You seem surprised.'

'Well yes. I wouldn't have expected you'd have finished with it so quickly.'

'The coroner's verdict came in today. It was death by misadventure.'

'Really?'

Stone looked puzzled. 'Why should that surprise you?'

'Tell me, how did the man die?'

The question seemed to throw the Inspector. 'An overdose of insulin. He was a diabetic. Either he accidentally overdosed or did it deliberately.'

'In the left side?'

Stone frowned uncertainly. He tried to recall. 'No, the freshest mark was on the right side.' He did not care to admit that when the office was deserted, he had carefully studied the autopsy report in an endeavour to pick holes in a case McBride had dealt with.

'Is that where the other injection marks were?'

The CI's eyebrows rose. 'No, they were on the left side.'

'Then don't you think that's odd?'

'Odd?'

'The man was left-handed. Surely he'd inject his left

192

side, would he not? The same side as the hand he would hold the pen in. Why the change?'

Stone began to feel he was now in the witness stand. 'Well, his left hand was severely bruised.'

'But it wasn't just his left hand was it? Both hands looked to be in a real state when I saw him.'

Stone considered for a moment. 'That's true, I suppose. There's another thing, he was travelling under an alias. His real name was Gabriel Montand.'

Amanda's shrewd eyes narrowed. 'Curiouser and curiouser. Was he the one who attacked and killed Theo Patterson?'

Stone stiffened. 'I'm not a liberty to discuss that case. He stared at her, somewhat dumbfounded. 'How do you know he was left-handed?'

'His spilled glass was on the left-hand side of the body. The syringe was on the right side and his wallet was in the right inside pocket of his jacket. Also, his right wrist bore a paler band of skin where he wore his watch. I asked myself why would he take his watch off, as if he was about to go to bed, then decide to commit suicide?'

'And how do you know all this?'

'Because I took a good look around when I discovered the body. And before you ask, no I didn't contaminate the crime scene.'

'Well, since you and Mrs Craddock were the only ones with access and have alibis, the inquest presumed he locked the chalet and did the deed, accidentally or deliberately.'

'I'm still not convinced it was as straightforward as that. I did try to mention it to DS McBride, but he didn't want to know.'

'Did he not?' Stone let out a smile. 'Well, that was all

pretty observant of you, Miss Sheppard,' *and pretty dumb of McBride if he had not spotted the man was left-handed.* Stone was confident that he would certainly have noticed it.

Amanda smiled. 'I think we've got past the Miss Sheppard stage by now, with all we've been through, don't you, chief inspector?'

He looked embarrassed. 'I suppose so, Amanda.' He rose, an apparently happier man than the one who'd arrived. 'Thank you for the tea and the information.'

'There is one other thing that bothers me.'

'What's that?'

Amanda shared her concerns over the apparent disappearance of Marcia and Roland Hawtry.

'Perhaps they've both gone away, separately. On holiday or something.'

'It seems a bit coincidental, plus the fact that neither of them mentioned it. And that's not all.' She went on to describe Charlie Pembroke's overheard conversation.

Stone appeared to tense up at the mention of his name. 'I can't believe that for a moment,' he replied, indignantly. 'He was a fine officer, and still is a good bloke.'

'So, you won't do anything?'

Stone now looked decidedly averse. However, Amanda had given him a steer that he would look into further, which might well give him something over his cocky DS. He supposed the least he could do would be to look into the matter and make some enquiries. 'Very well, I'll see what we can uncover.'

As he drove home Stone was struck by two different emotions. One of elation that it looked like his high-flying subordinate might just have dropped a brick. The other one of regret that he had not taken the opportunity to glean Amanda's thoughts on the murders of Patterson and Lagrange. Instead, he had slammed the lid down. That woman after all was one sharp cookie and had her finger well and truly on the local pulse.

Chapter 10

OCTOBER

Dripping wet, even though he had only dashed up the stone staircase from his car, Selwyn shrugged off his raincoat in the hall and breezed into the kitchen. 'What a foul night eh, Mrs S?'

The housekeeper, bowed over the range on which a number of pans were in various stages of some sort of volcanic action, turned, her face flushed. 'Hello commander, better get into something dry.' She cast a critical eye on the newly polished wooden floor where droplets of water had started to form from the commander's shoes.

'Quite right, capital idea. Any tea going?'

'Of course, whenever is there not a pot ready for you?'

'Quite true, then we'll have it in the... well, wherever Miriam is.'

Mrs S looked perplexed. 'She isn't 'ere.'

'What do you mean? Where is she?'

'Gone to 'er council meeting.'

His eyes widened and jowls drooped. 'What? In this, and at this time of night? She never told me about it.'

Mrs S put her hands on her hips, always a bad sign. 'It's on the calendar if folks'd read it.'

Selwyn held his hands up. 'Okay, okay, point taken. Where is this wretched meeting?'

Mrs S turned to stir one of the pans and turn the heat down. 'It's on the calendar,' she repeated, over her shoulder.

He strode over to the notice board and consulted it. 'I won't change just yet. Never know, what... Where's Sebastian?' the commander's tone was now far more serious.

'Probably in the cottage. I haven't seen 'im yet.'

'I'll have the tea in the study,' Selwyn decided and marched off. He took out his mobile, punched in a number and talked as he walked. 'Sebastian, can you get over here please.' He listened. 'Yes it is urgent. Bring your car.'

'What's the problem?' asked Sebastian, once seated with his uncle.

Selwyn looked distraught, his jowls still drooping. 'It's Miriam, she's out at a council meeting, on her own.'

'And?'

'I'm worried about her.'

'Guv, you can't keep her wrapped in cotton wool.'

Selwyn shook his head, irritably. 'I know but I'm scared to death something might happen to her. Even Stone recommended she shouldn't go anywhere alone, if she can possibly avoid it.'

Sebastian placed a hand on his uncle's arm. 'What do you want to do about it?'

'I'm not sure. I'd go and meet her from the meeting but I've got the dashed architect coming at seven and it's too late to put him off now.'

'You want me to go?'

'Would you?'

'I can, but I'm not sure it's the right thing to do. If everything's OK and Miriam finds you've sent me to look out for her, she'll have a real humour failure. You realise that?'

'Yes, yes, I know, but it's a stinker of a night and I'd rather be safe than sorry. I'd never forgive myself if something happened and I'd just let it.'

'Well alright, but we'll have to come to some sort of compromise on how far you're going to mollycoddle her. Where's the meeting? The town hall I assume?'

'Yes, thank you dear boy,' Selwyn's relief was almost palpable. 'Make sure you take the tracking stuff.'

'I'm on it.' He rose and made to leave. At the door he turned and smiled. 'Heaven help you when she finds out about the device.'

'Then she'd better not. Take care my boy and thank you. You're a first class chap.'

***

The quietness that had descended on the council car park, once the meeting had started, was punctuated only by the footsteps of very occasional passers-by, generally hurrying past under the shelter of an umbrella. Over an hour had passed by the time Sebastian arrived and parked at a discreet distance from Miriam's car.

Time ticked slowly by. Sebastian noticed a figure which, unseen to him, had alighted from a van. It sheltered under a golf umbrella, by the side of the town hall, adjacent to the entrance. Not long after the councillors began to leave the building, Miriam appeared, in conversation with another woman as they hastened across the car park. The figure immediately set off to follow her and as soon as the two women parted, he moved alongside Miriam.

Sebastian assumed this was just one of the councillors offering shelter to her car. At the Mercedes, Miriam appeared to unlock it, give something to the other, then get in. The companion then moved round to the other side, lowered the umbrella and got into the car.

Must be giving someone a lift, thought Sebastian as she pulled away, her car one of first to leave the car park. It took Sebastian four attempts to start by which time a queue had formed at the exit. By the time he turned into the road there was no sign of the Mercedes.

***

On Amanda's arrival at the hall that evening, her day's tally of missing people appeared to increase by one when Sebastian was not there. All Selwyn would say was that he was out but he knew not where. It was only when Amanda enquired if Miriam would be with them that evening, that Mrs S confided she was at a council meeting and that the commander was worried 'something chronic' at her absence.

Thus there were only Selwyn and Amanda there to enjoy a subdued aperitif before dinner, each cloistered with their own worried thoughts.

Throughout the day, an anxious Amanda had repeatedly rung Marcia. She had also tried Roland Hawtry's number, but with an equal lack of success. When questioned, Eleanor had confirmed that Roland had attended the meeting, but there had been no sign of Marcia. Nor had Roland mentioned her, or her absence.

At lunchtime, Amanda had visited Marcia's address, obtained from the Committee members' database, but there had been no answer to her knock, nor any sign of her car. After work she had tried again, with the same result. She had even tried Roland's address but there were no lights on, no car and no reply. She was still wondering

199

whether she should have reported their absences to the police, but concluded more time would need to elapse before they would act.

All this she had wanted to share with the commander, but from his expression it appeared he already had enough to worry about.

The timing of dinner, much to Mrs Soames' annoyance, became a moveable feast. Her grumpy mood had been enhanced, she confided to Amanda, due to having suffered something shocking all day with her 'various veins'.

'They should have been here by now,' Selwyn later observed with a glare at the mantlepiece clock as he paced the drawing room, casting envious glances at the drinks cabinet he had denied himself access to that evening.

'Maybe the meeting went on longer than usual?' Amanda eventually suggested, her own concern mounting over Sebastian's absence. Any further conversation was interrupted by the housekeeper's arrival with the ultimatum that if the meal was not going to be served directly it wouldn't even be fit to feed a dog. As if on cue, Mustard then bounded into the room and made straight for Amanda who bent to distractedly fondle his head and ears.

'Alright Mrs S, please serve it up and try and keep something warm for the others,' Selwyn conceded.

***

'Just drive, you bitch,' hissed McNabb, the point of the knife pressed against the terrified councillor's side. 'I'll tell you when to turn off. Any false move and you know what'll happen.'

Miriam bit down on her lip to try to control her trembling mouth and keep back the tears impatient to flow. 'You won't get away with this,' she eventually managed to utter.

'As if I fucking care, anymore. You've ruined my life and all I want is revenge.'

'You managed that all by yourself. Don't blame me for your mistakes.' She cried out as she felt the knife point jabbed into her side.

'Shut your stinking mouth or I'll do you right here. Just drive.'

Now in the unlit country lanes, the rain unceasing, McNabb had become less certain of his navigation. Twice they had halted, returned in the direction from which they had come, then turned off onto a different road. All the time McNabb's anxiety and frustration was growing as he peered through the windscreen and side window for something. 'Where is it? Where the fuck is it?' he mumbled to himself.

'Where's what?'

'My fucking motor bike,' he hissed into her face. 'Slow down, fucking slow down.'

Terrified as she was, Miriam tried to rationalise. He intended to leave her and her car and drive back on a motor bike, presumably back to a vehicle he had left near the town hall. Did he intend to kill her? He must or he would not have mentioned the bike. Or was that just a slip? She could feel a dampness on her side where the knife point had entered. Was she losing much blood? If he was going to knife her in the car, she should be ready at any moment, to try to get out and run just before he did it. Or, if he got out first, he would probably demand the key, as he had when she had unlocked the car at the car park. What should she do then? Lock the car as soon as he got out and try to keep it locked? But he had taken her mobile phone so she couldn't summon help. Nor would she know where to direct anyone to. Was there anything in the car she would use as a weapon? Not that she could think of anything. Maybe if…

What the hell's she doing? thought Sebastian, as he came to a stop to study the screen. *She's going around in bloody circles.* He had followed the dot for several minutes now and once more it had backtracked on itself. He drove on, pulled off the road into a farm track entrance and watched as the dot appeared to approach. He quickly turned off the headlights and ignition and waited, watching the dot and scanning the lane in each direction.

'Stop,' McNabb's command sent a shudder through Miriam. 'Switch off, turn the lights off and give me the keys. As he spoke, he jabbed the knife point into her side.

Miriam winced and let out an involuntary cry. She obeyed and handed over the keyring.

McNabb pulled a torch from his jacket pocket and shone it at her. Miriam's eyes blinked almost shut as she turned her face away from the glare.

His stare fixed on her, McNabb felt for the doorhandle. He opened the door and still staring at the terrified woman, slid to the edge of the seat and got out. As he did so he growled, 'If you move it'll be the worse for you.' He shone the torch beam along the verge until it lit up the tarpaulin with which he had covered the motor bike.

All the while Miriam trembled. With one hand clutched

on the steering wheel, her other felt her side. The clothing felt damp. She looked at her hand but could see nothing in the darkness. She eased off her high-heeled shoes and grabbed the bendy slip-ons she kept in the glove compartment for long journeys. When he returned and got back in, this would be her only chance to get out and run. She could feel the prickle of tears in the corners of her eyes. If only Selwyn were here, everything would be alright. He would make sure of that.

Through the windscreen Sebastian saw a slim figure emerge from the passenger side of Miriam's car and walk along the verge. His torch light initially and briefly reflected off something he held in his hand. A gun or a knife, Sebastian surmised. Without a moment to lose Sebastian emerged into the blackness and crept as quietly as he could towards the Mercedes. He crouched in front of it. He wanted to let Miriam know he was there but it was too dangerous. He lowered his head as far as he could, whilst still retaining visibility of the man who now returned. Sebastian had expected him to go to the passenger door but instead he approached on the other side. With the torch grasped in the same hand as he held the knife, he opened the driver's door. In the beam, through the windscreen, Sebastian could see Miriam's terrified face as she flinched away from McNabb. With the torch now transferred to the other hand, his arm was pulled back to deliver the knife thrust. 'This is for the hell you've put me in.' he snarled.

Sebastian sprang up and with a shout of 'Move away, you bastard,' flung himself at McNabb. The man looked momentarily stunned. However, he was quick enough to swing the torch round and lunge at Sebastian. At that moment Miriam's voice screamed out, 'No, McNabb.' The knife went home and as McNabb withdrew it Sebastian fell to the ground, coughing. A deep ache blossomed into a bloom of cold spreading through his middle. His sight narrowed to the knife, the manic expression on the man's face, then Miriam's horrified expression. The assailant merely glanced at his victim then turned his attention to the car. Miriam could only stare in horror at the knife and the look of evil fixation on McNabb's face.

Just as he thrust into the interior, as hard as he could, Sebastian slammed the driver door shut with his heel, thudding against the man's side and head.

McNabb let out a howl of pain, pulled away from the car and bent to retrieve the dropped knife.

Seeing her chance, Miriam slammed the door back open. It connected with McNabb's head. With another bellow of pain he tottered backwards, tripped over Sebastian and fell to the ground. Sebastian lurched onto his knees and in agony, reached for the knife now illuminated by the torch. He dropped onto McNabb and with trembling hand held the knife point at his neck. 'Just move, please just move then I can stick this right into you,' he panted, but all McNabb could do was to try to roll over in his pain.

Within minutes, McNabb had been bound with some rope Miriam had obtained from Sebastian's boot and bundled into the back of her car. She then began to thread her way through the country lanes in search of Hopestanding hospital. Despite his great pain, Sebastian called 999 to alert the police to their arrival there, with a prisoner, then rang the hall.

***

Miriam had already arrived by the time Selwyn's jaguar screeched to a halt in the hospital car park. Her Mercedes was obscured by two police cars with lights flashing. Nearby, next to his own car stood DCI Stone giving instructions to a PC who then headed off. 'Commander, Amanda, I'm so sorry. You'll want to go straight in. We'll speak later.'

The compassion in his voice fuelled Amanda's anxiety. 'How bad is he?' she pleaded.

Stone shook his head. 'I really can't say. You'll have to ask the doctors.'

Selwyn nodded to him, put his arm round Amanda's shoulder and accompanied her into the building.

The A and E area was unusually quiet, other than for a child lying on a trolley, being read to by his mother. In a screened off bay, a groaning patient was being treated.

'He's in theatre,' the staff nurse advised them, 'If you'd care to take a seat at the end of the corridor over there, the surgeon will speak with you when he comes out.'

The two-tone cream and pale green walls, in the fluorescent light, brought a chill to both of them as they made their way in numbed silence to the seating indicated. Selwyn remembered the final days when he had visited his dying wife. To Amanda, the foreign nature of these surroundings seemed to place her beloved Sebastian even further from her reach.

They waited and waited. With each minute that ticked slowly by Amanda feared her chances of seeing Sebastian alive again were receding. The longer the wait, the more serious the surgery, she kept thinking. Selwyn's numerous attempts to bolster her confidence, and indeed his own, therefore bore little comfort and success.

Once Miriam had given her statement to the police, she immediately went in search of Amanda and Selwyn who, Stone had informed her, were there in the hospital. She was conscious of the surgical dressing that covered the wound McNabb had made in her side. The right side of her coat and the dress were heavily stained with blood, some of it hers, some Sebastian's. It had taken a lot of convincing to persuade the staff that she should not be held overnight for observation.

The click of her heels in the corridor as she approached Selwyn and Amanda — she had been able to persuade the police to let her rescue her shoes from the car – caused their heads to instantly rise and look in her direction. The instantaneous hope of news, the sound of her arrival had brought, was instantly dashed.

Amanda rose and the women embraced. 'He'll be alright,' Miriam tried to reassure her.

'Of course he will. Solid as a rock, that man. Comes from good stock,' Selwyn added. Comforting smiles passed between them. Miriam volunteered to go in search of some refreshments and retraced her steps back in the direction of the hospital's café.

Shortly after she had disappeared, a green-gowned surgeon approached from the other direction, a surgical mask slung below his chin. 'Amanda Sheppard?' he enquired.

She sprang to her feet, her enquiring eyes fixed immediately on his. 'Yes,' she almost gulped.

'Sebastian is out of surgery but not yet out of the woods. The next twenty-four hours will be crucial. He had a very narrow escape. If the wound had been a fraction higher it would have been instantly fatal. He's lost a lot of blood. He's sedated and in intensive care, but you can see him from the window, if you wish. I'll take you there.'

Amanda thanked him profusely and glanced at Selwyn.

'You go on ahead and I'll wait for Miriam then join you,' he said.

The tears Amanda had valiantly suppressed for so long coursed down her cheeks as she gazed at Sebastian's inert form, surrounded by transfusion and monitoring equipment. She was then joined by the others. On each side of her, Selwyn, grim-faced, and Miriam also weeping, looking on and sharing in her anguish.

Chapter 11

The following day, Amanda's call to the hospital, as soon as she woke, was initially greeted with a coolness bordering on hostility. When, however, she explained it was her fiancé she was enquiring about, the nurse informed her he had passed a comfortable night and his condition was stable. She apologised for her initial unfriendliness and cited the repeated calls she had received from the badgering press. The consultant would examine the patient on his morning round, if Amanda would care to call back later.

Amanda relayed the news to Selwyn who was able to brighten his housekeeper's day. She removed the hand that had shot to her mouth when the commander began to speak about Sebastian, then fished in her apron pocket to apply the already-mangled handkerchief to the corner of her eye. 'Thank gawd for that,' she sighed.

'He's not got a clean bill of health yet,' warned Selwyn.

'No, but he's a Fitzgerald aint 'e. I know. I'll go and make some broth to take him.'

'I'm not sure he's as bad as all that,' Selwyn was tempted to respond but thought better of it. Mrs S' broths were not her strong point, though Selwyn had discovered that Mustard was partial to them, when she wasn't looking. Let the dear lady busy herself. It would keep her mind off things.

After she and Selwyn had recovered Miriam's car, Amanda returned to her office, having battled through the gaggle of reporters who hung around outside the library. Her thoughts now returned to Marcia and Roland. Both reception and Eleanor confirmed there had been no messages for her. During her coffee break she again rang their numbers, but without success. It had now been a week and there had been no word from DCI Stone, nor could she get through to him. She had been tempted to contact Charlie Pembroke to see what he knew, but if Marcia's fears had been true she would hardly get anything constructive from him. Furthermore, if Marcia had indeed gone off on holiday, or her absence was otherwise quite innocuous, Amanda felt the very last thing Marcia would want would be to draw Charlie's attention to it.

***

The points Amanda had raised about the scene at the fishing chalet, whilst not sufficient or serious enough to cause a re-opening of the case, certainly enabled DCI Stone to put his subordinate back in his place. Not to have noticed the man was left-handed was something of a schoolboy howler. Stone had also made sure this snippet reached the ears of Superintendent Nelson. He now realised he had possibly backed the wrong horse in McBride.

It was therefore a less ebullient DS who asked, 'What about interviewing McNabb?' as Stone grabbed his coat to go out.

'The weasel made enough of his so-called injuries to get off being interviewed yesterday so let him sweat until I get back.'

'Do you want me to interview him?'

Stone snorted his disapproval. 'Not bloody likely. You get on with liaising with the French Embassy over Montand. Make enquiries about next of kin and whatever formalities we'll need to go through for the return of the body, once we and the coroner are through.' As he strode down the corridor, he chuckled to himself at the peeved expression on McBride's face.

The DCI got into his car and drove to the outskirts of Hopestanding and Pembroke's apartment. He recalled the alleged conversation Charlie had had on his mobile. Only after he had left Amanda had Stone reflected further on the death of the drink driver and the cast iron alibi that Pembroke had had. Almost too good to be true, he thought as he drove into the car park of the block of flats. In the hope of catching Pembroke off-guard, he had not called him and taken the chance that he would be in.

He rang the intercom and waited for nearly two minutes before there was a reply and he was buzzed through. Crossing the mirror-lined entrance hall, heading towards the lift, he caught sight of his profile and in particular, the paunch he was dieting to lose. With a grimace he veered away in the direction of the stairs.

Charlie came to answer the door. Full of bonhomie, he vigorously shook Stone's hand and led him into the spacious lounge, its walls generously covered with several David Shepherd wildlife pictures.

'Originals?' the DCI queried as he took them in.

'I should be so lucky,' Charlie replied, 'Do have a seat. Can I get you something?'

Stone sank down onto the leather sofa and shook his

head. Francis Mboko entered the room from what Stone assumed was the kitchen. He rose, shook his hand and sat down again. Mboko took the armchair at the other end of the glass coffee table and Charlie the one adjacent to the DCI. There he sat back with his hands casually clasped on top of his belly. 'So, to what do we owe the pleasure of this visit?'

Stone glanced at the two men in turn. Whereas Charlie looked completely at ease, Mboko appeared less so, a frown creasing his brow. 'It's about a couple of your committee colleagues. Roland Hawtry and Marcia Phelps.'

Charlie gave him a quizzical smile. 'What have they been up to?'

'Disappearing, it would seem. When was the last time you saw them?' He turned to look at Mboko whose eyes were fixed enquiringly on Charlie.

Charlie scratched his head. 'Now, let me think. Roland we saw just about a week ago, at the committee meeting.'

'And Marcia Phelps?'

Charlie looked across at Mboko. 'She wasn't there at the meeting, so it would be the one before that, wouldn't it?'

Mboko readily agreed.

Charlie reached for his mobile and scrolled through it. 'That'd be the twenty fourth of September.'

Stone turned to Mboko. 'And what about you? Have you seen them at any other time, recently?'

'Nope, it's as Charlie says.'

'Did Mr Hawtry say anything at the meeting about going away?'

Both men shook their heads.

He regarded them both for several moments then rose. Mboko looked decidedly uncomfortable. 'Are you okay?'

Francis gave a weak smile. 'Yes, I'm fine. Sorry, I'm just a bit pre-occupied. A few business problems.'

'Well, I hope they get sorted out.' He glanced back at Charlie who was just fractionally too late in banishing a look of concern. 'If either of you do see or hear from either of them, do let me know.'

The two men both got to their feet. 'Of course we will,' Charlie smiled his assurance. 'Sure you won't stay for a drink?'

'No, I must get back. We'll meet up again soon.' He nodded to Mboko who gave a fleeting smile. He headed down the hall escorted by Charlie. At the front door he turned. 'I don't suppose you've had any more thoughts about the drink driver's corpse we found after the Lodge meeting?' he said, his voice loud enough to carry over to Mboko. Over Charlie's shoulder Stone noted the anxious look on the man's face.

'Can't say that I have,' replied Charlie and extended a large hand which Stone shook. On his way down the DCI deliberated. Something was definitely not right. He needed to question Mboko separately, but without any definite theories and solid evidence he would need to find a subtle pretext to get him on his own. In the meantime, he would put a search out for Hawtry's and Marcia's cars and get Amanda to file missing person's reports.

***

'Local hero saves Wisstingham's leading lady,' Amanda read out to Sebastian.

Propped up in his hospital bed by a generous supply of pillows. he could only smile his joy at the sight of her beautiful almond eyes and smile. Eyes and a mouth that

212

he and others at one stage feared he might never see again. Gone were the monitoring equipment, the blood transfusion, the IV paraphernalia and several days out of his life, but Sebastian was now safely and happily on the road to recovery. What's more, he was being feted as a hero by the local press and even a couple of the nationals.

Amanda finished reading the article to him, folded the newspaper then bent to give him a kiss, her cleopatra hairstyle almost enclosing his face. The kiss lingered until Amanda broke off, her face still close to his. 'God, it's so good to have you safe, I was frantic with worry. Selwyn was an absolute brick the way he put up with all my anxiety.'

'Couldn't have been any more anxious than I was. When I lay by the car I thought I wasn't going to see or touch or kiss you ever again. It made me realise how idiotic I've been.'

She closed in for another long kiss, fondled his ears then broke off again to ask how he was feeling. He grinned, raised the bedclothes and glanced down his body. 'Well, everything's certainly working.'

She returned his grin. 'Down boy, you'll need to be in better fettle for that, believe me.'

He put his arm round her neck and pulled her towards him. 'I think you're probably right. We've a lot to make up for.' His smile said it all. Her Sebastian was finally back.

It was a very happy Amanda who, two days later in the late afternoon, drove to the hospital to liberate her fiancé.

She carried the hospital's prescribed shipping order of dressings and medicines as Sebastian gingerly mounted the stone staircase, entered the hall and passed into the tender care of matron Soames. Without invitation, Mrs S was delighted to reinstate her role. Selwyn cast a sideways smirk at the unconvinced patient as the housekeeper fussed about fetching pillows, blankets, and a large tray for the inevitable jigsaw she believed would materialise during his recuperation. Much to her vexation, Sebastian insisted that Selwyn and Amanda should set up his laptop, printer, and other electronic devices, to enable him to work on his part of the hall project.

'That there work 'n strain isn't going to help 'im get better,' Mrs S warned, as she regarded with dismay the cables, extensions, connections and small tables being imported to host the equipment, files, drawings and stationery.

'As if a body 'asn't enough 'ardship working round all these tradesmen and their dirt and dust, 'ow on earth am I going to keep this place clean?' she complained. Only when Amanda had gently reminded her that since it was her fiancé, the matronly role should really be hers, plus that fact that his recuperation would so essentially depend upon the regular provision of refreshments and good food, did Mrs S somewhat relent.

'Then I'll go and fetch a pot of Rosie and some Dundee cake for you all,' she grudgingly conceded and bustled out of the room.

Seated on the chaise longue, Amanda next to him, Sebastian gazed at the rather chaotic transformation of the drawing room. 'A home fit for heroes,' he commented, with a smile. Amanda stealthily pinched his bottom, cast him a sideways, cheeky glance then leaned towards him. 'Don't milk it Munchkin, or I'll give you a real seeing to,' she whispered into his ear.

'Chance'll be a fine thing,' he whispered back, with a grin.

Selwyn turned from straightening a chair. 'Quite right, that man. We've got a real hero at the hall. And here's another,' he added, as the door opened and Miriam walked in, evidently amused at something.

'Mrs S suggests we get hold of a wheelchair for Sebastian. She intends to look in the attic for the old one she believes is stored up there.'

Selwyn's gaze shot heavenwards. 'Oh my giddy aunt! This caring malarkey's going too far. That thing's an absolute antique and probably full of woodworm. It'd be a veritable death trap. I'll have to disabuse her of that notion.'

***

'There's a Professor Ingrams on the phone, wants to confirm your two-o-clock meeting with him here is still on?' Mrs Soames announced as the commander descended the staircase.

Selwyn gave a puzzled frown.

Mrs S put her hand over the mouthpiece. 'Says he arranged it with you about two weeks ago, about the priory.'

Selwyn's eyes closed as he briefly clapped a hand to his forehead. 'Tell him I'm looking forward to seeing him,' he hastily responded.

'Getting more and more forgetful, 'e is,' Mrs S muttered to herself, after she had confirmed the arrangement and rung off.

Selwyn continued his descent of the staircase, remembering the conversation he had had with the professor.

Two-o-clock arrived and so did Ingrams. Though portly, he stood very erect and gave the impression of being quite fit, perhaps emphasised by his short-cut white hair. His round rim glasses perched on an aquiline nose and his mouth displayed an impressive array of teeth.

'Commander Fitzgerald, I appreciate your seeing me at such short notice,' Ingrams boomed, as he entered the library, his hand held out in greeting.

'Not at all. Would you care for some refreshment?'

Mrs S retreated from the room with the order.

'Do sit down,' Selwyn continued. 'You mentioned you thought you might be able to give me some useful advice about the crypt at the priory.'

'Well, I should start by saying I only just found out about Archie Fox and the villainy he got up to here. He was an undergraduate friend of mine and always something of a wild card, but what happened was far beyond what I would ever imagined him capable of. I came as much to express my apologies for anything untoward that might have resulted from my meeting him at the priory site.'

Selwyn's widened eyes invited the guest to enlighten him further.

Ingrams explained how, unbeknown to the commander, he had inspected the priory site at Fox's invitation and commented upon the absence of a crypt. A crypt which subsequent developments showed that Fox had later unearthed.

There was a pause in the proceedings as Mrs S entered with the refreshments and cakes. She cast Selwyn a questioning look which he interpreted as a query on the opinion he had formed on the visitor. He smiled in an attempt to put her mind at rest.

Selwyn assured his guest that his apology was unnecessary and described the chaos that Fox had wreaked generally, from the attempt to bleed the estate dry, to his attempt to murder Selwyn's prospective niece-in-law Amanda, and friend.

Ingrams looked suitably horrified.

Selwyn then outlined the history of the family's missing treasure and the attempts he had made to find it.

'And you think it might be hidden somewhere in the crypt?' Ingrams eventually queried.

'It's about the last place I can think of that it might be. The place has always been hidden and empty, apart from the coffins, though I've never seen any sign of a hidden door or anything like that.'

The professor thought for a moment. 'If it would be of any use to you I'd be most happy and intrigued to visit the place with you and share any thoughts I might have.'

'By Jove, would you really?'

'Of course. I'm touring in the vicinity for the next few days, so I'm at your disposal.'

Selwyn sat up. His eyes positively shone, 'Well, would tomorrow afternoon be too soon for you?'

'Not at all.'

Conversation continued amicably until the two men rose, a time was fixed and the delighted host showed his visitor to the door.

By mid-afternoon the following day they stood in the cold crypt, illuminated by lamps the commander had brought. He eagerly watched the professor as he wandered round the space. He closely inspected the coffins and then paced the dimensions of the room. At one stage he returned to the steps and climbed back up to the top, followed by Selwyn. He then did some more pacing and sat on a low wall to think.

Back in the crypt, Ingrams paced some more then walked the perimeter, inspecting the walls. Finally, he heaved himself up onto one of the coffin lids and sat there. Selwyn stared at him as if he were the oracle at Delphi.

'There's something not right down here,' the professor finally pronounced. 'The dimensions are wrong. The place looks to be too small.'

'How do you mean?' Selwyn was barely able to contain his excitement.

'For monasteries of this size there would normally be a larger crypt to ensure enough space to bury more than the three abbots that were interred here.'

'Are you saying the place has been foreshortened?'

Ingrams inhaled as if sniffing in the air. 'It's difficult to say in this light, but it could well be possible.'

'Where do you think it might have been foreshortened?'

The professor scratched his head. 'Again, it's difficult to say. We really could do with some more light on the job.'

Selwyn folded his arms and sighed. 'I did previously have a close look at the walls and floor but there didn't appear to be any difference in construction or any unusual overlapping of the floor slabs.

Ingrams waved away the observations with a flap of his hand. 'Oh, they'll probably have built new walls and floor all round.' He looked up. 'It's the vaulting of the ceiling that'll be the best giveaway. Though they'll have been very clever about the way they built out the columns at the corners.'

Selwyn held a lamp aloft but Ingrams once more shook his head. 'It really needs some better lighting to see what's what, and some accurate dimensions.'

The commander's spirits and jowls sank. Ingrams raised his arm to consult his watch by the light of the lamp. 'Goodness, is that the time? I'm afraid I'm going to have to get a move on. I'm sorry I haven't been of more use. I'd be happy to take another look at it all, if you could get some better lighting rigged up, or if you could send me some good photos and dimensions.'

His spirits somewhat restored, Selwyn confirmed he would oblige and with effusive thanks and an invitation to stay at the hall, whenever the professor might care to, he accompanied him to his car and waved him off. He then returned to study the crypt before he sealed the entrance once more and returned to the hall. Now, with a faint glimmer of hope, there was definitely work to be done as soon as Sebastian was sufficiently recovered.

***

Mrs Soames had indeed been disabused of the notion of a wheelchair for Sebastian, nor did he need it or any other aid. His recovery was quick and several days later he was more than ready for his first outing, away from the hall. Selwyn had suggested they take a look at the crypt. 'Nothing to carry and no exertion,' he had hastily assured Amanda, when the trip was suggested over dinner. 'I want to make a plan and need someone to hold the silly end of the tape measure. We might need some heavy equipment in there and I want to make sure we can get it in.'

'You're sounding pretty chipper about things, Guv. Is there something you've not been telling me?'

'You bet your sweet life, dear boy. All will be revealed

on our way there.'

'You just make sure you wrap up warm, me dear,' Mrs Soames urged. Her sideways glance at the commander clearly registered disapproval of the venture. Nevertheless, she had done them proud with a bulging picnic hamper and flasks of hot soup and coffee, 'To keep out that there chill,' she explained.

Sebastian's neck was reluctantly swathed in a shawl the housekeeper had produced.

As the Jaguar disappeared from view, down the drive. Mrs S turned and entered the hall, grim faced in anticipation of further run-ins with contractors wreaking havoc with the daily cleaning programme, tidiness and cleanliness of her domain.

***

The morning's hectic programme of a meeting at the Hopestanding council offices, followed by staff appraisals, managed to keep Amanda's thoughts clear of the mysterious disappearance of Marcia and Roland Hawtry. However, over her lunch break Amanda once more found herself pondering on what had happened and where they might be.

Dark thoughts surfaced again that Hawtry, and or others, had silenced Marcia. If that was so, where was her car and more importantly her body?

It was when Amanda began to picture Marcia dead in some cold and dark place, that the memory of her own previous entombment in one of the crypt coffins re-surfaced.

Her thoughts began to follow the train of events associated with that dreadful night and as she re-lived the experience, she recalled how she had shared it with members of the steering committee, during a break, when she had touched upon her knowledge of Wisstingham Hall and the discovery of the crypt. Unlikely though it was, she went cold at the thought that such a fate might have happened to Marcia. 'Oh my God! Surely not,' she exclaimed. Nevertheless, it was a possibility that needed to be debunked.

***

Sebastian switched off the engine and glanced through his side window towards the priory site.

'So, there's a real chance we might find something, even if it's only another load of coffins.'

Selwyn gave him a cold stare. 'Your negativity does you no credit, young Sebastian. Let's just have a bit more optimism and less of the naysaying, eh?'

'You're absolutely right Guv. Treasure here we come.'

'And a toning down of the flippancy wouldn't go amiss, along with your shirts.'

'I suppose you understood fashion once upon a time, Guv,' Sebastian smirked.

Selwyn thought best to ignore this new slur on his excellent sartorial taste. He was only too glad to see his nephew transformed back into his old self. 'Okay, let's get going and get the place fully surveyed and photographed.'

'Right-ho boss.'

From the boot Selwyn took out his old briefcase, the digital camera, and video camera, which he gave to Sebastian. He lifted out the two lamps and they set off across the undergrowth, well-trodden down by the recent activities on the site.

At the priory ruins he refused his nephew's offer of assistance and huffed and puffed as he removed and set aside the wooden beams that closed off the entrance to the crypt.

'Weren't we supposed to secure these?' asked Sebastian, as he looked on.

'Reggie's working on it but I daren't ask Mrs S to get on his case. He's spending more time than she likes on restoring the launch. What with that and the contractors…'

Sebastian gave a warning shake of his head. 'You're going to have one unhappy bunny on your hands with her, if you're not careful.'

'Don't I know it.'

They took out their torches and began to descend the steps. Sebastian's torch beam picked out the wall recesses and coffins as it scanned the room. He wrinkled his nose as they entered the darkness. 'Stinks a bit.'

'Hmm,' Selwyn's beam swung slowly across the walls then came back to bear on the briefcase. He took out the tape measure, notebook and pen which he placed on one of the coffin lids. The two heavy duty lamps were then switched on, their beams fixed onto one of the walls, across the two other coffins.

'I'm not sure even these are powerful enough to do the job,' Selwyn remarked.

'Hold on!' exclaimed Sebastian, 'didn't we leave all the coffin lids partly open?'

Selwyn aimed his beam at the coffins. All three lids were fully closed. He furiously tried to remember how things had been on his last visit with the professor. Hang it all, they had sat on the coffin lids. He was almost certain at least the one they had sat on was closed. Memories of a much earlier evening, when they had found Amanda and Martin both entombed, came flooding back. 'Oh crikey!' he moaned, 'what the devil's been going on?' He glanced across at Sebastian and they moved towards one of the coffins. For a moment they stared down in apprehension at the closed lid then exchanged uncertain glances.

'Let's do it then,' murmured Sebastian.

Selwyn frowned. 'You stand aside, I'm not taking the chance of you doing any damage to yourself.'

'You sure you can manage?'

'Of course I can, they're not that heavy.' He took a deep breath then heaved against one of the lids. It grated aside. Sebastian shone a light inside. It was empty. They moved on to a second coffin and Selwyn pushed that lid aside. They both peered in and instantly drew back, repelled by both the sight and smell of what they saw.

'God almighty,' gasped Selwyn.

Sebastian gave an involuntary cry as his mobile rang out. He fumbled for it, connected and listened. 'How the hell did you know? Yes, we're down here and we've just found a body in one of the coffins.' He held the phone away from his face and mouthed, 'Amanda' in answer to Selwyn's querying frown. He returned to the call. 'No, I don't know who it is. No, don't come, there's nothing you can do…Amanda, Amanda?' He glanced at the mobile then at Selwyn. 'She's on her way here,' he sighed.

Selwyn reached reluctantly into the coffin and gently touched the face which was as cold as the coffin lid. He instinctively wiped his hand on his jacket and slowly nodded his head.

'Stone is just going to love this, and us,' Sebastian

observed, as he took out his mobile and punched in the police station's number which he knew only too well.

It seemed an eternity before they heard the sound of footsteps on the stone staircase. Selwyn swung his torch to the silhouettes that appeared at the entrance. It picked out the faces of DS McBride and DCI Stone, whose expression was set hard. As both men approached them, there was the sound of further footsteps on the staircase. Four pairs of eyes turned to the entrance as Amanda appeared, panting.

'Don't come any further,' ordered McBride. 'This is probably a crime scene.'

Stone signalled for her to come forward. 'Come on in. Will you be alright?'

Touched by his solicitous tone she forced a smile, nodded and approached the coffin, hesitantly. There, Sebastian enfolded her shivering form in his arms. 'You shouldn't be here,' he murmured.

She gazed up into his eyes. 'I'm the only one who knows what she looks like.' Before he could say anything more, she steeled herself and looked over the edge of the coffin. Her hand shot to her mouth.

By now, Stone was at her side. 'Can you identify—' His question was cut short as Amanda's eyes glazed over, her legs buckled, and she collapsed to the ground before Sebastian could catch her.

***

It was lunchtime. Mrs Soames could tell that without looking at any clock. The din of carpenters, plasterers, masons and other workers, the whine of machine motors and the external rumble of construction traffic had all ceased. She took a sip of her tea and gazed around her kitchen. The sweet apple and cinnamon smell of the tarte au pomme, made for dinner that evening, assailed her nostrils and brought a fleeting smile. Only fleeting, as her apprehensive thoughts dwelled, as they had done all morning, on the changes just round the corner. Next week she would leave her kitchen, never to see it again in its present state. She was to have exclusive use of the new cafeteria kitchen whilst hers was being refurbished. 'Shake down' was what the Architect had told her the use of the new kitchen would constitute. 'Testing it all out,' he had explained.

'I'll shake 'im down if it don't work proper,' she muttered to herself. She rose, waddled out into the hall and down the corridor. As she did so, she ran her fingers along the surfaces of furniture and ornaments and glanced despairingly at the films of dust that now coated them. They had only been cleaned a couple of days earlier. This was all getting too much. She was losing the battle to keep the hall clean and tidy, no matter how diligent and hard-working her team of cleaners still remained.

Outside, the noise of an engine starting up was echoed by sound of a generator as it throbbed into action somewhere in the hall.

She sighed and promised herself that tomorrow she would definitely make up her mind about whether a future in this changed hall would be one for her, then slowly, sadly, retraced her steps back to the kitchen.

Elsewhere, in Wisstingham, another lady pondered recent events and her future. Seated in her father's high-backed chair, Eleanor gazed into the yellow flames of the coal fire. Gone was the woman with whom she had hoped and intended to spend the rest of her life. Her future now seemed to be slipping away from her.

She had done her duty to her family by her return to Wisstingham. Now her father no longer recognised her, his health in rapid decline.

Outside, a blast of wind buffeted the wooden window frame in competition with the driving rain that spattered the glass. She yearned for the warmth and light of spring. Yearned to see the poppies bloom on the French country roadsides and to once more witness the fresh growth of the vines. To smell the bakeries, visit the markets, drink early morning coffee in one of the village café bars and taste the baguettes and croissants that were never the same in England. She wanted to stroll through the quaint cobbled streets of medieval Pezenas and gaze into the windows of the artisan shops with their wonderful, unique wares.

The settling of the coals broke into her reverie. She could feel the moistening in her eyes as she continued to stare sadly into the fire.

After several minutes, she shook her head as if to dispel the thoughts and wishes that still lingered. There were things to be done and her lips tightened as she contemplated them.

Chapter 12

Seated on the stone step, Amanda stared incredulously at the beaker of coffee nestled in her hands. Alongside her sat Sebastian, his arm round her shoulders, whilst Selwyn, Stone and McBride looked on, from the bottom of the staircase.

'You okay now?' asked Sebastian.

'Yes. It's Roland Hawtry,' she almost whispered in answer to the DCI's questioning look. Her eyes widened. 'What about Marcia?' She moved to get up but Sebastian held on to her.

'The other coffins are empty, we've checked,' Stone reassured her, 'which brings us back to the question of where Marcia is.'

It was a sombre procession that later made its way through the hallway to the drawing room and a totally mystified housekeeper who took their orders for tea and coffee. She waddled back to the kitchen in her little cloud of muttered confusion.

'So, when you rang me, what made you think there might be someone buried at the crypt?' Sebastian asked Amanda. At her wretched expression, he squeezed his arm around her shoulders. 'I know you've got to go through all this again when Stone and McBride emerge from the crypt, but it's probably a good idea to get your thoughts in order before the snappy Scot starts barking questions at you.'

'With no sign of Marcia, I feared Hawtry had done away with her and if he had, I wondered where he might have hidden the body. Then I suddenly remembered that I'd told the committee about the crypt and what happened there. That's when I rang you.' She paused and stared down at the carpet. 'I was so sure Hawtry was responsible for her disappearance.'

Selwyn turned from his customary vantage point at the French windows. 'Perhaps he was.'

'Then who killed *him*?' queried Sebastian.

Amanda absent-mindedly fingered a strand of her hair as she stared at him. 'There's only one person I know who was close to him and that's Charlie Pembroke.'

Further discussion was halted, as much out of confusion as due to the arrival of Mrs S. She carried a laden tray and homed in on Sebastian. 'I reckon as 'ow you might well do to have a tot of whisky or brandy in your tea, to warm you up, after all yer gallivanting,' she suggested.

Selwyn's jowls lifted with his smile. 'Sounds a capital idea,' he remarked and raised questioning eyebrows to his nephew. Without waiting for a response he headed over to the drinks cabinet and took out a bottle of Glenfiddich.

Mrs S caught the gleam in her boss's eyes and smiled inwardly. *Might 'ave known 'e'd be all in favour. Just as long as 'e doesn't get the taste and end up sipping till late.*

The fortification was not to be, however, at the resonant ring of the doorbell, the housekeeper headed for the door. 'It'll be them policemen and their muddy boots,' she muttered, evidently intent on some preventative measures for the latter.

Once they were all settled and Mrs Soames had disappeared to bring more tea, Selwyn opened the conversation. 'Before we start, chief inspector, what's the latest on McNabb? Has he been charged?'

'Not yet, commander, we're waiting for psychiatric reports.'

Selwyn pursed his lips. 'I see. Blighter's not going to get away with anything is he?'

'I can't say. If the reports are bad enough, as it were, he may never come to trial but be put away in a psychiatric unit.'

Selwyn snorted disapproval. 'Fellow wants hanging after what he put Miriam and Sebastian through.'

'I'm afraid we don't do that anymore, commander.'

Selwyn sighed. 'More's the pity.'

'What have you found out, Inspector?' asked Amanda.

'Other than that, we now know the body is indeed Roland Hawtry's, we can't tell you anything more at this stage.'

'Can't or won't?' demanded Selwyn.

Seated with his legs crossed, Stone looked down at his trouser leg and began to brush away some invisible intruder. He slowly lifted his gaze and fixed it on the commander. 'Both,' came his firm reply. The men stared at each other in an ominous silence, as if battle lines were being drawn.

Grim-faced, Selwyn rose and broke the silence. 'Then I think you'd better make a start with the interviews, then we won't take up any more of your time.'

Once they were finished and walking to their car, McBride turned to Stone. 'That seemed a bit tense when you talked to the commander.'

Stone halted and looked at him. 'After what we've found today and what's previously gone on here, the press are going to have a feeding frenzy. So, the less these people know the better and the safer for us. Okay?'

McBride nodded his accord.

'I think you'd better go back and warn the commander, if he hasn't already realised it, that he's likely to have a gaggle of journalists on his doorstep at any moment.'

McBride meekly complied and Stone watched him go. With regret he reflected on the distance and possible barrier he felt he had now put between himself and Amanda. She was savvy, someone he had come to trust and whose opinion he valued. However, by keeping a professional distance he would not give any inkling or opportunity for McBride to cause trouble for him back at HQ. He no longer trusted the man after his last attempt to undermine him.

***

True to Stone's prediction, early the following morning the press hounds were once more baying at the closed and locked gates of Wisstingham Hall. Fortunately for her, Amanda had returned to her own cottage the previous evening. So far, none of the press had made the connection with her. Kathy however, Amanda's friend and reporter on the Chronicle, had phoned her first thing. Amanda had given her information which she considered would not embarrass the DCI or his enquiry.

Seated in her office a few hours later, she brooded on whom she might persuade to take over Roland's role as chair of the festival committee. She became concerned when reception rang to say Detective Chief Inspector

Stone had arrived and wanted to see her.

'So, how can I help you?' Amanda asked in as casual a manner as she could, fearful that she might just have given too much away to Kathy, which had got back to him.

Her concern subsided when she saw that Stone looked ill at ease.

He rubbed a hand over his mouth before he spoke. 'I, er, I hope I didn't... er, I wasn't too abrupt yesterday, when the commander asked about the incident.'

Amanda was heartened by his evident discomfort. 'I'd hardly call it an incident, Inspector, the chairman of my festival committee interred in the commander's crypt.' She flashed him a disdainful look from narrowed, almond eyes. 'I should think the commander had every right and entitlement to want to know more.'

'Well, be that as it may,' Stone blustered, 'there's previously been too much loose talk to the press and I wasn't going to take the chance of there being any more, particularly if it might compromise our investigation.'

Amanda drew herself up in her chair. The small 'o' her mouth was now set in and the exhalation through her nose was intended to subdue. She had successfully used this ploy many times, mainly in the subjugation of errant youngsters in the library. 'Very well, if that's how you wish things to be...'

Stone hastily raised his hand as if to ward off the threat that would follow. 'I wouldn't want to jeopardise the working relationship that's developed between us,' he interrupted.

'I'm sure it won't come to that.' Amanda's smile was immediately reciprocated. Emboldened by her success she pressed on. 'So, have you spoken to Charlie Pembroke?'

'Why do you think we should talk to him?' The question was guarded.

'Because he was close to Roland, plus the mobile call that Marcia overheard.'

'He is on my list,' he grudgingly admitted. He reached for his ringing mobile. As he listened, despondency registered on his face. He gave various instructions and rang off. 'I'm going to have to go,' he announced.

'What is it?'

With his hand over his mouth, he studied her with a frown of indecision.

She in turn gazed back in growing alarm. 'What's happened?

He lowered his hand. 'There's been another development. A burnt-out car's been found, the same model as Hawtry's and there's a body alongside it. Very badly burned.'

Amanda swallowed. 'Marcia?'

'We don't know yet. Our forensic team are on their way. I shouldn't have told you this but since you raised the alarm about her it's only right you should know before the press get hold of it. Not a word though, understood?'

With pursed lips, Amanda meekly nodded.

'I'll let you know as soon as I can whether or not it's her. I must go.'

Amanda held out her arm to pause his exit. 'What about Pembroke? Surely he must be the missing link.'

'Maybe, but we can't find him. He's not been at home for several days.'

'Since the night Marcia and Roland went missing?'

'Since I saw him just a few days after.'

'In that case I reckon he's either also dead or on the run. Have you searched his place?'

'We haven't enough to go on to get a warrant.' He bristled at Amanda's derisive snort. 'That's procedures for you. Policing may have been modernised but it's not necessarily made it easier and better. We got away with far more, in the old days.' He put a finger to his lips. 'But I didn't say that.'

There was a knock at the door which slowly opened to reveal Eleanor. 'Oh, I'm sorry, my dear, I didn't know you'd got company.'

'That's okay, I'm off.' He turned to Amanda. 'I'll be in touch and if there's anything you think of that may help, let me know.'

She nodded and watched as he hurried off.

'Problems, dear?' Eleanor asked as Amanda sat down at her desk.

'I think you'd better sit down. Have you heard about Roland?'

Eleanor regarded her, anxiously. 'No, what's happened?'

'He's been found dead.'

She looked away, as if trying to take it in. 'Oh my goodness. That's just awful. How on earth did it happen?'

'The police aren't certain yet and I can't really tell you anything more.'

'Was it an accident, or heart failure or something?'

'No, I'm afraid it wasn't.'

'You're making it all sound very mysterious. Where was this?'

'Again, I can't tell you.'

Eleanor fixed her with a puzzled stare. 'What about Mr Pembroke? Is he alright?'

'The police want to speak to him.'

'Oh dear, he's not in any trouble is he?'

Amanda nibbled at her lip. 'I'm not sure. He appears to have gone missing.'

'Oh heavens above, surely not, dear. What a mess it all sounds to be and no mistake.' She looked away again and stared idly across the room. 'He was very keen on Christine,' she observed, after a pause.

'Who? Charlie?'

'Oh yes, dear. I think they were what you young people call an item.'

Amanda glanced quickly, unseeingly, from side to side, as she grappled with this new information. Other myriad thoughts now flitted through her brain. They all led to the man's possible implication in the recent deaths. 'Has he been in touch with you?'

'Certainly not. Why would he? I didn't approve of the relationship and I'm sure he would have known that, and resented it. I imagine he's quite a possessive man.'

'I'm sorry. I didn't mean to…'

Eleanor nodded, reassuringly. 'That's quite alright dear. No harm done.' Her gaze fell to her lap. She looked decidedly uncomfortable.

Several moments passed before Amanda asked, 'What is it, Eleanor?'

She looked up. 'It's all a bit awkward now, what with all that's happened.'

'Tell me.'

'I intended to tell you I'm going to go away for a short while.' Her enquiring eyes met Amanda's.

The librarian did her best to hide her surprise and disappointment. 'I see.'

'I made enquiries about the release of Christine's body but it looks like the police won't be in a position to do that for some time. Not until they've completed their investigations and after the coroner's hearing. It's like this,' she continued, in answer to Amanda's puzzled frown. 'I suppose, if there are no living relatives, it will be up to me to make the funeral arrangements. I would want to do that anyway. So, I thought I'd better go to France to see if I can find any relatives.'

'But can't the French consulate do that?'

Eleanor's look cast doubt on the notion. 'There's also the sale of Christine's Domaine. The Agence and Notaire need to be informed and I need to find out and obtain what documents they will need.'

'Well of course you must go.'

'But my dear, the timing's so bad. You have so much on your plate now, what with the festival and organising a new chairman.'

'Eleanor, it's very kind of you but it's my problem and I'm sure everything will be fine. Of course, I'll miss you and your most valued contribution, but your plans must take priority.'

Eleanor gave her a sheepish look. 'If you're absolutely sure, my dear?'

'Very much so. When do you intend to go?'

'I'm going to drive there and take my time over it. See some places in France I've always wanted to visit. I'll probably leave on Sunday.'

'What about the pottery?'

A look of apprehension flitted across the old lady's face. 'It's all closed up and I'm going to try and sub-let it.' She gave it a moment's reflection. 'It's all so very sad. Never mind.' She brightened. 'It's life, I suppose.'

'Yes, I suppose so. I hope you'll have a really wonderful time. You deserve to.'

Eleanor leaned forward over the desk and put a hand on Amanda's arm. 'Now are you sure you're going to be alright if I go, my dear?'

Amanda patted the hand and smiled her appreciation. 'Absolutely. You just pack your bags, teabags and HP sauce and don't give it a second thought.'

'Tomato ketchup as well,' the old lady quipped. 'Seriously though, work-wise I've completed the schedules you gave me, so everything's up to date. I've also done you some notes on where all my files are stored.'

'Thank you, Eleanor. You're a real diamond. If everything's up to date you might as well pop off now.'

'There's just one thing. I've got a favour to ask.'

'Fire away.'

'I wonder if you might please be able to put my bin out on Tuesday evening and get it back in on Wednesday. I've no one else to ask.'

'Of course I will.'

She rummaged in her handbag and pulled out a key. 'You might as well hang on to this whilst I'm away. Also, there are a couple of pot plants if you could possibly find a home for them?'

'Thanks. I'm sure we'll find a corner for them in the hall. You take care and look after yourself. Travel gently, eh?'

'I will.' They embraced and Eleanor departed, leaving the librarian to stare thoughtfully at the closing door.

She had only just resumed her seat when there was a knock and Miriam entered. 'How's it going?'

'Could be better.'

'Is there anything I need to know about?'

'I rather think so. How much time have you got?'

Miriam shrugged. 'As long as you need. I've nothing very pressing.'

Amanda proceeded to fill her in on the events regarding Marcia and Pembroke. When she had finished, Miriam gave a low whistle. 'I hope all this isn't going to put the kibosh on the festival, particularly now we've geared up the hall opening to coincide with it.'

'I can't see why it should. I've already co-opted a couple more people onto the committee and I've ideas for a couple of people who could take over as chair. I also intend to get my friend Kathy to do a piece in the Chronicle about the contribution Roland made to the festival and that it'll still be going ahead as planned.'

Miriam considered, for a moment. 'No publicity is bad publicity eh? It could be a clever move but it might be as well to park some of it until we see that there isn't any negative fallout from the police investigation. Maybe just a piece to assure people the festival will still be going ahead. Then, if nothing adverse comes out about Hawtry's past life and Pembroke reappears after an innocent few days, maybe a second feature about them, also promoting the festival again.'

'Two bites of the cherry. Good idea. I'll get onto it.'

***

Kathy Turnbull was only too glad of the chance to meet Amanda that evening, in their usual haunt the Ferret and Wardrobe. As well as a good catch-up there was the prospect of a possible steer on the recent murderous happenings. As the Chronicle's reporter on civic affairs, among other things she would deal with the press release on the new appointment of a committee chairman. However, news had already leaked about the discovery of a body and a burned-out car and if anyone, other than the police, was likely to know something about it, it would be Amanda.

'So, tell me what gives on the body and the car?' Kathy enquired as Amanda placed the drinks and packets of peanuts on the table.

Amanda feigned surprise. 'What body?'

Kathy spluttered, but before she could respond Amanda's mobile started to ring.

'Hello.' As she listened relief registered on her face. 'Thank God you're alright.' Her eyes narrowed and lips tightened at what she heard. 'And you didn't think to tell me? After our last conversation did you not think I'd be worried?' she now railed.

Her ears pricked up, Kathy put the bag of peanuts down and watched Amanda who had now got to her feet, her hand impatiently tapping the table.

'I don't know, maybe it is dangerous but I think you'd better get yourself here as quick as you can and report to the police.' With a glance across at Kathy, Amanda bared her teeth as she listened further. 'I don't care Marcia, it'll be a lot better for you to volunteer yourself than have the police coming to drag you here. I imagine they'll be pretty hacked off when I tell them you're alive and well after all the searching they've done, so I suggest you make things as easy as possible for them from here on in.' The call ended, Amanda slumped down onto her seat, took a deep swallow of her spritzer and stared angrily at the table. 'Unbelievable!' she eventually murmured. She looked across at Kathy. 'Here I am worried sick about her, and all this time she's been cosseted with her mother in Cornwall. Just heard about Hawtry on the news, she said.'

'And the background story?' prompted Kathy, as she dived into her bag for notebook and pen.

Amanda's sightless stare remained fixed on her. 'Then whose is the body with the car?' she murmured.

'Cooee, I'm here. Penny for them?'

Amanda finally saw Kathy and shook her head back to reality. Kathy was watching her like a dog waiting for its owner to put the food bowl down.

'This is all off the record, for now but you might as well have some background, to save time later,' warned Amanda.

'Misery guts. Fire away.'

Amanda filled her in on the conversation Marcia had overheard and her subsequent disappearance, along with Hawtry's.

Kathy finished jotting. 'So, it sounds like Charlie Pembroke's got some explaining to do, once he surfaces.'

'If the police are really interested in finding him at all,' was Amanda's dry response. 'The main thing is who the hell was with the car?' She decided to call Stone. He, however, had gone for the day, so things would have to wait until the morning. 'Time for another?' she asked.

Kathy glanced at her watch. 'No. I'd better get a move on.'

'Don't forget the piece about the new chairman and the festival.'

Kathy rose, slung her bag over her shoulder and blew Amanda a kiss. 'No, I won't,' she called back, as she hurried off.

***

DCI Stone strode resoundingly into the general office. His humour had improved after the interview with a very contrite Marcia Phelps, who had hastened back. He had had to admit to himself that Hawtry's fate appeared to have justified her fears for her safety. In her circumstances maybe even he would have gone into hiding and maintained radio silence.

'I think yer man was nearly as scared as me,' she told him, after she had related the incident of Pembroke's overheard conversation. 'We never got to the Mazawat. Didn't Hawtry just stop the car and tell me I should go away and lie low somewhere until he could find out what the craic was and sort things out. So, I never got to the meeting. He drove me back to the library for me car, I drove off, packed some things and went to Cornwall that very night. I reckon he must have challenged Charlie Pembroke that evening. Roland was a fine man. Pembroke's yer man to talk to.'

By now, McBride and a couple of officers, armed with a search warrant, had already forced entry into Pembroke's house, only to find it empty as expected. Neighbours had confirmed that he had not been seen since just after the middle of October.

'Did you find anything at Pembroke's place?' Stone quizzed McBride.

'No luck there, looks like he's scarpered.'

The jingling stopped. 'Holiday?'

'They didn't think so. He's not one for that, they said.'

Stone gave a sigh of resignation. 'Then let's get him found.'

'We've got everything covered.'

'Also, bring in Francis Mboko. Let's see what he's got to say for himself.'

Superintendent Nelson had now appeared in the doorway. In his hand he held a folder and on his face an expression of acute displeasure. 'I think you'll find it a little difficult to do that,' he observed.

Stone turned quickly to face him.

'On account of his being the charred deceased.'

Stone's jaw started to open.

'My office please,' Nelson instructed him and turned to go.

''Take a seat,' he ordered as Stone followed him into the office. He passed a folder across the desk. 'It's the pathologist's report. Mboko was identified by an inscribed medallion. Seems he died of a lethal injection. It's fortunate for us the body wasn't too badly burned for that to be picked up.'

Shocked, Stone put his hand to his chin and started to read the file.

'Read it later. What's happening about bringing Charlie Pembroke in?'

'We've alerts out everywhere. It's only a matter of time.'

'Which we haven't got.' Nelson made no attempt to hide his irritation. He was quietly seething that a former officer and colleague was making mugs out of *his* force. Furthermore, any suspicion that might now attach to the him and Mboko, and hence the steering committee, might prove an embarrassment if word got out that his wife was also on the committee.

'You'd better come up with something pretty dammed quick, Roger, bottoms upstairs are getting very twitchy.'

Stone gave him a cold stare. 'There's one person I'd like to take into our confidence.'

'Who's that?'

'Amanda Sheppard, the librarian. She's in charge of the festival and its committees and has her finger firmly on the pulse of the whole shenanigans.'

'As long as she can be trusted to keep her mouth shut with the press. Go ahead, but on your head be it.'

Isn't it always? Stone reflected as he rose to go. Despite the camaraderie of strange handshakes, afternoons on the golf course never happened for him. Outside the Lodge he felt himself to be very much a loner.

Back in his office, he put a call through to the library.

***

Pandemonium had been reigning for what seemed an eternity.

Contractors had muddied freshly polished floors and created layers of dust on recently polished surfaces. Rooms and corridors, to Mrs Soames ever-anxious dismay, were littered with cable drums, boxes of electrical fittings, cable trays, buckets, bags of plaster and tins of paint. The expression 'final fix,' the Architect had assured her was the stage the contract had reached, looked to be nothing but a sick joke.

Even Selwyn, very conscious that the opening was now only just over three weeks away, would issue comments and utterances compatible with his looks of despair, when he frequently patrolled and inspected his domain. These sorties were carefully arranged to minimise any chance of coming into contact with Mrs S, whose belligerence now knew no bounds. Any such encounters inevitably resulted in a severe ear-chewing.

This particular morning, the routine chaos received a boost with the arrival of a large consignment of signs, boxes of promotional leaflets, posters, panels, guides and other marketing accessories. Not to be left out, a van bearing the safety, security, and instructional signs also rocked up. The custodian of this particular delivery got very short shrift from Mrs S when he had the temerity to mention that he was 'parched'.

'As if folks 'ave nothin' better to do than make tea for tradesmen,' she growled as she shuffled indignantly away from the disconsolate man.

Sebastian, being the man in charge of the IT installation, came in for a fair amount of stick, Mrs S having long since abandoned her matronly role. 'If you don't keep them blokes in better control, I'll 'ave yer guts for garters. And theirs,' she had threatened on more than one occasion.

Miriam's role had been to interview the applicants for reception and other duties. These candidates were carefully chaperoned into the drawing room, past the eagle stare of Mrs S. Nevertheless, she did provide the necessary refreshments, although her visual inspection of each candidate was invariably frosty and mirthless.

Mistakenly, Selwyn had thought it would be a good political move for Mrs Soames to sit in on the interviews for the manager and café staff. When given the opportunity, her questions to these candidates, particularly for the manager's job, had been relentless and ruthless, her later condemnation of the candidates total. Fortunately, Gustav, the favoured applicant for the manager's post, had found the least disapproval from Mrs S, so the man had been appointed.

Two further elements of the hall opening remained to happen, which had not yet been drawn to the house-keeper's attention. Of lesser significance was the erection of gazebos and installation of external lighting, tempo-rary toilet facilities, generators and fencing. These did not directly affect her and would be supervised by the estate manager.

The other element was the sponsors' and dignitaries' evening to be held two days before the opening. Whilst this would take place in one of the marquees, the catering was to be done in the new café. As such, this was likely to incur not a little displeasure in the hall kitchen, which left Selwyn and Miriam to continually rack their brains on how Mrs S could be involved and thus minimise any friction.

Thus, the planning and work for the big day continued. Its frustrations, hindrances, upsets and delays led Selwyn to contemplate the installation of and offerings to a statue of the Hindu God Ganesh, the remover of obstacles.

From Amanda's point of view, over the whole proceed-ings now hung the shadow of the deaths and disappear-ance of two members of her festival committee, together with the glaring questions of who had been responsible for doing what and to whom.

As she prepared to go to bed that evening, her mind was still alive with these thoughts as she entered the bathroom and opened the cupboard to get her tooth-brush and paste. Yet once more they lay hidden behind Sebastian's bottle of FCUK.

During the dark hours, she lay awake next to the gently breathing form of her fiancé. She pondered the involve-ment of Charlie Pembroke and possibly Francis Mboko, not only in Roland's death, but also possibly those of the other recent murder victims. Nevertheless, try as she might she could discern no logical connections with these. Although the police had concluded that Montand had killed Lagrange, as far as Amanda was concerned, the Frenchman himself had been murdered. Had Pembroke's hand therefore been in on this? Had it just been revenge for Lagrange's death and if so, how would Pembroke have found out so quickly? And where was Francis MBoko in all of this.

Unresolved questions finally gave way to sleep, though a dream-filled one where the grounds of the hall were invaded by manic, grinning and rampaging reporters chasing her in and out of marquees, demanding quotes for their scoops about 'The Festival of Murder'.

***

It was late in the morning by the time a bleary-eyed Amanda made it to the library. She had arrived after an uncomfortable meeting with Miriam and a representative of the Arts Council. Word had got out about of the recent murders and their linkage with members of the festival committee. Accordingly, the representative was most anxious to ensure that no adverse publicity or implication might attach to their offices through the grants they had awarded. It had been intimated that funding and the associated sponsorship could still be withdrawn if matters went the wrong way. There had also been a hint that this might affect the funding promised for the opening of Wisstingham Hall.

Nor was it just the Arts Council that the two women were concerned about. It was only a matter of time before the news would filter through to the festival sponsors, some of whom had already contributed or promised substantial sums.

When she did finally sit down at her desk, with a very welcome mug of tea, the first thing Amanda noticed was a scribbled message that Stone had called and would she ring him back.

'DCI Stone,' came the curt response, when she finally got through.

'It's Amanda Sheppard. You rang?'

'Amanda, yes, I thought I should update you on matters. Can you come round to the station? I've had clearance from above to share information with you. On a confidential basis, of course.'

Amanda was only too keen to take up his offer and at lunchtime presented herself at the desk. The glance she received from DS McBride, through the corridor window, as Stone escorted her to his office, did not bode well for convivial relations.

Once seated in Stone's office, the windowpanes battered by wind and driving rain, the DCI began to share information. 'We now know that the burned-out car was Hawtry's and that the body is that of Francis Mboko, who died from a lethal injection.'

'Oh my God,' Amanda gasped. She stared incredulously at Stone for several seconds. 'I suppose it's some comfort that he died of the injection, I suppose. Better than being burned alive.'

Stone merely grunted his agreement. 'Anyway, we now also know that Theo Patterson spent some time in France as part of a European hitch-hiking tour. He returned to the UK from Bordeaux in December 2010.'

'So that's the possible link with Montand and Lagrange.'

'Possibly. We're making further enquiries but the French authorities aren't very forthcoming.'

'From what Eleanor told me she doubted if Christine had any living relatives, though I suppose she wouldn't know about Montand.'

'We can wheel her in and see what she can tell us.'

Amanda let out a sigh of exasperation. 'You don't 'wheel in' a lady like her. Anyway, it wouldn't be very easy, she's gone to France.'

Stone stiffened. 'What? Who the hell authorised that? Why's she gone there?"

'Oh, come on! She's not a suspect surely to goodness. She's gone to see if she can locate any relatives of Christine's and sort out her affairs. I can call her.' She tried the call but there was neither a reply nor could she leave a message. 'She's probably driving, I'll try her later.'

'She never told us she was going.'

'I don't suppose she knew she had to, unless you specifically told her.'

'I'm sure someone would have done.' He sounded uncertain and distinctly unhappy. 'We wanted to speak to her.'

'What about?'

'There was a call made to her house from Patterson's surgery, the night he died.'

Amanda stared at him in disbelief as she pondered this. 'Of course, it could have been Christine Lagrange he phoned. She was living there too.'

'Did either of them have a pet?'

'I don't believe so.'

Stone rose. 'Follow me.' Hands in pockets, he led her

from his office to the now-empty incident room. In silence they scanned the evidence board, photos of all the recent victims pinned up along a top line. Arrows led off in all directions to notes, names, dates and photos of other people, including Pembroke, Mboko, Marcia and even Eleanor.

'Can I take photos of this?' asked Amanda, 'It'd be so useful.'

Stone shook his head, his eyes still fixed on the board. 'Can't take any documents out of the building.' He turned to her. 'Would you like another cup of tea? I'm sure you would.'

'Well yes, thank you.'

He glanced around the empty room and into the corridor. 'I might be a little while. The kettle will probably be empty.' He winked and strode out of the room.

Amanda quickly took out her mobile and with occasional, furtive glances around, systematically photographed the board, section by section. She had only just pocketed the mobile when McBride sauntered along the corridor, entered the room, caught sight of her and scowled.

'And what would you be doing in here, Miss Sheppard?'

'DS McBride, what a pleasure to see you again. DCI Stone just popped out for a moment.'

'Did he, indeed? So you're having a good snoop around are you? He focused on the board. 'Hoping to put us straight and show us the error of our ways, are ye?'

'I think the expression's 'Assistance of the general public'.'

'Just as long as it stays that way and does nae stray into wasting police time.'

Stone re-appeared and leaned his head round the edge

of the doorframe. McBride almost stood to attention.

'Tea's up, my office,' he told Amanda, then he regarded the DS with a cool expression. 'Keep at it, sergeant.'

McBride grunted and went to his desk. With a grin, Amanda exited the room.

Amanda took a sip of her tea. 'It still looks to me like Charlie Pembroke's very much a person of interest.'

'It does, and you're dead right, but God knows where he is. However, he's not in the frame for Patterson. It's only a matter of time before we apprehend him.'

'As the Met said to Mrs Biggs.'

Stone evidently did not appreciate the quip.

She gave him an apologetic look. 'So how do you think the deaths of Patterson, Lagrange and Montand all fit in?'

'We don't, as yet. That's a separate kettle of fish. We found Montand's prints at the surgery, so he ties in with Patterson and Patterson ties in with either Lagrange or Delaney. That's the French connection.'

On hearing the phrase, something stirred in Amanda's mind, but she couldn't nail it. 'In that case, who might have killed Montand? You must now agree that it's a distinct possibility he was murdered.'

'Let's just say we haven't ruled it out, though it makes life very awkward for us, having had his death declared as misadventure. As for who killed him, if he was murdered, I don't know. What are your thoughts?'

'I can't see how...' She broke off and frowned at the sudden memory of Pembroke as he bent to unlock his bike outside the doctors' surgery.

Stone stared at her, his head cocked, like a curious bird. 'What is it?'

She was still frowning as she turned to him. 'I saw

Pembroke with a bike, the other day. What if it had been him and not Montand who was seen cycling away from the vet's surgery and the pottery? They'd be similar in build.'

'But the bike at Montand's cottage had been used.'

'He could have just gone for cigarettes, or shopping.'

Stone shook his head. 'No. I'm not buying it. For reasons we don't yet know Montand kills Patterson then Lagrange.'

'And Pembroke kills Montand.'

Stone snorted his disbelief. 'Why?'

'Because apparently, Pembroke was in a relationship with Lagrange.'

The CI's eyes widened. 'Was he indeed? Where's this come from?'

'Eleanor.' Amanda looked round startled, as Stone slapped his hand on the desk.

'I want that woman here. We've only got half a flaming story.'

'She'll be well on her way to France now. The best you'll get is a telephone conversation.'

'Fat chance of that, I reckon.' He began to pace up and down, the concerto for coins more allegro than the usual andante. He came to an abrupt stop. 'If it was Pembroke he must have found out bloody quickly about Lagrange's death.'

'Well, he was a policeman,' Amanda offered, somewhat hesitantly in view of Stone's downturn in mood.

'That's true, and a good one too. What's more, when it comes to leaking information this place is like a colander.'

'And on that note, if there's nothing more, I'd better get back to work. It's a similar situation there with people whispering about how much time I'm spending on murderous matters.'

Chapter 13

The idea had occurred to Selwyn in the early hours of the morning, when he woke for one of his increasingly frequent trips to the bathroom. Had it not, he would probably have been able to get back to sleep. The brain however, was now in full flight on the eternal riddle of the hidden family treasure. Professor Ingram's comments had reinforced his view that the crypt was now very much his best bet, despite previous failures to discover a hidey-hole there.

The day before, a police officer had rung to arrange the collection of their lighting equipment from the crypt. 'Dunno why it's taken 'em so long to pick it up,' the officer had said. 'A bit like scaffolders. They get the stuff up quick enough, but it's a pain trying to get 'em to shift it when it's finished with.'

Selwyn had completely forgotten about the equipment. He had agreed he would arrange to secure the entrance to the crypt, while it was there and access was still restricted.

'Would the day after tomorrow be okay? Say around noon?' the officer had asked, to which Selwyn had agreed.

Thus, the idea to use the police lighting to get a really good look at the whole place, to take photos and thoroughly search for any tell-tale crevices or signs of concealment, had ensured the continuity of his wakefulness. It would certainly save him time and money in not having to install his own equipment.

Before dawn, he was up with the larks, thankful for Miriam's absence at her own house. At least he had not disturbed her with his restlessness and early rising. Doubtless, Miriam would have considered this a manifestation of his fixation. Indeed, his first wife would no doubt have signed up to the same notion, but they were not here and the opportunity was.

As he descended the staircase, the cleaning ladies, laden with vacuums, cleaning caddies, brushes and mops, were already moving off to their separate locations.

'Good morning, ladies,' he acknowledged them with a smile, and received a chorus of responses.

Before he had reached the bottom step, Mustard came bounding towards him, fresh from his first outing and breakfast demolition. Selwyn squatted to greet and fondle the beagle then rose, picked up his Telegraph from the salver and proceeded to the dining room. He shouted his customary, cheery 'Good morning Mrs S' in the direction of the kitchen.

'Morning Commander,' Mrs S later greeted him as she shuffled into the room, with the tea tray. 'Up early this morning, aren't we? It's muesli and kippers, today,' she warned. 'Full English isn't till weekend,' she reminded him in response to his crestfallen look.

Resigning himself to the menu, he offered an appreciative smile as the housekeeper poured. He glanced at his watch, reached for his mobile and tapped out Sebastian's number.

'Morning, what's up?' came a sleepy voice.

'Good morning, dear boy, I think it's called the sun.

How are you today?'

'I'll let you know when I find out. What do you want?'

'If you've nothing urgent on, I'd like you to come with me to the crypt.'

'Again?' yawned Sebastian. 'What for?'

'Again indeed. We've got just today to use the police lighting to search the place before it's taken away. Get yourself over here for a spot of breakfast. I'm sure Mrs S will rustle up some more muesli and kippers for you.'

'Not likely. I'll grab something proper, over here, and see you shortly.'

With a smile Selwyn disconnected and turned to his paper.

A while later, the two men, laden with exploratory equipment and a camera, descended the stone steps to the crypt. It took some time and several curses before Sebastian finally got the generator to cough into life. The powerful arc lights flooded the room.

Selwyn surveyed the space and smiled. 'I don't know why I didn't think of this earlier.'

Pity you thought about it at all, grumbled Sebastian, inwardly.

Selwyn pointed to the lights. 'We'll start from this corner. You swing that light round to focus on the wall, I'll take the photos, then we'll work around the whole room like that. Afterwards, we'll focus on the ceiling in the same way.'

Sebastian stifled a yawn. 'Right you are Guv.'

It took them a good two hours to take the photographs and measure the crypt, noting the positions of the coffins, the spacing of the support columns to the vaulted ceiling arches, the entrance and wall heights. By the time they were finished, Selwyn could feel the cold creeping into his very bones. He turned to Sebastian who now looked to be flagging. 'Let's call it a day and attack that picnic hamper.'

Sebastian readily agreed, gathered their things together and turned off the generator.

As they sat eating in the car, the engine and heater on full blast, Sebastian glanced over to the site. 'Do you really think we'll find something?'

'From what the professor said it seems there might well be a good chance. I'll do a dimensioned layout of the whole place, get some prints of the photos and send them off to him. Hopefully, he'll be able to guide us as to where we should start the excavation.'

***

'There's a call for you Amanda,' said the receptionist, 'It's Detective Chief Inspector Stone and he doesn't sound in a very good mood.'

Par for the course, 'Thanks Mary. DCI Stone, what can I do for you?'

'I can't get through to that blasted Delaney woman. Do you know what her travel arrangements were, and have you got any other number I might get her on?'

'She was due to set off by yesterday, so she'll probably be crossing the channel now, or in France.'

'I wish to goodness you'd told me she was going. She might have valuable information. What about a French contact number?'

'No can do. She never gave me one.'

There was a short silence before Stone spoke. 'Okay, I

suppose at least she's out of harm's way from Pembroke.'

'You think he'd be a danger to her?'

'He could well be. Hawtry was almost certainly endangered by Pembroke, and look what happened to Mboko. And the two were supposedly friends.'

'But Eleanor didn't have anything directly to do with the committee, other than refreshments and making arrangements.'

'From what you said, she was on friendly terms with most of them, and of course Lagrange. If she'd seen, heard or knew something she shouldn't…' Stone tailed off and left her to consider the implications.

'Yes, I suppose you might be right. Maybe it is a good job she's out of it.'

'Just make sure, if she does contact you, that you tell her to get in touch with me as soon as possible. And, if for any reason she hasn't left, tell her she needs to stay. Warn her she might be in danger and tell her to contact me personally, asap.'

Amanda agreed then rang off. She pondered where Pembroke might have gone and who else might be in danger from him. She tried to call Eleanor but there was no answer.

'Do you really think she's in danger?' Sebastian later asked when Amanda related her conversation with Stone.

'Not if she's already left, I imagine. Stone certainly sounded concerned for her. Made me wonder if he knows more than he's letting on.'

'I'll have a quick check round when I do her bin tomorrow and collect the plants. Don't forget to leave the key.'

She nestled close and looked up at him. 'How could I forget anything you might want, Munchkin?'

He smiled. 'A kiss maybe, but just park those come-to-bed eyes until later.'

'Spoilsport', she complained, in a whisper, and gave him a lingering kiss.

'Are you staying tonight?'

'You bet,' though her kiss and smouldering eyes had already said as much.

***

Dressed only in a pair of pyjamas liberated from Sebastian's cupboard, Amanda stifled a contented yawn and padded downstairs to the kitchen. The teapot still warm enough, she poured herself a cup and returned to the bedroom.

Sebastian had left much earlier, on a search for equipment that took him to Hillingden.

Reluctantly, she abandoned the warmth of the bed and in the bathroom, peered at herself in the mirror. Dishevelled didn't quite cover it but happily dishevelled it most certainly was. She broke into a smile as she remembered her teasing behaviour the previous evening and Sebastian's friskiness when he finally lured her to bed. 'Like sleeping with an octopus,' she murmured to her grinning reflection. Certain that those bad days were behind them both, she bared her teeth and examined them. Still beautifully white, she congratulated herself. Yes, she was in fine form, as indeed Sebastian had been. *Perhaps too fine,* she stifled a happy yawn.

Amanda stepped out of the shower, towelled herself and reached into the bathroom cupboard for the deodorant. Her eyes lit once more on Sebastian's FCUK stick of deodorant. It triggered an instant reprise of the vague mental ping she had experienced the last time she had seen it. She mentally dislodged the notion and went to get dressed. It was an easy day ahead, a check-up at the dentist and the rest of the day unusually unencumbered with meetings.

On the way from the dentist, after she had tried another unsuccessful call to Eleanor, the image of the deodorant stick once more entered her mind. 'French connection UK,' she murmured to herself. She recalled the film 'The French Connection' and the slippery villain that had eluded Popeye. Her thoughts drifted to the recent events at home and an idea formed in her brain. How much did she and the police really know about *all* the players in this puzzling, murderous spectacle. She needed to do some digging into backgrounds.

When finally ensconced in her office, Amanda once more tried Eleanor's number, in vain, then opened up the laptop and began her search in earnest.

***

NOVEMBER

Sebastian's elation at having been able to acquire all he needed from the Hillingden supplier was short-lived. On arrival at the hall, he learned that the power was off and not expected to be reconnected until later in the afternoon. Mrs Soames' very respectable impersonation of Henny Penny, when it happened, was partially curtailed when the electrical contractor produced a generator to power the fridges and freezer. Still, the sharp end of her tongue would await Selwyn's arrival in the kitchen.

In the absence of power and the electricians' monopoly

of the areas he needed to work in, Sebastian decided to abandon his programme. Instead, he could make better use of his time by a visit to Eleanor Delaney's cottage. He would sort out her bin and rescue the plants.

Disaster being a somewhat greedy rascal, it decided to have another go at Sebastian. The car that had so reliably taken him miles on his errand and brought him equally reliably back, now resolutely refused to start. He slammed the door and stomped back to the hall in search of his uncle whom he found in the drawing room, with Miriam. They were poring over the final proofs for some of the hall's advertising literature.

'Hello Miriam, Guv, the blasted car won't start,' he announced.

'Selwyn glanced up. 'Hello dear boy. Sorry to hear that. How can I help?'

'Any chance of borrowing yours?'

'Why not take mine? I'm not going to be using it,' chipped in Miriam.

'You sure?'

'Certainly. He's covered on the insurance, isn't he Selwyn?'

'Absolutely.'

Miriam bent to fish the keys out of her handbag and handed them over. Sebastian thanked her and gave an assurance that he would not be long.

***

A call from Kathy Turnbull alerted Amanda that not only was it nearly lunchtime, but that the journalist had something for her. 'I'll see you in the Mazawat at half noon,' the reporter suggested.

After they had exhausted the chit chat, Kathy became her usual enquiring self. 'Have you heard anything more about Charlie Pembroke's whereabouts?'

'No, as far as I know he's not been found yet.'

'And do you think he had anything to do with Hawtry's and Mboko's deaths?'

Amanda regarded her through narrowed eyes. 'What is this? Did you get me her just to interrogate me? All of this is off the record, as usual, isn't it?'

Kathy flushed. 'Yes, of course. I'm sorry. I didn't mean to try and put you on the spot. I'd never use anything you tell me unless you were agreeable. You should know that, don't you?'

It was now Amanda's turn to be embarrassed. She nodded. 'Yes, I do, I'm sorry.'

The arrival of the food halted further discussion.

The subsequent silence was eventually broken by Kathy. 'I hear the police are now looking for Celia Rossiter, another of the festival committee. Do you know her?'

Amanda lowered her fork and stared open-mouthed at her friend. 'Yes I do. I saw her only just the other day, at the cemetery. Is she missing? Do they suspect her of anything?'

'They won't say. From what I could gather from my source, she seems to have just upped sticks and left. What were you doing at the cemetery?'

'I was with Sebastian. We took some flowers for his mother's grave. Celia caught sight of me then hurried away, I tried to catch up with her but she got into her car and zoomed off before I could reach her. It didn't seem right to be legging it through a graveyard. It's funny, I was going to ring her later to find out what was wrong.' She gazed aimlessly across the café as she turned things over in her mind. This was broken only when Kathy waved a hand.

Amanda looked up and gave an apologetic smile. 'Sorry, I was miles away.'

'I think you should mention it to Stone. Do you think she's been involved with what's been happening?'

Amanda shrugged. 'For all I know she could be. The whole ruddy village could.'

Kathy eyed her keenly. 'It all seems to be centred on that festival committee of yours.'

'Hey, don't start trying to lay it all at my door. They all seemed normal, respectable citizens when they came on board.' Amanda had started to feel as if everything was about to come crashing down around her. Despite her dogged determination to keep the event going, after the disappearance of key committee members, and the need to avoid any whiff of scandal which would imperil the funding, she was not prepared to cancel the festival. Not only would she lose credibility with the council, but expenditure of some of the sponsorship money had already been committed to. There was no turning back.

On top of all that, she had lost the support of a good friend and reliable, hard-working ally in Eleanor, now away in France until goodness knows when.

Kathy leaned across the table and took hold of Amanda's hand. 'Hey, this is your friend speaking. I'm not having a go at you and never would. Whatever has happened is nothing to do with you. Unless, of course, you bumped them all off,' she added with a smile. 'If there's anything I can do to support you, you know I'm here for you.'

Amanda eased and returned the smile. 'Thanks Kathy,

sorry for the brittleness. Anyway, you said you had something for me.'

'Well, not for you. For that lovely old lady Eleanor. You know the time I met you here with her and she mentioned she'd lived in Beziers? Well, I had to do some research on the place for an article and got into the old photo archives. I did a bit of digging and, lo and behold I came across a photo of her old home. I'm sure it's hers because she said it was a shop and backed onto the church grounds. Anyway, I got a copy of it for her.' She slid over an envelope.

'Aw Kathy, that's very kind of you. I'm afraid you've missed her though. She's gone back to France and I don't know when she'll be back.'

Kathy looked crestfallen. 'I tell you what, you hang onto it for her.'

'I'll do that. Thanks again.'

Just then Gwen arrived at the table. 'Have you two ladies finished?'

Kathy glanced at the clock and reached for her bag. 'Sure have. You'd better let me have the bill. I need to scoot.' She turned to Amanda. 'It's on me this time.'

Amanda thanked her and within minutes Gwen had cleared away, the two satisfied customers on their way back to work.

Not for the first time after her return did Amanda look at the envelope that lay on her table. I don't imagine she'd mind my opening it, she thought as she reached for the paperknife. She could always seal it in a new envelope.

She was interrupted by the phone ringing. 'It's Detective Chief Inspector Stone for you,' said the receptionist.

'Hello chief inspector, how are you, today?'

'Amanda, I'm okay. I just wanted to let you know that we checked with all the ports and your friend Delaney hasn't appeared, so far. Is there a possibility she may have travelled under a different name? Was she ever married?'

Amanda's pulse started to race as did her thoughts. *Oh my goodness, where on earth can she be. She should be in France by now. What's happened to her?* No, I don't think she was ever married. She might have travelled under her first father's name but I don't know what that was. She's always been Delaney as far as I was aware. The father's address is Brackshaw Cottage in Wisstingham.'

'Don't worry, we'll track the name down. We're just hoping nothing's happened to her on this side of the Channel. If she contacts you, stress that she could be in danger and should return and see us immediately.'

'Of course, I'll do that.'

'Also, I'd like to have a word with you about Celia Rossiter, if you could call in tomorrow.'

'I hear she's gone missing,' She could hear the sigh on the other end of the line.

'Like I said, this place is like a sieve. Yes, though it looks like she's packed her bags and gone.'

'I saw her only the other day, at the cemetery.'

'You did? What was she doing?'

'Putting some flowers on a grave.'

'Was she indeed? Would you be able to locate the grave?'

'I think so.'

'Right. Can you get away for a short while?' Stone sounded very determined.

Amanda hesitated. 'I suppose so, if you're saying it's essential, to assist your enquiries.'

'I'll vouch for you. I won't come blaring up to the front door. I'll pick you up just outside the car park in ten minutes.'

The drive to the cemetery was a short one. Amanda's initial confidence that she could find the grave began to flag. She took her bearings from Sebastian's mother's grave and threaded her way, followed by Stone. Once they had found the approximate location, her search was aided by the fact that only one grave bore a bunch of relatively recently laid flowers.

'I'm sure it's this one,' she declared, rather relieved.

Stone stooped down and read the card with the flowers. 'This is it.' He studied the headstone, which was new.

Amanda waited for him to speak but he merely stared at the stone and rubbed his chin.

'Well, does this shed any light on anything?' she felt compelled to ask.

'It certainly does but it also raises yet more questions. This is the grave of the woman who committed suicide last March. The wife of the man found hanged at Sebastian's office block.

Her gaze now rooted to the headstone, Amanda gave a shudder.

'Another can of worms,' murmured Stone. 'Still, at least we now have a new link to pursue. He turned a solemn face to Amanda. 'Not a word to anyone, right?'

Amanda nodded. On his mobile, the DCI took photos of the gravestone, and location of the grave, then placed the card in an evidence bag before the two of them headed back to the car.

Once back at the library, Amanda sat for a while and pondered the implications of what Stone had revealed.

Abstracted, she reached for the envelope she'd abandoned earlier and opened it. She stared at the black and white, grainy photo. There was a man and woman, both wearing long, white aprons, with a little girl, between them. It was the sign above the shop window that seized Amanda's attention. Her eyes narrowed as her brain went into overdrive picking through memories of recent conversations and events. Of what could, could not, might or might not have been. Images came thick and fast. Impossibilities morphed into possibilities and then probabilities.

One by one the pieces started to fall into place, though the reasons for many of them remained elusive. 'FCUK. French Connection UK,' she murmured as she reached for her mobile to call Sebastian.

***

By early afternoon Selwyn had had quite enough of the privations the lack of power had brought about, not least the absence of the housekeeper whom he had earlier sent home. There at least she would not be deprived of central heating.

'And just 'ow are you and your good lady going to manage?' she had argued, in initial resistance to his suggestion, diplomatically omitting the words, 'without me'.

'That's not a problem, Mrs S, I'm going to take Miriam out for a late lunch then we're going to see James Bond. 'Skyfall' is showing at the cinema in Hopestanding.'

Mrs S had a fleeting regret she had not been included in the luncheon party, under the exceptional circumstances that prevailed. However, James Bond sounded far too violent for her liking. Hence, she had graciously accepted the offer to return home.

As a consequence, there was no-one present at the hall to answer the call Amanda made later that afternoon, after her call to Sebastian had yielded no reply.

***

Eleanor Delaney's cottage appeared to be quite deserted when Sebastian entered, after an unanswered ring on the bell. A tray containing the plants sat on a table in the hallway, accompanied by fairly lengthy advice on their care and positioning. There was also a note from Eleanor to thank Amanda for taking care of them and for all she had done for her.

More like a note of final farewell, thought Sebastian as he pocketed it and lifted the latch to the adjacent door. He had to duck his head as he entered the lounge. The room was cold, the coal fire on the opposite side of the room empty and dark. On the central, large coffee table were neatly stacked large books which probably contained impressive photos of exotic places around the world. Cushions on the large sofas and in the high wing back chair were neatly plumped.

On the pretext of ensuring all windows were secured and electrical items turned off, he satisfied his curiosity with an exploration of the rest of the cottage.

In what he took to be the main bedroom, he peeped into the wardrobe in which only a few dresses hung. Similarly, the shelves were sparsely taken up with folded clothes.

He wandered into the kitchen and looked in the empty fridge, which had been turned off. He tried the light, the electricity was still on, but a turn of the taps indicated the water had been turned off. The kitchen waste bin was empty, as were the waste baskets in each of the rooms. Everything was totally neat and tidy.

Sebastian ventured outside, sought the waste bin and trundled it down the drive to the public footpath. It was after he had locked up the cottage and was ferrying the plants to the car, that he noticed a red Fiesta parked slightly up the road. Inside, in the driver's seat, sat a large man whose face seemed familiar, but it was the 'HEN' registration that seized his attention. Mother Hen… Eleanor's car.

He glanced again at the occupant and recognition came. It was the man, Charlie Pembroke, that Amanda had previously pointed out to him outside the doctor's surgery.

***

'Lost another one then, have you, Roger?' Superintendent Nelson carped when the DCI walked into his office.

Stone clenched his teeth. 'If it's Celia Rossiter you're referring to, her departure was some time before she became a person of interest to us.' How he wished he could swipe that smug look off his boss's face.

'And why is she a person of interest now?'

'She was one of the festival committee members.'

'You should have wheeled the whole lot of them in for questioning, long before now.'

Stone smiled inwardly. Nelson had taken the bait. 'Would that have included your wife, sir?'

Nelson felt the barb. 'Of course not,' he replied, irritably.

'There are over fifty people involved in the various committees. I really don't think it would have been a best use of our resources.'

'And what about this old woman who's tottered off to

France?' Nelson's smile was back.

How the hell does he know about her? 'She's not a suspect…'

'Just a witness you want to speak to,' the superintendent cut in.

McBride, the bastard! It's got to be him blabbing to the admiral. 'She's not checked in at any of the ports yet.' *if she's not already dead.* 'We've put out alerts.'

'And what about Pembroke?'

'No sign of him so far. We've got everywhere covered. It doesn't help that we're looking for one of our own.'

'Hmm,' Nelson reluctantly agreed. 'Well, keep on it Roger. Let's have some of those results you've been promising me, eh?'

'Yes sir,' came the reply, through clenched teeth.

Marching along the corridor Stone was livid. So, McBride was up to his old tricks was he? *Just you wait until tomorrow, you Scottish creep!* He steamed into his office to reflect on the latest developments.

Chapter 14

NOVEMBER

Sebastian climbed into the Mercedes and glanced through the side mirror. The other driver showed no sign of setting off. To stay there would be something of a giveaway, so he decided to drive off and park round the next corner. This road he knew was a cul de sac, so the red car would have to pass the junction and he would follow it.

He had only just turned to park facing the junction, and started to reach for his mobile, when the other car drove past. The call would have to wait.

He did his best to keep a discreet distance from the Fiesta, though the fact that he was tailing an ex high-ranking policemen did little for his confidence.

If Pembroke was in Eleanor's car, what had he done with her? Where was she and was she still alive?' He desperately wanted to call Amanda but could not stop and lose the other car. He tried to pull the mobile from his jean's pocket but it was desperately tight. He tugged and tugged then had to stop to change gear as he slowed down. The Fiesta, three cars ahead of him, turned onto the Hopestanding road. One of the cars in front of him drove straight on, the other also turned, which he followed. He tugged once more and finally the phone came free, only to hurtle out of his fingers' grasp and fall onto the passenger side floor. He cursed. *Trust it to land as far away as possible.*

The Fiesta was now pulling away, on the open road. The car in front stubbornly stuck to the speed limit. At last, there was a straight stretch clear of oncoming traffic. Sebastian gunned the accelerator and swung out to overtake. Ahead, in the distance he could just see the red car before it disappeared round a bend. Thankful that this was Miriam's new car and not his old banger, Sebastian made the most of its acceleration and sped along. He was unnerved by a flash of light in the rear windscreen. He had been caught by a speed camera.

He sped on for another half mile. A sigh of relief went up when he caught sight of his quarry on another straight stretch. The outskirts of Hopestanding loomed. This would be a real test of whether he could keep the Fiesta in his sights.

As they entered the built-up area, the traffic lights went red. Pembroke was at the front of the queue, Sebastian now two cars back. On the opposite side was a police car. He judged there was not enough time for him to run over and alert them to Pembroke. Sebastian willed the officers to spot the fugitive, but to no avail.

With his seatbelt on, a stretch for the mobile was just too far away. He was just about to undo it when the lights changed and the traffic started to move off again.

Three more sets of lights later, all fortunately on green, the red car turned right. It was now headed out of town, in a direction and neighbourhood Sebastian was not familiar with.

There was now no more traffic between them, so he held back. They passed through a council estate and into a country lane. From this the red car turned onto what appeared to be a farm track, signposted a cul-de-sac. Sebastian hesitated to follow. He pondered whether to stop and make that call, but didn't have a clue where he was. He turned onto the track and drove at a snail's pace. To his right he could see the backs of a line of buildings. Eventually, the track petered out and gave onto an entrance to a walled yard to what was the last building in the row. The gates to the yard were open. He stopped. To his left, the space next to the track, which would have enabled him to turn round, was taken up by a stack of empty wooden pallets. He would either have to reverse the whole way or turn in the yard. If he was confronted he could just say he had taken a wrong turning.

But what if Pembroke had seen he was being followed? Sebastian would just have to say he had mistaken the ownership of the car. That he had thought it was someone else's.

He cautiously drove into the yard. There was no sign of the Fiesta. At the far side of the yard there was what appeared to be a rear extension to a building. Central to it were large, wooden double doors, one closed the other slightly ajar. Other than for another small stack of pallets against one wall, the yard was otherwise bare. There was a light shining through the louvre blinds to one of the two side windows to the doors. The window on the other side was in darkness. The place looked deserted.

Sebastian did a three-point turn to leave his car facing the lane for a quick getaway. He reached for the mobile. About to call, he heard a voice call out. 'Can I help you?' He swung round to see the garage door had opened further, though the speaker was in the shadow it cast.

Sebastian wound down his window. 'I, ah I think I got lost. I must have taken the wrong turning,' he shouted.

'Well, come on in and I'll get you back on your way.'

'Not to worry, I'll just go back the way I came and find my way from there.'

'No, I really think you should come and let me help you.'

'That's alright, I…' The appearance of the barrel of a gun, through the shadow, cut further conversation short.

'Over here.' The voice now had a menacing tone.

Sebastian wondered if he should try and make a break for it. Pembroke was now approaching. As a senior policeman he would have been trained with firearms at some point. Sebastian now knew he had left it a split second too late. He got out of the car, raised his hands and slowly walked towards the doors.

Inside, when his eyes had become accustomed to the darkness, he saw the smile on Pembroke's face.

'You just come and sit down over here.'

Nervously, Sebastian approached, turned and sat down in the chair behind which Pembroke stood, the gun aimed at his prisoner. Sebastian felt a coldness that began to rise through his body starting from his feet. He believed that by the time it reached his head he would die. It never got there. He felt a sharp sting in his neck and the last thing he saw was Charlie Pembroke's face grinning at him as he slipped away from consciousness.

Moments later, Miriam's car was nestled in the cavernous garage, the doors firmly closed and bolted from the outside. Inside, next to Sebastian's body lay the smashed remnants of his mobile.

***

On their return from the cinema, Selwyn had had just enough time to rush to the ringing phone before the call was cut off. 'Wisstingham Hall, Commander Fitzgerald speaking. Oh, hello Amanda, how are you dear girl?'

'I'm fine. Is Sebastian there?'

'I'm afraid not. Not seen him since this morning. Anything wrong?'

'I'm not sure. I've tried him a number of times but there's no answer.'

'You sound concerned. What is it?'

'Oh, I'm probably worrying unduly.'

'Are you here for dinner?' Selwyn enquired.

By now, Mrs Soames had joined the commander, a look of consternation on her face

'I was going to be. Sebastian said he'd tell Mrs S.'

Selwyn put his hand over the receiver. 'Did Sebastian tell you Amanda would be dining with us?'

She shook her head. 'No matter, there's plenty.'

Selwyn resumed the conversation. 'I'm sure there's nothing to worry about. We'll look forward to seeing you. You can tell us all about it. No doubt Sebastian will have turned up by then, anyway.'

But turn up Sebastian did not. It was Amanda who finally cut through the silence after the discussion on where he might possibly have gone, other than to the suppliers in Hillingden who had closed much earlier. 'So, what do we do? How long do we give him before we contact the police?'

'I think the police need a forty-eight-hour absence before they'll act,' Selwyn offered, gloomily.

'But surely, if we have a word with Stone he might be able to get something done.'

Selwyn drummed his fingers on the table as he considered. 'I think the first thing we should do is see if we can use the tracking device to locate the car, assuming it's still active, though goodness only knows how it works. Do you know how to work it, Amanda?'

She looked totally baffled. 'I haven't a clue.'

Selwyn exhaled his exasperation. 'The device homes in on the tracker on the car. It shows you where it is on...' He stopped mid-sentence. With a grimace he slowly shook his head.

Alarmed, Miriam held out a hand to him. 'Selwyn, are you alright? What's the matter?'

He looked up and gave her a wry smile. 'I was just about to say it shows you where it is on your mobile screen.'

'Which is with Sebastian,' added Amanda. 'So that idea's a non-starter.'

Miriam brightened. 'Unless he also connected it to his laptop.'

Selwyn rose, looking more hopeful. 'Right. Amanda, can you go and find his laptop and bring it here. Also, the original packaging and instructions, if you can find them. I'll go upstairs and see if he left anything in his room here. It's worth a try.'

Amanda dashed off to the cottage, though it was some time before she returned with only the computer. 'I couldn't find anything else.' She started it up and began to scroll through the desktop ikons until she found what she thought was the one. It demanded a password upon which a communal groan went up from the trio huddled round the screen.

'Why does this technology have to be so blasted complicated?' complained the commander.

Tired, Amanda sat back in her chair and hung her head in despair. Miriam comforted her as Selwyn, his jowls hanging very low, persevered in trying to input possible passwords, without success.

A call to the police station revealed that DCI Stone had left for the night, though DS McBride, who was still there, was offered as a substitute. At that point Amanda thanked the desk sergeant and rang off.

'It's no good, we're going to have to leave it until tomorrow morning,' Selwyn finally admitted defeat.

'We've got the radio interview first thing, Selwyn, then the reception and television feature at the town hall,' Miriam reminded him.

'Hang it! Yes, I'd forgotten.'

On the verge of tears, Amanda got up and started to pace the room. 'I can't just leave it like that. I've got to go and try to find him.'

Selwyn raised his hands. 'But where? He could be anywhere.'

'I'll start with Eleanor's cottage. If the bin's out, I'll know he at least went there. Maybe a neighbour will know when he was there. It's a start.'

Selwyn jumped to his feet. 'I'll come with you.'

'You two be careful,' Miriam warned.

Amanda turned at the door. 'I'm not sure if I'm going to make it into work tomorrow, if we don't find him.'

'That's the least of our worries. Don't give it another thought. I'll alert the staff. Sebastian's the priority.'

The bin was found out on the footpath at Eleanor's cottage. Amanda and Selwyn wandered round the outside of the cottage. They peered in through the windows with the aid of a torch. Amanda then went to approach the next-door neighbour. 'You'd better stay here,' she told Selwyn. 'If it's an old dear she might get spooked if we both go.'

The neighbour was indeed an old lady who confirmed that a young man, answering the description Amanda gave, had indeed been to the cottage. He had deposited the bin and taken away a number of plants. That was in the afternoon, but she could not add anything more, other than that a well-built man had called just a little earlier. No, she hadn't seen a car because it was only a fleeting glance, on her way to the bathroom. Nor did she know if he had been in the cottage.

Without even knowing what she was looking for, Amanda scanned the road outside the cottage with the torch then reluctantly accepted there was nothing more they could do there.

It was late by the time they got back to the hall. Miriam was busy at her computer with correspondence to sponsors and contributors to the hall opening fund. The anxious housekeeper had stayed on and busied herself in the kitchen, hopeful of positive news. She offered to make the trio a cup of tea or chocolate, but Selwyn's thoughts were on stronger stuff. So, having invited Mrs S to join them, they partook of a nightcap before they called it a day and retired to their separate beds, Amanda staying in the cottage for the night.

Chapter 15

The face that the librarian saw in the bathroom mirror, the following morning, was a totally different one to that of the previous day. There was no smile, no sparkling eyes and not a trace of happiness. She had had barely a wink of sleep, the brief periods of repose tortured with vivid, shadowy dreams that echoed her loss of Sebastian. It was still dark and tired though she was, to return to bed was totally out of the question.

Though early enough, and knowing that Mrs S would delight in cooking her a delicious full English, Amanda breakfasted alone at the cottage. She barely finished the meagre portion of cereal she poured out for herself.

A call from Selwyn mutually confirmed that the status quo remained unchanged. It was too early to phone DCI Stone, so Amanda resumed her search for the instructions and password for the tracking device. It was only after a lengthy, fruitless search that she dialled Stone's number and got through. Although sympathetic to her plight, the DCI reiterated what Selwyn had said the previous evening. It would be 48 hours before the police could record Sebastian as a missing person and initiate action. However, he would have a word with the uniformed section to look out for him.

It was only after the call she realised the one place she had not searched was the glove compartment of Sebastian's car.

By this time, Selwyn and Miriam had departed for their interview. Amanda sped over to the hall and with a hasty, 'good morning' to Mrs S, hurried to the drawing room and Sebastian's computer. She logged on to the system and the screen opened up to reveal a map of the area and a red pin-point which Amanda had to assume was Miriam's car. Logic dictated she should inform Stone, but unluckily he had left the building and she was put through to DS McBride. His snotty tone, on learning it was Amanda, did not bode well. She tried as best she could to explain the situation and urge assistance.

'So what you're saying is he's only been missing overnight and that you've located where the vehicle is. Is that right?

'Yes, but he might be...'

'Since it's unlikely our men would get there before you do, I suggest you make your way there and if you find there's a problem, give us another ring. Goodbye.'

Amanda made to protest but the line had gone dead. There was nothing for it but to set off on her own. This time she paid more attention to the location shown on the map. She expanded the view on the screen and took a screenshot on her camera. She hastily jotted down the name of the road she was going to and gave it to the anxious housekeeper.

'This is where the tracker shows Miriam's car is. I'm going there now. If I'm not back when the commander returns, please tell him and give him this.'

'Oh my gawd, Shouldn't you wait till 'e gets back?'

'It won't wait. Anything can have happened. Also, get him to ring DCI Stone and also tell him that I think I know where Charlie Pembroke might be.'

'Oh lummy, I do 'ope as you're doing the right thing. Do take care dearie.' She followed Amanda out of the front door. Her fingers quivering at her mouth, she watched as the librarian sped away.

***

Navigation and map-reading not being some of Amanda's strong points, it took several wrong turnings and deviations before she finally came to a halt at her destination.

She could not remember ever having been to Cawthorn Lane before. From the image on her phone, the precise location of Miriam's car should have been further up the road, but there was no sign of it. What did register with her was the pottery with its 'To let or For Sale' sign.

She sat in the car for several moments, her impatience to get out and continue the search curbed while she ordered her thoughts. Finally, she got out and walked towards the building. She peered through one of the windows. The place was in darkness, the door locked. She peeped through the second window. There appeared to be no sign of life inside. Several strides further on, she arrived at the end of the building and found a passageway. Along it she reached a set of open gates set into a brick wall. These were open. From the side wall she cautiously leaned forward to look into the courtyard beyond. The rear of the property appeared to be an extension and into the back wall were set two large, closed wooden doors. In front of them stood a car she knew well. A car that should, by now, have been travelling along the highways and byways of France. But what of its driver? Amanda wondered and feared.

***

'They've nabbed the lassie sir,' McBride announced as Stone entered the open office.

'Nabbed who?'

'The Rossiter lassie. She was spotted in London, yesterday. Our lads are bringing her in.'

'Woman, McBride. You're not in the Highlands now. What time are they expected?'

'Anytime now.'

'Well let me know as soon as she arrives and we'll interview her.' He turned to leave. 'God save us from bloody Rob Roys,' he murmured to himself on the way to his office.

Less than two hours later, Stone and McBride were seated opposite a nervous but defiant Celia Rossiter.

***

For several minutes Amanda kept watch on the courtyard but no one appeared and nothing happened. She retraced her steps to the front of the building, summoned up her courage and knocked on the door. She expected no reply but after several moments there was the sound of a key turning in the lock and the door slowly opened.

'Hello, dear. How nice to see you again. Do come in,' Eleanor greeted her, with a smile.

'I thought you were going to France,' was all Amanda could muster as she was led into a sitting room.'

Eleanor invited her to sit. 'I was, dear, but there were one or two things I needed to take care of which took longer than I expected. I was just about to set off. Would you care for a cup of tea or coffee?'

'Not at the moment. What are you doing here, anyway?'

'As I said, one or two things to clear up. Did you come looking for me?'

Uncertainty and confusion stole into Amanda's mind. Here was Eleanor, as calm and kindly as always. Could it be that she was ignorant of what Amanda was there for? 'No, I've come to find Sebastian.'

Eleanor gave her a questioning frown. 'Why would you think he'd be here?'

'Because the tracking device on the car he was in indicates it's here.'

'Goodness gracious. Are you sure? Surely it must be faulty. How could he possibly be here?'

The innocence of the reply fuelled Amanda's uncertainty. 'I don't believe so. Do you mind if I have a look around?'

'Not at all, I'll give you a guided tour, but let's have a cuppa first eh, dear?'

Amanda agreed. She needed to buy time to re-order her thoughts. She remained seated as Eleanor disappeared into what presumably was the kitchen.

In the kitchen, Eleanor ground her teeth as she stared at the kettle, waiting for it to boil. This was a dilemma she had really not wanted. She was so close to her goal to return to France and leave everything behind. She could not fail now, but to have two more murders on her hands and innocent people at that? And one of them Amanda, of all people. The kettle whistled. She had made up her mind. If they had to die too, so be it.

'Coffee okay?' she called out.

'That'll be fine,' came back the reply.

Coffee was better. Stronger. Would hide the taste better. She made the coffees, reached into her handbag and took out a small bottle of pills. She regarded it for a moment. No, it would not work. Amanda was too clever to fall for a drugged drink. She replaced the bottle, loaded the tray with the coffees and biscuits and returned to the sitting room.

Amanda felt herself tingle in anticipation and dread. 'Where's Sebastian?' she demanded.

Eleanor stared at her and gave a slight frown. She thought for a moment then gave the slightest of shrugs, as if in resignation. 'Yes, you're right. He is here, safe and sound, for the moment.' Her voice sounded surprisingly even.

Amanda jumped up. 'Take me to him.'

'All in good time. I need to speak to you first. Sit down.'

Amanda was so tempted to use force, but in view of Eleanor's age and her determined tone she relented and sank back down in the chair. A feeling of relief at Sebastian's apparent safety now supplanted her anxiety. She pulled an envelope from her bag. 'I had lunch with my friend Kathy, the other day. She'd been doing some research about Beziers and discovered a photo she thought you might like to see.' She passed it across.

Eleanor viewed it with birdlike curiosity. 'How very kind of her.' She opened the envelope and drew out the photo which she studied, without any sign of elation.

'That *is* you with your parents, isn't it?'

Eleanor merely nodded.

'Standing outside Pharmacie Delaney?'

Another nod.

'The pharmacy that you worked in, which you described to me as a shop.'

Eleanor pointed across the table. 'You're not drinking your coffee. It'll get cold.'

'I'm not thirsty.'

Eleanor lifted her mug and took a drink. Amanda refrained. 'The pharmacy in which your step-father supposedly committed suicide, after your mother died.' Another snippet of information Kathy had later uncovered.

'He was a brute,' Eleanor murmured. 'He abused me and when I told my mother she never believed me. At least I like to think she didn't believe me, though I feared she just didn't want to.'

'How did he die?'

'Poison.'

'Which I assume you had learned a lot about.'

'Amongst other things.'

'Like the expert way you dealt with my wound in the office.'

Eleanor smiled. 'I was only too glad to be able to help out, dear.'

Amanda's impatience for finding Sebastian was mounting. She now wanted to stand up and compel the woman to take her to him. She wanted to rampage through the building, but she had to go through with this rigamarole. She had to find out about Pembroke. But there were other things she also needed to know. She forced herself to remain as cool as she could. She had to play this out.

'Tell me about Christine.'

'Christine was the one love of my life, after my real father. I would have done anything for her. I always loved her, but she didn't feel the same way.' She shrugged. 'It didn't matter in the grand scheme of things.'

'And Montand?'

Eleanor's eyes narrowed to slits. She related how Christine had blackmailed Patterson and, unbeknown to her, pocketed the money that was supposed to be sent to his deserted wife and child. How Montand must have traced Patterson from the postmark of the one payment that got through and had come to exact his revenge on the vet. 'You know that he killed Christine,' Her declaration carried a strong note of self-vindication.

'Is that why you killed him?'

'Yes, Charlie and I killed him. Charlie had the gun, I talked to Montand in French and told him he had no chance of getting back to France. Charlie threatened to hurt him badly before he finally shot him. The alternative was for him to take an overdose of his insulin. He refused to do it because he didn't want to die a suicide, so I did it. I knew he was diabetic from a letter Christine had sent me, but I did have other drugs available.'

'How very cold-blooded of you, Eleanor. And I suppose you locked the door with a key copied from the master key I gave you to take to Mrs Craddock.'

Eleanor's glance was as cold as the arctic. 'Yes, dear. I took that precaution when I saw Montand had made the booking. He made it under a false name but his email address gave him away, also his flight details. Goodness knows why he bothered to give those. So, I thought the key copy might come in useful.'

'I can't believe that you killed him in cold blood.'

Eleanor's face convulsed into a malicious sneer. 'He killed the one person I loved.'

'Possibly not. She suffered from a bleed at the thinnest part of her skull. Apparently, there was a broken pot that the pathologist proved had been in contact with her head.'

Eleanor gaped at her. She stared, unbelieving as her jaw

dropped. The eyes closed and her head drooped. Tears that welled up in the corners of her eyes began to slowly trickle down her wrinkled cheeks. She reached into her bag for a tissue and dabbed her eyes. 'Oh my god,' she finally murmured. 'Oh my god. I threw the pot at her in the heat of the moment.'

Amanda felt herself weaken at the pathetic spectre of this aged woman who had previously been so kind to her. She braced herself to continue. 'Did you kill Patterson?'

Eleanor regarded her. She sniffed away further tears and the fire appeared to reignite in her eyes. 'He threatened to ruin Christine, to expose her as a blackmailer. He rang me after Montand had beaten him up. I went to persuade him not to do anything but he refused. So, I injected him.' She gave a dismissive shrug. 'Montand had all but killed him anyway.'

'Tell me about Charlie Pembroke.'

Eleanor's eyes softened. 'He's my cousin.'

The surprise came like a hammer blow to Amanda. She looked at her in astonishment then leaned back in the sofa as she took the news in. She leaned forward again and regarded Eleanor with a cold stare. 'Where is he?'

The question was ignored. 'He's got everything planned out and he's determined to join me in France.' Her voice was eerily calm. Her filmy eyes turned to the door then back to the librarian. 'So many questions dear, but I'll explain everything.' She settled back in her chair. 'My original family name was Crawley and I had a younger brother Jonathan, whom I adored. He was murdered, well as good as murdered. Plunged to his death off a railway bridge wall. The boy who bullied and killed him was Roland Hawtry. That's what was widely understood, but nothing happened to him. There was never any proof. It broke all my family's hearts, especially my mother's and mine. She never recovered and the loss drove her and my father apart. They divorced, she took me to France and the rest you know.'

Amanda's hands went to her mouth. She gazed at the old woman as if mesmerised.

'I never forgot Jonathan or forgave what Hawtry did. I swore if I could ever find him I would avenge my brother.' Her eyes narrowed at the thought. 'Then Charlie, whom I was so fond of, wrote to tell me Hawtry had turned up in Hopestanding. Charlie's always been protective of me, the dear boy, and was so close to Jonathan. More like a brother really. So, with mother dead, I decided to come home and find a way to kill Hawtry. Looking after my father was only part of the reason to return. The festival committee membership just fell into Charlie's lap. An ideal way to get close to Hawtry. It was so fortunate, particularly as I had already got involved with you. It really was the ideal opportunity.' She leaned forward and gave Amanda a warm smile. 'I did enjoy working for you, you know, my dear. It was a wonderful experience. I'm only sorry I had to deceive you. It didn't sit easy with me.'

Amanda almost found herself melting. 'It was nice having you on board.' She murmured then frowned as she returned to the present. 'What about the others? Did you have anything to do with those other deaths?'

Eleanor nodded, quite unfazed. 'Yes. We formed a Hanging Committee all of our own and I was the leader, I suppose. Francis and Charlie lost their sons in a motor accident caused by a drunken driver who came out of prison. He never uttered a word of repentance or regret.

285

It broke both of them. Celia Rossiter was a close friend of the poor woman who committed suicide. Her husband regularly abused her. Then the brute had an affair with a married woman.'

'But Charlie and Francis had alibis for when the man was killed.'

'Quite so. That was me and Celia with some help from a gun and an old prison lag that Charlie knew.'

'And what about Francis. You killed him as well, did you?'

'Of course not, he was our friend! He had an accident when setting Hawtry's car alight and the fire savaged him so fast that all we could do was put him out of his misery. Honestly, that was a mercy killing. Of course, Charlie then had to burn his remains with the car, to delay the discovery of who it was, as long as possible.'

'So you collectively decided to take the lives of three people, in cold blood, the abusive husband, the drunken driver and Roland Hawtry.'

Eleanor's head rose in defiance. 'Yes we did. It was justice. Three people who one way or another were responsible for the deaths of innocent people and had ruined the lives of others.'

Amanda eyed her coldly. 'I could never have conceived of what a ruthless and calculating person you were, Eleanor. A cold blooded murderer.'

'Don't give yourself such airs, my dear,' Eleanor snorted. This is real life. People die all the time. We all have to go at one time or another. Does it really matter when? When it does it is nearly always too soon, if you ask the person doing it. Once it's done you either move on to a better or worse place, or you're nothing at all. In fifty years no one will know or care one jot who died when. Life goes on, the world goes on. we're just temporary phantoms. Were any lives going to be the worse for the loss of these people? I think not. The world's best rid of them. Those who suffered because of them will feel the same and be glad that the vermin can no longer harm anyone else.'

Amanda was taken aback by her vehemence, a side of the woman she had never seen before. 'And what does Charlie intend to do? That erstwhile upholder of the law?'

Eleanor's eyes cut to the door that led further into the building. Her voice softened to almost a whisper. 'He has terminal cancer. The prospect of being in prison as an ex-police officer is something he can't and won't face. His plan was to escape, if he could. Failing that, he'd commit suicide, take responsibility for everything and enable me to return to France. I don't expect I have much more time left anyway, but I yearn to spend it in the sunshine and warmth. My job here to avenge Jonathan has been done.'

Amanda now had it all. 'And Sebastian?'

Eleanor stared at her, but not unkindly. 'He came here yesterday. He followed Charlie who'd gone back to the cottage. I'd left behind some things I needed. It was foolish. I should have gone but he said he was going stir crazy, I believe that's the expression.'

Amanda glanced round in alarm and rose. 'Pembroke's here? Where's Sebastian? What have you done to him?'

Eleanor waved down her anxiety. 'He's alright. He's not been harmed. It wasn't my intention to do so. I was going to contact you when I was safely out of the country, to tell you I feared Charlie might have gone to hide out in the pottery. He would have gone by then. Sebastian only saw Charlie, yesterday, but not me. He doesn't know I'm here. But now you've messed up our plans.'

Amanda advanced towards her. 'It's all over now, Eleanor. Show me where Sebastian is or I'll…'

Eleanor's lips tightened. 'I don't think so dear.' She reached into the handbag, by the side of her chair.

'You'd be no match for me,' warned Amanda.

'Perhaps not, but this would.' She levelled a revolver at Amanda, rose and backed away. 'And don't make the mistake of thinking I can't handle this. It's my father's old service revolver and I've had plenty of practice with it. Not on people, I hasten to add, but there's always a first time.' There was now distinct menace in her voice. 'I think it's time for you to join Sebastian, but first things first. Place your mobile on the table, please, dear.'

Amanda reluctantly obliged, watchful for any opportunity to overpower her captor, but she stood too far away.

'Alright, go on through that door.'

Amanda opened the door with some trepidation. She toyed with the idea of slamming it back on Eleanor but found herself staring at Charlie Pembroke.

***

For Mrs Soames, the day's happiness was unfortunately marred by her anxiety over Sebastian's disappearance. She remembered how she had let the family down on a previous, crucial occasion, by forgetting to pass on a message. She tried a few times to ring the commander but there was no answer. Similarly, she had been unable to get through to DCI Stone.

The pleasant part of the day had started when husband Reggie had woken her with a tray bearing a cup of tea, an anniversary card and a small glass vase bearing a solitary red rose.

Reggie, not normally a man for sentimentality and with an atrocious memory for birthdays and other important dates, had astounded his wife with this act. Not only her but himself, in having remembered the date and that it was a special event.

'You soppy ha'p'orth,' she greeted him, with one of her rare smiles. Nevertheless, she savoured the moment and warmly reciprocated the kiss he stooped to give her.

As she later bustled about the hall, she tried one more time to get through to the commander and left a copy of Amanda's note on the commander's desk, the original tucked safely in her apron pocket. She then decided to make some of Reggie's favourite cheese scones. These would be part of the picnic she intended to take down to him, together with a bottle of prosecco she had bought to celebrate their 40th anniversary. She had merely told him she would bring a sandwich to the boathouse, where he was putting the final touches to the refurbished launch, but they would lunch in style.

His agreement with the commander, when he undertook the project, had been that he would be left in peace to do the work. Selwyn would not visit the boathouse or view the launch until it was completed.

Promptly at noon, Mrs Soames, laden with the picnic hamper, bustled to the boathouse and surprised her husband. The spread was tremendous, their happiness such as they had not experienced in a long while. The prosecco disappeared and it was in a very happy frame of mind that the rather woozy Mrs S eventually packed up the hamper, kissed her husband and set off for the hall.

'Mind how you go,' he called out to her.

'Don't I always?' her head turned to respond, thereby

missing a mooring cleat which she tripped over. With a cry she ricocheted off the side of the launch and landed awkwardly on the path. She let out a cry. Happiness was instantly replaced by fear and acute pain. Reggie rushed to her side and saw the abnormal angle of her arm.

Ten minutes later, after much effort, further cries of pain, and curses worthy of a sailor, the stricken woman had been eased into Reggie's car and was on her way to the hospital. The note for the commander was safely tucked away in the pocket of the apron Reggie had left in the boathouse.

***

Both Selwyn and Miriam were elated at the way the radio interview had gone. There had been one or two early, awkward questions along the lines of money perhaps being better spent than on a festival and supporting the public opening of Wisstingham Hall. Selwyn had begun to fear they had been allocated an ambulance chaser for an interviewer, but thereafter things had improved. Miriam managed to get a plug in for the Arts festival, with the emphasis on the coordinated events which would be also take place at the hall.

Selwyn had been previously drilled by Miriam to refrain from mentioning the missing family treasure. However, since he had received a prompt and positive feedback from Professor Ingrams on the photos and plans he had sent him, the commander had already decided to keep his own treasure-seeking agenda a secret, for the present.

Once out of the radio station, Selwyn checked for messages from Amanda. In their absence from the hall he put a call in to her, but there was no answer. 'Perhaps she's driving, I'll try later,' he told Miriam. There was a missed call from Mr. Soames, but by now they were already almost late for their next deadline at the town hall.

The television coverage and Mayor's commentary on the opening of Wisstingham Hall and the council's support for it, was everything the couple could have wished for. Calls made both to Amanda and Mr. Soames, at appropriate opportunities during the event, had worryingly gone without answer.

After the buffet reception in the Mayor's parlour, with sponsors, contributors, and the great and the good, it was well into the afternoon by the time Selwyn and Miriam returned to the hall. On their arrival, the commander was both mystified and alarmed that the housekeeper was nowhere to be seen, nor any note to say where she was. He set off for her cottage but no one was home. The boathouse was also empty.

As he walked back to the hall, he made another call to Amanda but there was still no reply.

***

'Hello Amanda,' said an unsmiling Pembroke as he rose from the table he'd been sitting at and approached her. 'I suppose Eleanor's told you all.'

Amanda merely nodded, her mouth downturned.

'I imagine it must make grim hearing. I'm glad you've not tried to harm her in any way. That would be unforgiveable.'

Amanda shuddered inwardly at the menace in his voice. 'Mr Pembroke, you're certainly not the person I believed you to be.' Nor the man you used to look, she mentally added, his beard, reduced frame and drawn features now a striking contrast to the man she had first met.

Pembroke shrugged. 'That probably applies to all of us in one way or another. We choose our paths and follow them.' He looked at Eleanor and the gun she was holding. 'I think I'd better take care of that, Eleanor.'

A furrow flickered on the old woman's brow. she appeared hesitant and reluctant to hand it over. 'I don't want you to use it. There's no need for that.'

He gave her a cold, challenging stare then appeared to relent. 'Alright, not unless it proves necessary. Nothing's going to get in the way of your safety.' He gave a warning glower at Amanda. 'Or mine, if I can help it,' he added.

Eleanor handed over the gun, squeezed his arm and smiled up into his face. 'You're a good man.'

Not from where I'm standing, thought Amanda. To her right was another door through which Eleanor motioned her to go. Inside, about half of the unlit, windowless room was a taken up by a metal structure that Amanda took to be a cage, inset with a steel door. She presumed it had at one time been a secure storage area. Behind the bars, in the borrowed light from the open door, she could vaguely discern a body on the floor. On the floor on the outer side of the bars stood a metal beaker and a water bottle. Alongside that sat an empty plate. The form did not stir and Amanda's pulse once more began to race.

All the while, she was conscious of Pembroke who held the gun and barred the outer door. Eleanor signalled Amanda to stand with her face to the wall whilst she took out a key and unlocked the steel door. 'Inside,' she ordered, without a hint of compassion. She locked the door and disappeared through the outer door which was locked behind her.

In the pitch blackness Amanda groped for Sebastian, though he did not stir. She put her hand on his chest and sighed with relief as she felt its rise and fall. He was alive but presumably drugged. She now recalled a comment he had once made, some while ago, about drugs and poisons being the weapons of choice of a woman. Why had she not remembered that before now?

Sebastian stirred. She shuffled round, cradled his head in her lap and gently stroked his cheek. 'Oh my poor Munchkin, what have they done to you?' she murmured, her eyes moistening with mixed emotions of sympathy and joy at his still being alive.

Sebastian stirred again and groaned. He lifted his arm and felt for her face.

'Hello Munchkin, how are you?' she whispered.

He groaned again. 'Pretty muzzy,' he croaked, 'is there any water?'

She disentangled herself from his grasp and felt for the bottle from which he drank greedily.

'Ah that's better,' he said, his voice now a smoother sandpaper. 'What's happened?'

Amanda recounted, as best she could, the events of the past day.

'What do you think's going to happen?'

'I really don't know. I wouldn't put it past Pembroke to do away with us both, commit suicide here and take the blame for the lot, once Eleanor's gone.'

Sebastian let out a sigh. 'Holey moley, it's not sounding good.'

'Unless, of course, he decides to make a run for it also and try to join her in France. But that leaves a witness behind who's seen her with him.'

'So, it all depends whether his instinct to stay alive is strong enough.'

Amanda felt for the comfort of Sebastian's hand. 'And whether it's stronger than the family tie of keeping Eleanor in the clear. Also, of course, if Selwyn gets my message from Mrs S and when he might turn up.'

'Let's hope he brings the cavalry with him.'

'If it's left to McBride we can forget about that.' When there was no reply from Sebastian Amanda squeezed his hand. 'Are you okay?'

'I was just thinking.'

'About what?'

'About how you always keep getting me into sticky situations. It's a bit like being a punchbag, really.'

'Yes, I'm sorry. I'll make it up to you when we get out of this.'

'That's going to take some making up.'

Amanda smiled in the darkness. 'Just you wait and see.'

'Do I have to wait?'

'A kiss is all you're going to get for now.'

Now Sebastian smiled. 'Oh alright, there's nothing else to do, I suppose. Let's see where it goes.'

Chapter 16

It was during the second interview that Celia Rossiter's resolve to answer every question with a 'no comment' finally broke down. The disclosure by DCI Stone that DNA found on a tissue at the scene of the first crime, at Fellowes House, matched hers, was a major factor in persuading her to talk.

Although it came as little surprise to Stone and McBride to learn that Charlie Pembroke and Francis Mboko had been involved, the absence and non-involvement of Roland Hawtry was something they had not bargained for. That Eleanor Delaney was the mastermind behind the whole thing came as a complete shock. It was she who had organised the group, and decided where the murder should take place. It appeared she had been to the building on a previous occasion, on legitimate business.

'Stone the crows, that old harmless-looking lady?' Stone exclaimed when Celia had been charged and led to her cell. 'Who would have thought it? I'd better have a word with Miss Sheppard.'

McBride, who was looking distinctly uncomfortable, said nothing.

Stone glanced at his ill-at-ease subordinate. 'What is it McBride? Cat got your tongue? Come on man, spit it out.'

McBride eyed him timidly. 'Er, Miss Sheppard rang earlier on to say that Sebastian had been missing since yesterday evening. He hadn't been seen since the morning.'

'And what did you say?' Stone's tone was ominous.

'She did say she'd located his car on a tracker.'

Stone sighed. 'Bloody amateurs again. What the hell are they up to? What did you say?'

'I told her that since she'd probably get there before our men could, she should go and find it and call us if there was any problem, or if she did nae find him.'

'And you didn't see fit to tell me until now?'

'I didn't think it was important.'

'Did you get the location from her?'

'No I didn't.'

Stone's eyes shots heavenwards. 'Jesus! What the hell were you thinking of? Correction, you obviously weren't thinking at all. If anything's happened to either of them, you'd better start looking for a transfer. I'd better go and ring the commander and you'd better give some thought to where that car might be.' Grim-faced, the DCI marched down the corridor towards his office, leaving a humiliated and embittered DS.

***

'Commander Fitzgerald it's DCI Stone,' the voice on the other end of the phone announced. 'I've just learned that Miss Sheppard rang the station this morning to say that Sebastian had gone missing yesterday.'

'That's right. There's no sign of him or Amanda. What can you do to help?'

'I'm also informed that she'd found out the location of the missing car, on a tracker. Is that correct?'

'We tried to find it last night but had no success. She

must have tried again this morning. Miriam and I have only just got back. We've been out since first thing.'

'I'm assuming Amanda's gone off to find the car and Sebastian. Has she left a message or anything?'

Selwyn scratched his head. 'I've not seen anything. Mrs Soames is also missing.'

The day just keeps on giving, thought Stone, with growing exasperation. 'Do you think she's gone with Amanda?'

'I shouldn't think so for one minute, but I couldn't swear to it.'

'Well, if you find out anything let me know and I'll keep you posted.' He rang off.

**

Still inwardly seething, McBride sat at his desk. He ruminated on the possible whereabouts of the couple that had caused him so much trouble and aggravation. The office was deserted. There was therefore no one to turn round at the sound of his tea mug being thumped on the desk as he came to a realisation. The pottery! The one place that was linked to that wee biddy.

He sprang to his feet, grabbed his coat and set off. 'I'll show that coin-jingling sassenach,' he murmured darkly as he strode down the corridor and hurried down the stairs, too impatient to wait for the tortuously slow lift.

In the car park he jumped into his car and headed onto the Hopestanding roads. The traffic being sluggish, through the side window he mounted the blue flashing light onto the roof, started the siren and began to thread his way through and round the heavy traffic.

**

Eleanor lay on the sofa. Her last memory was of her panic at shortness of breath and the floor rushing towards her. Her slowly opening eyes narrowed as her brain began to process where she was and how she had got there. She looked up into Charlie's anxious face.

'I thought you were a goner,' he murmured, with the shadow of a smile.

With a weary effort she heaved herself up into a sitting position and glanced at her watch, horrified at how much time had passed. 'It's just another of my attacks,' she murmured.'

Charlie now sat down opposite her. 'What can I do? What can I get you? Is it serious? Will you be able to drive?'

She spied the gun on the side table next to her cousin's chair, and frowned. 'It's alright,' she reassured him. 'I just need a little while and I'll be alright. I have some pills in my bag.' Her hand limply gestured in the direction of the chair she had been sitting in earlier. Charlie reached for the bag, handed it to her then went to fetch some water.

We'll carry on as planned,' Eleanor stated once the pill had been swallowed.

'But she's seen you. It won't work. They'll catch up with you.'

'So what do you propose?'

Pembroke leaned forward and glanced quickly at the door. 'We could silence them. Then it would all be back on track.'

Eleanor's lips tightened. 'I don't want my freedom at that price. Do you understand?'

He gave her a challenging look then succumbed with a curt nod.

'If you were to kill them, there would be such a hue and cry you'd never have the chance to get away,' Eleanor persuaded. 'Leave them to be found and the hunt for you will be no worse than it already has been. Anyway, you have your exit plan.'

'And what about you? They'll probably be waiting for you at the ports.'

'I'd already thought about that, dear. I'll drive up to Scotland and get a ferry over to Northern Ireland then across the border to Eire. I'll have a better chance that way.'

'You'd have an even better chance if the girl wasn't able to spill the beans about you.'

Eleanor stamped her foot. 'No! We set out to do three things and we did them Murdering her and the boy is not an option.'

'Very well. I'll use Christine's car. You'd better get going, if you feel up to it.'

She gave him a kindly smile. 'I'm fine, dear. I'll go and wipe my prints off everything then get my things together.'

'And I'll get your car out.'

Pembroke disappeared into the other room. He unlocked the door to the secure room and switched on the light, his angry gaze fixed on Amanda's narrowed and blinking eyes. Sebastian lay with his head in her lap, his eyes closed.

Pembroke jabbed his finger in her direction. 'If I had my way you two would be dead. Everything was going to plan until you showed up. If anything happens to Eleanor and she doesn't get away, I'll kill you, my God I will, make no mistake. You'd better just hope we're lucky.'

Sebastian stirred but did not open his eyes.

'Charlie, you're not that kind of person,' said Amanda.

Pembroke gave a snort of derision. 'Maybe I wasn't, but no longer.' He switched off the light, stepped into the other room and locked the door behind him.

Amanda could just about hear the creaking sound of the large garage doors as they opened, then a car was started and driven out into the courtyard.

***

DS McBride pondered his boss's words as he drove to his destination. Perhaps he should put in for a transfer. Stone had no intention of retiring and even if he did, there was no guarantee he would get promotion. The possibility of a position in Scotland would suit him just fine, though it might not be too easy to secure that.

Still angry, he growled as he had to stop for a doddering pedestrian on a zebra crossing. *He'll be reported as a missing person by the time he gets across,* thought the DS. Once safely on the pavement, the man gave him a wave of appreciation which fuelled a pang of guilt.

Hopestanding's urban sprawl gave way to more open countryside and eventually Cawthorn Lane. McBride approached the pottery with caution and parked well away. He stepped out of the car and walked towards the building. It looked decidedly closed and bereft of occupation. His knock on the door received no answer. Through the windows he could make out little in the interior darkness. He stood back on the pavement and looked at the upper floor. Blinds were drawn at all windows.

After another unanswered knock, he walked on and found the side passage. The doors to the courtyard were open and there, parked with its engine running, was a Corsa. A man he instantly recognised as Charlie Pembroke was about to go back into the building.

Hearing footsteps, Pembroke turned to see DS McBride walking towards him. He felt a surge of alarm and panic. His adrenaline started to pump.

'Mr Pembroke, we need to ask ye a few questions. You'd better come with me,' the Scotsman called out as he approached.

Pembroke snatched the revolver from his waistband and aimed it at the DS who came to an abrupt halt, his palms splayed towards the man.

'Don't do anything ye'll regret. Put the gun down, Charlie.'

'Stay where you are,' Pembroke growled, his lips narrowed. 'You're on your own, aren't you?'

'No, the team are round the front,' McBride called back, flushing like the improvising liar that he was.

The giveaway sign was not lost on Pembroke whose pulse was throbbing in his ears. His mind was fixed on the hot French sun and his determination for both Eleanor and him to reach it. 'Put your radio on the ground, kick it over to me then go and lie down next to that wall, facing it.' He gestured with his other hand.

McBride smiled. 'Now come on Charlie it's all over. Put the gun down. You know it does nae make any sense now.' He started to walk towards him, slowly.

Pembroke's mind raced. He had to get away. He would be the one they would concentrate on and Eleanor could slip quietly away. He felt the tremble in his hand. He would shoot close to the DS, then maybe he'd see sense. He raised the gun. McBride's expression instantly morphed into shock. He sprang to one side just as the deafening explosion came.

***

'Where the hell is McBride?' Stone demanded as he stormed into the open office.

'Don't know, boss. He was gone when I got back,' Johnson replied, hesitantly.

'Then put a call out to him. Tell him I want him here, now.'

Johnson made the call but there was no answer. The other officers stopped what they were doing and watched. There was now a palpable feeling of concern in the room. Johnson tried the call again, with still no reply.

The DCI glanced at the faces round him as if to assess their perceived gravity of the situation in comparison to his. He turned to Johnson. 'Get a trace put on his radio.'

All eyes swung towards the phone on McBride's desk as it rang. One of the officers took the call, the eyes now rivetted on her. 'It's the desk, sir. A message for you from Commander Fitzgerald. He says he believes Amanda and Sebastian are at the pottery on Cawthorn Lane.'

'My sainted, bloody aunt,' exclaimed Stone. He took a second or two to process the information. Was McBride already there and if so, why had he not been in contact? Would they need armed backup? He hesitated. All he had at present was a missing officer and two missing civilians. He would investigate the scene first.

He scanned the office. 'Clive, you come with me. Steph and Tony you bring another car. We'll meet up at the end of Cawthorn Lane. Let's get a move on.'

***

Selwyn's frustration was slowly mounting. He had encountered every traffic light on red and now found himself in unfamiliar territory. What is more, he had not even thought to bring the satnav. Nor did it help that the directions he was given, when he stopped to ask the way, had apparently sent him in the totally wrong direction, when he stopped again to enquire.

Finally, his eyes lighted on the Cawthorn Lane sign, just as there came a sound like a car backfiring. He came to a halt behind a vehicle, the model and registration of which he knew only too well. He looked around, checked his revolver and tucked it in his waistband, under his jacket.

Selwyn noted the drawn blinds through the pottery window and moved past the building, deciding to reconnoitre further along. He found the side alley. Summoning the nerve and posture of his services experience, some thirty years earlier, he moved on. As he rounded the open gate, he froze. The first thing that had caught his gaze, some distance into the yard, on the ground, was a body from which a pool of blood had spread. His attention was then drawn to the noise of a revving engine. When he looked up, a Corsa was hurtling towards him, driven by someone he did not recognise. For an instant, Selwyn did not know what to do. Was it an accident? Had the man been run over? There was surely danger.

He jumped back to the safety of the wall, by the gate, as the car came to a halt alongside him. The driver's window, next to him was already down. The driver levelled a gun and another shot rang out.

***

DCI Stone, had only just left the station when a call was put through to him from commander Fitzgerald, requesting immediate police presence to an armed incident at the rear of the pottery in Cawthorn lane. Stone immediately called for armed back up and activated his siren.

As he swung into the lane, he sped to a halt behind what he assumed was the commander's Jaguar and jumped out.

Stone reached into the boot for a loud hailer then went through the same ritual of the earlier visitors to the pottery, that day. He and Johnson were joined by the two other officers, one of whom had found the side alley and alerted the others. They ran down it and found the commander leaning against the edge of the wall by the gate. When he saw the officers, he headed off to find Stone. Quietly he warned him that he was terribly sorry but feared DS McBride may have been killed in the rear courtyard. 'A fairly bulky fellow, with a gun, just drove off in a white Corsa. He stopped to fire a warning shot at me. From the look of him, I don't think the man's firing on all cylinders.'

Stone looked round the corner of the gate and saw McBride. 'Have you seen him move at all?'

'No, it doesn't look good.'

'Is there anyone still in there, do you know?'

'Don't know for certain. I assume Sebastian and Amanda must be there, alive I hope.'

The DCI called in for an ambulance. 'Steph, get the adjacent buildings vacated of people. Tony, you go and set up a road block at the end of the lane and keep the ambulance there until further notice. Johnson, you bring the car down to block off this exit then go and keep watch on the front of the pottery. Keep me informed of any movements or sightings whatsoever. If anyone appears with a gun, you know what you're trained to do. No heroics, right?'

Once they had gone Stone turned to Selwyn. 'I suppose you've come armed, have you?'

Selwyn gave him a knowing stare. 'You might think that, I couldn't possibly comment.'

Stone grunted. 'Just as long as I know, though of course I don't. But if you were armed, for God's sake I wouldn't want you to use it or show it unless it was absolutely necessary.'

'Understood.'

'I'll try and …' Stone broke off as one of the doors partly opened. Someone stood in the shadow of it. The person appeared to be looking into the courtyard, but neither man could make out who it was.

'Is that you, Amanda, Sebastian?' Selwyn shouted out.

The door slammed shut and they could hear it being locked.

Selwyn looked at the DI. 'What now?'

Stone sighed, 'All we can do is wait until back up arrives.'

Selwyn glanced down at the loud hailer. 'Can't you call whoever it was and tell them the place is surrounded?'

Stone gave him a tired look. 'And have them possibly fire pot shots out of the windows? I'm not putting anyone at risk. We have to wait for the armed response unit to arrive.'

***

Eleanor's horror, when she saw McBride's body, held her spellbound for a few moments, after she had locked the garage door. Yes, she had seen the other bodies but they deserved their ends. Not this man. It had all gone horribly wrong. Although Charlie had fired the shot, she felt she had crossed a divide and was now no longer the person she believed herself to be.

To get away now seemed impossible. She had to think. There were two men at the yard, one she recognised as DCI Stone. She was sure there would not be enough time for her to get into her car and drive away before they would be on her. She was panting. Not from exertion but the fear and uncertainty that now gripped her.

Eleanor almost stumbled into the living room and collapsed onto the sofa. Unconscious of what she was seeing, she stared at the potter's wheel, through the open door into the workshop. She hoped Charlie had got away. Even if he had, the dream of their both being in France together was vanishing. There was no way she could go through capture, interrogation, a court hearing and imprisonment. She knew now what she must do. To delay the inevitable as long as possible, to keep the pressure off Charlie.

She rose and hurried back to the garage. She unlocked and opened the door, ensuring that she stayed within the shelter of it. She called out as loud as she could, 'I have two hostages here. If you try to enter, I will kill them. If you all go away, I will release them safely, later today.'

Eleanor saw Stone step forward from the cover of the wall. 'Release them now, Miss Delaney and no one will get hurt. You know it's hopeless to expect to get away from here.'

'I know that, but I mean what I said. Stand your men down and I will release Amanda and Sebastian later today. I do not intend to give myself up so I have nothing to lose.'

'Bugger!' muttered the DCI, 'a potential suicide. The worst-case scenario.' He stepped forward. 'We want to attend to the injured man. Will you give us safe access for that?'

'Yes, but any tricks and you know what will happen.'

She watched as Stone and the other man cautiously approached McBride's body. After they had determined he was dead, they withdrew, but not before Stone had cast a furious glance back at the garage door.

They'll know there's only me, Eleanor reasoned. They don't know if I've also got a gun but they will know it'd be impossible for me to cover both entrances.

With the garage door once more secured, she hastened to the living room.

It was another ten minutes before the tactical support team arrived. Once briefed on the situation, Sergeant Selkirk, the officer in charge, instructed and deployed his men. Only then did Stone raise the loud hailer to his lips and call out for Eleanor to let her hostages go. There was no response so Stone instructed Selkirk to proceed. He instructed his men and with some coordination of timing and much shouting, they forced entry into the building.

The last room they arrived at was the secure room. The door was forced open but would not fully open, being partially blocked by a dead body.

Chapter 17

After his escape from the pottery, Pembroke drove to the new mooring, loaded the bicycle into the car then motored to a country pub which had been closed for some years. He left the car at the back of the building then cycled back to the canal.

Within half an hour he had slipped his mooring and the narrowboat was slowly and gently cruising down the canal, a large hat on his head and a whisky in his hand. But there was no smile or happiness. His concern for Eleanor and her safety were uppermost in his mind, some might say to the degree of irrationality.

***

The tired librarian's statement to CI Stone, once she had been released from hospital was, of necessity, a very lengthy one. She was then free to drive to the hospital to catch up with Sebastian. He had been taken there in the ambulance, for a check-up on the drug he had been administered. His statement would have to be given the following day.

By the time Amanda returned to the hall with Sebastian, Reggie had long since arrived back with Mrs S who sported a plastered arm in a sling. She brusquely ignored her husband's imprecations to rest, and more politely, those of Miriam. She immediately wheeled the trolley into a prominent position in the kitchen, to facilitate the continuation of her regular tea service.

This proved surplus to requirements when the commander arrived. He insisted they sat round the kitchen table with Miriam, to catch up on the housekeeper's antics, then narrate the events of the day. Between many 'ooohs' and 'aaahs', the good lady, with staunch refusals of all offers of assistance, served up teas and cakes aplenty.

That evening's meal was surely the strangest that Wisstingham Hall had seen or was ever likely to. Seated round the table were the commander, Miriam, Amanda, Sebastian, having narrowly escaped from being kept in hospital overnight, Reggie, and a very confused and uncomfortable Mrs Soames.

The mood was mixed. Overlaid by the relief at the rescue of Amanda and her fiancé was the sadness at the death of DS McBride. Added to this was Eleanor's suicide, Amanda strongly suspected by poison.

For Mrs Soames, as well as her physical discomfort was the added confusion and discomfort of being also seated at the dining table, and the estrangement from her usual position and role.

Through the invalidity of the hall's catering supremo - and more relevantly, the immediate reluctance to invade her empire, which it was believed would greatly agitate the poor woman - it had been Sebastian's idea to send out for a Chinese takeaway meal. Whilst this, at least temporarily, safeguarded her domain, it had caused yet another cause for concern for Mrs S. She had never before tasted that cuisine.

Despite Reggie' reassuring squeezes of her good hand, under the table, Mrs S brooded on how she could possibly sit there and be waited on and how, and by whom, the food would be served. They won't warm the plates, I just knows it, was just one of the negative thoughts that crossed her mind.

Nevertheless, the evening saw her tentatively taste the various dishes and thoroughly enjoy them. Also, that Reggie had partly waited on her had somewhat eased her concerns and conscience. Furthermore, the commander had ensured that the wedding anniversary was toasted with champagne.

'DCI Stone took McBride's death very badly. I think he might have throttled the woman if she hadn't already saved him the job,' the commander observed, at one stage.

'A bit tactless, commander,' Amanda remarked, careless of whether he would be offended. Try as best she could to hide it, Pembroke's last threatening words to her, should anything happen to Eleanor, weighed heavily.

Selwyn glanced across at her. 'Yes, I suppose so. I'm sorry.'

'This 'ere speckled rice tastes good,' ventured Mrs S, which immediately eased the tension.

The meal and conversation continued until Miriam regarded her fiancé and whispered, 'Penny for them, Selwyn.'

He looked at her through moistened eyes and spoke low enough for just her to hear.

'There was one thing today, that took me back to that night with Lucian. I suppose it was to be expected, but who should arrive with the armed response unit but Sergeant Selkirk? I'm certain he was here at the hall for every crisis that's arisen. He took one look at me, smiled and said

'We've really got to stop meeting like this, commander.'

Unsurprisingly, Mr and Mrs Soames were the first to take their leave with profuse thanks, and an undertaking she would be back in business on the morrow. This Selwyn firmly rebuffed with a promise to discuss with her what temporary arrangements they would come to while she was in plaster.

After the women had cleared away, Sebastian and Amanda were the next to say their goodbyes. Tired though they appeared, Selwyn wondered what sort of night's sleep they would enjoy, now they were back together.

Finally, after a nightcap, Miriam convinced Selwyn, with great ease, that it was time for bed. The next day promised to be a busy one with the imminent opening of the hall looming large.

***

The night was not however to go as had been expected. Miriam immediately fell asleep while, through the hours she slumbered, Selwyn lay wide awake. He wrestled with exactly how they would search for the treasure at the crypt. Up until now it had all been very much a gung-ho affair, his normal penchant for organisation and planning overtaken by enthusiasm.

If the crypt was indeed where it was buried, there was a lot of work involved in breaking through the wall. This would need some pretty heavy-duty equipment and a generator. There was also the structural stability to consider. He was not concerned whether the roof would be affected since, according to Professor Ingrams, the walls would have been built later. He did not relish knocking the whole wall down, if it proved unnecessary. Timber supports would therefore have to be taken in to ensure the remaining wall above did not fall on top of them.

Then came the aspect of security. Ideally, if they did discover the treasure, they would need to get it to safety that very day. But there was no knowing what or how much there was, or how heavy it might be. A nice problem to have, he mused. Although the site was off a country lane, there was still traffic and there would not be the opportunity to sufficiently secure the site if they found themselves unable to move everything in a day.

There was also the historical significance of the whole enterprise. Although not Tutankhamun's tomb, the find should be properly documented and recorded, particularly if this was to feature in an exhibition at the hall. Someone would need to be there just to film, photograph and record all that happened. It was only appropriate that Amanda, as a librarian and historian, should be involved and she would probably need Miriam's assistance, so the full team was now accounted for.

Selwyn glanced at his sleeping partner and quietly slipped out of bed. He padded down to the kitchen and had started to make a cup of tea when he was startled by a sound in the doorway.

'I'll have one of those too, please, my love.'

He turned. 'I thought you were asleep.'

'No, the whirring of your brain woke me.'

He walked over and kissed her.

'What is it that won't wait until tomorrow to think about?' she asked as they sat over their tea at the kitchen table.

'The treasure, what else? I was wondering about the financial aspects.'

'A bit previous, isn't it?'

'Nevertheless, it'll need to be insured and what about the tax implications?'

Miriam straightened in her chair. 'I'd never considered that.'

'Odds on we'll find ourselves liable to inheritance tax.'

'Oh my God! Surely not?'

'I reckon so. What's more, suppose the devils were to try and charge it for each generation it's passed through?'

'Never.'

'Well let's hope not. We could end up owing more than the treasure would be worth. Anyway, we have to find it first.'

There was now a doubtful expression on Miriam's face. 'As long as you think it's still worth looking for.'

The look he gave her warned her off any further exploration of that option. He got up and went in search of the biscuit tin and returned with it and a smile. 'It'll be totally worth it. Bound to be more valuable than what the taxman will try to get his hands on. Anyway, it's my family treasure and I'm determined to find it.'

'You're going to need some help in digging it all out, aren't you?' Miriam suggested.

'Exactly. I'd thought about hiring some labourers but I don't think that's on from a security and privacy point of view. Once word gets out the whole place will be swarming with all sorts of intruders, many toting metal detectors. I think we'd better rely on our own staff. We'll have to keep mum until the site's been adequately secured.'

'Then there's the press. That'll have to be carefully controlled and managed.'

Selwyn fixed his gaze on her. 'What I would really like, if we do discover it, would be to have an exhibition curated here in the great hall, in time for the opening.'

Miriam's eyes wrinkled at the joyous thought. 'Oh yes, that really would be the icing on the cake. And what icing! It'd be a very tight thing to achieve though.'

'Then let's try and make it happen, old girl. We'll have a council of war, tomorrow and start to get everything ready.'

Miriam set their empty mugs by the sink and linked her arm in his as they crept back to bed.

***

The heads-up Amanda had given Kathy on the breaking news of what was to be billed as 'The pottery siege', had enabled the reporter to maximise her opportunity and coverage.

Amanda Sheppard, her fiancé Sebastian Fitzgerald and their successful release, unharmed, from capture, featured prominently as the main good news aspect of the saga. Both had limited their comments to expressions of relief at being freed and appreciation to the police officers who had taken part. They of course regretted the tragic death of detective sergeant McBride whom they greatly respected.

Charlie Pembroke also featured prominently in the article as a person the police were anxious to learn the whereabouts of and question. The man was considered dangerous and not to be approached by members of the general public.

Equally, the death of detective sergeant McBride had prominent coverage, together with moving tributes paid by his immediate superior, Detective Chief Inspector Stone and the Assistant Chief Constable.

Not so prominent was mention of the discovery, at the pottery, of the body of an Eleanor Delaney, who was suspected of having taken her own life.

This latter snippet of news, through the same evening's radio broadcast, was to reach the ears of the man the police were searching for. As he listened, his was indeed a grim countenance matched by an equally grim determination to fulfil the threat he had made.

**

The suicide of the woman who had so successfully fooled everybody was of no consolation to the Hopestanding constabulary. DS McBride's death hung heavily with the station, in particular with his CID colleagues. That he had acted off his own initiative, without orders, or informing the station of his whereabouts, did nothing to minimise the feeling of loss or lessen the guilt that DCI Stone harboured in his heart. Whatever their differences and the sometime undesirable traits the officer showed, he had been Stone's partner and one the DCI somehow felt he should have taken better care of.

The grief the station felt was matched by the determination to apprehend Charlie Pembroke, his act made more despicable by his having at one time been one of them. An officer gone bad. The worst and most dangerous breed of all.

'I don't care what it takes, I want Pembroke found and charged,' Superintendent Nelson instructed Stone, when they met in the Super's office after a bruising press interview.

'I'd already assumed that.'

'It wasn't too clever that no one connected him with the pottery. He must have been holed up there all the time.'

Stone was not for being browbeaten, this time. 'Hindsight's always twenty-twenty. There was nothing to indicate the old woman was behind it all.'

Nelson let out a loud sigh. 'What the hell was McBride thinking of, going off on his own like that?'

The CI cleared his throat. 'I think it was an attack of conscience. I'd bawled him out earlier for having ignored Miss Sheppard's call for help. Her fiancé, the commander's nephew, had been missing since the previous day. Apparently, she'd found the car's location with a tracker but McBride just told her to go and find it and call if she had any problems.'

The Super pondered. 'I can see that might have been a reasonable response in normal circumstances, but the Sheppard woman is a bit of a different kettle of fish.' He examined his fingernails for a few moments then rubbed his chin and fixed his gaze on Stone. 'Now listen to me, Roger. There's going to be an investigation and we'll all be giving evidence, so we've not had this conversation. You're too near your pension to be putting it at risk with careless admissions of having bawled a dead officer out. If you've got a fault,' he paused, 'well, one of your faults is that you're not political. McBride was a good officer but he's the one that stepped out of line, going off on his own without reference or warning to anyone. He was a grown man and senior enough to be able to dish it out and take it, when necessary. So, don't you go throwing yourself under any buses, okay? I hope you understand what I'm saying.'

'Stone nodded. 'I appreciate it, sir.'

'I'd better have your report about what happened and what led up to it, asap.'

'It'll be on your desk first thing tomorrow.'

'The one thing you can congratulate yourself upon is having cleared up two complex murders and their respective trails of death in one day. That's got to be up there with the national records.'

Stone pulled a face. 'That's somehow of small comfort, under the circumstances. And we've still got Pembroke at large.'

Nelson sought to lighten his gloom. 'We've got everything fastened down as tight as a drum. It's only a question of time before we get him.'

This brought a smile to the DCI's face. 'That's something I'd normally be saying to you, isn't it? In any case, we had it like that for some time and he still evaded us.'

'Let's leave that for tomorrow, Roger. If you haven't already done so, go and tell the team what a good job they did today. Got to keep them motivated, especially as they've still got the task of finding and apprehending Pembroke.'

At the door, Stone turned to speak. 'Just to say, I do appreciate what you said about the investigation.'

Nelson waved it away with a smile. 'Off you go.'

***

Mid-pour of their tea, Mrs Soames glanced across at Amanda. 'You're looking a bit peaky dear, are you alright?'

Amanda ran fingers through her cleopatra fringe and affected a smile. 'I'm not sleeping well,' was the evasive reply.

'Probably worried about the festival, I shouldn't wonder.'

Amanda seized on the excuse. 'You've hit the nail on the head, there, Mrs S. We're too near to the big day and too much money spent and committed to turn back now. We've just about managed to keep our backers on board after the recent bad press over the recent deaths.'

'Well don't you go worrying that pretty 'ead of yours. It'll all turn out fine and be tip top, I'm sure. Tell me all about what's planned.' The housekeeper's shoulders wriggled like those of a child anticipating something delightful about to happen.

'We've arranged for the celebrations and events to take place in the library, the village green and here, at the same time. We've got the arts and crafts exhibition, not surprisingly in the exhibition hall, and downstairs, round the library, a Punch and Judy show and some art and modelling classes...'

A look of shocked surprise appeared on the housekeeper's face. She leaned in closer to Amanda. 'Not... er... nudes?' she interrupted, in a whisper.

'No. Modelling. Making models. It's aimed at the children to keep them amused whilst the parents visit the exhibition.'

Mrs S looked humorously abashed.

'There are also street theatre groups at key locations in the village, through the market and on the green.'

Mrs S sat up. 'There's a market?'

'A Christmas market. It's coming from Germany. There'll be gluwein, German sausages, sauerkraut, stalls selling candles and votives, Christmas carousels. There'll also be a few French stalls selling cheese, tartiflette and the like.'

Mrs S appeared to award some of the offerings a look of suspicion. 'And this is going on all day?'

'And into the evening. To connect the hall opening and the other events, shuttle buses will run between the green and here, and Hopestanding's town crier will make frequent announcements round the market.'

'Tell me what's happening here. Noone tells me anything.'

'As well as the visits round the hall there'll be events taking place outside. A bouncy castle for the children, some more market stalls, street theatre, one or two games stalls like hook the duck, a crepe stall and ice cream van.' She smiled. 'The commander drew a line at having a burger bar. He thought it would be too much competition for the cafeteria.'

Mrs S gave an indignant shrug. 'Quite right too.'

'And, of course, there are the trips round the lake on the launch. We hope they'll will raise some money to cover the cost of its repair.'

'Reggie's given his time for free as his contribution,' the housekeeper proudly boasted.

'That was very good of him. Then of course there's the opening of the cafeteria.'

Mrs S sniffed the topic away. 'Well we won't mention that. What's this 'ere street theatre stuff?'

'We've hired professional acts to perform either in one spot or move about, to entertain the crowds. Mostly humorous.'

'But what if it rains, dear?'

'We've got wet weather contingencies and anyway, it won't be a problem. We're British.'

Mrs Soames' concern was instantly swept away by this patriotic assertion. The Dunkirk spirit welled up in her. 'We certainly are, dearie.' She glanced at the clock and frowned. ''ere, shouldn't you be at work by now?'

Amanda reached for the milk and began to pour another cup. 'Not this morning. I'm helping Miriam with the scripts the guides will be using for the visits round the hall. We're going to go through them at each location. She should be here anytime now.'

Right on cue, the bell rang, announcing her boss's arrival. At least, that is what Amanda sincerely hoped it was, fearful of something far more sinister.

Chapter 18

Up to the event at the pottery, Pembroke's planning had been meticulous, so he thought, granted that this had been his back-up plan.

The narrowboat had been hired for three months, through the friend of a dubious character. It had been well provisioned and moved from its normal mooring to a quiet and convenient location on the canal. It came complete with a bicycle and all mod cons such as radio, generator, central heating and wifi. It also came with one of two pay-as-you-go mobiles, courtesy of the friend, the other having been given to Eleanor. Added to all this was Charlie's laptop. The false passport was something another even more dubious connection was working on. The necessary financing had been through Eleanor's French account and Charlie had been thankful that the criminal fraternity's loyalty to money transcended any other.

His plan had been to slowly, discreetly make his way through the canal system of England, while he waited for the commotion to die down, then quietly slip out of the country under a new identity. After what had happened, this was now in question.

He cut the engine and after he had secured the canopy to the deck, went down below. The narrowboat's interior was temporarily bathed in silence until noisily broken by a couple of disputing ducks, but that, to Pembroke, was a pleasant intrusion. His ears now accustomed, he could hear the lapping of the water on the sides of the hull.

He knelt on the seat, drew back the net curtain and wiped away the condensation on the window. Outside, the towpath gave way to a low hedge and beyond, at the back of a field, a copse of trees. Leaden clouds dotted the sky and in the hedge he watched, with a smile, the antics of two blue tits as they darted in and out of the defoliated branches. To the right, in the far distance was the outline of what appeared to be a farm, to the left, stone steps ran up from the towpath to a country road which crossed the nearby canal bridge.

He felt a sharp pang of regret that this might well be the last time he could enjoy such scenery. He straightened the curtain and moved to the back of the boat, to put a log on the wood-burning stove, then settled down at the small table. The light from a small table lamp cast an orange glow on his immediate surroundings.

For several minutes Pembroke studied one of the set of Nicholson waterways guides he had got one of his associates to buy online. He needed to convince himself he had navigated to the best location, a location to offer maximum isolation and closest access to a road. The steps were not too many or too steep to carry up the bicycle, even now despite his weakening condition.

He reached for the laptop, switched it on and brought up the website for the Hopestanding Chronicle which he flicked through for the latest local news. The annual online subscription he had thought exorbitant, but since it was funded from his uncle's account, it did not matter. It had been Eleanor's forethought to give him access to her father's account. Confined with his dementia to a care home, Mr Crawley would certainly not be aware of any transactions, nor were the police likely to think to put a trace on the account.

He scrolled down and reached a special feature on the festival and opening of the hall. As he read, his anger flared up that these events should still be going ahead when Eleanor and so many of the committee were either dead or in custody. All down to that wretched busybody of a librarian whose interference and actions had snatched the most precious thing out of his life.

He was now faced with a choice, either to continue his journey to a new identity and escape to freedom in France, or to remain in hiding to extract his revenge on Sheppard, at the best possible opportunity, which could only be the launch of the festival and hall opening.

A coughing fit overcame him for a couple of minutes. To stay would mean waiting for over three weeks and lying low for that time. Even on the narrowboat that would run the distinct risk of being found. He would have to get his underworld contact Torrence to pick him up, late one night, and shelter him.

The way the cancer was going he feared the option of killing the woman and then escaping was not a realistic one. In a month's time, he doubted he would have the energy left to navigate the locks and waterways despite his determination to try.

The desire for revenge won through. If it was the last thing he did, and it might well be, - it no longer particularly mattered to him - he would make sure Sheppard paid. Doubtless she would be there at the forefront of the launch so he would be handed his victim on a plate.

His attention was then caught by an advert inserted by a security company with which he was familiar. They were proud supporters of the festival and Wisstingham Hall. This advert the Chronicle had doubtless persuaded them to take out, since they had presumably been drafted in to provide stewards and security guards. He knew from experience that the security demands of both events would be far too much for the local security companies to satisfy. He sat back and smiled. That suited him just fine.

His attention turned to the narrow cupboard at the far end of the cabin. Hanging in there was what he would wear on the day. He had done his research thoroughly and now the timing was set. The grand opening of Wisstingham Hall was to coincide with the start of Wisstingham Arts and Crafts festival in a month's time. Even the civic party's programme was set out, with times and locations.

All he had to do now was to be there to deal with Sheppard. Once the deed was done, he would slip away back to the narrow boat and embark, as best he could, on his slow journey to the Thames. He very much doubted he would reach France. It no longer even held the lure for him. It did not even matter if he was too ill to continue his journey. He would be content to live out his remaining days as a water gypsy, assuming he avoided capture.

***

Although he was not to know it, Pembroke's luck had continued to hold out. Two days after he had been driven to the refuge of Torrence's rather shabby abode, a routine police search patrol of the canal found his narrowboat padlocked and checked off their list of possible hiding places for the fugitive.

***

The planning and organisation completed, early morning of the great day of excavation saw a small fleet of three cars and the estate truck make its way from Wisstingham hall to the priory site. Selwyn had decided to co-opt Sean the estate manager and the gardener, to swell the ranks, sworn to silence, though their loyalty and dependability hardly necessitated it.

With Professor Ingrams' advice and recommendations to hand, Selwyn directed operations, from the unloading and assembly of equipment and lighting, to the location where the wall should be attacked first. Miriam and Amanda were in charge of the photographic department and the generously filled hampers of food and drink Mrs S had conjured up in the early hours.

Being the businessman he was, Selwyn had forewarned his staff that in the event of that substantial treasure was found, this did not imply he was suddenly going to be rich. It would not enable him to lavish pay rises on staff who might then go off spending money like drunken sailors. None of the treasure would be sold off but incorporated as estate assets, most of which would probably go on display to the general public. Fortunately, the message did little to dampen the genuine enthusiasm of the two men as they began to lay about the crypt wall.

Progress was slow. The stonemasons had done an excellent job, all those years ago. Nevertheless, after a break for elevenses accompanied by Mrs Soames' delicious scones, one large stone was displaced to reveal a gap behind. Selwyn grabbed a torch, knelt, shone it through the aperture and peered into the void.

As he was to subsequently recount on many an occasion, he then fully understood how Howard Carter must have felt when he discovered Tutankhamen's tomb. He spied a cavernous space in which chests and caskets were piled on top of each other. From what appeared to be a woven basket that had fallen over on its side, had tumbled an array of chalices and metal plates. Pikestaffs and muskets leaned against the farther wall and nearer the front was a large trunk on which were piled folded materials. To the very back, in the shadows, there was the very dim outline of three large containers, side by side.

All this is going to take some shifting, he thought, with some alarm, as he rose and made way for Amanda to take photos and video through the opening.

Within the next hour, an opening was made, wide enough to take the supporting beam and props whilst allowing a single person to pass through.

'Blimey O'Reilly,' Sebastian exclaimed as he adjusted the lighting to play on the interior.

'Absolutely,' echoed the commander. He could now see that the containers to the back of the large void were in fact coffins, he assumed from the monastic order.

Much as they wanted to seize upon everything and look into the boxes, it had already been agreed that Amanda and Miriam would systematically label and cross reference each item, supported by a schedule of detailed descriptions and photos.

Whilst this was in progress, to save time the men tucked into the picnic hampers and Selwyn opened a bottle of champagne for all present to toast the find. Whilst the women lunched, the men would load the treasure into the vehicles.

By the time the site had been secured and the party were ready to return to the hall, darkness had long since descended.

It was a very happy commander that greeted the housekeeper and regaled her with the events of the day, but not before Reggie had been called in to share in another bottle of celebratory champagne.

Over dinner, Selwyn looked over to Amanda. 'It's going to be very much down to you now, dear girl.'

She frowned.

'The cataloguing and curation of the exhibits,' explained Selwyn.

Miriam cut in. 'I think the first thing to do, if it can be done, is establish the provenance of the find, that it does belong to the Fitzgerald's.'

Amanda murmured her agreement. 'I think I'll start with the caskets. There may be some documents or letters to substantiate that. It'll have to be at the weekend though.'

Miriam overruled her. 'I'm making an executive decision. Since this treasure is of such historical importance both to the hall and Wisstingham, I'm allocating you to the work as a matter of priority. I'll fill in for you on your festival commitments and get Mary to help me.'

'Yes ma'am.' Amanda replied with a smirk.

Selwyn glanced round the table. 'Until we've got all our ducks in a row and are ready to go public, we all keep mum, right?'

All agreed and the meal continued in the highest of spirits.

***

It was not only Amanda who, once the treasure had been transported to the hall and secured there, began to burn the midnight oil. They were now all under severe pressure to photograph, catalogue and clean as necessary the find, as well as going through the appropriate formalities. The opening of the hall and festival were now only less than a month away. Not only that, publicity leaflets, posters and banners had to be produced for the exhibition, as well as the acquisition of display stands, tables and cabinets.

Amanda beavered away, alongside her Sebastian, an accomplished photographer, took numerous photos and developed a website for the treasure. Miriam prepared the press releases that would follow, in due course. Their graphic design company, that had worked on the Hall marketing material, took up the challenge for the publicity material, with gusto.

Selwyn consulted with his insurance company on what additional security measures might be required at the hall, to cover those additional contents that would go on display.

Gold and silver coins and chains, jewellery and trinkets had been discovered in the caskets.

One of the chests revealed silver chalices and plate whilst the other held scores of documents. Some of these fortunately evidenced that the treasure was in fact that of the Fitzgerald family. It was also fortunate that Selwyn's previous research into the family history had established that the family line had run straight down to himself. Therefore, any future potential claims to the fortune, from other Fitzgeralds, could be effectively rebutted.

As legally required, the Coroner was advised of the find and the Treasure Valuation Committee also contacted for its valuation.

Until such time as the Committee's representatives were able to arrange a visit, the manager of Hadwin's bank agreed to store the precious metals, jewellery and smaller, valuable items in their vault. An approximate value had been quickly assessed on the basis of the weight of gold and silver and a local jeweller's evaluation of the stones. Naturally, being a bank, head office insisted that Selwyn should pay the additional insurance premium whilst the goods were stored. His fists had been clenched in annoyance and frustration at this short-sighted manifestation of the bank's greed, as he left it's Hopestanding branch. Selwyn's premonition of the costs his find would incur now loomed large in his mind.

As for Selwyn's own insurance company, once they had been acquainted with the nature and value of the treasure, a representative was despatched to investigate the security measures already installed at the hall. Sebastian was to deal with this aspect and the introduction of any further, necessary measures. Fortuitously, the measures already introduced, to open the hall to the public, proved virtually sufficient in themselves.

'I can't see that there'll be any complications in your ownership being accepted, Selwyn,' Amanda reassured him, after discussions with the relevant authorities. 'How you'll stand on the tax side of things is quite another matter.'

'I'm beginning to wonder if it was worth finding the treasure in the first place,' Selwyn grumbled,' at the thought of what the tax inspector might come up with. However, this was something Selwyn had been only too glad to task his accountant with finding out, and on learning that he might expect to clear over four million pounds in assets, the commander was not only relieved but almost bowled over.

As for the various paintings that had also been uncovered, these were inspected by an art expert whom Amanda knew. Her opinion was that whilst they were not in the same league as the world's top flight paintings, they were of national interest and worth considerable sums. These too were therefore temporarily consigned to the bank vault. This left the pikestaffs, chalices, muskets, smaller arms and, to Mrs Soames' complete dismay, more armour.

'As if there aint enough of the blithering stuff to dust,' was the least uncomplimentary comment she could offer.

It was left to Amanda to lead the charge on the dating, cataloguing and labelling of the items that remained at the hall, the agreed consensus being that the precious goods would remain under lock and key whilst the empty caskets and chests would go on display, with appropriate descriptions.

***

SATURDAY 8TH DECEMBER

The chaos and near panic attendant upon the morning of the great opening of the hall appeared to be no less than that which had reigned during the preceding week.

Then, contractors had been all over the place like ants, finishing off last minute touches, the cafeteria kitchen equipment engineers sorting out glitches. The signage suppliers' men had also been very much in evidence, their ladders a constant hazard to access as they moved about the building erecting signs.

Each time she left her kitchen, Mrs Soames felt like she was going over the top in the first world war, scurrying into no man's land with her trolley, dodging materials strewn on floors, workmen bent at their work and step-ladders creaking under their occupants.

Now, on the great day, an army of cleaners with their battery of vacuums, dusters and spray polish were engaged in making the place as spotless as a very elderly stately home could be. Soldiers of the other army of attendants and guides were busy erecting the stands and silken, twisted ropes of crowd control barriers. The two receptionists busily set out neat piles and stands of tour guides and information leaflets.

Selwyn busied himself with his master key, checking that all the doors to the private rooms were securely locked.

Once Sebastian was happy with all the public address systems and internet connections, he and Selwyn joined Sean the estate manager on a tour of the grounds and public domain.

Miriam reminded the staff of their roles, positions and procedures whilst checking on the background coordination and care of the civic dignitaries, sponsors, and key supporters of the opening and ceremony.

Amanda's role now centred on the launch and coordination of the festival itself.

And what of the catering? The battle royal over this had already been fought and won by Mrs Soames. Plans for the serving of the dignitaries' champagne and canapes from the cafeteria had been bitterly contested by the housekeeper in a campaign worthy of a medal.

She and Gustav, the cafeteria manager, had been at loggerheads for days, obliging the commander, on more than one occasion, to seek solitude and refuge in a glass or two of Jura, his favourite whisky.

'If I aint good enough to serve them dignitas people with champagne and food, at a time like this, I'm not good enough to be 'ere,' the housekeeper had argued.'

'Dignitaries,' Sebastian had foolishly tried to correct her, which caused Selwyn to cringe at the thought of the outburst that would follow.

'I knows what I mean,' Mrs S had rounded on him with a look Medusa would have been proud of.

Got off lightly, there, lad, thought Selwyn.

Gustav's high ground had been the legalities of serving food from a kitchen not yet signed off by the health officials. Fortunately for him, this argument had been put at a discreet distance from the housekeeper.

'I'll 'ave the ears off 'im,' she had threatened and reached for one of the kitchen knives, when she got wind of this. 'They already told me it was fine to make me cakes an' the like, for the café, as Mrs Soames delicacies, so what's different about canapes?'

Gustav had thus been disabused of this argument and verbally abused, at a distance. Eventually, after the war had entered a phase of denial of biscuits to the commander, on the grounds that they might poison him, Mrs S had won the day.

She was therefore left to leaf through her Mrs Leith and with Rose, the new addition to the kitchen staff, to set about making the reception food.

***

Charlie Pembroke had returned to the narrowboat the night before the festival opening date. As he waited by the canal bridge, in the early morning, a cap pulled well over his head and the security hat and high vis jacket secreted, with various other nefarious items in a rucksack, he pondered on the task ahead. He drew on his previous police training and experience to curb his apprehension. Succumbing to another coughing fit he steadied himself against the bridge wall. He looked up at the summit of the bridge and smiled. *At least Eleanor and I got our revenge for Jonathan.*

It had all the makings of a bright, sunny day, the surface of the canal like that of a millpond, only disturbed here and there by the antics of the moorhens, ducks and the more stately passage of the odd swan.

Pembroke was so glad to be outside. He had been cooped up inside for over three weeks, with only his books and laptop to keep him occupied. Only in the small hours of the morning had he been able to venture into Torrence's secluded garden, for some limited exercise and fresh air.

Presently, he heard the sound of an approaching car which came to a stop in an unmade layby near the bridge. On hearing the toot of the horn, Charlie slowly heaved himself up the stone steps from the towpath, crossed the road towards the car and got into the passenger seat, panting for breath.

'Alright, chief,' the gaunt driver asked as he slammed the car into gear and drove off. He turned his pockmarked face to the passenger, his yellowed crooked teeth showed through a leering smile.

Pembroke raised a cautionary hand. 'Give me a moment,' he wheezed. 'I'm okay, Torrence, how about you?' Pembroke eventually replied, once he had got his breath back.

'Could be better and richer.' He peered through the windscreen, the smile vanished.

'You always say that. There's plenty in it for you, don't worry.'

'How're we doing this, then?'

'You drive the car to the hall, leave the keys on the rear wheel, wander round the place for a while and when the buses start to take people back to the green, you get on one. Catch a taxi home and I'll bring the car back, later tonight. Then you take me back to the bridge.'

The driver cleared his throat, wound down his window and spat out. 'What time you reckon you'll be back?'

'I don't know. Maybe by nine, I hope.'

Torrence dropped his passenger off in one of the quiet lanes close to the village green. From there, Pembroke walked slowly in the direction of all the noise and came across a security van parked alongside the green. Elsewhere, no-parking cones had been set out along the road.

Previous experience with the same security firm, when he had been a chief inspector, Pembroke hoped would stand him in good stead. The only question was how well aware any of them might be, as to his identity and wanted status. He was taking a great risk being there but this would be the very last place the authorities might expect him. Also, his appearance was now so changed. The pounds had fallen off him, his face was much thinner, now sporting a moustache and full beard. His hair had also receded.

As the number of stewards and security staff was high, for a double event such as this, the majority of them would be bussed in from further afield and mostly be strangers to each other. As to his identity, he had a false one ready, if needed. He would just have to play it by ear.

Now wearing the high vis jacket and peaked cap, Pembroke slid the knife and revolver into the jacket's deep inside pockets. In his trouser pocket nestled the small box Eleanor had given him.

With his head bowed, he headed round the edge of the green and looked amongst the shuttle buses for the one marked for the security team. Yes, there it was. Business as usual. There was quite a crowd of people teeming through the fair and at regular intervals high vis jackets could be spotted.

Pembroke took up a position close to one of the stalls, which afforded maximum visual protection but enabled him to keep an eye on what was happening at the area where the mayoral party would assemble.

The 10 am formal opening of the festival was to take place in the library's large foyer. The Mayor of Wisstingham, together with the representative of the Arts Council, would officiate at the opening itself, after brief speeches from Amanda and her boss Miriam, the councillor with portfolio for cultural services.

'Thank goodness that's over with,' Miriam whispered to Amanda after they had departed the launch and settled into their seats on the special shuttle coach to take the civic party to the village green. 'I thought your speech was excellent. Just hit the right note. Let's hope the general public take up the invitation to go to the hall.'

A formal opening of the Christmas fair seemed hardly appropriate as everything was already in full swing. Despite the relatively early hour, the gluwein stall was almost packed, an aroma wafted from the grilled bratwurst and in the open area by the Christmas tree, the Hopestanding Salvation Army were playing carols.

Nevertheless, the town crier insisted on announcing the arrival of the Mayoral party as they began a tour of the festivities.

The ringing of the town crier's bell alerted Pembroke to the mayoral party's arrival. He spotted Amanda and smiled to himself. All was going to plan. However, there was a long day ahead of him. The big unknown was the woman's intended movements. He knew she would travel on to the hall for the opening. Thereafter, he imagined she would remain there, but exactly whereabouts he did not know, nor could he be certain she would indeed remain there all day. If she did not, she would certainly return for the evening fireworks display. The deed would preferably have to wait until darkness but he would just have to take his chances and deal with her at the first available opportunity.

Between the stalls the grass thoroughfare was occasionally made almost impassable by crowds of spectators enjoying various street theatre performances. At one of them, seated on the knee of his puppeteer, a large puppet, dressed in a smock and beret, attempted to paint a volunteer's portrait, to smiles and howls of laughter from the audience, at his running dialogue.

The nervousness that Amanda had felt prior to her speech, had temporarily blotted out a different anxiety that had been with her since Pembroke's threat to kill her. Since his escape, try as she might she could not convince herself that Eleanor's suicide had had nothing to do with her and, more importantly, that Pembroke would not risk getting caught in trying to get at her. After McBride's death, the press coverage and police presence in the area were high and no doubt the police had spread their net very wide.

However, Amanda's fear remained, though she had still kept it secret. After all, Sebastian and the police had enough to do without playing chaperone to her. She could look after herself, would be careful and ensure that she was in the company of others at all times.

Amanda therefore tagged on to the mayoral party as it slowly made its way, with frequent stops, through the market. At one point she was convinced she spied Pembroke in the distance, through a gap between stalls. As she cleared the stall, she took a second look but considered she had been mistaken. The only person in the vicinity was a security guard in a high vis jacket with a torn pocket, who faced the road with his back to the green.

By now, the VIP party had arrived in front of the band. Amanda glanced at her watch. Another five minutes and they would need to make their way to the coach, for the onward leg to the hall. From the other side of the group Miriam caught her gaze and raised her eyes questioningly. Amanda held up her hand by her side and splayed her fingers, to which Miriam nodded then closed in to whisper something to the mayor.

As the mayoral party moved off into the market, Pembroke feared Amanda had caught sight of him. While he was out of her vision, he hastened to join another steward and start a conversation with him. This he soon broke away from to wander closer to the security shuttle bus, still close enough to the market so as to not look conspicuously out of touch with the proceedings.

When the VIP party began to head to their coach, Pembroke joined the small group of stewards on their way to the security shuttle bus. A small fleet of buses awaited the growing queue of people now destined for the opening.

Pembroke climbed aboard the bus and chose a seat on the opposite side from the green, where he stared out of the window for the entire journey to the hall.

***

Not for many a year, perhaps since his military career, had Commander Fitzgerald felt so excited and nervous. His earlier stroll through the grounds with Mustard had done little to calm his nerves. Even the time he spent on his favourite seat in the rose garden, as he gazed out over the lake whilst Mustard bounded backwards and forwards chasing ducks, did little to improve his composure.

He wandered over to the boathouse where he found Reggie buffing up the launch's highly polished woodwork. Selwyn pumped his hand in grateful appreciation of the magnificent job he had done on the craft.

'I'll give it a run on the lake then moor it up at the staging, like you said,' Reggie affirmed.

'That'll be just fine, my dear fellow. You've done a splendid job on it, absolutely top hole.'

Reggie beamed and resumed his polishing.

At the hall, Selwyn found Mrs Soames directing her little army of helpers in the assembly and arrangement of glasses, plates, and cutlery. Bottles of Dom Perignon were stored in the café's wine chiller, under Gustav's testy supervision. Rose was busy at work on the vol-au-vents, under the ever-watchful and critical gaze of her boss.

Mustard scampered into the already crowded kitchen. Mrs S flicked her kitchen towel at the beagle to shoo it out. He was followed by Selwyn in a cheery mood, judging by his appreciative smile at the work in progress.

'Don't you think you ought to be getting' a move on with changing?' the housekeeper suggested.

He glanced at the kitchen clock. 'Crikey, is that the time?'

'Will you be wanting a cuppa before you get too involved?'

Selwyn gave her a wink. 'Something a bit stronger I fancy, Mrs S, thank you.'

Twenty minutes later found him fully transformed in his formal attire. He stood in the drawing room, on the right side of a glass of Jura, and gazed through the window in the direction the VIP's coach would arrive. He had already walked through the great hall and examined, yet again, the exhibition of treasure Amanda and Miriam had so excellently curated. He had also inspected the reception area where Sebastian was again testing out the PA system and reception area equipment.

'All that gimcrackery working alright, dear boy?' Selwyn's enquiry was only rewarded with an engrossed grunt. 'Hmm, well, that's fine then,' he added and made himself scarce.

The contingent of stewards and security officers was due at any moment, to take up their positions in accordance with the previous day's briefing there.

'It's going to be an interesting and challenging day,' the commander murmured as he watched for the coach.

***

Pembroke made sure he was one of the last to leave the bus. All the others appeared to be headed towards the front door to the hall, so he took up the rear. It was when he was on the threshold that a voice from behind caused him to freeze. 'Hey, you there.'

Pembroke turned slowly round. His eyes widened slightly as he recognised Jack Silverdale, a police officer he had briefly known, many years earlier.

Looking perplexed, Silverdale stared at him for a moment then appeared to visually search for an identity badge. 'Sorry, I thought for one moment you were someone I knew. Where's your ID? Didn't you pick it up at the briefing, yesterday?'

Pembroke was glad of the cue. He raised his fingers to his cheek, puckered his eyes in mock pain and affected a gravelly voice. 'Couldn't make it. Had a problem with the teeth. Root canal job.'

Silverdale grimaced. 'You poor sod. I had one of those. Never again.' He fished into his pocket, pulled out a pass on a chain and offered it. 'Here, use this. One of the lads went off suddenly. Wife having a baby. There's no photos so you're under an alias for the day.'

Pembroke could hardly believe his luck. He took the pass and put the chain round his neck.

'So, you won't have been assigned a particular location will you?'

Pembroke shook his head.

'Then you might as well have a roving brief. Just maintain a high profile and look out for any scallies or people in need of assistance. I'll no doubt catch up with you later.'

Pembroke turned to go inside the hall. *Better and better.* He needed a few moments to assess his bearings so he positioned himself at the large notice board in the hallway and started to read the literature about the opening event and attractions.

One particular poster caught his attention. It advertised trips on the lake in the newly refitted launch, with times and the names of the captains sailing her. Amanda had previously shown a keen interest in the refurbishment work Reggie had undertaken, occasionally helping out and even sailing the launch with him, during its trials. She had also volunteered to captain some of the timed trips during the event.

The sun's certainly shining on me today, thought Pembroke as he moved off to discreetly blend in with the surroundings.

***

As DCI Stone entered the office, only one of the officers glanced up then turned back to the file she was reading. Although nothing had been said, he had a feeling that he was held partly to blame for McBride's death, due to the reprimand he had given him just before the man had set off. He certainly felt the unspoken accusation was at least partly justified. He pursed his lips as he stared at the empty desk then turned to study the incident board for a few moments. Stone then directed his attention to one of the DCs. 'Johnson, any new leads on Pembroke?'

'Afraid not sir. Seems like he's gone to ground.'

'Anyone else?'

All heads rose. 'There's been a reported sighting in Nottingham,' one officer volunteered.

Stone gave an unenthusiastic nod then turned back to the board and stared at Pembroke's photo. *Where the bloody hell are you? Far from here, I imagine.* He turned again to the team. 'Keep at it,' and with that walked quietly back to his own office.

***

The smooth coming together of the Wisstingham 'family' at the opening event never happened as planned. Amanda expected to find her fiancé join her but he was out of sight, busy with a last-minute hitch on one of the computers. Similarly, Miriam found herself distanced from Selwyn, having been cornered by the Arts council representative. The commander, standing centre-stage with the mayor, felt bereft of his fiancée's support and struggled to remember his speech.

Mrs Soames, divested of her pinny and sporting a smart frock, new hairstyle and broad smile, stood next to Reggie. He had swapped his customary overalls for grey slacks and a navy blazer, set off with a pale blue shirt and naval themed cravat. All it needed was the captain's hat which indeed was at the boathouse.

Eventually, somewhat flushed, Sebastian appeared and sidled next to Amanda who gave his hand a relieved and affectionate squeeze. 'You will stay close by me?' she whispered, with not a little hint of nervousness, though he was unaware of the true reason for it.

'Course I will,' he responded, through the corner of his mouth.

Amanda started as the first flash went off from the phalanx of photographers.

The speeches and acknowledgements started. The assembled audience took it all in with smiles and occasional exclamations or laughter, depending on the content.

Miriam managed to stealthily reposition herself next to Selwyn. He was splendid in his praise for one and all, not forgetting all the workmen and staff and, in particular, his indefatigable and most-loved housekeeper, Mrs Soames. She immediately turned bright red at the praise and the volley of applause that followed, which necessitated a search for her hanky.

Miriam and Sebastian came in for lavish praise and gratitude. The final accolade was saved for Amanda and her brilliant work and achievements in the organisation of the festival, as well as the promotional literature and the magnificent exhibition of the treasure. This latter topic was the subject of a separate presentation, naturally closest to the commander's heart.

Finally, as the speeches came to an end and the ceremonial ribbon was cut – which lasted two or three minutes, to accommodate the photographers - the opening was concluded to thunderous applause.

The crowd then dispersed, divided between those who made for the cafeteria, those to the reception area, to purchase tickets, and those who preferred to do the grounds first. Pockets of the mayoral party stood in conversation as Mrs Soame's own army of stewards sallied forth with the champagne and canapes.

As Amanda happily stared at Sebastian, the torn pocket of a high vis jacket registered with her as it receded into the shadows of a darkened corridor, but when she turned back there was no steward in sight. Not that Amanda could be completely certain that it had been Pembroke wearing the jacket in the first place.

***

Sebastian's well-intentioned promise to stay close to Amanda was broken only too soon by an urgent call from one of the box office staff, to attend a faulty computer.

'Sorry Mandy,' he apologised as he put down his plate and champagne flute and hurried off.

She surveyed the room and headed over to join Miriam and one of the leading sponsors. Selwyn had been led off by Reggie, to join him and some of the sponsors and supporters on the maiden voyage of 'The Wisstingham Belle.' Tickets to the general public were to go on sale after the launch had set off.

When Miriam agreed to give some of the sponsors a conducted tour of the hall, Amanda, anxious not to find herself alone, made her way to the great hall, crowded with more visitors than she had anticipated. Security staff were stationed at regular intervals around the room and a queue had already formed, waiting for the next available guide. Amanda was therefore happy to take over a group and begin a tour of the exhibition. She had, however, already rapidly scanned the faces of the security staff in the room, as well as the faces of her group. If the exhibition was going to remain as busy as this, she was happy to contemplate the rest of the day to be spent as a guide, alternating with piloting the launch.

Meanwhile, Pembroke had left the hall and made his way towards the boathouse to familiarise himself with the layout. There were, as yet, no visitors assembling for the first trip. Only on his return did he see a few eager customers approaching. To avoid them he wandered off the path into the woods. He headed towards some buildings which he discovered were the stables and paddock. The path to these had been barriered off from public access. Here, there would be no one to bother him. With his back to public view, he would be a distant visible deterrent to anyone who might be tempted to approach the area. Here he could stay until the time for the action he had now decided upon.

***

At Selwyn's prior suggestion, he, Miriam, Sebastian and Amanda all met up in the drawing room at precisely quarter past five. The hall was now closed to the general public and all the guides, reception staff, and the majority of security staff and stewards had departed. There was still a security presence outside, where the market and attractions were in full swing.

Mrs S had also been primed to arrive at the drawing room at the same time, wheeling her trolly laden with a bottle of champagne and five glasses. Reggie, unfortunately was engaged on one of his launch trips.

'My heartiest congratulations to you all on a first-class effort. The day's been a brilliant success, I reckon,' the commander toasted them all.

'Here, here, Guv,' Sebastian responded in unison with murmurs of approval from the others.

Selwyn turned to Miriam. 'Any idea how many visitors we've had, my dear?'

'Over seven hundred.' Her smile said it all.

Selwyn's eyes widened. 'Good Lord, that's phenomenal.'

'Mind you, it is the first day open and we've had bags of publicity,' warned Amanda.

Selwyn would not be put off. 'Even so, that's ruddy marvellous. A toast to Wisstingham Hall and all who live and work in her.' He raised his glass then turned to Amanda.

'Talking of sailing, you've got one last trip out, haven't you?'

'Yes, at six twenty.'

'Many punters?'

'It's been virtually full each time I've taken it out and Reggie's returns looked about the same. I reckon it'll slacken off though, with only the outside ticket kiosk.'

'I takes it you're all going to be ready for a bite to eat soon?' enquired Mrs Soames.

'You bet,' replied Sebastian, 'I'm famished.'

Selwyn nodded his agreement. 'Yes, I think we'd better eat soon, we've got the fireworks display at seven.'

***

It was the last trip of the day. Nearly late, Amanda had hurried her last dinner course. At a brisk pace she passed seven people who had been out on the launch with Reggie, the two children chattering happily about the experience.

Reggie was waiting for her at the mooring. Already on board was a man and his two young children.

'Reckon that's the lot for the day,' Reggie observed as he handed her the keys. 'You've done a great job, Amanda. I'd have found it a real slog to do it all on my own.'

She smiled and patted his arm. 'It's been great fun. See you later.'

As Reggie headed back towards the hall, Pembroke slowly approached through the woods and watched as the launch headed out onto the lake. He ducked into the shelter of the boathouse, removed the high vis jacket and sat down on the bench to wait.

***

Hands in pockets, DCI Stone paced noisily back and forth across his office. He was distinctly uneasy. There was nothing in particular to cause this, other than the continued absence of any trace of Pembroke. It was just a gut feeling.

There had been no reports of any disturbances at the festival and the opening of the hall, which he had very much wanted to attend, and indeed had had a personal invitation to. Instead, he had been obliged to attend non-productive meetings that had almost bored the pants off him, change and all. Perhaps it was because things had been so quiet that he was edgy. That and the fact that it was Wisstingham Hall where events were taking place. He recalled many other 'events' there, with which he had been personally and regrettably involved.

Johnson and Garrick had been annoyed that he had asked them to do a late shift. Hopefully nothing would come of it, but just in case, they were there. There was plenty of work for them to get on with, anyway.

He glanced at his watch. Six thirty. Sudden inspiration brought him to a stop. That's what he would do. He would take the two officers to the hall. The fireworks display was timed for seven. If anything was going to happen he would put his shirt on its being at the hall. The display would be good to see, his officers would appreciate it and there would be some fast foods to bribe them with.

He switched off the light and strode down the corridor. 'You two, come with me,' we're off to Wisstingham Hall.'

Chapter 19

Amanda looked up from the mooring cleat to which she had tied up the launch. Her three passengers were already some distance away. The two boys had scampered off down the path, ahead of their father who had quickened his pace to catch up with them.

From the shadow of the boathouse emerged a dark form that now walked towards her.

Amanda caught her breath. Her heart began to pound. She instantly regretted not having warned anyone about Pembroke's threat. She had even omitted to mention that she thought she had sighted Pembroke at the market, not wanting to cause any unnecessary alarm. Her fear had been that the police would arrive mob-handed at the hall, just when the opening ceremony was to take place. It would have ruined the day for those she loved. Perhaps Sebastian would come to meet her. But no, there was no sign of anyone. All these thoughts flashed through her mind in an instant.

By now, the figure had reached a bulkhead light on the side of the building. Amanda could clearly see it was Charlie Pembroke. A wicked smile of triumph played on his face.

She cast around. Where to run to? At least she was familiar with the grounds. Pembroke continued to approach. She dashed off in the direction of the quarry road, intending to skirt the lake garden and hide in the woods beyond.

She ran as fast as she could. From behind could be heard the pounding of her pursuer's feet on the path. Along the edge of the lake garden she ran. At the trees she took out her mobile. She tried to call Sebastian but running made this impossible. She would have to stop. In the gloom, Amanda could make out a large tree behind which she might hide. Breathless, she pressed her back against the trunk and stabbed out the numbers, but in the dark pressed the wrong ones and had to repeat the process. From somewhere nearby came the sound of heavy panting and the rustle of undergrowth. Oh God, please answer, please answer, she silently prayed.

At last, Sebastian's voice. 'Hi Mandy, where are you?'

'He's here, Pembroke's here and he's after me…' was all she could pant before a strong hand wrenched the mobile from hers and another grabbed her arm.

'You won't be needing this,' Pembroke gasped, 'we're going on a cruise.'

Seeing the state of the man, Amanda thought to run off. He would never catch her. Then she felt something hard pressed against her side and her head drooped in frightened despair.

***

'What's happened?' asked Selwyn as he caught the look of horror on his nephew's suddenly drawn face.

Sebastian stared at him, momentarily gathering his wits. 'It's Amanda, Pembroke's somewhere here and he's after her.'

Selwyn and Miriam shot to their feet. 'Get Stone here,' he ordered.

But Sebastian was already calling the number. The call

connected and he waited for a reply. He listened. 'Well call him up on his radio, this is urgent, Charlie Pembroke's been seen here at Wisstingham Hall and Amanda Sheppard's in danger. I think they'll be somewhere near the lake. Tell him to get here as soon as he can.'

Selwyn took control. 'Miriam, you take charge here and see the place is secure. Get Sean over here and get him to keep a lookout in case Amanda tries to get in. Warn Mrs S. You'll have to officiate at the lights switch-on without me. I'm going for the revolver. Sebastian, wait for me at the front.' As he dashed up the stairs, the most appalling sense of déjà vu overrode his shortness of breath caused by the unwanted exercise. The last time he had run upstairs in search of his revolver was the night his brother had been killed. He sped up.

Feeling almost sick with terror, Amanda stepped shakily onto the launch, at gunpoint. In trepidation she watched as Pembroke, his eyes and the gun trained on her, single-handedly untied the moorings then clambered aboard.

'Head out in that direction,' he wheezed and gestured with the gun.

She switched on, throttled the engine and set off.

The door firmly locked behind them, Sebastian and Selwyn dashed to the lake, their progress soon impeded by the crowds who had arrived for the fireworks display. 'We'll cut through the lake garden,' Selwyn puffed as they now ran along a deserted stretch of the path.

At the shore they could make out the silhouette of the launch as it headed off across the lake. Under the light of the wheelhouse lamp they could discern Amanda as she steered the launch. Alongside her, standing in the shadows, someone who could only be Charlie Pembroke.

At the sound of shouting from the shore Pembroke and his prisoner looked behind. Amanda gave a sharp intake of breath as she saw Selwyn and Sebastian at the jetty. They stood, their arms waving as they stared in the direction of the launch, their forms slowly receding into the distance.

***

DCI Stone's car had just arrived at the gates to Wisstingham Hall when the call came in from the station. Johnson relayed the message to his boss who immediately instructed him to call for armed back-up, a precaution he hoped they would not need, but he was not going to take any chances.

Waving away the steward's signal to park in the car park, Stone drove on. The car slowly threaded its way past the somewhat annoyed pedestrians. Previous knowledge of the layout of the grounds now served the DCI well. He drove as far as he could, past the pedestrian barriers that enclosed the wildflower meadow where the spectators were corralled.

The three officers alighted from the car and hurried to the lakeside. They joined Sebastian and Selwyn who were helplessly watching the disappearing launch.

'Who's out there and how long's the boat been out?' Stone demanded.

'Pembroke's taken Amanda on the launch. Only a few minutes ago. God knows what he intends to do,' Selwyn replied through gritted teeth, his eyes fixed on the dim outline of the craft.

Moments after the launch had disappeared from view, the small group of onlookers was joined by Sergeant Selkirk and three of his armed response unit. The Sergeant gave a nod to Selwyn as he made for the DCI. 'What's the situation, sir?'

Stone pointed out to the lake. 'We suspect Charlie Pembroke has taken a young woman, Amanda Sheppard, hostage on a launch. We think he's armed. Noone else on board, as far as we know.'

Selkirk turned to Selwyn. 'Any other boats we can use, sir?'

'Yes, there's the inflatable in the boathouse,' Sebastian cut in.

The sergeant directed one of his men to go with Sebastian and the two of them sprinted off.

As the small group waited, Selwyn paced up and down, his progress suddenly halted by the arrival of the dinghy. Selkirk replaced Sebastian in the boat and the two armed officers headed out over the lake, the anxious group onshore watching the engine's white wash as it receded into the darkness.

***

Amanda finally summoned up her courage. 'What are you going to do?' her voice tremulous.

Pembroke gave her a glacial stare. 'I warned you at the pottery.'

'It wasn't my fault that Eleanor committed suicide.'

'If you hadn't interfered in the first place we would both have got away.'

She turned and, in the dim light of the canopy lamp, fixed her eyes on his. 'You were a policeman Charlie. You committed murder. Do you really believe it would be right for you to get away?'

Pembroke averted his eyes and frowned. 'They were scum. Criminals. They caused the loss of innocent lives and virtually got away with it. So, it was proper justice. An eye for an eye.'

'And DS McBride? What did he do to you? What was his crime?'

'I didn't murder him. It was an accident. I aimed to miss him and warn him off but the man suddenly dodged right into the bullet.'

'I'm sure he'd be most understanding about that.'

'Shut up. Just keep going,' Pembroke snarled.

Except for the steady throb of the engine and hiss of the wash from the launch, silence reigned. Amanda stared ahead. She felt as if Pembroke's stare was boring into the back of her neck. She furiously tried to envisage the various scenarios that could unfold and how she might respond to save her life. Pricking the man's conscience appeared to be futile.

By now she had lost sight of any landmarks. Another fear, that of colliding with the island, now manifested itself. She peered into the gloom and throttled back the engine.

'What the hell are you doing?' demanded Pembroke, who had risen and approached her.

'I'm not certain where we're headed. It could be easy to run aground in this part of the lake.'

Pembroke stared about them then grunted. 'Alright, keep your eyes peeled and no funny business.'

The engine now cut to a much slower speed, Amanda peered into the blackness, lit only immediately in front of the craft by its light. 'Where are we heading for anyway?' she asked, over her shoulder.

'The other side of the lake. That's the closest point to the canal.'

This indication of his destination both surprised and worried Amanda. That he had offered it would indicate he would not be letting her use it. You've got to be ready, she told herself. Mentally, she desperately rehearsed the advice and moves she had gleaned from the self-defence instruction course Stone's retired colleague had given her.

'The number of scrapes you seem to get yourself into, I can't imagine anything better than taking the course,' Stone had urged her. True, she had learned much from it, but in this real-life situation her confidence was ebbing. As surreptitiously as she could she glanced around for any suitable weapon, all the while staring ahead.

Presently, Pembroke spoke, his voice much softer. 'I loved Eleanor. I'd always loved her. I was so happy when she came back home, even though things were far from ideal.'

'But you had a fling with Christine.'

He gave a dismissive shrug. 'That was nothing. Nothing physical happened. It was just friendship and, in a way, it brought me a little bit closer to Eleanor. She told me stories about what they'd got up to in France.' His expression eased at the recollection.

'And how do you propose to get away now?'

Pembroke glared at her. 'I'm not sure but I'm bloody well going to try.'

'And one more proper murder will make it better, will it?'

The cold stare had returned. 'I don't really care anymore. You were the cause of all this. Cut the engine.'

She obeyed and turned to face him. The muscles in his face appeared to tighten, his lips compressed. The launch drifted slowly on and everything seemed eerily still.

A lump came to her throat as dread and panic started to surge through her body. *He's made his mind up. This is it.* She struggled to keep as calm as she could. The terrible memory of the bullet that hit her at Fellowes house, which seemed so long ago, now flooded back.

'This is as good a place as any,' Pembroke said as he approached his victim and squared up to her. Amanda could see his jaw was now tightly clenched. The gun was slowly raised. Pembroke took a deep breath.

Over his shoulder, she caught sight of a tracer. It would be from the first rocket to start the fireworks display.

Pembroke caught the distracted glance and instinctively paused. Almost simultaneously there was a loud explosion and an instant flash of light in the sky above. In the split second that the distracted man looked up, Amanda lunged to deflect the extended arm. The gun went off then clattered to the deck. With her other arm, Amanda drove her fist into Pembroke's solar plexus. He let out a gasp as he bent forwards, winded.

She snatched up the boathook she had spied earlier and thrust it at him. He however, managed to grab the other end, took the force from the lunge and levered the pole. Unbalanced, Amanda fell to the deck. By the time she had scrambled to her feet, the sky now illuminated by the starburst of another rocket, she froze for an instant as she saw Pembroke reaching for the gun.

***

The sky was now brilliantly lit up by a procession of fireworks, in sharp contrast to the dark foreboding that, like a sledgehammer, had suddenly hit the small group at the sound of the gunshot. Sebastian instantly cupped his hands round his face at the sound. Selwyn exchanged a fearful glance with Stone. In the sky there was now one explosion after another, each accompanied by flashes of cascading or starburst light. Then came the sound of a another much louder explosion from across the lake.

Sebastian gave a loud gasp. Selwyn closed his eyes, as if in excruciating pain. Stone raised his hand to his brow. From the lake there was now silence. Suddenly there was the sound of cheering as behind them, Christmas lights came on. Moments later, the sky was lit up by greens, reds and blues as a crescendo of rockets streaked through the night sky and exploded in brilliant varieties of explosions, coloured bursts and crackles. Beyond could be heard the delighted cheers and yells of the spectators. Silence only reigned by the lakeside and over the dark water.

***

The fireworks display was an at end. Sebastian felt cold and terrifyingly helpless as he stood on the jetty and stared despairingly over the lake's surface.

It seemed an eternity before the watchers could discern the distant, faint sound of an engine. As it gradually got louder, the launch's outline could now be made out. At the helm, Selkirk's outline could be made out, but there was no sign of Amanda, nor of the inflatable.

By the time the launch was moored, further police reinforcements had arrived and were busy keeping back a small group of spectators, stragglers from the fireworks display. Further off, the majority of spectators were heading away, ignorant of the events at the lake.

Sterling cut the engine and stepped onto the jetty.

Behind him lay a body slumped across the seating under the canopy.

'Pembroke's dead and there's no sign of the woman,' he advised Stone who cast a quick glance at the anxious Sebastian. 'The men are scouring the lake but we'll need some proper lighting and another boat. There are no signs of any superficial wounds on the deceased, from what I can see.'

'I'll call up more support and forensics,' said the DCI. He moved over to Sebastian and Selwyn.

'What can we do?' Selwyn asked him.

'Perhaps if you could rustle up some torches and then search along the lakeside, in case she's got ashore. If you've got a whistle that might be useful to alert us if you find her.'

The two men set off apace for the hall.

By the time they returned only a small number of the more determined spectators remained, halted where they were by a couple of PCs. Sebastian and Selwyn agreed to set off in opposite directions round the lake, to cover ground quicker.

'Courage, dear boy,' Selwyn comforted him before they split up, 'we'll find her and she'll be okay.'

Sebastian forced a smile and strode off.

In the pitch blackness, his way only lit by the slowly swinging beam of his torch, Sebastian plodded through the rough grass for some considerable time. At one point he was startled by a nearby rustle and the squawk of a bird as it flapped away into the sky.

Eventually, as his torch beam lit up a large boulder in the near distance, Sebastian knew where he was. It marked the point where the old quarry road made its closest approach to the lake. He was now approximately a fifth of the way round the lake's perimeter.

With renewed anxiety and determination, he called out again 'Amanda, Amanda.' He held his breath and listened, but there was nothing. Not a sound in the stillness. With a sigh he straightened and started back on his search.

Some five minutes later, the arc of his torchlight revealed the outline of something near the edge of the water. It was dark, solid and chillingly still.

Sebastian crouched down and reached for the inert form that lay face down. He could see no injuries to the back. As gently as he could he lifted and turned the body over. Nor could he find any other signs of injury. He gazed mesmerised at the pale face, tears now coursing down his cheeks. Relief surged through him as he felt the distinct gentle throb of her pulse. Then there came a faint moan. Open-mouthed he stared at Amanda's face as the eyes flickered open.

'Is that you, Munchkin?' Amanda whispered.

'Yeah, it's me alright,' he enthused. 'You're safe now.'

Her eyes tightened and face creased, as if in pain, as he blew ferociously on the whistle.

'Do you have to?' she demanded, faintly.

'Yes I do,' he insisted, with a smile, and bent to kiss her.

***

A not infrequent visitor to Wisstingham Hall over the past few years, the ambulance sped along the old quarry road until it reached the officer who had stationed himself at the closest point to the lake.

Shortly after, Amanda, now fully back in the land of the conscious, was stretchered into the vehicle which set off for the hospital, Sebastian seated next to her.

The still anxious fiancé stroked her hand and gazed into her eyes. 'I thought you were dead.'

Amanda shook her head, as if to activate her memory. 'So did I, for a moment. Pembroke was about to shoot me so the only thing I could do was jump into the lake. Even then he took a pot shot at me. I swam without a clue as to where I was headed. I made it to solid ground then the next thing I knew was seeing you. What's happened to him?'

Sebastian squeezed her hand. 'The man's dead. When the police picked up the launch from the inflatable he was already a goner.'

Amanda breathed a sigh of relief. 'He must have killed himself. Probably with something Eleanor gave him, I imagine. He'd certainly no intention of being caught.'

'Probably just as well. He certainly did enough damage. You didn't get to do your Kung Fu then?' he smirked.

She gave him a playful frown. 'Don't you knock it, Munchkin. It taught me enough to keep alive, I reckon. Any more of your cheek and you'll find yourself on the receiving end of it.'

'Gee, that's real scary,' he mocked, 'but let's just get you checked out first, before we get up to anything physical.'

'Is that your one-track mind at it again?'

He returned her grin. 'Just might be.'

Chapter 20

DECEMBER

It was a grey, chilly day when DCI Stone came to visit Commander Fitzgerald. The housekeeper's announcement of him, as she showed him into the drawing room, sounded like the greeting of a long-lost friend.

Selwyn rose as he entered the room. 'Good morning, Chief Inspector. Can I offer you some refreshment?'

Stone nodded. 'Tea would be fine, please.'

Mrs S nodded, gave him a wide smile and departed.

Selwyn motioned him to sit. 'I'm delighted to see you again, in better circumstances.'

'I'm not sure whether it's this place or Amanda Sheppard that's the magnet for skulduggery,' Stone observed, lightly.

'Probably both, but she's a smashing girl, for all that.'

'Agreed. I only wish I could have her on my team. I take it she's fully recovered?'

'Absolutely, the quacks put it down to hypothermia and sheer exhaustion.'

Stone nodded. 'Changing the subject, it was very kind of you to offer to arrange the funerals for Miss Delaney and Charlie Pembroke.'

'Well, there appeared to be no living relatives, so someone had to step in.'

'Nevertheless, it was a kind gesture. DS McBride's funeral is next Thursday afternoon. Three o clock at the crematorium, if you want to be there or represented.'

'I will. I'm sure Sebastian will also want to attend and possibly Amanda, if she can make it.'

Mrs S arrived with the tea, a plate of buttered scones and a warning look to the commander which he well recognised as an indication that he should only eat one.

'I'd like to give you a tour of the hall sometime, if you'd like that. There's far more to see than the rooms you've already been in.'

Stone lifted the scone he was holding, in a gesture of appreciation. 'I'd like that. Perhaps even a trip in the launch?'

'Naturally. Just give me a ring to fix a date. Is everything cleared up then regarding the murders?'

'Yes, it was a very mixed bag. It turns out there *is* a living relative of Christine Lagrange, so the body will be handed over to the French authorities. Oh, I meant to ask you, what's the situation with the crypt?'

'It's all sealed off at the moment and the site's been fenced, though I don't expect that's going to stop the really hardcase detector wallahs. We found four tombs at the back of the area where the treasure was hidden. A professor is looking into the history of them, for us. We'll eventually repair the walls, put a gate in and open the crypt as an extension of the hall tour.'

'So, you've plenty to keep you busy.'

'Rather.'

Stone rose to leave. Selwyn also got to his feet, motioned for him to stay for a moment, then went over to the desk. From the drawer he withdrew an envelope. 'I was intending to give you this. It's an annual pass for the hall for you and a guest, should you wish to use it at any time, but my personal tour still stands. Keep it under your hat though, you're the only officer I've given one to.'

Stone pocketed it with a smile. 'It's much appreciated. I'll be in touch very soon.'

Selwyn showed him to the front door and watched as he drove away. Back inside, he returned to the drawing room and started to list the tasks he had ahead of him. There was much to do.

***

It was Amanda's idea that started the ball rolling. With the nightmare occurrence at the opening of the hall well behind them, and the relatively smooth running of operations, thoughts had turned to wedding plans, both for Miriam and Amanda.

'Wouldn't it be lovely to get married here,' Amanda rather dreamily suggested over dinner one evening, at the hall. Silence fell as the diners stopped to ponder the suggestion.

'Now that could be a rattling good idea,' observed Selwyn, unmindful of all it would set in train. 'We could apply for a licence to hold weddings here.'

'A grant of approval you mean?' queried Miriam.

'If that's what it is.'

Miriam's brow wrinkled. 'But we'd have to be able to cater for receptions.'

'And why not?' beamed Selwyn. 'We have the café and just think of the publicity.'

'And the money,' Sebastian chipped in.

Amanda looked pensive. 'People would also want accommodation.'

Another silence ensued, broken by Selwyn. 'Well, the place is dashed large enough. Why not?'

Miriam raised a hand. 'Whoa, let's not get too carried

away. How would all this square with Mrs S?' The elephant in the room had finally trumpeted its presence.

Selwyn's jowls drooped a bit 'Crikey, never thought of that. Perhaps we could get the licence for just one or two weddings?'

Miriam shook her head. 'That's not possible, Selwyn. It's all or nothing.'

'Guv, with the café *and* Mrs S's new kitchen for the catering, perhaps the catering could be shared between her and Gustav.'

'Could be a tricky balancing act that, but let's not rule it out as a possibility.'

Amanda finally put the whole discussion into context. 'Why don't we discuss this with Mrs S and see what she feels about it, and what might have to be done to make it happen. It'll mean additional staff, doubtless some changes in the building, here and there, and the additional publicity material and officialdom. We've plenty of time before the wedding…' She gave Sebastian an indulgent smile and patted his hand. 'Don't worry, Munchkin, I've got it all planned out.'

Selwyn rubbed his hands together. 'Alright then, let's wheel Mrs S in and see where we go with it.'

The housekeeper's reaction was far from what the little committee had anticipated.

'I reckon's it's a cracking idea,' she enthused, 'since I'm housekeeper I can be in charge of the catering and the room staff.'

'But you wouldn't be able to do it all. Perhaps the catering could be shared between you and Gustav?'

Mrs S pursed her lips. 'Well, we'll 'ave to see about that,' was her guarded reply.

'Unless you wanted to leave all the catering to him?' Selwyn suggested. 'It would make life easier for you.'

Mrs S sat up straight, aghast at the very idea. 'Most certainly not! I'm blooming certain we'll be able to sort things out between us.' Her tone clearly brooked no further discussion on that topic.

Heaven help poor Gustav, thought the commander. 'Very well, it looks like we have an agreement in principle.'

Mrs Soames patted her hands onto her apron. 'That's that then. I'd need some additional 'elp with the catering and the 'ousekeeping,' she insisted.

'Only if the figures stack up,' Selwyn warned.

'I'm sure we could provide adequate support from within the resources we have,' Miriam suggested.

'And there would also be an uplift in your salary to reflect the added work and responsibilies, Mrs S,' Selwyn added with a smile, which was not quite as big as the one that now appeared on the housekeeper's face.

'I think we've just cleared our first major hurdle,' Miriam observed, once the happy housekeeper had taken her leave.

***

It was two months later when the four were once more at dinner, that Amanda and Sebastian announced the intended date for their wedding. Champagne was immediately called for and happiness reigned, other than for Miriam's gentle reminder to Selwyn that it was about time that they fixed a date.

'How about a double wedding, Guv?'

'I think that'd be pushing things a bit too far, dear boy. We couldn't all go off on honeymoon at the same time.

There'd be no one to look after the bally place.'

Miriam turned to Amanda. 'Any idea where you'll be going on honeymoon?'

'I've found just the place. It's on the Peloponnese in Greece. A place called Tolo. The hotel, which is small, quaint, and has sea view rooms, is literally right on the beach. The water's calm and crystal clear and there's a lovely Italianate town called Nafplio close by. It'll be just perfect.' She gazed eagerly into Sebastian's eyes. 'You'll just love it, I know you will.'

'I'm sure I will,' he smiled back, 'it sounds ideal. What could possibly go wrong?'

THE END

Acknowledgements

I should firstly like to thank Sam Kruit for her invaluable advice and support in the developmental edit of this novel. She has done such a fantastic job in guiding me through the various errors and omissions of the original script.

My grateful thanks also go out to Ted Rhodes for his continuing advice on police matters.

Also, my appreciation to Charlotte Mouncy of 2QT publishers in the publication of the novel and creation of the fantastic cover design.

Finally, my undying appreciation and thanks goes out, as ever, to my lovely wife Pat for her encouragement, advice and patience.

About the author

Nigel Hanson enjoyed an exciting and varied career, starting out as a Civil Engineer and later branching into project management for major British companies, both in the UK and Saudi Arabia.

His subsequent role of Commercial Manager for a group of Lancashire-based engineering companies eventually led to the role of General Manager of a major UK desalination plant company, involving world-wide travel.

For the last thirteen years of his working life, Nigel to took a totally different path in becoming Blackpool's first Town Centre Manager. This eventually led to his and his team's creation of the first Business Improvement District in the North West.

On retiring, seventeen years ago, having always wanted to be a writer, Nigel embarked on a creative writing course and in 2020, his first book in the Wisstingham Mysteries series, 'Murder Mapped Out' was published.

Publication of the second book in the series, 'Murderous Pursuit' followed in 2022.